Alexandra Campbell's first efforts at journalism saw her become a finalist for the Catherine Pakenham Award and the Vogue Talent Contest, which led to regular appearances on Radio 4's *Start the Week*. She subsequently worked on the staff of *She*, *Harpers & Queen* and *Good Housekeeping*, and has written for the *Daily Telegraph*, *The Times Magazine*, the *FT magazine How to Spend It*, the *Independent Magazine*, *You* magazine, and many women's magazines, winning the Individual Journalists Award from the National Home Improvement Council. This is her second novel. Her first, *The Office Party*, is also published in Penguin and was shortlisted for the Nottingham Arrow First Novel Award. She is also the author of *Spaces for Living* with Liz Bauwens and is currently the Beauty and Wellbeing editor at *Woman & Home*. Alexandra Campbell lives in south London with her husband David and twins Frederick and Rosalind. ·

The Ex-Girlfriend

ALEXANDRA CAMPBELL

PENGUIN BOOKS

PENGUIN BOOKS

Published by the Penguin Group
Penguin Books Ltd, 27 Wrights Lane, London w8 5tz, England
Penguin Putnam Inc., 375 Hudson Street, New York, New York 10014, USA
Penguin Books Australia Ltd, Ringwood, Victoria, Australia
Penguin Books Canada Ltd, 10 Alcorn Avenue, Toronto, Ontario, Canada m4v 3b2
Penguin Books (NZ) Ltd, Private Bag 102902, NSMC, Auckland, New Zealand

Penguin Books Ltd, Registered Offices: Harmondsworth, Middlesex, England

First published 2000
3 5 7 9 10 8 6 4 2

Set in 11.75/14pt Monotype Garamond
Phottypeset by Intype London Ltd
Printed in England by Clays Ltd, St Ives plc

To My Mother, Margaret Campbell

Acknowledgements

I'd like to thank my editors at Penguin: Louise Moore for her perceptiveness and invaluable advice, Harrie Evans for her enthusiasm and sympathetic editing, and Clare Parkinson. Also my agent, Sarah Molloy at A. M. Heath, for her unfailing support, and David, Freddie and Rosie for being generally wonderful, as are Graham, Jane, Peter, Hugo, Anna, Jack, Sam, Richard, Lizzie, William and Lucy. Doctors Claire Baker, Clare Gerada and Jeremy Gray helped with the medical facts – although any mistakes are mine entirely. And Graham and Jane Campbell made sure I haven't libelled anyone – although, of course, any resemblance to any real person is entirely coincidental, so libel was not, I hope, an issue.

And in memory of Stafford Campbell, George Wilson and Hugo Tobias, who are doubtless holding a cracking good party somewhere else.

Prologue

'Would you divorce your husband if he had a one-night stand?' I looked at Maeve, who was running a lacquered fingernail disapprovingly down a menu in All Thai'd Up, a restaurant which specialized in unlikely and faintly distressing combinations of Eastern and Western ingredients.

She gave me a sharp look, and opened her mouth to say something. Maeve has had three husbands, or at least, three she admits to, and everyone is uncertain of the status of her current walker.

'It's an article we're thinking of running.' I backtracked, suddenly regretting that I'd introduced the subject. Still, as the editor of *How?*, a glossy women's magazine with the slogan 'Beautiful living made easy', I can talk about almost anything, and pretend it's work.

'Indeed?' Her eyes, with their slightly drooping hoods and glistening with pastel pearl eyeshadow, made it clear that she didn't believe me. I'm very bad at even the whitest of lies.

The waiter took our order for two pastas, stir fried with ginger and gorgonzola and served with beetroot marmalade – the least menacing of many alarming options, two side salads, and, at Maeve's insistence, two glasses of ice-cold white wine. Still, Maeve's own relationship with the truth was often one of distant politeness.

'You were half-dead in the office this morning.' She and I worked for the same company, Maglife. 'Now what's really up?'

I swallowed and fiddled with my napkin.

'Will's had a one-night stand?' Maeve took no prisoners.

I felt a kind of sick terror curdle in my stomach at the thought. 'I think so.'

It seemed mad to confide in Maeve, *How?*'s publishing director, a colleague – even a boss of sorts – and therefore someone who shouldn't be allowed into the inner recesses of one's soul on principle, in case they find something there that is a sackable offence. But Maeve's sparkly pink glasses – which she kept concealed whenever possible, in order to maintain the fiction of youth – had seen it all. She rarely judged and never gossiped.

'Are you sure you're not just imagining things? You look very tired.' The sympathy in her eyes made me feel even worse.

'I know what imagining feels like.' My smile was rueful. 'If this is my imagination, I think I've probably lost my mind.'

I paused painfully, before adding, 'It was while I was away in Paris for that perfume launch.'

The words 'perfume launch' jetted Maeve instantly into work mode, and had her sniffing around for advertisers with huge budgets. 'Which perfume?' she asked me, rather sharply.

'Affair.' I wondered if the name of the fragrance had put ideas into my head. Sub-consciously. Whether it had inspired me to change my flight to the first plane out on Monday morning, instead of sleeping in, amidst the fin-de-siecle marble and crystal splendour of the Bristol Hotel.

Perhaps I had slipped my key into the handsome blue-painted front door of 37 Branworth Terrace at 7.45 a.m., instead of swanning into the office at noon as I'd planned, because the strapline for the advertising had been something absurd like *Everybody's at it*.

'The house smelt empty,' I told Maeve. 'And the bed was untouched. Will let himself in five minutes later. He wasn't dressed for work.'

'What did he say?' Maeve, looking relieved because she already had vast sums in advertising promised from the Affair budget, put her hand on my arm sympathetically. 'Maybe it didn't mean anything.' Although it was unlike her to parrot platitudes like that. She must have seen the strapline for Affair too.

'He said it didn't mean anything.'

I pushed a piece of straw-like salad into my mouth, which refused to register it as food. But it saved having to explain any more about Will's expression. He had looked . . . well, 'bereft' is the only word that comes close to the memory of his bleached-out, heavily shadowed face.

'Or do you think it was more than just one night? That he's about to leave you?'

'No, it really has only been once. So far.' It was ironic. Will setting up home with someone new would be so simple. Extremely painful, admittedly, but relatively uncomplicated. 'No,' I repeated. 'It's only happened once. I'm sure of that.'

'Well, then.' She took a sip of wine. 'I had a spot of trouble like that with Timmy. You know, my second husband.' She looked distantly out of the window, as if she'd spotted the past getting off a bus at the very end of the street. I followed her gaze, but only saw a pregnant woman looking in a shop window. I turned my head away quickly, shielding my eyes as if they hurt. Everything hurt.

'We stayed together,' she sighed. 'Then, of course, he did have to go. One of the happiest times of my life.' I wasn't sure if she meant his departure or their years together, and briefly wondered why he had 'had to go', but I knew from experience that this was as much information as I was likely to get out of Maeve.

She turned her attention back to my problems. 'Did he explain why? Not that there are any excuses, but it's always interesting to see how men justify themselves.' She sounded like a zoologist studying the habits of some rare breed. 'Where did he meet her?'

'It was Saffron Perry.'

'Oh, Leonie.' Maeve put her wine glass down

sharply and a bit slopped on to the table. She met my eyes. She knew how bad it was. 'Oh, my dear, I am so terribly sorry.'

I

It can be difficult to know when some stories really begin. Perhaps when I met Will, eight years ago. It might even have started earlier, when he first met Saffron, but I don't know anything about that. He doesn't speak of it at all. Maybe it was the day I stood by the pool in the south of France, with the blue water glittering so hard on my eyes that they hurt, when I sensed that the enraptured, perfect time Will and I had had together might already be threatened. Or perhaps it was the damp, drizzly day we married, while we sheltered under the thatched lych-gate of the local village church as the photographer struggled simultaneously with an umbrella and a tripod. Everyone screamed with amusement, their best shoes getting muddy and their high heels sinking into the soft grass around the mossy gravestones. We'd looked at each other as if there was no one else in the world, but I'd caught a shadow of someone else, someone who wasn't meant to be there, coming out of the church door. When I'd turned my head to see her more clearly, I'd realized I'd imagined the slender, fragile outline. It was somebody quite different. Then Will and I had kissed under the lightning of the photographer's flash, and we'd raced, laughing, to the car for the reception.

But I think this story began just three months ago, when I got the call I'd always dreamed of. I had finally got tired of waiting, of putting my life on hold, of expecting everything to happen in a certain order. It was when I stopped believing that tomorrow would come automatically and that stages in your life revolved like terms in the school year, offering promotions and challenges as a matter of course. I'd finally decided to take matters into my own hands. About three weeks earlier, I had applied for a new, demanding, prestigious job.

'Could I speak to Leonie Lucas, please? It's Peter Rennie here.'

Peter Rennie, the Managing Director of Maglife Magazines, does not make person-to-person calls very often. He has three secretaries who usually dial for him.

'Leonie speaking.' I tried not to squeak. Women's voices, according to the experts, get higher with tension, which is why, apparently, we get asked to pour the tea at board meetings.

We how-are-you'd, interrupting each other slightly, while my heart thumped so noisily I was surprised he couldn't hear it down the line. I calmed down by focusing on my desk, a sea of designer rubble, according to Will. Glossy magazines, even glossier press releases and, glossiest of all, the invitations, inscribed wittily on to paper, plates, balloons, mugs and even, worryingly, a potty. These were punctuated with pieces of memorabilia, each eminently forgettable, sent to remind me of a new book, store or product about to be launched. I could see a stick of rock with the words 'British Gas' etched through its core, and a dying Bonsai tree from a paint company, amid the mound of notebooks and page proofs.

'We're very impressed with your presentation, Leonie. Your vision of how you'd like to see *How?* develop was outstanding. Absolutely outstanding. The art of living beautifully. The best in interiors, food and craftsmanship. Glorious photography. A "How To" magazine as upmarket as *Harpers & Queen* or *Vogue*. It's just what we had in mind. We'd like to offer you the editorship.' Peter Rennie's voice was measured but welcoming. 'Would you like to come in and see us some time?'

It was a rhetorical question. Of course, I'd like. I was virtually dialling Will, my husband, best friend and co-conspirator, on the other line before I'd put the phone down.

'Can I speak to Dr Bailey, please? It's his wife.'

'Oh, hello, Leonie. How are you?' Sally, one of the practice receptionists, stayed outrageously chirpy even when the surgery was full of raging drunks, crying children and a long procession of disgruntled, snivelling people complaining that they'd been waiting since 8.15 a.m. 'He's with a patient, I'm afraid. Can I get him to call you?'

Suppressing only the mildest disappointment – it would be more fun to tell him face to face, after all –

I said I'd talk to him that evening, and set about the pleasurable task of disentangling myself from my current job as the deputy editor of a teenage magazine called *Penny*. I looked forward to wearing little – well, biggish – black suits instead of embroidered cardigans, investing in power haircuts rather than a shaggy blonde bob, and realized that I'd never, ever come to work in jeans again. Still, most people get to that stage well before the ripe old age of thirty-seven, and if you aren't slim enough for navel jewellery, it's probably better to avoid the jeans in the first place.

Mind you, speaking of thirty-seven, it would be bliss, utter bliss, not to have to write every word, headline and caption for readers who could easily have been my daughters. Not that I have any, of course. Nervously I pushed the word 'daughter' to the back of my mind, where it could do no more damage.

I'm usually home after Will because there are so many after-work parties and launches that journalists need to see and be seen at. That evening I decided to miss a lavish thrash for a new spot-stripping tape. Instead, I went back to 37 Branworth Terrace, stepping into our hall – painted a shade of 'historic white' that my mother, irritatingly, insists on calling 'fawn' – with a sense of delicious anticipation. The best part of good news is coming home with it.

We'd bought the house – in a solid, red-brick terrace – in those heady, whirlwind days between the exchange and completion of our own contracts with each other, during that mad, social whirl known as an 'engagement'. It has two downstairs rooms knocked into one long, thin, difficult-to-furnish railway carriage, and, at the back a box-like extension houses a kitchen, which we plan to extend and turn into a big family room – even, perhaps, with an Aga – when the time comes. This, in turn, overlooks a garden the size of a large tablecloth. It's much the same as the houses around it, just larger than a few of them and smaller than most of the rest, perhaps differing only in that it retained more 'original features' than those whose windows and doors had been ripped out and replaced with plastic in the pursuit of lower heating bills. Together we'd planned the interior to anticipate any eventuality, planning for babies that would arrive at neat two-year intervals. And, of course, we kept one eye on what improvements would do to the re-sale value. 'We won't be there for ever, after all,' said Will, which makes it feel something of a temporary stopping-off point. So we went for safe choices, compromises. Things that wouldn't date, although occasionally I wondered if we shouldn't have given in to passion and painted the whole house Schiaparelli pink or tungsten orange, just for the sheer joy of living. We'd added a little dining conservatory at the side of the kitchen, and converted the top floor into what would one day be perfect children's bedrooms. These had slowly evolved into dusty box rooms, which was the one eventuality we hadn't planned for.

I was, unwisely, halfway through the bottle of sparkling fizz when Will wiped his feet wearily on the mat and looked up at me like a ghost. His skin was dry with exhaustion, and he'd turned his collar up against the cold and dark of a blustery, soggy March evening.

'God! What a day.'

I looked at him warmly, if fuzzily, from somewhere around the bottom of my glass of sparkling Cava. Tired or not, he was mine, all 6ft 2in of him, with his floppy, honey-coloured hair, baggy cord trousers and green waxed jacket. Young fogey, I'd said. Urban camouflage, he'd replied. 'Cities are full of people wishing they were in the country. Like me.'

I didn't usually agree. I love cities. So do lots of people. But today I'd have concurred with anything. I was floating.

'I got it!'

'Wonderful!' He swung me off the ground. 'Well done.' I slid back to my feet, as he added. 'I knew you would.' It was a joint victory in some ways, because Will has always been my sounding box, listening carefully, then interrupting with a crucial question. These sometimes made me slow down for a second, then I'd shriek with realization. 'Of course!' I'd cry. 'That's it!'

So, in a way, this promotion was his victory, too. I danced around, filling in the detail of who'd said what to whom, while he stowed away his battered leather case, and sank back into a shabby old chair with bits of horsehair stuffing falling out. A larger salary would mean we could re-cover that.

I could see his mind beginning to drift, the way it does when you get back to the sanctuary of home, when you can stop pretending to listen to everything anyone says.

'And I get a company car,' I concluded.

He was silent for a moment. 'Three cases of measles, on top of everything else.'

'Measles!' Irritated by the change of topic, I suppressed the ignoble thought that three cases of measles did not exactly sound like an outbreak of plague or a mass medical emergency. After all, the person whose desk flaunts a reproduction china lavatory the size of a salad bowl with the words 'Come to the launch of our new sanitaryware range' inscribed round the rim is scarcely in a position to accuse others of being trivial.

But Will, as he has always said, can read me like a book. I caught his expression and amended my interjection to: 'I mean, nobody dies of measles, do they?'

'They can do.'

I opened my mouth to say something, but he raised his hands in mock surrender.

'Okay, okay, it's very rare. But the bleeding heart journalists who write these anti-vaccination stories don't exactly stress that it *can* happen, do they? And then, three years later, we get a classful of preschoolers who haven't been vaccinated against *anything*.'

'If I was a mother . . .' A small, slightly dangerous pause hovered between us, so I moved on hastily. 'If I was a mother, I'd want to know the facts. So I could make a choice.'

'I wouldn't mind the facts,' he retorted, as I edged around the kitchen, bursting with desire to re-hash Peter Rennie's conversation another fifteen times. He shuffled through the post I'd passed him, ditching a few medical magazines without opening them, before resuming the argument: 'It's the hysterical headlines I can't stand. And those sentences blown up big . . .'

'Pull-out quotes,' I interjected.

'Okay, pull-out quotes saying things like "Like every mother, Cathy wanted to protect her daughter. Instead, vaccination left her in a world of her own."'

'You don't protest when publicity means three times as many men check themselves for testicular cancer or people over forty start asking their opticians for glaucoma tests.'

He grinned, his face crumpling, like a piece of paper, into lines. Too much sun, I always told him. Bollocks, he'd tell me back. For a doctor, he really doesn't look after himself. 'Yeah, yeah, yeah. All I get is mothers determined to get their little monsters diagnosed with dyspraxia or as hyper-active to avoid having to make them behave.'

I have noticed that people, even very nice ones like Will, love to blame mothers. I must admit that I do myself sometimes, when buggies are blocking the escalator in the rush hour or I see nine-year-olds smoking on street corners. Basically, though, I believe that women should stand up for each other, so I took a deep breath.

Before I could speak, he took my hand and squeezed it. 'But this is your big day, so let's not argue.'

I grinned. 'Let's. I'd like a flaming good row.'

'But I wouldn't.'

'I would.'

'Wouldn't.'

'Would.'

'Wouldn't.'

We finished up in a tangle of tickles on the sofa, breathless with laughter.

'Okay, okay.' He's stronger than I am, and had my arms pinned down by my sides. For a moment, I thought he was going to kiss me, properly, but he just pecked the tip of my nose, then jumped up and dusted himself down.

'Men!' I pretended to be disgruntled. 'They all think they can solve an argument with violence.'

We hugged for a bit, and I added, 'I've also made the first appointment at the infertility clinic. We've only got five weeks to wait.'

Will broke away, and went over to the window with that long, athletic stride I could recognize from miles away. He stared out at the green-tinged city darkness, as if he was looking for something amongst the jagged skyline of tower blocks and terraced roofs.

'Isn't that a bit soon? Won't you have problems getting away?'

I hesitated, halfway through rummaging in the fridge-freezer for something to eat.

'Well, obviously I'm not going to tell The Suits at a new company that I'm about to try to have a baby. Much less by IVF or whatever. I'd be out on my ear before I could say "maternity leave". But there's no reason why I can't have a long-standing dental appointment.' I closed the freezer door. Man cannot live by frozen peas alone. Woman certainly can't. A candle-lit meal at the local Italian restaurant beckoned alluringly.

'I just think it's a bit soon, that's all.'

I felt a sense of panic pressing on my chest. Perhaps he didn't really want a baby. Is reluctance a form of birth control? For all I knew, it might be.

'This is hardly soon.' I suppressed the note of panic I could hear in my voice. 'I've put my life on hold for the last five years, staying at *Penny* far longer than I should have in order not to jeopardize my maternity leave. That's how long it's been, since we started trying. Five whole years. I'm just sick of waiting. Waiting for a baby, waiting until the right time comes for everything. There isn't a right time.' I didn't want to add any clichés like 'I'm not getting any younger, you know.'

I replenished our glasses of wine, and took them over to the window, stroking the soft sleeve of his sweater. 'Please. I want to stop being cautious. I want to go for it, for everything.' I didn't dare ask him if, perhaps, he no longer wanted children, because as far as I knew he did. Just as much as I did. But if he'd changed, I wasn't sure that I wanted to hear it, not at this point when I was almost ready to admit desperation. 'Don't be cross.'

He took the wine glass from me. 'I'm not cross.' He put his arm round me again, and we looked at our reflections in the dark window glass, transparent, ghostly versions of two people standing side by side, with the shadows of the garden outside and the furniture inside mingling in a double-layered world. 'I'm just worried about you taking on too much.'

Relishing the feeling of my own arm around his familiar, solid, warm shape, I was aware that, far from taking on too much, there was a huge sense of relief that, at last, I was moving things forward, both in my professional life and on the baby front. So many people had told me stories of couples who'd tried everything to have children, adding, 'Of course, once they gave up and forgot about it, they relaxed and she found out she was pregnant in the middle of a round-the-world sailing race/house move/starting her own company.' The underlying moral seemed to be that, as there's no convenient time to have a baby, the more *inconvenient* you can make the time, the more chance there is of your getting pregnant. And it's always plain sailing from there. Two or three children would follow without difficulty. So, perhaps, in a sense, I had applied for the Maglife job on the grounds that this new challenge was just what was needed to shift our luck. Perhaps I would be pregnant within six months, and be faced with a whole different set of worries.

I reached up to kiss his sandpaper-rough cheek. 'I do love you, you know.'

His grip tightened round my shoulders in recognition, drawing me close to his side and enveloping me in the safe, comforting embrace of lemon-scented soap. 'Sorry.' He ran his other hand through his hair, rumpling it, and then sweeping down his face as if to wipe away his tiredness. 'I didn't mean to be a bear. Just one hell of a day, that's all.' He sighed. 'I'm very proud of you, you know.'

'I know.' And I did know.

He kissed the top of my head. 'Be careful. That's all I meant to say. Be careful.' I moved away. Will likes to look after people. Occasionally I feel suffocated by it.

The next best thing about good news is sharing it with everyone else, but before I could start dialling I had to check my messages. There were three lights winking.

The first was from my sister, Lindsey. 'I'm just ringing to see what you were thinking of organizing for Mum's birthday,' she'd told the answerphone briskly. She is the arch-delegator of all time. She has one of those high-powered jobs that involves moving loads of money from one place to another and making sure that as much of it as possible sticks to her fingers on the way. It's all quite legal and I don't begrudge her it, but when people say, 'Isn't Lindsey *wonderful*, that demanding job, woman in a man's world, such a lovely husband, those sweet children – I understand they're terribly clever – and isn't it amazing that she also finds time to be a school governor and non-executive director of all those companies, I can't think how she finds the time . . .' and so on, I do murmur, 'She delegates.' The few who actually hear think I'm being mean.

The second message was muffled. 'Hi, Leonie, it's Laura here . . . (sounds of screaming in the background) . . . Zack, stop it, I'm on the *phone*, no it's not YOURS (sound of thump, crash and more screaming). God, sorry, I'll have to call you back.'

The third message was like the second. 'Hi, it's Laura again, Mum's birthday, what were you thinking of doing about it, of course I'll help in any way I can . . . for GOD'S SAKE, Phoebe, *oh no*, speak to you, bye.'

When I was born, Mum was just sewing her first lot of school name tapes for Lindsey, and she found it so traumatic she vowed that all her children would have the same initials so she'd only ever have to order one batch. And it would be easier to pass down clothes. So we became Lindsey, Leonie and Laura Lucas, which is almost too good to be true. Lindsey was a whippet – she was thin and strained-looking, with that high tensile strength and constant shivering that you often see in small women who go far. Laura was a King Charles spaniel, very pretty and curly, but not really all that bright. At 5 ft 8in I felt like something galumphing between them – a golden retriever perhaps, with shaggy blonde hair and big shoulders. Middle children always compare themselves. On a good day I was thinner than Laura and prettier than Lindsey, on a bad day I wasn't as clever as Lindsey and not as pretty as Laura.

Lindsey and I kept the Lucas (Lindsey, who likes to think ahead, tacked it on to her husband's name as the most straightforward way to emphasize her professional identity without the risk of having to cope with muddling calls to schools who didn't know she had a different surname to her children) but Laura couldn't wait to get shot of it the minute Paul Parker proposed on her twenty-fifth birthday. So she is now Laura Parker and she spends her time looking after the two little Parkers, Phoebe and Zack, who trash the place and rule her life in a way that Lindsey's three little Lucas-Whites, suppressed by expensive nannies and lots of extra-curricular activities at their top school, would never dare to.

I looked at my watch, amazed that Lindsey had suggested I could call at any time up to 11.30 p.m. She's at her desk in the City by 7 a.m., but perhaps she's discovered how to delegate all her bodily functions, like sleeping and eating. Still, it was barely nine o'clock now.

She even answered the phone as if she was at work: 'Lindsey Lucas-White. Oh, Leonie. It's you.'

I told her my news.

'Well!' She sounded pleased. 'Have you got a decent package?' Lindsey was an instinctive negotiator. However much she'd wanted a job, she'd always have improved on the terms offered. I'd simply accepted everything with unquestioning enthusiasm.

We chatted for a bit, and she moved on to Other Matters Arising, the part of the agenda referring to Mum's birthday. I tried a counter-proposal, implying that she, rather than I, take the role of hostess on this one.

'Mm. Mm. Yes, well I *would* do it only Profitbank are going through a merger and I've got the children on holiday that week, a school governors meeting and an AGM for Smiths Stores that non-executive directors are meant to turn up to.'

I considered pointing out that she also had a secretary, a housekeeper, a nanny, a woman who came to clean four times a week, and someone to manicure the garden on a monthly basis. The five-storey mansion in Parson's Green sparkled, gleamed and glowed, unsullied by toys out of place, papers or greenish-fringed milk bottles. Our mother was fond of saying she didn't know where she'd gone wrong, the only one of us with the faintest concept of keeping the house looking nice was Lindsey. She usually added, 'Although Laura wasn't too bad until she had the children.' However, I meekly volunteered to have Mum's Sunday lunch at my house.

There was a brief silence. 'Mm. Mm. That'd be fine. And, for God's sake, get Laura to help you. She's got nothing else to do. She won't be able to pay her whack though, we'll have to stump up as we're the rich ones.'

I wouldn't call myself rich, certainly not compared to Lindsey, but I knew this was shorthand for 'I'm rich, and you don't have any children to pay for'.

I decided to counter this with a criticism of Laura's much-flaunted status as a mother. Really, she positively *wears* her children like jewellery: round her neck, at her ears, clasped round her wrists – wherever you look there's a child draped artistically to show off what a wonderful person she is.

'Laura always *says* she'll help,' I whinged, 'but at the last minute one of the children gets an ear infection or she's too tired because she was up six times in the night.' Phoebe and Zack appeared to require drinks, card games, stories, three-course meals and entertainers between the hours of 10 p.m. and 6 a.m. as far as we could see. Will had once asked her what was wrong with roaring at them, offering to tan their hides if another word was heard out of them before breakfast, then slamming the bedroom door. Laura's eyes had filled with tears, and she'd said quietly, 'Well, I don't expect you to understand, but I don't believe in hitting children.' So I knew that even their most minor needs would be a higher priority than helping us with Mum's birthday.

'Oh, well, sis,' said Lindsey cheerfully. 'You know what they say about doormats. They get trodden on.'

I started to point out that I wasn't a doormat, I was

just about to be a top editor with fifteen staff working for me, but I could hear the dialling tone. I wondered if you could be a success and also be a decent person, rather than the kind of mini-Hitler Lindsey was turning into. I intended to prove you could.

One thing I had discovered about success, however, is that when you reach the penthouse suite of whichever great, big gleaming tower block you've designated your particular goal, you suddenly discover that it's only the mezzanine floor after all, and there are still another forty floors to go. I'd tried to ask Lindsey if she'd found that too – that when she moved two million dollars from Switzerland to Tokyo, she suddenly realized that it was peanuts compared to what she ought to have moved from the US to Germany. She'd given me a baffled look, and said: 'But it *is* peanuts.' And when I asked Laura whether she felt as if she'd be incomplete unless she went on to have three, four or five children, she'd uttered a short bark of a laugh and said, 'You really don't understand what's involved in having one child, let alone five, do you?' This is the sort of thing mothers say to keep the moral high ground.

Laura and Paul were in the middle of supper when I called with the news.

'God, everyone's getting so grand.' Laura's voice was slightly muffled by a mouthful of pasta. 'And I'm just sitting at home doing nothing. I feel awful.'

'Well,' I took a deep breath, trying to remember what Laura would consider the approved retort for this kind of complaint. She is completely impossible sometimes. 'You're not doing nothing, you're . . .'

'It's dreadful having to say you're just a housewife at dinner parties,' interrupted Laura. 'People switch off immediately and turn to the fascinating little investment banker flirting on the other side.'

'Well, don't *say* you're just a housewife,' I snapped. 'Call yourself a maternal consultant or something. Try to have some pride in yourself.'

'It's all very well for you to talk,' countered Laura. 'It's all so easy for you.'

She did not, I know, really envy me. This was just crude blackmail to get me to admit that she, by being a mother, had scored as many – if not more – points in the Great Game of Life than I had.

But I refused to play. 'It's only a question of time. When Zack goes to school, you'll be able to . . . well, do whatever it is you want to do.' Laura faffed around talking about becoming a teacher or taking a degree, but she never did anything to make it happen.

'I can't just pick something up like that. You don't understand.'

No. I didn't. And I wasn't going to give her the satisfaction of agreeing with her. I changed the subject to Mum's birthday, and extracted, surprisingly easily, promises to ring round the cousins and find out who could bring what.

Feeling slightly better, I rang my parents.

'How wonderful!' exclaimed Mum. 'Is Will pleased?'

'Of course.'

'He's very good like that.' She sounded approving. 'Your father would have had a fit if I'd gone out to work.'

Far from having a fit, he boomed satisfaction down the phone. He'd probably have been just as pleased for Mum if they'd lived in a different age.

It was too late for the candle-lit supper. Will made us both cheese on toast, savoury and perfect, just like nursery food. Far better than a restaurant for my current mood. I sighed in satisfaction and snuggled down with him to watch the news on television, my legs curled up and my stockinged toes wedging comfortably under the edge of his long thighs, as he sprawled over the sofa. We were like two pieces of a jigsaw puzzle slotting together. That was what our lives together had been, I thought, like parts of a puzzle that had slowly been fitted together bit by bit until the picture became clear. Sometimes we were very similar in our tastes, like endless almost-identical cut-outs of sky or grass, at others there were distinctive differences and highlights that showed what the picture was really about. It had been as intensely absorbing and satisfying as doing a jigsaw, too, but now I was aware that, as a couple, we were almost complete. There were just a few pieces missing.

But I was too excited to concentrate properly on anything except *How?* and he was too tired to stay awake, so we propped ourselves up against each other facing the television and were left with the vague impression that some Royals had opened a flood somewhere in India and that American warplanes were on standby to bomb a Cabinet Minister's mistress.

2

Will sent me flowers on my first day at my new job. His world is not one where people send flowers to each other on an almost daily basis. In mine, however, exquisitely extraordinary combinations of flowers and vegetables are cleverly wound into interesting, fashionable containers, and despatched all around London on bikes as congratulations, sympathy or even just a thank-you for lunch. For him to send me flowers, therefore, required as much careful consideration as I would need if I was to find myself suddenly delivering a baby or watching an operation. Well, not quite, but you get the picture. Sometimes I thought our worlds were so different that it was amazing that we'd ever managed to find each other.

I'd managed to get away from *Penny* remarkably quickly. What with having holiday outstanding – both Will and I got so tangled up in our various work commitments that we hardly ever took any – and the usual management paranoia at *Penny* that I might talk to Maglife about how many paperclips they were planning to order, it only took me just two drizzly, grey March weeks to escape from my job and join *How?*. I moved from a dull little office in a dull little street to the air-conditioned marble foyer of Maglife;

a gleaming testimonial to urban regeneration just south of the river. It had been a part of the city that no one had even known about until the urgent need to build four million more homes was discovered, along with great tracts of industrial wasteland, and the wonderful stainless steel Maglife Towers. This was a 1960s design classic that had become outdated so quickly that it had never actually been occupied until it was made a listed building in the early 1990s, whereupon it was lavishly refitted to fit the newly expanded Maglife group. Now it was twenty-first century city round here. The blueprint for the future. Although it was so windy that I couldn't help thinking that all the new little yellow-brick terraced houses might just be blown away one day, and that the urban wasteland, like the jungle, would ultimately triumph.

Three uniformed receptionists, all male, smiled at me and nodded. A quick glance at the two smoked-glass coffee tables on either side of the reception area confirmed that they were suitably scattered with copies of *How?*, along with the other titles: *My Life*, *Rural Life* and *City Life* – known, unsurprisingly, as the Life group – and a selection of smart young women's magazines with deliberately downbeat names like *Eric*. The biggest earner of the group was *My Life*, billed as the 'magazine for today's woman, with all your contradictions'. I was longing to turn *How?* from a dismal rag containing knitting patterns and twenty ways with mince into a chic interpretation of homeliness like 'Martha Stewart Living', but I was uneasily aware that however 'outstanding' my vision was, I knew virtually nothing about managing a team of staff. My mouth dried up with nerves at the thought of addressing a roomful of people, although Maglife had picked up this weakness in my CV and sent me on a couple of weekend management courses.

The lift swished up to the top floor, where I was met and pampered, then offered tea which came on a tray with white porcelain cups, a proper teapot and even a plate of biscuits. 'We employ the cream among women journalists,' Peter Rennie told me with a sweep of his hand, leaning back in his leather executive chair and surveying his domain. 'We pick the best, then we look after them.'

I could believe it. I was now, officially, 'the best'. It was a terrific feeling.

'You'll find you've inherited a brilliant creative team,' added Peter. 'All they need now is a good leader.' I hadn't inquired too deeply into the fate of Martina, my predecessor, but I gathered she'd disappeared into some netherworld of freelance journalism. So here I was, editor of *How?*, with a brief to turn round falling sales and take the magazine upmarket in order to collar the lucrative glossy ads. I'd fought for the interview, been thrilled by the eventual offer, flattered by the challenge, and I now believed the MD when he told me that *How?* had a great, talented, authoritative team but that there had been problems of leadership. I wanted to believe him. I didn't want to be one of those editors (or marketing directors, managing directors, technical directors – you get them in every industry, in any department) who immediately clear out the team they inherit when they take over and replace everyone with their cronies. Without even giving anyone a chance. I'd show the team that I'd be fair. Just. Good to work for. Inspirational. I leant back in my chair and sipped the Earl Grey tea.

I faced the 'brilliant creative team' once Peter had ushered me downstairs, introduced me, and scuttled off. The staff gathered their chairs round in two semi-circles of heavy, oppressive silence. They looked like two rows of bag ladies: pale, wary and so immersed in layers of wool in shades of brown and grey that you couldn't see if they were thin or fat. Or pregnant, as two of them later turned out to be. They eyed me with undisguised suspicion. Nobody seemed to have brushed their hair that morning.

I pulled my stomach in. I'd blown about a quarter of my new monthly salary on an understated black suit from Harvey Nichols that minimized my broad shoulders and seemed to lengthen my slightly stumpy legs. I felt a good two inches taller than my usual unremarkable, cumbersome 5 ft 8in.

Everyone's eyes seemed focused on the two main desks where I knew that I, and my deputy editor, would sit, rather than on me. My desk, which had been pointed out to me on a previous tour of the building by one of Peter's secretaries, was piled high with files and miscellaneous personal possessions, all carelessly dumped on top and slithering off to the sides. My predecessor's perhaps? Feeling conspicuous, I removed most of them to the windowsill or the floor and sat on the desk facing them, arranging myself to look (I hoped) caring and approachable, while totally in control. Nobody moved, but there was a ripple of something – I couldn't quite tell what – as a tall, dark girl strode in, with endless legs clad in blissfully soft leather trousers and topped with an outrageously expensive-looking, yet simple, cream silk shirt.

Her eyes flicked over me, price-tagging the suit and finding it wanting.

'Oh!'

'Hello? I'm the new editor, Leonie Lucas.' I tried to sound welcoming, but her dismissive gaze made me feel about as chic as a traffic warden about to write a ticket.

She didn't reply for a moment. 'Why are my things on the floor?'

'I don't know,' I replied. 'Someone put them on my desk, so I had to clear them away. I'm sorry.'

She sighed with irritation. I got the impression that everyone behind her was craning their necks. For a moment, I thought she was going to say something else, but she tossed her head and flung herself down at the deputy editor's desk, positioned to one side of mine, and uncoiled the long legs to place immaculately leather-booted feet on its surface. Aha. This must be the deputy editor, Camilla Carstairs. Peter had told me about her, describing her as 'a very talented and hard-working young woman'. The bag ladies' eyes swivelled round from her to me and back again.

I had a carefully scripted speech, written after the weekend management course. 'The art of leadership,' my course trainer had stressed, 'is knowing when to be assertive and when to be collegial.' I had been advised to start off collegial, 'using less direct ways of guiding or influencing staff' in order to engender team spirit. 'It's important that people feel heard,' he'd said.

I spoke warmly of the good things I'd heard about them all, and promised that talent would be promoted. Feeling a bit of a fool, I followed the course manual's suggestions that I let them know that I intended to nurture their creativity by allowing them to become 'pilots of their own destiny'. Empathy, I had been told, was central to good management – even crucial to success – so I urged them all to regard me as a friend as well as a boss. The tall dark girl's lip curled, and she looked almost amused.

I explained that I intended 'to turn the craft of how to live beautifully into an art form', which had been the phrase I'd devised to inspire the staff. Although I had to be careful when using the word 'craft', as the snootier ones would regard craft magazines as deeply inferior. I thought, though, that there was scope for a stylish 'how to' in the market. From wonderfully naïve pots of jam and wooden bowls to finely embroidered linen and herbal remedies for beautiful skin. Shot to look aspirational. Nothing else. No celebrity interviews and society weddings, no features on how to change your life, no introverted pieces on domestic life in Islington or Stoke Poges.

'No money pages?' Peter Rennie had asked wistfully, mindful of the huge advertising budgets of the financial services companies. I thought of those desperate photographs from silent movies that would be used to illustrate pieces called 'Time is running out to complete your tax form', and stood my ground. 'No money pages,' I re-iterated.

'No books?' asked the sub-editors, who had mostly got into the world of magazines because they loved reading and had been good at English at school. I felt a pang. I loved reading and had been good at English myself. But principles were principles. 'Glossy books on homes, fashion, food and beauty only,' I'd told them regretfully.

'No travel?' Camilla asked, her eyes slanting sideways, doubtless thinking of the freebie press trips that would be denied her if travel disappeared from the pages of the magazine. I'd paused. Ah. You couldn't have fashion teams whizzing all over the world without some reciprocal help from the travel industry or you'd go bankrupt. One thing that Will had drilled into me as he rehearsed me for my interviews for the job was that the bottom line was, well, the bottom line, even for doctors nowadays. 'Very beautiful travel only,' I'd told her. 'Preferably with a homes, food, fashion or beauty angle to it.' She hid a smile. The lead-lined cloak of leadership settled on my shoulders with a dull rustle.

The rest watched me impassively, and had no questions. It was like addressing a sea of treacle, when you know you're going to have to jump in soon and swim through it to the other side.

My smile was very fixed by the time I came to the end of the meeting.

Things improved slightly when everyone dispersed, and people started to emerge from the grey/brown woollen herd as individuals in their own right.

'I wondered . . .' A square woman – who, on closer inspection, turned out to be an incredibly pretty, slim-but-pregnant one – approached my desk, to ask 'if we could discuss my future'.

I leant forward with interest. 'Of course.'

She introduced herself as Deirdre, the homes editor, about to go off on maternity leave in a surprisingly short time. She was concealing her pregnancy amazingly well, considering she was due in three weeks.

All she really wanted to know was whether her job would be safe when she got back, and I assured her that it would be. 'Oh, I won't take long,' she assured me blithely. 'Just the basic six weeks.'

I rallied. 'I think you owe it to yourself and your baby to take the full Maglife entitlement of four months. And your job will be quite safe, you know.'

She looked doubtful.

'Please,' I said to her. 'Think about it.' I thought of my elder sister, Lindsey, scuttling back to her big City job six weeks after giving birth, like a rabbit in the headlights of redundancy. And the quiet, well-behaved faces of her children, Ella, Oliver and Daisy, above their neatly ironed blouses with Peter Pan collars and grey skirts or trousers, which made my heart twist uncomfortably with love and pity every time I saw them. Laura's Phoebe and Zack Parker, who rioted about in mismatched dungarees and torn woollies, cushioned by constant love, mess and shouting, simply didn't affect me in the same way. In fact, I was always very relieved to see the last of them. Will called them 'the contraceptive devices', and I secretly agreed with him.

'I've always thought my elder sister went back to work too early,' I said, casually, in the hope of developing the conversation, but I could see that there was no point going on. It wasn't going to sink in. Deirdre was a woman dreaming of a perfect life, baby and briefcase, and she wasn't going to listen to anyone telling her it might not be as bright and crisp as a washing-powder advertisement. But I had resolved that one thing I would do as a boss was to support working mothers. I'm not religious, or even particularly political, but this is something that does seem right, and now, at last, I was actually in a position to do something about it.

'By the way,' she rose out of the chair with heavy, awkward movements, 'well done about the desk.'

'The desk?'

But she'd gone, called to an urgent phone call across the other side of the room.

Two more people sidled up to discuss their futures, one of them, unsurprisingly, Deirdre's deputy, Kate, who seemed worried about taking on twice as much work while Deirdre was on maternity leave without any increase in pay. I promised to see what I could do for her. On the other hand, Kate was getting an extra leg up the ladder doing Deirdre's job while she was on maternity leave, and she ought really to think of it as paying her dues. She'd probably be pregnant herself one day.

'The desk,' said Kate, who seemed a bright and capable girl, 'I'm glad you got it back.'

'Back?' I looked at her questioningly.

She blushed. 'I shouldn't have said anything.'

'But you have.'

'Well,' she took a deep breath, 'Camilla moved her things on to your desk, when Martina left. She said, well . . .' Kate fiddled with the cuffs of her sweater. 'Well, she said you'd be sort of co-editing together, and as she'd been here longer, she deserved the better desk.'

'Really?' I felt confusion rise up my neck: and blotch across my face. How was I to deal with this? I'd just introduced myself to them as editor. I couldn't call them all together again to say, 'Now listen, I really *am* the editor.' They would think I was demented. Particularly after having told them they were the pilots of their own destinies. And, of course, Kate might not have got the story right. Or Peter Rennie might have said something assuaging to Camilla –

who had, after all, been short-listed for the editorship – that she'd misinterpreted. And, anyway, it was only a desk. Absolutely nothing when you thought about the wider picture, like property disputes between the Serbians and the Bosnians.

A nasty clutch of fear gripped my insides. Perhaps Peter Rennie really had made her co-editor without telling me. You could never tell what management might regard as suitably collegial and empathetic, and who they might decide to be empathetic to.

'Well, it's the first I've heard of it,' was the best I could manage. 'I'm sure there was a misunderstanding.'

'Of course.' Kate rose efficiently, adding, 'I'm sorry.'

Sorry for what? That I wouldn't be co-editing with Camilla?

I was about to go straight up to Peter Rennie and complain, until I realized that it was up to me to sort it out. I was now the boss. And there wasn't much he could do, except fire Camilla, and even I could see that it would only be fair to give her a chance.

Will laughed when I got back that evening, rifling through the wine rack to find something drinkable that hadn't been offloaded on to us by someone else trying to get rid of it. I swear there's a dusty bottle of Liebfraumilch dating back to the 1970s that has probably been taken to parties around London and not drunk, only to be taken on to another until eventually finishing up in honourable retirement in our wine rack while we sanctimoniously buy something a bit nicer whenever we take a bottle to people. I told Will he should be more ruthless in this vinous pass-the-parcel but he just grinned and said, 'Ruthless? Come, come, I have the fondest memories of Ruth.' This is his kindly way of telling me he has absolutely no intention of taking any notice of me.

I finished the story about Camilla's desk takeover by asking his advice on what I should do about it.

'Do?' He'd found a bottle of Argentinian red, quite respectable really, even drinkable, and poured us both a glass. 'Nothing, I should think. After all, you've won your first round. You've recaptured your desk from the invading hordes. You're Rome beating back the vandals.'

Dunkirk, more like, if you're going to compare it to history. I sat there, slumped in depression until he said, 'Cheer up, Kitty. Where's all that optimism and cheerfulness I married you for?'

I bet Tristram didn't hanker after Isolde for optimism and cheerfulness. Romeo wasn't declaiming about cheerfulness and optimism under Juliet's balcony. And what about Heathcliff and Cathy? Not exactly cheerful and optimistic.

I pointed this out to Will, who thought it was terribly funny.

3

So why did Will marry me, I asked myself grumpily on my way upstairs to cleanse, tone and moisturize my skin in the vain hope of a restful, early night. I'd taken to slumping unconscious at about 10.30 p.m., only to wake with a thudding heart at 3 a.m., worrying about feature ideas and promotions and whether the *How?* staff, like thoroughbred racehorses, would detect my lack of management experience and instantly pitch me off.

And why had I married Will? According to the vicar at a recent wedding we'd attended, you should spend a little time every day thinking kind, loving, romantic thoughts about your other half, particularly when you've been together for long enough for the romance to be swamped by the welter of daily detail. Daffodils in a blue vase in the bedroom nodded their heads in agreement.

Well, for a start, I remembered as I creamed my face, I'd been really pleasantly surprised when I first set eyes on his rangy form and sandy hair on a blind date, set up by Corinne Wells, a former schoolfriend.

'I've just met the most divine man,' she had breathed down the phone. 'Simply perfect for you.'

'Why isn't he perfect for you?' I'd had a series

of disappointing experiences with divine men, all of whom seemed to have ex-wives, ex-girlfriends or even wives and girlfriends who were not exactly properly exes yet. And, as for men who had been described as 'perfect for me', they mostly turned out to have some kind of problem. Impotency, alcoholism and sheer boorishness were the easiest to spot and label. I'd already told Corinne that I was planning to have a sign made for my front door, like the ones that used to read 'No Hawkers or Circulars', only inscribed 'No Broken Hearts, No Guilt Trippers, No Catholics'. Not that I've anything against Catholics in general, but they're real liabilities when it comes to romance. As, of course, are Jews, Muslims and most of the other world religions. Today's version of No Hawkers or Circulars is a blue stick-on label from Neighbourhood Watch which says 'WE DO NOT buy from this door, YOU MAY BE ASKED to wait while we confirm your identity.' I'd love to have one made that said 'I DO NOT BUY that explanation about commitment, YOU MAY BE ASKED to wait for me to get around to ringing you.' Admittedly, it had all been great fun, too. Life had been one long, giddy party, but the stream of unsatisfactory endings was beginning to leave me hungover and jaded.

Corinne had told me several months earlier that she was ready to compromise: 'Settle for Mr Almost Right.'

I'd shuddered. 'I'm not. That kind of marriage is the definition of a disaster waiting to happen.' I believed, against all the evidence, that true love conquered all. That it lasted for ever. And all that.

Corinne had laughed. 'There's no point in being a romantic in this day and age. You need to be practical if the species is to survive.'

'I am being practical,' I'd murmured through gritted teeth.

So why, if Corinne was so ready to compromise, was she so generous over an apparently perfect man?

'Well,' she'd hardly contained the triumph in her voice. 'I've got lots to tell you. I'm, well, pretty much fixed up at the moment. So I thought we could make a foursome. Me and Mike, you and Will Bailey.'

Will Bailey. It was rather a nice name. More importantly, though, it had sounded as if Corinne was slipping away into that undiscovered country from which a few travellers do unexpectedly return, battered and bruised, but only after some time away. Marriage. Oh dear. That was why I hadn't heard much from her for the past few months.

I'd agreed to meet Will Bailey in the foursome, but only in order to size up this Mike person and decide whether I thought he was good enough for Corinne. I hoped that she wasn't compromising.

'Why is he free?' I'd asked. Forewarned is forearmed.

'He's had some unsatisfactory on-off relationship for years with a pianist, or a dancer, I'm not sure which. Apparently she's absolutely ghastly. He was terribly upset for a bit, but it's over now and she's with someone else.'

Corinne loved disaster stories. The fact that she had so few details was a good sign. It probably meant that this unsatisfactory love affair had been resolved to the satisfaction of all parties. She knew what I was worrying about. 'He doesn't seem to have a broken heart if that's what you're thinking. He laughs a lot. You know. You'd better snap him up before someone else realizes he's free.'

So, Will, marked out as reduced by love like a sale bargain, was sold to me as a good impulse buy.

I'd visualized a man who laughed a lot as a rubicund, jocular rugby player with rosy cheeks and sturdy, muscular thighs.

Back then, I had resolved to have nothing to do with him.

I had not been prepared for the floppy hair and the intense, blue-eyed gaze, or the large quantities of excellent wine that he'd poured down my throat.

'And you a doctor,' I teased him.

He poured me another glass. 'You know what Oscar Wilde always said about good advice?'

I shook my head.

'Pass it on.' He laughed confidingly. 'That's what I do. Pass on good advice.'

I felt him watch me for most of the evening. It was a warm, dangerous feeling. Corinne's eyes gleamed in satisfaction. She could see which way things were going, and she approved.

I thought, however, that I could see some kind of reserve – or even a warning – in the way Mike spoke to me, in the slight stiffness of his profile as he leaned back and watched Will watching me, but then, I hardly knew him. And some men don't like their drinking buddies to get serious.

But here we were, eight years later, and I had the job I wanted and the man I loved. I pitched down into the pillow and instantly fell asleep, occasionally waking to hear the rain drumming on the window like a call to arms, with the eerie cry of the wind echoing down the street in the anguish of those left behind.

Yet I woke refreshed, bolstered by Will's opinion that I had, albeit inadvertently, won The Battle of The Desk. The optimism and cheerfulness, the qualities that he seemed to consider so essential in a wife, were restored.

'I'm all cheerful and optimistic again, darling,' I told him chirpily, sniffing the milk before I poured it into my tea.

He looked up from his newspaper as if down from a great height. 'Mm, good.' He sounded vague, and then added, 'Hope you like your second day at work,' as an afterthought. I tripped out the door feeling totally in charge again.

This mood lasted until I met my new PA, Lucy, a mousy-looking blonde with a great bone structure and huge glasses. She twitched like a frightened rabbit when we were introduced and looked at her desk as if the piles of paper might explode and swallow her up. Peter Rennie had appointed her for me, explaining that she was 'a very experienced editor's secretary. She's worked for quite a few people in the building, so she'll know the ropes.' She jumped nervously every time the phone rang, and went bright red when Camilla asked her to pick up some dry cleaning. I considered telling Camilla that, although the arrangement was that she could ask Lucy to help her if necessary, that did not extend to fetching dry cleaning and sandwiches. We could all do that ourselves. However, I didn't want to come on heavy in my first week ('Collegial, collegial,' I muttered to myself) and decided that we'd probably work together better if she liked me.

I also met my fellow editors, gathered together in the boardroom for a weekly 'internal communications meeting'. They looked like living incarnations of their magazines: there was a dumpy housewife of a woman called Belinda Bracken who edited a magazine called *Home Life*, a raddled-looking girl of about twenty-four, smoking defiantly in the corridor and wearing a short silver lamé dress with masses of eye make-up, who was introduced as Loulou Steel, editor of *Night Life*, and Edward Taylor, a rumpled middle-aged man with a stained tie, who looked as if he'd slept in his clothes and who edited *Redundancy Today*. Most alarming of all was Elaine Brown, the editor of the flagship title *My Life*, whose elaborately tousled hair and discreet, sassy little suit from some newly discovered British genius were far more terrifying than any smart Bond Street label. My black suit, smart as it was, did not reflect the personality of *How?* or what I hoped to turn it into. I felt like the new girl at school who hadn't managed to visit the uniform shop yet.

'We must do lunch,' Elaine told me, waggling her fingers at me in a way that was supposed to look welcoming. 'I'll get your girl to ring my girl.' Feeling like a speck dusted off her jacket I was alarmed by her next statement. 'I hear you've stolen my Lucy off me.'

'I have?' This was bad news. Office politics were such a minefield, and accidentally pinching someone's secretary was not a good beginning. 'I'm terribly sorry. You must have her back, I didn't . . .'

'No way.' Her smile reminded me of a shark in lipstick. 'A sweet girl, absolutely delightful, but dead from the neck up, if you get my meaning.'

'Didn't you bring your own PA with you?' asked Belinda Bracken, sounding sympathetic but slightly surprised. Now I was the new girl who hadn't even brought a proper pencil case with her, and had been forced to find a ropey old one in the Lost Property Box. 'Oh well, I'm sure you'll bring out the best in her. I'm afraid I failed to bolster her confidence enough, and she used to panic a bit . . .' She broke off and looked at me kindly, obviously regretting having told me that Lucy had been rejected by two editors already.

'Lucy?' Another woman, whose name I couldn't remember, shook her head in amazement. 'You've got her as a PA?' She laughed. Belinda gave her a gentle, warning smile, and they both changed the subject.

Feeling as if this was the first time I'd been allowed to stay up to have dinner with the grown-ups, I sat down nervously at the big boardroom table, rifling through the agenda set in front of me. Peter Rennie had just started to speak when the door opened and a majestic woman, dripping with gold chains, sailed in.

'Sorry I'm late, Peter. Frightful traffic.'

He frowned slightly over his glasses. 'Maeve. Can I introduce you to your new editor, Leonie Lucas? Leonie, Maeve is in charge of the sales and advertising side of *How?*, and is also a board director.'

A heavily be-ringed hand, discreetly liver-spotted, shot out and grasped mine firmly. I had heard of Maeve, the only woman on the board, and with a terrifying reputation for brilliance and tenacity. She sat down beside me at a spare seat.

'Can I borrow your agenda?'

I moved it across halfway between us, as the chatter broke out around us again.

'Ghastly waste of time these meetings,' she confided to me, barely dropping her voice. 'Still it keeps The Suits happy.'

Peter shot her a look, cleared his throat and resumed. I was longing to go down and be an editor. It seemed impossibly dazzling and exciting, while sitting up here was, in my view, just fiddling about.

After the meeting I managed to have a quiet word with Peter Rennie, who ushered me into his office. He confirmed that Camilla had indeed campaigned vigorously for my job, and had been deeply disappointed when she didn't get it. I suspected that she intended to undermine me at every opportunity and suggested that she be re-deployed – preferably out the door, or to be absolutely fair to her, somewhere else in the building where she couldn't do any damage.

Peter Rennie steepled his fingers thoughtfully before saying anything. He pushed the black leather director's chair away from the desk, allowing me to note a very well-cut grey suit, and a surprisingly fit-looking body, considering his grey hair. According to the gossip, he jogged to work every morning. At the age of fifty-five. The chauffeur brought the suit, with a clean shirt and, presumably, underpants and socks, to the office. The thought was enough to distract me from Camilla Carstairs, but only briefly. I waited for him to sketch out my rescue scheme.

'Hm. Well, it's not quite that simple. She hasn't, in fact, actually done anything wrong, has she? I feel that any decision taken during what one might call the "honeymoon period" could prove a mistake. And she's very well thought of generally. Anything that looked like a major editorial blood-letting might frighten the advertisers. And *How?* can't afford that at this stage of the game.'

'She tried to take my desk.' I felt petty-minded as I spoke.

He laughed. Then he shook his head. 'Dear me. You ladies can certainly beat us chaps at war-games.' There was a pause, before he continued. 'I really don't think it's fair to sack someone for an unsuccessful desk takeover, do you?'

'That's not exactly the point. I need a deputy I can rely on. It's a key position. It should be someone who can get inside my head, and second-guess me if necessary. And certainly someone who will support me rather than undermine me. That's crucial not just to my success, but to the success of the magazine.'

He agreed. 'You're right, of course. In an ideal world that's exactly what you'd have. A loyal, talented, hard-working deputy. But Camilla works hard and does have talent.'

I felt forced to nod, because, at that stage, I hadn't established that she didn't and she hadn't.

'Well,' he said smoothly, 'two out of three isn't bad. There's no guarantee that the perfect deputy is out there, ready to slip into her shoes, is there?'

This was a risky question on his part, because I could have had the perfect candidate lined up in the wings. In fact, I should have had the perfect candidate, but it's easy to be wise after the event.

'So you see,' he concluded, 'it really is better not to rock the boat at this stage, isn't it? Let's get your first year over with, and hope that the revenues and figures have improved so much that we can afford to make the staff changes we really want to make.'

As I left, he added, quite casually, 'By the way, you do know who Camilla's father is, don't you?'

I did. 'Daddy' was Brian Carstairs of Carstairs Quick Fielding. The advertising agency, who did all the creative work and media buying for a great number of high spending, glossy magazine clients. Whose combined spending power on advertising across the entire Maglife magazine group was awesome. It looked as if I had been saddled with the employment equivalent of a Trust Fund Babe. An ambitious one. The very worst kind.

Peter had winked at me as I left. 'A good person to get friendly with. Very influential. Have another go. I'm sure you can make it work. I have great faith in you as a people person. And Camilla is a charming child. When you get to know her.' What he meant, I suspect, was that she's pretty. Which she is, in a feline, creamy-skinned, almond-eyed, upper-class sort of way.

Will thought I was making too much fuss about it all, as we both collapsed over a Marks & Spencer curry at 11 that evening, washed down with a bottle of red wine that I knew would wake me up again with a thumping heart at 3 a.m.

'You've got to learn to work with all sorts of people. Even in your business.' He often implies that 'media types' are all the same.

'Be reasonable,' he added.

I am reasonable. At least, I thought I was.

'You are in charge,' he said. 'Just tell her what she can and can't do.'

'It's not that easy,' I mumbled.

'Yes, it is.' He picked up my hand and began massaging the mound of my thumb. 'What about an early night?'

I wondered if he meant sex. If I'd been honest – and I usually am – I'd have said I was too tired and it was too late. But that is not the way to get pregnant. Over the past five years – ever since we started 'trying' and certainly since I started worrying about it, which was about three and a half years ago – I had read every single book and article I could find on conception, and it was only recently I'd come across any really thorough discussion on the role of sex in the process. 'It has been an element so far overlooked in studies on infertility,' explained the writer. 'Very often, infertility clears up if the couple make love more often. The soaring infertility levels amongst professional couples today may simply be due to lack of time, lack of sleep and the consequent lack of sex.'

Well, that rang my bell. More sex coming up then. Much more sex. Even much much more sex. Bother.

According to recent research, apparently, sex is now getting less and less popular. Things like gardening or cookery – or snorting cocaine – are taking over, even in the traditional tabloid newspapers. I blame Bill Clinton, really, the Monica Lewinsky affair seems to have put a whole generation off sex for life. While teenagers, fizzling with hormones and free of responsibilities, must presumably be still at it like rabbits, grown-ups are clearly beginning to feel about sex the way they feel about chocolate-brown wall-to-wall 1970s carpets. Great in its time and probably due for a revival any time soon. Just not now.

I trailed upstairs after him with flagging enthusiasm. I don't think he noticed.

4

I only had eight days left to round up the sisters, cousins, aunts and uncles for Mum's birthday, delegate the makings of trifle, chocolate log and Banoffi pie to those who were efficient enough to achieve it, and pore over cookery books. It wasn't easy to find a straightforward, quick dish that would satisfy every taste from the older generation – who distrusted anything with too much chilli in it – to Lindsey and Sandy's sophisticated palates, honed to perfection by daily lunches at Marco Pierre White restaurants. Co-ordinating everyone's allergies was an added complication – all kinds of fish made Sandy extremely ill, which irritated him since so many ways of manifesting wealth, such as smoked salmon, oysters and caviar, are fishy. Laura had allocated herself a sensitivity to wheat, although I'd seen her secretly stuffing in bits of French bread when no one was looking, and Zack had one of those really frightening peanut allergies that mean you're supposed to carry a syringe around with you. Oh, and Cecily, our cousin, was a vegetarian, while her mother, Aunt Wendy, 'couldn't abide cheese. It brings me out in hives.' In the end I decided that it was the older generation's day, and everyone else could jolly well put up with a choice of coq au vin or sausages, ordering a lorryload of each from the organic butcher. (Lindsey was emphatic about the children's diets, pouring all her mothering down the telephone at the nanny in strict lists of permissible additives. Sausages, in her view, were a guaranteed shortcut to cancer or BSE and she had listed the disagreeable things the food industry did in their manufacture so graphically that I'd rather gone off them myself. However, the label 'organic' waved a magic wand over all objections.) A shop-bought quiche would have to sort Cecily out.

Will, pre-occupied with an unseasonal outbreak of a severe type of flu, emerged from his surgery late every evening waving off any attempts to get him involved. After all, it was a question of priorities. I didn't really mind, because each day he seemed more weighted down by the constant onslaught of misery he had to face, as surgery rolled in after surgery. But he said he loved the job, loved being a doctor, so I said nothing.

'They come into the surgery with a sore throat or whatever,' he explained, 'but it's always about something else really. Like they've been made redundant or their wife's having it off with someone else or their kid's in trouble.'

'Always?' I had read enough medical articles to know that many patients did have quite complex problems, but I couldn't believe that there really was no such thing as a simple sore throat. A small, disloyal bit of me, deep down, wondered if Will was bringing it on himself. I visualized a patient going into his little box of an office.

'Doctor, I've got a sore throat.'

'Fine, fine, what's really wrong?'

'Honestly, doctor, just a sore throat.'

I could hear him running through symptoms in that doctory way, but instead of rapping out, 'Bowels normal? Any blood in your stools? Chest hurt? Periods regular?' he'd be asking, 'Wife faithful? Getting it up? Job still there? Mother-in-law difficult?'

I wrenched myself out of my reverie to hear Will tell me that a sore throat was very, very rarely just a sore throat, and that people usually needed something much more fundamental than a pastille tasting of liquorice or a prescription for anti-biotics.

I contemplated telling him that, perhaps, sometimes one could be a bit too caring, but went back to the cookery books instead, trying to decide how to scale up coq au vin and get it cooked at the same time as heaven knows how many sausages. I suppose that, like all muscles, the ability to cook atrophies if you don't use it. We seemed to have slipped into takeaways and anonymous international dishes from the cook-chill counter. When I married Will, I'd sliced, cooked and chopped with the best of them. I'd hunted out exotic ingredients and hovered over them for hours. But then, when I met Will, I'd found the caring very sexy. Now it only made me cross, possibly because it was a bright light that was so rarely shone at me. He was acknowledged locally as a 'wonderful' doctor, and I was often told how lucky I was to have him. But I felt, sometimes, shut out, not ill or lost enough to be interesting.

Christ! Was that the time? I shot out the door in a flurry of dropped cookbooks, reminding myself that he *had* sent me flowers.

My brain not only reverberated with domestic detail and the family Sunday lunch, but also with all the thousands of issues, big and small, that I had to remember as soon as I stepped into Maglife Towers. Here I was, at the end of the first week, still feeling like a beginner. Even finding my office, I realized, as the lift doors opened at my floor, can require actually engaging the brain to remember whether it was left or right at every junction, and these minute decisions, added to the bigger things, meant that I was having to concentrate constantly. Particularly as, I had discovered, the boss is never off limits. Even when I slipped into the loo, one of the juniors would sidle up while I was washing my hands to ask if we could discuss her future.

Even once I'd finally settled in my seat, having said 'good morning' to fifteen different people ('Managers who show empathy to their team have been proved significantly more successful' according to the training manual), I couldn't suppress a niggling resentment that it was me who had to do everything about the family lunch in the first two weeks of an important new job.

I was only slightly mollified when Lindsey rang up to promise that Sandy White would go round to a wine warehouse, and deliver several crates to our door. She waved aside all suggestion of payment.

The next call was from Laura, who promised that Paul would make his signature chocolate dish. 'Will enough for eight be all right?' she asked anxiously. I thought of the trifles and Banoffi pies coming from the cousins and aunts.

'After all,' she added, 'you've probably got time to make any extra yourself, not having children.'

'Eight will be fine,' I said, as someone slapped down a prospective cover for the July issue of *How?* on to the desk in front of me. It was awful. 'I've got to go.' I dropped the phone so fast that it nearly fell off the hook again.

'I think, perhaps, that there are too many cover lines.'

'They came from you,' Mimi, the art director, pointed out, quite reasonably.

I tried again. 'Perhaps the yellow is a bit, er . . . vibrant?'

'You asked me to be different.'

If I hadn't been so determined to remain empathetic and collegial I think I might have shaken her. 'Not quite that different. Let's lose the bottom two cover lines, and get rid of the yellow.' I peered at the print. 'There's an awful lot going on in the background. Have you got a simpler photograph?'

'That's the one you chose.'

'Well, I may have made a mistake.' It's good management policy to acknowledge your mistakes and move on, had been another of the Executive Training dictums. I wondered what it had been like in the days when bosses were like gods, and never made mistakes.

'What about the shot without the vase of flowers in the foreground?' interjected Camilla.

I paused. She'd suggested that one at the time, but it had looked rather dull to me. Perhaps, though, she was right. 'Yes, try that one.'

It was much better. Camilla smirked.

'Well done, Camilla.' It almost hurt my throat to say the words, but I remembered how the stress was now laid on motivating staff, acknowledging their input and thanking them.

'Why don't you stop trying to be all things to all people?' grumbled Will affectionately, eight days later, having been reluctantly levered out of the centre of the mound of Sunday papers strewn all over our huge double bed. 'Just for a bit. Give us all a break.'

'You like it really. Can you open the wine?' I wrapped my arms round him, and leaned against his warm, firm body briefly.

'After I've shaved, I'll be at your service.' He stroked my hair for a moment, then shook himself into action, disappearing behind a layer of shaving foam, while I scurried round, pulling the duvet over the bed, and extracting a pair of shoes that were wedged underneath it. A bit crushed, but they'd do, I thought, as I tugged them on. Unlike Camilla, who, I suspected, could have done a thesis on Contemporary Accessories in her sleep, I found shoes and bags incredibly boring, and almost preferred the days when salesgirls pressed you to buy a matching bag every time you bought a pair of shoes. If Camilla found out, she'd be upstairs demanding my job immediately because I didn't even know which Prada bag was to die for this season. She'd probably get it, too. I peered at the rescued shoes again. They were a bit squashed, but no one would be looking at my feet.

Will and I moved around the house in comfortable tandem for the following two hours, slotting into our respective tasks with familiar efficiency. He gets things out of high cupboards and moves heavy tables, I slice and chop and season.

Finally, Will leant against me with a sigh and kissed the top of my head. 'Ready for them, superwoman?'

I wound my arms tighter around him, breathing in the scratchiness of his old sweater. 'I wish it was just us. Having lunch somewhere special.'

'So do I.' He tipped my chin up to kiss me. 'So do I.'

The doorbell shrilled almost immediately, and we jumped apart.

'You look very nice, Auntie Leonie,' said Phoebe, unusually politely as she stood on the doorstep with a runny nose and a fake-leopardskin pinafore dress. 'I like your outfit. But . . .' and she left a dramatic pause that Camilla would have been proud of . . .

'those shoes don't go.' At the age of four, she had obviously inherited Laura's sense of tact.

'Sh, sh, Phoebe darling, Auntie Leonie probably hasn't had time to change.' Laura hustled her in the door, dragging a reluctant Zack behind her, followed by Paul laden with enough equipment to keep them going for a week. She'd put on weight, I noticed, and was wearing a baggy V-neck sweater and unflattering black leggings with trainers. All that remained of the pretty dark girl who giggled out of a veil in the hundreds of wedding photographs they'd dotted around their house was a creamy cleavage and rather tangled black curls.

'I hope you haven't come to stay, ha ha,' said Will, obviously wondering where he was going to put everything. The contents of a Volvo Estate settled in the hall, in a mound that tripped everyone up at least once.

'Tat! Tat!' shouted Zack. Not another infant arbiter of taste, I hoped. 'Tat!' He rattled the letterbox urgently as Laura tried to drag him past it.

'No, darling, it's not Leonie's cat, and it probably doesn't like children.' Laura hauled him away from the doorway. She had a permanently exhausted expression, and responded to most attempts at conversation with a roll of the eyes and a sigh, usually responding with, 'Well, I'm sorry but . . .' Next-door's cat fled, indignation vibrating through its tail.

The Lucas-Whites stood behind Paul, a neat trio of clean children in navy and grey, each one bearing a small, immaculately wrapped present. Ella, I noticed, had braided a few sections of her hair into tiny plaits, with beads woven through them. I thought it was unlike Lindsey to allow anything so subversive, but then Ella must be nearly fourteen by now, and perhaps she was allowed small, insignificant rebellions. As she kissed me I realized she was now as tall as I was, although she still had the soft and fragile skin of a young child. I couldn't help smiling at the sight of her.

'You're so grown-up these days!'

She flushed and smiled, looking away in embarrassment. My glance flickered to Lindsey, hoping she wasn't going to make any of those terrible maternal confessions like 'We bought her first bra the other day.' I needn't have worried. Lindsey never got personal in public. Hardly ever got personal at all, come to that. She merely raised her eyes to the ceiling, and Ella, leaning in close to the wall as if she hoped it might conceal her movements, loped awkwardly towards the back room. Teenagers were so self-conscious.

The others followed more boisterously, with Lindsey looking drawn and tired behind them. Her skin always seemed to be tightly stretched across her bones, and she was dressed from head to foot in a fitted beige suit, American Tan tights and honey-coloured court shoes. Pressed against the 'historic white' walls, she faded into the background like a patch of damp. I caught sight of myself with her in the hall mirror, with my mannish blonde 'executive' hair and square shoulders, and wondered what had happened to the three pretty Lucas sisters.

The whole chaotic muddle transferred itself from the hall to the kitchen, which allowed everyone to spread out a bit but didn't exactly feel spacious. I could see my mother's sister, Wendy, booming in the background and waving a wobbling trifle.

'Where shall I put this? You girls always look so tired,' she shouted at us. We chorused in unison: 'The Tokyo stock market's been a bit unstable this week', 'Zack still gets up three times a night', and 'I'm fine, thank you'. We needn't have bothered. Aunt Wendy liked us to look tired, to reassure herself that her own daughter's placid lifestyle as a part-time librarian with one well-behaved eleven-year-old was a triumph in today's terms. 'Cecily has really got it sorted,' she told us every time she saw us. 'Not like you lot, chasing your tails all the time.' Laura was looking rather green under her usual pasty pallor, I noticed, and her hair needed washing. Lindsey's hair, like the rest of her, looked even thinner than when I'd last seen her, about a month ago. I could see the edge of Cecily's hair, just behind Wendy's formidable shape, as always, a shining, glossy curtain, a cliché-d raven's wing, echoed in the polish of her gleaming black shoes. Perhaps Aunt Wendy was right. Francine, the well-behaved eleven-year-old, had already been dispatched to 'look after the little ones', which she would do, as always, quite extraordinarily efficiently.

Lindsey was looking for somewhere to dump a

prettily wrapped patisserie box, clearly bemused by the piles of stuff and heaped plates on every spare inch of work surface. She had a huge, immaculately fitted kitchen and someone called Consuela who put everything away in its correct place as soon as it was delivered. I think it had been so long since she'd seen any clutter that she didn't quite know what it was.

I edged out of the kitchen with two bottles of sparkling Cava in my hand, and a jug of orange juice, and finally reached the sitting room where Sandy White was indulging in his favourite pastime of making Paul Parker feel insecure.

'My dear fellow, you've simply got to look at the larger picture. These chaps are heads of multi-million-pound corporations and they're not going to . . .'

Paul Parker looked rather strained and pale. Presumably he had to defer to old farts like Sandy White for most of the week, and found it hard to stand there politely while he was condescended to at weekends. He was trying to bleat a reply. Sandy swept over him, determined not to be interrupted.

Will, who was going round with a tray of glasses, caught my eye and we exchanged a gleam of amusement, until Sandy rounded on me: 'My dear, this is *very* good of you. You've obviously made a splendid effort at a very busy time.' He sounded as if he was thanking the mayor and the municipality for their hard work in erecting the refreshments tent. I smiled and slid out of his grasp, because I could feel his hand straying round my bottom. Getting trapped with

Sandy involved a jaw-achingly dull half hour of grinning and nodding while he lectured away, usually culminating in a fulsome tirade of embarrassing compliments. 'No, I mean it, you're one of the most intelligent, attractive women I know. If you weren't my sister-in-law . . .' I usually left him to Will, who didn't mind so much. Men are much more tolerant of each other than women are, I decided.

Returning to the kitchen to replenish the glasses, I saw Lindsey and Laura head to head, whispering something.

'She slammed the phone down on me when I mentioned children,' I heard Laura say. When Lindsey caught sight of me, she nudged her. Laura stopped talking and looked guilty.

'What's the secret?'

'Nothing,' Lindsey spoke in a bland tone that I recognized from childhood. She had always been infuriatingly good about keeping secrets. The sort of child who had so much self-restraint and discipline that she could make a bar of chocolate last a whole week, eating just one square a day. I'd be better off tackling Laura, who, like me, tore off the wrapping, wolfed the lot in one go and then regretted it.

Laura went scarlet. 'We weren't talking about anything.' Then, clearly hit by inspiration, she added: 'Well, Mum's present, if you *really* want to know.'

'Well, why couldn't you tell me openly?' I demanded, determined not to let her off the hook. There was a loud crash from upstairs, and I winced.

'Because,' there was a distinct note of triumph in Laura's voice, 'she's standing behind you.'

I turned round to hug my mother, dressed in her usual soft, heathery tweeds and smelling of Femme mixed with mothballs. My father, gentle and dignified, leant on a walking stick behind her. They brought in grace from a different age. I wondered if they'd ever been as crowded and cluttered and rushed as we all seemed to be. Still, Laura needn't think she was going to get away with it. When she was little, I'd tickled her to make her give in – and sometimes tickled her just to show her who was boss – and now, even without the tickling, I knew I could find out what was up.

In the end, by adding two card tables to our dining table, and covering it all with white sheets, we'd managed to work out how to seat all the grown-ups. The children, exhaustingly, ate earlier and had been dispatched to watch a video, except for Ella who went upstairs to my bedroom to thumb through magazines. I was surprised, when I went upstairs to the loo before lunch, to sniff the faintest waft of cigarette smoke, but Ella pointed out that Aunt Wendy, who smoked like a chimney, had been upstairs just five minutes before me. 'Would I, honestly?' she asked me, looking at me under her lashes in exasperation.

I sat down on the bed beside her, and just about stopped myself from wrinkling my nose as the smell of cigarettes grew stronger. Should I say something?

I decided not to. I could feel a chasm growing between us, as the little girl who used to jump on to my lap and fill my ears with detail about how she'd been the first to canter in her riding group was gradually replaced by this awkward, reserved creature. She used to hurl herself at Will, too, chattering away with excitement, and his eyes would meet mine over her head in acknowledgement, and even anticipation of having a beautiful little Ella of our own one day.

I stroked her arm. 'How're things?'

She shrugged. 'Fine.'

'School okay?' God, I hated myself for asking all the questions that seemed so idiotic when I'd been that age. But the easy old questions about her cat, Marmalade, or her ever-revolving circle of 'best' friends had somehow worn out. Marmalade was dead, and she no longer admitted to a 'best friend'.

'Boring.' She allowed herself a small smile, and began flicking through the magazines again, looking embarrassed.

'There are some more magazines beside the bed, if you want them.' I went downstairs and sorted out where everyone should sit. Lindsey sat between Aunt Wendy and my father, setting out to charm both of them with her perfect attentiveness. Laura had to sit as far away from Sandy White as possible, because tensions between them had never really been resolved since he pinched her silk taffeta-clad bottom on her wedding day and told her he liked women 'with a bit of flesh on them'. And Cecily always withered beside

Lindsey, who was inclined to sound bossy when discussing the pros and cons of full and part-time work. Will was easy to place as he seemed to get on with everybody, except very possibly Aunt Wendy, because she bombarded him with a continuous barrage of medical titbits she'd gleaned from *Woman & Home* which she 'felt he ought to know about'. So I allocated Laura to Will who always rather enjoyed gazing down her cleavage, and made a mental note not to let her escape before I'd nobbled her on the latest family secret.

Aunt Wendy wedged herself in across the table, her elbows invading everyone else's space.

'Now, Leonie,' she shouted. 'When are we going to hear some news?'

'News?' For a moment, I couldn't imagine what she was talking about.

'Now, now,' she went all coy, which was a frightening sight in a woman that size. 'Don't pretend you don't know what I'm talking about. You know,' she raised her eyebrows meaningfully, 'the patter of tiny feet.' She twinkled two fingers to indicate a running motion.

I darted a look at Will, but he had just got up to find another bottle of wine. 'No news, Aunt Wendy,' I said as firmly as possible. 'I've just started a new job, and . . .'

'Don't leave it too long. Time is running out, you know. You remember Daphne and Douglas Smith-Hastings from Thornton Peverill?' She hardly paused for me to nod or shake my head, mouth full. 'Their daughter, Lesley, went into the City, didn't get married till she was . . .'

I saw Lindsey and my mother exchange glances. Mum dived in to the rescue: 'That really was delicious, Leonie. I don't know how you always manage to make it so full of flavour. My coq au vins are so boring.'

The hubbub rose a few notches as Cecily gently put forward the case for free-range chicken, while Wendy, distracted by the challenge of the words 'free range', bellowed that it was all a lot of nonsense and just an excuse for charging more. Sandy reached out a hand towards the quiche, asking if there was any fish in it. Will had been too busy opening bottles and topping up glasses to spot the exchange, thank goodness. I certainly didn't want him chirping up about fertility clinics as we hadn't yet agreed how much we were going to say about it and who to.

'Have some more, Paul.' I decided to stick to the subject of food, and thought that Paul looked in definite need of feeding up. He was even paler than usual today. As the youngest of the three brothers-in-law, barely in his thirties, he looked relatively fresh faced and innocent, tall and thin with a shock of curly dark hair. I looked at him more closely. 'You look a bit worn out.'

'He's working late,' snapped Laura. 'Every night at the moment.'

In anyone else working late might be considered sinister or a code for something else, but Paul is the last man to be unfaithful. On the relatively junior rungs of the ladder as an accountant, he was working very hard in order to improve his prospects of a partnership in a few years' time. He constantly had to do exams, as well as deal with regular office overloads, but he still didn't earn what Laura thought he ought to.

'Oh Paul. That's rather a good thing, I suppose.' Mum always tried to be soothing. 'It shows you're in demand.'

Laura rolled her eyes. 'Unfortunately, being an accountant isn't like stacking the shelves at Sainsbury's. You don't get more money when you do overtime.'

I wondered why Laura was being even more vile to him than usual. He was usually like the tree that bends in the wind when she laid into him. I'd sometimes suspected that, as in the old parable, he was all the stronger for it, and their relationship seemed to be built on Laura's nagging and him ignoring it. He liked trailing round looking slightly cowed and being domestically hopeless, and she enjoyed getting infuriated by it. Occasionally, though, I did think she went too far.

Lindsey and Sandy starting rabbiting on about boarding school for Ella.

'Best thing for a child, I'd say,' he boomed. 'Wouldn't you agree, Will?'

'No,' Will's voice was quiet, but firm. 'No, I wouldn't send any child of mine to a boarding school.'

Sandy didn't even pause. 'But you're a Gorst boy, aren't you? You lot got buggered to hell and back.' I saw Lindsey try to nudge him with her foot, but he was too far away to reach.

Will's face set into a blank expression. 'Really? You seem to know more about it than I do.'

'The school says that Ella is being very difficult.' Lindsey was obviously trying to change the subject.

'I remember one headmaster went down for five years, haw, haw, haw,' chuntered Sandy, who was unstoppable once he'd seized on a topic. He slapped his hands on his thighs and roared at this particularly good joke. Lindsey, who looked as if she'd sucked a lemon, raised her eyebrows meaningfully at her husband, but it made no impact on Sandy.

Will simply roared with laughter. 'Sandy, you complete fruitcake, you haven't the faintest idea about anything.' He slapped him on the back, just slightly harder than was strictly necessary, and settled down beside Laura, who shot me a worried look. Sandy went on going 'haw, haw, haw' into his napkin for several minutes afterwards, but he'd lost everyone's attention. Honestly, Sandy is ghastly.

Aunt Wendy heaved herself to her feet and wheezed out into the garden to 'have a puff', grumbling about the way people today actually expected to keep their homes smoke-free, which more or less confirmed my suspicions about Ella. Will turned politely to Laura and offered her some more wine. She put a hand over her glass. He re-filled his own, and I saw his face light up as she murmured something to him. He gave her a quick, brotherly hug, but she pulled away when she looked over his shoulder and saw me watching them. Our eyes met. Laura did have a secret. I know Laura. And she was telling everyone except me.

Two hours later, we stood together on the doorstep waving them all off. Will put his arm around my shoulders.

'Well done. That went very well.' He kissed my forehead. 'It was a lot of work for you.'

I looked up to see affection in his eyes. 'Thanks for your help.' ('Isn't Will wonderful?' Aunt Wendy had said. 'You modern girls don't know how lucky you are.')

He closed the door softly behind us, and leant over me, dropping his lips gently on to mine.

Having spent the last – oh, I don't know how long – thinking of sex as a duty, a chore, something that had to be achieved between certain dates and followed by lying with one's legs up in the air and a pillow under one's bottom, I looked at him and felt the beginnings of warmth steal through me.

We forgot the washing up.

I lay on the bed, watching him unbutton his checked shirt with pleasure. His eyes met mine in mutual anticipation.

The phone burbled beside me.

I wish I'd let it ring, but answering phones is an involuntary reflex.

'William?' I knew that low, clear voice, with its faint resonance of hoarseness.

I automatically passed it to him, and then wondered why she couldn't at least have said 'Hello' to me.

'Saffron!' He sounded surprised. 'We haven't heard from you for ages.'

I liked the 'we'. I hadn't cared for the lightness in his voice, the way he'd straightened up, then leaned forwards towards the phone, cradling it under his jaw and turning his back on me.

'I'm sure we'd love to. Let me ask Leonie.'

Oh God. One of Saffron's zany schemes. Every so often, she'd ring up and say 'We're all having a picnic in the bandstand in Hyde Park' (this in November) or 'Let's all go and celebrate the Mexican Day of the Dead.' She'd be the Christmas tree fairy, the centre of attention as she sparkled at everyone. I'd be toiling away in the rear with a coolbox full of sandwiches, because she was hopeless at organizing anything and knew that someone else would pick up the practical bits.

I felt the pleasure I'd felt five minutes earlier shrivel inside me.

He turned back to me, mouthing, 'Sunday 27 May's fine, isn't it?'

I shook my head vigorously. I'd always fallen in with these plans before, because I didn't want to cause a scene or behave like an unreasonable, jealous wife. Now, suddenly, I felt it was time to stake my own claims.

He turned back again. 'Yes, I'm sure it'll be great, but I can't find Leonie just now. I'll call you back.'

I didn't fancy that, not a long, intimate conversation when they both had time to laugh and flirt, so I hastily signalled agreement before he could ring off.

I turned my back on him, as he put the phone down.

'For God's sake,' he sounded mildly exasperated. 'You don't even know what she was asking us to.'

'Well? It's bound to be something completely extraordinary. And I'm too tired for weird.'

'As it happens – ' his voice was patient, as if talking to a child, as he continued unbuttoning his shirt.

I wondered whether to jump up and insist we did the washing up after all, but that would be going too far.

' – there's a special rehearsal of a concert she's going to be playing in at the Albert Hall,' he explained. 'It's an exclusive preview, and they're selling tickets to raise money for the Special Care unit at Tommy's.' Will had trained at St Thomas's and originally wanted to go into gynaecology. Even I had to admit that you didn't have to be an ex-girlfriend to know that this was a cause close to his heart. And he loved music. It was how they'd met apparently, when she'd come to play at some student concert when he was at medical school.

'She's suggested we all go out for a meal afterwards. We can miss that if you like.' There was a slight edge of resentment in his voice, but I knew he meant it.

'But I would like to go to the concert if you don't mind.' As he unbuckled his trousers, he added, 'I'm quite happy to go on my own if you don't want to come.'

The washing up suddenly seemed a lot more alluring than spending the rest of the evening in bed with him. However, I tried to think of the Buddhist story about the two celibate monks crossing a river. One saw a beautiful girl stranded on one side and carried her, leaving her on the other bank. The two monks walked on in silence for another twenty-five days and eventually the second monk said, 'Brother, having taken a vow of celibacy you should not have carried that girl across the water.' The first monk replied, 'Brother, I left that girl on the side of the river bank. But did you?'

Will seemed to have left Saffron quite happily on the telephonic river bank when he put the phone down. It was I, it occurred to me, who could not let her go.

I made a massive effort to smile and put out my arms to welcome him into bed. 'Fine.'

'Good girl.' He jumped under the covers beside me. 'Brr! Move over and warm up my side of the bed.'

I moved over and, eventually, parted my legs dutifully, but the call rattled round my head, splintering into icy little thoughts that, I kept telling myself, were inconsequential, meaningless, worth nothing.

I concentrated on telling myself that she hardly ever phoned and that she hadn't been in touch for nearly a year. Last time she'd rung it had been to ask Will where he thought her stop tap might be, which had been far more irritating than an invitation to a concert.

5

Eight years ago I'd never heard of Saffron Perry. That was when Will took me to Rosse Manor, a country house hotel built in golden Cotswold stone – as brochure-speak would have it – nestling romantically amongst the fields just outside the village of Rosse, and overlooking some of Britain's most spectacular countryside. At dinner the waiters, experts in synchronized dome-lifting, fussed about us with suppressed excitement, but I was so happy I didn't notice. Just the bare fact of being on a country house hotel weekend with a boyfriend was my idea of perfect romance. And, although we'd only known each other for six months, Will had already engineered to meet my parents, had invited me to join him and some friends in a villa in Provence that summer, and had planned a weekend in New York together.

I'd liked Will immediately when Corinne had introduced us. He'd been easy and relaxed, and had taken me home that night without seeming intrusive. He'd taken my number as if it was the most natural thing in the world, and I'd known he'd ring. He'd been gentle and easy, funny and sharp, and, most importantly, hadn't manifested any of the usual run of problems. No hang-ups about his mother, his sexual prowess, his earning power, his role with women. Instead he was kind and courteous, occasionally bringing me delightful little presents or suggesting something unusual, such as a trip down a canal, rather than an ordinary Sunday lunch in a restaurant. The simplest things – a walk in the rain, a shared joke, the sight of a bird skimming over the Thames at dawn – had been enveloped in a golden, magical haze. We'd talked and talked. His family had come from Scotland, he'd told me, but had had to sell their home, White Gates Farm, when he was ten because his father had died, and his mother couldn't keep the small family business, selling paraffin heaters, going. 'I've always wanted to buy it back,' he'd told me, 'or at least find a place with open skies and fish leaping up in the water.' Our first few weeks together were like making friends on a long train journey – intense, but removed from reality. Yet I'd felt, for some reason and pushing away deep pangs of regret, that it was a journey that would end.

So when the waiters, quivering with excitement at being involved in our future, removed our domes with a flourish and mine had an engagement ring twinkling on a salad bed of rocket and lamb's lettuce, I never stopped to ask him properly about the 'pianist or dancer' that Corinne had briefly alluded to. And he had never brought the subject up so I assumed that it no longer mattered to him.

Instead, I looked into his eyes and said, 'Yes.'

It had been magical. We'd stayed up all night talking

about our plans, unravelling great, glorious vistas of a golden life together. It wasn't until later on in the weekend, when my mind was befuddled with thoughts of flowers, dates, bridesmaids and white dresses, that he slipped her name into the conversation for the first time.

'You'll like the crowd in Provence,' he said. 'Did I tell you who's coming?'

I shook my head as I wondered whether we should go for a church or a registry office.

'Whatever you like,' he said, absent-mindedly stroking my hair behind my ear. 'It's your day.'

I paused. Surely it was *our* day. But, with a pretty rural church just yards away from my parents' home, and a vicar who I'd known since childhood, it wasn't really something we talked about any further. We fell into a church wedding.

He went on to list the couples on holiday, with a distant, spiritual look in his eyes that I attributed to our brief conversation about church. 'Saffron Perry and her boyfriend, James Walker.' He then gabbled out the other names.

'Who are they?'

'Oh, James is a merchant banker, very good tennis player . . .' he reeled off the careers and hobbies of the others. Then he paused and said, 'Saffron Perry is my ex-girlfriend. She's a very talented pianist. *Harpers & Queen* did a double-page spread on her last year.' If I hadn't been so dazed with emotion I'd have realized that everyone else had been defined by their achievements. It was only when it came to Saffron that he had outlined a relationship to himself.

As it was, I briefly halted in my excited mental list-making, and sniffed the air for danger. Will picked up the *Sunday Times* Business Section and said, 'My God, old Henry's got himself into hot water. This I must read. I always thought they'd find the bugger out.'

I relaxed. Another distant, safely-partnered-off girl-friend. No threat. And, if she'd been in *Harpers*, she might even be quite interesting.

6

A few days after the family lunch party, I saw Rosse Manor again. In a set of fashion pictures brought in by Fortune, one of our top photographers. Like many fashion photographers, he was so sensitive about his image that the words 'artistic temperament' simply didn't touch the sides of some of his worst tantrums. It had taken me – and Mimi – several telephone calls to convince him that *How?* was moving sufficiently upmarket for him to deign to work for us. Had I still been at *Penny* he would have slammed the phone down on me. When he was very difficult, I comforted myself with remembering that he had been christened 'Colin', which he didn't think was cool enough, and was why he insisted on being called just 'Fortune'. Fortune and Saffron – why couldn't people be called sensible things like John and Margaret these days?

It took me a while to realize what I was looking at, as I put the transparencies on the light box in *How?*'s art department. They depicted models in various wispy clothes, hunched against crumbling stone walls or sharp topiary-cut hedges, in positions that suggested being shot by a firing squad rather than a camera. Their wide-eyed, over-mascaraed terror was obviously intended to indicate that the New Florals were cutting-edge. I peered closely at the first shot, and saw a dark green Gothic bench in the background, under a wrought-iron pergola. There were leaves winding up through the metal, and, although these photographs had been shot just a few days ago in April, long before roses even budded, I knew what rose it was, climbing vigorously through the black metallic curves.

It was called Paul's Himalayan Musk, the rose that had cascaded all over us on that weekend eight years ago, almost stifling the clear June air with a sweet, narcotic scent of old roses. It was a fragrance which would signify the colour 'pink' to me for the rest of my life. Will and I had sat on the bench – holding hands, each with a glass of champagne in the other hand – as my mind drifted through essentials such as the wording of the wedding invitation and those delicious ivory silk shoes with rosebuds that you can get from Emma Hope. Will had sketched out our future to me. It sounded wonderful.

'I've never really thought about what I want until now,' he said, squeezing my hand. 'But now it's time to stop lurching from pub to party and back again. Time to put down roots. I want to see my children grow up and run around. I'd like to take them fishing.'

I, too, had fantasies, but they went no further ahead in time than thinking how Lindsey's darling little Ella was absolutely the right age at six to be a bridesmaid. Ella is, and always has been, special to me. I can't explain why, but my heart beats faster when she locks her fragile arms around my neck and I can feel how silky her cheeks are. Her kisses are like butterfly wings fluttering against my skin.

'I could be a consultant in ten years,' he leant back with satisfaction, lifting the glass, and closing one eye to look at the Cotswold hills through the champagne bubbles. 'If I stop messing around.'

I was glad to hear it, although the arcane world of hospital politics was a foreign one to me. It would be busy, I supposed. I was sure that Will's prankish nature fitted in well to the joky world of medicine I'd seen on the TV. Medical students were always playing japes, I thought. I wondered whether we should go somewhere reliable for the wedding list, like Peter Jones, or be a bit more stylish with the General Trading Company. Or perhaps both.

But that was still in the future, sitting on the bench under the Paul's Himalayan Musk, as Will sketched out the house we would buy, the children we would have ('of course, I don't mind boys or girls, as long as they're healthy'), and even cautious, long-sighted things like pension schemes. But he never told me – and, with my head full of sashes and engraved lettering, rosebuds and lace, I never thought to ask – anything more, really, about what he'd been like before I'd met him, why he'd driven battered sports cars far too fast, gone on all-night drinking binges, and never ever managed more than two months without an overdraft. Looking back, I now think that Will, at some point, had turned himself into a man with a future, but in doing so, he seemed to have erased the past. Not that it mattered, I thought, then. All that wildness belonged to young men. He, in the words that were so often read out at weddings, was putting away childish things. We talked and talked, until the sun went down on our dreams. The sky darkened very suddenly, and I shivered as the evening breeze raised goose-pimples on my bare arm.

'Let's go in,' I tugged Will's arm. In the half-light, the outlines of the topiary that lined the Rosse Manor gardens stretched several acres away from the house, and cast long, dark shadows along the endless lawns. I didn't like the odd rustling I could hear in the hedges. Peaceful suddenly felt deserted. I remembered that someone had told me that a famous person, possibly connected with the Christine Keeler affair or some other ancient political scandal, had apparently hanged himself from the Monkey Puzzle tree in the centre of the rose garden. But that was a very long time ago.

'Hang on until I finish my drink,' he said. 'Or you go on ahead. It's quite safe here. There's none of your inner-city violence in Gloucestershire.'

My inner-city violence? I rather thought that anyone who worked in a hospital might know more about that than I did, cosseted and protected as I was within my glittery media life. I'd call it his inner-city violence. Still, I just didn't want to walk back across the deserted gardens on my own. I'd got very sick of being alone over the past few years, in spite of the parties.

There would be no more of that. Happiness washed over me like a refreshing cloudburst on a hot August day.

'No, I'll wait,' I said, suddenly loving him very much. 'I feel like telling the whole world our news. Let's do some phoning when we get back to the hotel. Who shall we call up first?'

Will treated me to a quizzical half-smile, and turned my hand over as if to read my palm.

'You tell me. Who would you like to phone first?'

'My parents.' They knew Will, and had been cautiously welcoming.

'Well, we'll tell your parents then.'

'What about your mother?'

That smile again. 'I'd rather we told her face to face. This is too important.'

He was right, of course, although I felt obscurely disappointed. I felt our engagement was too important to wait. I was bursting with it. And I wanted to know what his mother was like, and to hear about what he'd been like as a little boy. When I met her, though, eventually, I found a querulous old woman who had lost most of her memories. She never quite grasped who I was.

My parents were delighted, calling each other in from the garden and fussing round so that they could both talk at once down two separate extensions. I could almost see them on the other end of the telephone – my father in his tweed jacket with the leather patches on the elbow and his gardening corduroy trousers, my mother dressed in that indeterminate floral sludge skirt that seemed identical to every other in her wardrobe and all those worn by her friends. I wondered where they found them these days. A dusty boutique called Maison Pamela in some High Street, I supposed. They loved the thought of another wedding. Even the cost of it faded into insignificance at this point. Laura had married almost as soon as she'd left home, and Lindsey straight after Oxford, so I was the last to go. They had been getting worried.

'I think he's certainly sowed his wild oats,' my mother had said, 'probably several sackfuls. But he's awfully sweet.' Sweet? Yuck. Marrying a man your parents think is sweet? I couldn't care less. I loved him, sweet or not.

'Well, he seems a good man,' said Dad. 'Always knew you'd go for someone a bit different.'

Different? I was too happy to analyse it.

'Come down soon,' said my mother. 'The roses are wonderful at the moment.'

'I know,' I put the phone down, and started to get ready for dinner. I sang in the shower, in my tuneless voice, with the door shut tightly and the shower full on. Not that Will was marrying me for my singing, but the sound of me belting out the lyrics to 'Stand By Me' in a flat C was something I'd prefer him not to hear.

With my back still tingling from the jets of hot water, I stepped back into the chintzy bedroom, wearing one of the white towelling robes provided by the hotel. It was a pity, I thought, catching a glimpse of myself in the pier glass, that they stopped at exactly the point that made one's legs look like milk bottles. Will was just putting the phone down.

'Oh, who was that?' I wondered if we had any messages.

'I was just telling someone our news. As you suggested.' Looking back, I thought I remembered an edge in his voice, but I was too happy to take much notice at the time.

'Who?' I hadn't intended it to come out quite so sharply, and he raised an eyebrow.

'Saffron Perry.' He made it sound very casual. 'And James. To tell them to expect a happily engaged couple in Provence.'

That was all right then. But I could feel my forehead puckering in tension. Just slightly.

'She wasn't . . .? I mean, there isn't . . .' It occurred to me that I hadn't asked him when he and Saffron had split up, or who had ditched who. Perhaps she would be devastated. Or angry.

Will read my mind. 'God, no. Saffron's not the marrying kind.'

'Why not?' It made being 'the marrying kind' sound second best.

'She's too . . .' He screwed up his eyes and sighed, as if he couldn't quite explain it.

'Damaged,' he concluded. 'No, that's not the right word. Fragile.' For a moment, his eyes went all shuttered, as if he was a long way away, in another time, a million miles from the leisurely sunset of Rosse Manor. In a different kind of twilight altogether.

For a brief second, something tightened my throat, and made it hard to swallow. I've since decided that Saffron is the kind of woman that men see as vulnerable, mysterious and enigmatic, but who women usually find self-obsessed, depressive and phoney.

'No,' he repeated, in a much more normal tone of voice. 'No, she wouldn't be any good at marriage. Anyway, she's with James, I told you. He seems to be doing her a lot of good.'

I stood there uncertainly, until he reached up and pulled me down to the bed, unwrapping and parting the thick white towelling, so that the rounded curves of my pale, naked body gleamed whitely in the fading light. Pinning my hands down behind my head, he moved his lips close to mine.

'No more questions?' Was he asking, or was it an order?

'No,' I whispered, knowing that in a few moments he would release me and take his clothes off, and that we would miss our booking for dinner. The waiters would have to dance their quadrille with steel food domes for another couple.

But he unbuckled his jeans and, with a few short, sharp thrusts, it was over. I gasped with shock, as if drenched with icy cold water, and then rose to meet him, clinging and meeting his thrusts as if my life depended on it. Just two minutes later, we both lay breathlessly looking at each other, drained, limp, sated.

'Well,' he said. 'Well, well. My little Kitty has claws, after all.'

With an effort I brought myself back to the Maglife art department. I realized that everyone – Camilla, Fortune, Lucy and Mimi – were all looking at me, waiting for me to pronounce on the pictures.

'Lovely,' I said, automatically. 'Brilliant as usual, Fortune.'

He smirked. '*Vogue* are thinking of putting me on contract. So I might not be able to do any more work for you.'

I could feel a worried look tighten all the muscles of my face in spite of knowing that he always said this. It was difficult to get really good photographers to work for *How?* and the pictures were central to what I was doing with the magazine. Photographs appearing in *Vogue* and *Harpers & Queen* guaranteed Fortune the lucrative advertising contracts that really brought in the dosh. If it came to a battle, I would lose every time.

After Fortune had disappeared, kissing Camilla noisily on both cheeks and waving at the rest of us, we sifted through the other fashion pictures for the issue. There was a knitwear shoot using anorexic schoolgirls, all cowering away from the camera as if they had been successively starved and beaten. I wasn't sure that these images really spelt cashmere to me, but Mimi praised the lighting, and Camilla pronounced the clothes 'sexy'. It was the look of the moment. Then we looked at the catwalk shots, which were the usual irrational combinations of colours and textures with the regulation smattering of models minus their underwear, and then, rather unusually, a line of stout women promenading in rubber bathing suits, Argyll socks and walking shoes. For a minute, I thought that Mimi had called in some pictures for a piece on walking holidays we had considered doing (as a way of toning your thighs), but when Camilla saw them she let out a sigh of ecstasy: 'Haiku Brown. They're so directional.'

I wondered if she was taking the mickey, but she pored over them, apparently genuine. 'They're up for the fashion awards,' she murmured reverently.

I didn't know what direction this cross-channel-swimmer look indicated, but I knew it wasn't going to do me any favours when it hit the High Street.

'I think, perhaps, it might be best to major on Galliano, Chloe and Dior,' I laid them firmly in front of Mimi. 'And John Richmond.'

If Camilla wanted to look like a Russian shot-putter that was her problem. I certainly wasn't making it mine, or the readers'.

7

It hadn't all happened exactly the way we'd planned. Instead of becoming a consultant, Will had decided a couple of years after we married, that he'd have a more varied life as a GP. He'd be able to 'make a difference' more effectively at a local level. I'd wondered, briefly, if there'd been some kind of disappointment behind this decision.

He'd laughed and kissed me, then quickly found a practice not far from 37 Branworth Terrace, doing eight surgeries a week.

'When we have children,' he'd told me five years ago, when we thought an easy pregnancy was just months away, 'it'll be useful not to have to travel too far. I'd like to get really involved in bringing them up.'

But the years went by and I still wasn't pregnant. The word 'baby' started to drench me in an icy shower of panic. Every time I opened a magazine there seemed to be an article on falling fertility in the West or a photograph of a smiling, triumphant mother with a bouncing baby acquired in the face of terrible odds and an almost torturous series of treatments. Even the newspapers went through cycles of proclaiming the baby an essential accessory. Family life, I had thought, was a baton that you handed down the generations, the way Lindsey and Laura did. I'd visualized pregnancy, birth, how I'd arrange my day with a small baby, what I'd do on my maternity leave, how I'd organize a nanny, everything. Everything except the prospect of stalling at the aunt level, and then being promoted merely to great-aunt. Even being a successful great-aunt didn't seem to have any compensations. Every time I went to a supermarket it seemed to be full of pregnant women. Suppose I couldn't get pregnant? I wasn't sure I could face it.

Three years ago, Will had quietly done a few basic blood tests on us both, and our hormone levels seemed to be fine. Up until a few months ago, we'd decided that the key to success was not to get too wound up about it all, and we'd reassured each other that we had plenty of time. We'd argued about what we should be doing, and never quite felt the same way at the same time, but eventually we'd seen the sense of the ruling that doctors can't treat their own family, and formally made the appointment at the infertility clinic.

Now three weeks into my new job, the appointment loomed, making me feel hunted and guilty. There was bound to be something I was doing wrong, drinking too much coffee for example, or red wine, or some really illogical or irritating diktat would be foisted on me like having to eat – or not eat – something apparently harmless like bananas. I did not want to be interfered with. I had visualized birth as a natural, wholesome process, the ultimate fulfilling trip. I associated it with curves and softness, not the hard, sharp, straight lines of needles and medical instruments.

I didn't say any of this, of course, when I kissed him goodbye and set out into the crisp April air. The breeze had just the edge of softness about it, a brightness rather than warmth, with sharp shoots of green bursting out on stark wooden branches. I thought I could hear birdsong, although as I got closer to the Tube, I decided it was probably a mobile phone, or several, trilling in people's briefcases and handbags.

Maglife Tower felt like home now. I said good morning to Maeve, and, just as the lift doors were about to shut Peter Rennie stepped in.

'Morning, Maeve. Morning, Leonie.' He peered at me as if confirming my identity, and then said, 'Are we seeing you at the House of Commons lunch today?'

It was the first I'd heard of it. 'I . . . er . . . haven't checked my diary. I've got a lunch of some kind in, certainly.'

'Good, good. Very important to be seen in the right places.'

I was bewildered. House of Commons lunch. It sounded most unlikely, unless some perfume company had managed to hire the whole chamber for the day and re-create it, complete with actors, as it would have been in the fourteenth century for the launch of a perfume called 'Freedom' or 'Liberty' or something. Anything was possible in the over-the-top world of perfumery.

My diary did not have any such lunch in it. There

was a sandwiches-and-mineral-water session booked for the boardroom on training. 'Lucy?'

Lucy hadn't heard anything about it either. I was just about to work out which of the other editors was friendliest, and might be prepared to enlighten me when Camilla arrived, looking stunning in cream Armani.

'You look fantastic,' I told her.

'Thanks.' Compliments about clothes were about the only safe exchange between us.

'Are you going somewhere?' Perhaps, with any luck, for a job interview.

She shrugged minutely. 'One of those dull lunches. You know.'

'You don't know anything about a House of Commons lunch, do you?'

Her eyes widened. 'Oh, that's the one I'm going to. Have they invited you, too?'

Challenging Camilla could be dangerous, so I thought carefully before my next question.

'Weren't they inviting all the editors? Peter Rennie seemed to think so.'

She had lifted her phone and started dialling, signalling that she was not available for a long conversation. 'I've no idea. They called me personally.' I gave up, as I heard her shriek a greeting down the phone.

The sandwiches-and-mineral-water training session was full of deputy editors. '*How?* is so lucky to have an editor that takes an interest in junior training,' the personnel director told me warmly as I left. 'I can't tell you how difficult it is to get editors to turn up in person, and really, unless you get the grass roots thing right, the boat's all top heavy.'

I smiled, trying to decipher the mixed metaphors, and couldn't help wondering how I seemed to be where Camilla was supposed to be, and she had finished up where I should be, if Peter Rennie was correct. I decided to risk some possible loss of face and asked Lucy, who went scarlet.

'Do you think . . .' she was almost stuttering, 'that she raided your post tray?'

I was startled. Surely not? I wondered how desperate she was, and felt a stirring of pity under the anger at having my mail invaded. 'Do you think she could have done?'

'She could have done,' admitted Lucy. 'Sometimes she's quite . . . er . . . helpful . . . about the post.'

This, I suspected, was code for Camilla's impatience at the way Lucy floundered over the toppling pile of mail that came into the office every day. I'd seen her flicking expertly through the envelopes, picking out with an unerring eye anything that was hand-written or on stiff card. She usually let the boring brown A4 envelopes slip to the floor, from where Lucy eventually picked them up.

'Well, keep an eye on it. We'll be sharing all the invitations out between us anyway, so there's no need for her to be secretive about it. It's not as if we can get to half of the parties as it is.'

Lucy looked relieved.

I contemplated an escalation of hostilities by asking Camilla outright if there were any invitations she'd accepted that I really ought to be going to. I cast a look at her diary, sitting in leather-bound splendour on her desk, and wished I was the sort of person who thought it was all right to inspect it closely.

But I wasn't. Petty, I reminded myself. Very petty. The phone rang again.

'It's your sister,' snuffled Lucy. I decided not to ruin her day by asking which one. She'd probably crumble. Anyway Lindsey only ever did secretary-to-secretary calls, which involved lengthy, echoing technological silences while you got put 'on hold' and then accidentally diverted to the bought ledger department. So probably Laura.

It was. She sounded unusually subdued.

'I wondered if we could have lunch. Tomorrow.'

Something was definitely up. Laura's idea of the perfect child-free lunch was a salad sandwiched between two serious shopping expeditions. There were no shops in the urban wasteland around Maglife, except for a few newsagents and an expensive, but tiny supermarket. But then, knowing Laura, she'd expect me to get into a cab and come to her.

'Well . . .' I just couldn't waste time grappling with London's traffic. I couldn't really waste time having lunch, for that matter. 'Couldn't we make it Monday?'

'I go to the playgroup on Mondays.'

This hardly seemed pressing. 'Couldn't you miss it?'

'Routine,' Laura spoke unusually sanctimoniously, 'is essential for children's security.'

That was rich. While Lindsey's children were so regimented that they virtually goose-stepped downstairs in formation every morning, Laura had never paid the slightest attention to routine, breast-feeding on demand for years and apparently letting the children go to bed at midnight if they felt like it. I began to protest.

'Please . . .' said Laura. 'You could just pop into a cab.'

I rallied. 'I can't pop into a cab. I really can't. There's the most dreadful panic on.'

She sighed, a short puff that indicated how much she always did in the face of massive ingratitude from the world. 'Okay. I'll come to you. See you in your reception at one? Bye.' Laura would usually have manoeuvred me into finally getting a taxi and spending about three hours in a traffic jam, but she'd caved in so quickly that I realized the cab had been a diversion to take my mind off saying 'no'. That girl's talents are wasted at home, they really are. She ought to be out selling encyclopaedias or double glazing or becoming a politician or something.

The following day, I took her round the corner to an old print-works that had been converted into a restaurant, erratically painted in ice-cream shades to emphasize how super-cool it was. Laura, who was wearing her up-to-town outfit – a too-tight navy blazer over a bulging pair of jeans, settled herself on a caramel-coloured banquette and tore at pieces of rosemary focaccia the minute it arrived.

'God, I'm starving. Did I tell you,' she said, with her mouth full, 'that I've signed on as a distributor of children's books? I'll be selling them at school fairs, and giving coffee mornings. I can't tell you what a hassle it all is. God!' She munched a bit more. 'I don't know how I'll stand it really. Still, I earned £54.10 yesterday which is, apparently, brilliant for your first time.'

It was good news because they were always terribly broke, but hardly earth-shattering.

'But that's not why you wanted to have lunch.'

She flushed, and opened her mouth, but obviously didn't want to continue with the waiters hovering over us, waving menus and pressing drinks on us. Once everything had settled down a bit, she started fiddling with the pepper-pot.

'I'm pregnant again.'

What I had dismissed as pudgy self-indulgence in her face now seemed like a halo of radiant fertility, veiling her features in a new softness. I felt a short, sharp stabbing pain that it was never – perhaps would never be – me. It was like being the last to be picked for rounders, and having to sit most of the game on the sidelines. For a moment I felt the hand of real terror clutching at my heart, squeezing it so tightly I could hardly breathe.

I was suddenly struck by an even worse thought. 'You weren't thinking of ... er ... ?' I could only assume that she'd come to me to find out how she could arrange an abortion. The rosemary focaccia in my stomach heaved and bubbled sickeningly at the thought. 'I mean, I know you're broke and knackered, but I'm sure . . .' More awful options piled in thick and fast, stacked up like planes waiting to land at Heathrow. Perhaps she was expecting Will and me to adopt it – it was absolutely the sort of solution my family were likely to come up with, after all that whispering on Sunday. I suspected our ongoing child-lessness was under constant discussion.

'Oh, no!' There was a pause. 'I just thought you'd be . . .'

'Be what?' I didn't like the sound of this.

'You know . . . be . . .'

I thought of the way she and Lindsey had excluded me on Sunday, and leant back in my chair, folding my arms. 'No, I don't know.'

She ran her hands through her hair in an unnecess-arily melodramatic way. 'For God's sake, Leonie, don't make this so difficult for me.'

'I'm not making this anything.' I now knew exactly what she meant, and I hadn't been so angry since . . . well, since . . . Lindsey, in the throes of her first adolescent clearout had passed down all her old dolls, including one I had coveted for years, to Laura, because, at five, she was still a baby. Lindsey always had to know what was best for me. She'd decided I was too old for dolls at ten, and that was that. No question of asking me if I'd like to make up my own mind. Laura, in turn, had followed Lindsey like a little dog, with an unquestioning devotion that made me sick. I glared at her. 'You're the one who started the conversation.'

We both stared at the white linen tablecloth for a moment, and I wondered if Will was also part of the plot to break things gently to me.

'Did Will know we were meeting for lunch?'

'What do you mean?'

I took an exaggerated deep breath. 'Did you, or did you not, tell Lindsey and Will you were having a baby at Mum's birthday? And did they, or did they not, tell you that I might be rather upset about it, and that it would be better if you told me yourself, privately, at a lunch, rather than hitting me with it in front of everyone?' Sympathy from one's family was the ultimate humiliation.

She wouldn't meet my eyes. 'Not exactly.'

'Not exactly. But pretty close?'

'Well, you see, you are upset.'

I could feel my jaw seizing up. 'I am NOT UPSET.' The two diners next to us, whose table was rammed so fashionably close to ours that we could practically see up their nostrils, stopped talking and looked round at us.

'Sh,' implored Laura. 'Please.'

'I'm not upset. I'm FURIOUS.' Two women on the other side, both dressed in beige (currently this season's 'new grey' or 'new white' or whatever), twitched nervously, but were clearly too cool to acknowledge any sign of a scene. Laura looked around, and I almost expected Will to step out from the pistachio-tinted shadows and calm us both down. 'I'm furious,' I repeated in a more normal tone of voice (at least, I thought it was more normal. Laura's eyes widened in terror, but then she was always a wimp). 'I'm furious because you think I'm such a mean-minded, selfish sister that I can't be pleased for you when you've got good news.' Suddenly I was back in the garden at home, aged about eight, with the three-year-old Laura bawling, and my mother scold-ing me for pushing her over, while I tried to explain that I hadn't pushed her, I'd been helping her up and trying to stop her falling over. Nobody ever listened and I used to be treated to sensible, patient, understanding lectures about not being jealous of her because she was so little. It's just not fair. I felt a choking at the back of my throat and my eyes stung.

'Well, it's not good news,' said Laura, in that old familiar voice of someone who always gets the raw deal. 'We haven't got another bedroom, and we can't fit three children in the car, not with Pongo (their massive labrador, quite unsuitable for a two-bedroom inner city cottage) and we don't have any money. In fact, I cried when I got the test result.' The waiter laid down two plates of roasted vegetables in a pesto sauce. 'It's all such a muddle.'

Irritation at the chaos of Laura's life cheered me up. 'But you're not thinking of . . . er . . .' We seemed to have got right back to the beginning of the conversation in a giant loop.

She shook her head miserably.

'And what does Paul think?'

'Paul?' She tore impatiently at another piece of bread. 'What's he got to do with it? He's never there.'

'Why not?' Paul always seemed so amiable, and, in his quiet, gentle way, a devoted father.

'Because,' she spoke venomously, 'he has to work until midnight some nights in the hope that one day – one day, mind you, not this year – he'll be made a partner. If he doesn't get made a partner we have to manage on his pathetic salary.'

I didn't think this was very fair of her. After all, lots of people manage on a junior accountant's salary and count themselves lucky. But I knew that the loss of her wages had hit them hard when Phoebe was born, and they found the mortgage payments on their little terraced cottage a great strain. I also knew that without him getting a partnership, they'd always struggle. Until Laura could get back to proper work, which she showed absolutely no sign of doing. She'd never earned enough to pay for childcare, so it'd have to be something that fitted in with school. Heaven only knows what, and it occurred to me that she blamed Paul for her lack of options. That's the way she treated him now anyway.

However, options or no, she was always too tired to think about work because of the way the children trooped in and out of their bedroom all night. I wondered if she was going to give birth to a third sleep-defying fiend.

'I just hope this one sleeps.' She was obviously thinking along the same lines.

I refrained from suggesting sleep clinics or pressing on her review copies of books on getting babies to sleep (you wouldn't think they'd send these to magazines about home decorating, would you?). I was quite sure that if only she was a little firmer and more disciplined then Phoebe and Zack could be just as angelic as Lindsey's poppets. It must be just a question of parenting.

'Well, Lindsey manages three, and none of hers has ever woken up,' I pointed out, which I thought was very restrained of me in the circumstances. She could draw her own conclusions. Lindsey had told me that the midwife had said that babies would sleep through the night 'from 13 weeks or 13 pounds, whichever comes earlier'. And hers had. That's what good management does for you.

'Yes,' Laura's voice was conspiratorial. 'But I've always suspected that she paid someone else to have them, and just stuck a cushion up her executive suit for the whole nine months. I mean, you can't imagine her in the labour room in those court shoes and American Tan tights, can you?'

'And you can't imagine her ever taking them off,' we chorused. We laughed.

We enjoyed ourselves dissecting Lindsey for a bit, woven together as we were in a cat's cradle of criticism, disapproval and mutual support. I knew that Laura and Lindsey must mutter about how I really ought to get a move on if I wanted children, and I'd be telling Lindsey how irresponsible it was of Laura not to be more careful with contraception, what with two children already and that enormous dog. (Pongo was absurd, and led to endless exhaustion on Laura's part as she trundled the buggy round the Commons with a reluctant Phoebe hauled along in a grizzling trail behind.)

But I envied Laura her life. It seemed uncompli- cated, without choices, and almost Zen-like in its simplicity. If she wasn't my sister, I wouldn't believe that people like Laura still existed. She and Paul had spotted each other the minute they popped out of the egg at twenty-something. It seemed as if she had never had to fight for her survival on her own, as she had moved smoothly from Mum and Dad's to a flat in London with four other girls. She'd met Paul in the first week of independence and married him four years later. She'd left her job at the Fulham Road boutique at the age of twenty-eight when Phoebe was born. Laura had never had to ask herself difficult questions like whether she should have a baby by a man who was still helping his ex-girlfriend find her stop tap.

I wasn't in the least upset about Laura's pregnancy, not really, of course. I just wished everyone else could have been a bit more grown-up about it. I hated to think of people being sorry for me behind my back.

With a massive effort, I tried to get this across to Laura.

'I really am pleased for you, you know. I really am not in the least bit worried about the whole thing. If it happens, it happens . . . you know.'

'Mm.' Laura squeezed my arm. 'Thanks.' She had to remove hers when the waiter began hoovering up the crumbs on the table with some funny little electric gadget. 'But have you thought of IVF? I've got this friend who tried for simply years, and now she's . . .'

I waved my hand for the bill, and shrugged. I was not in the mood for lots of advice and uplifting tales of Couples Who Had Finally Succeeded. People sought me out more vigorously every year to tell me such tales.

'This is nice,' observed Laura, hardly bothering to conceal her envy as she glanced round the restaurant. 'You're so lucky. You really don't know how good your life is, with that expense account of yours.'

I thought of a story I'd read recently in some magazine about a woman who'd finally had a 'miracle' baby after six years of IVF. She'd cycled up from Dover to Hammersmith every morning before work for an injection. Something like that anyway. Will and I just didn't have time for endless hospital waits, and feeling sick after injections, and another whole raft of appointments to be fitted into our diaries. Perhaps, I thought, for about the hundredth time in the last few years, nature would just take its course. It often did, according to lots of magazines, the best treatment was just to forget about the whole thing and relax.

I resolved to relax. Properly. My jaw set like concrete at the thought of it, and I could feel the sinews of my neck stand out with the effort of this fresh goal. Relax, I repeated, mentally trying to make the space between my eyes wider, a tip we had recommended recently in *How?*. Much better to relax. The only trouble was, there were just a few hours left in which to relax before I got sucked into the system. Our appointment was at 4.30 this afternoon.

I felt a fraud tiptoeing along the linoleum corridors of the hospital. It was a place for sick people, not for spoiled women who couldn't quite manage a baby exactly when they wanted one. I passed a woman holding a tiny, crumpled newborn baby up against her shoulder and felt a sudden, painfully sharp pang. Perhaps there was something terribly wrong with me, after all. Nobody else seemed to be having these problems. It was a frightening thought. Will strode confidently, one half-step ahead.

'Don't worry,' he told me as he sat down on a shiny metal seat, shaped like a pelvis and obviously designed to make sure no one lingered on it any longer than they had to. 'It won't hurt.'

I looked at him and honesty forced him to qualify it slightly: 'Well, there may be some discomfort with some of the procedures. But not today anyway.'

Squeezing my knee, he added, 'I'll be with you all the way, don't forget.'

I smiled at hearing him slip into doctor-speak. 'It must be funny for you being on the receiving end of hospitals for a change.' I was determined not to show that I was scared. Just slightly. And it was nothing to what anyone coming in for cancer tests would feel, I reminded myself, to get everything back into proportion.

'No, not really.' He didn't explain why not, and picked up an old copy of *Woman's Own*, getting instantly engrossed in a story about a woman who'd been born with a third breast.

I looked cautiously round the room, determined not to meet anyone's eye. This was too private. In one corner, a woman dressed in a navy wool coat sobbed silently into a tissue. Everyone tried to pretend she didn't exist. No one wanted to reach out to her. We were just hanging together ourselves.

Will and I didn't talk any more. We were both edgy, wary of being blamed, I suppose. I worried that tests might find something really wrong with me – or him – that couldn't be fixed. I really dreaded them asking us difficult questions like 'How many times a week do you have sex?' Or even 'Do you have orgasms?' The whole area seemed fraught with things I did not want to talk about. Over his shoulders I could see he was reading the inevitable 'Miracle Baby' story, with its happy ending. But happy endings, I was beginning to think, belonged to other people. They were distant, foreign-sounding events, like elections in obscure Bavarian states.

We'd been there forty minutes, and read several copies of *Woman's Own*, plus *Chat*, *Woman's Weekly*, *Girl About Town* and even a cheering copy of *Woman & Home* that someone had left. I looked around for something that Will might enjoy and came up with a sepia-tinged and curling copy of *Caravanning Today*. A couple opposite me, who had been holding hands and talking in whispers, looked away when our eyes met.

Will flicked through *Caravanning Today* with amusement. A door opened. We all stiffened upright, noses pointed hopefully towards the uniformed nurse. Will squeezed my hand. She flicked through her papers, looking for the name. 'Mr and Mrs . . . ah . . . Pemberton.' The other couple sprang up, beaming like lottery winners, while we slumped back on the uncomfortable metal pelvises. Another forty minutes to go, probably. Perhaps we should just forget about the whole thing. Will squeezed my knee. 'Not long, now.'

I looked at him and we exchanged a secret smile. Suddenly, I felt it was all going to be all right. We were together.

We read the notices for the tenth time. Diabetes and pregnancy fact sheets, infertility groups, HIV counselling. A hand-written note asking everyone giving samples to use the Toilet on the right-hand side and to pass their bottles through the hatch to the laboratory. Worst of all, there was a noticeboard with photographs of babies born in the IVF unit over the past five years. There were lots of them, dog-eared and fading, pinned roughly to the board. 'Our babies', said the notice. I counted them to pass the time. There were around thirty of them. I knew that not everyone would have sent a picture of their baby, but even so, considering there must be about forty-five appointments a week, I felt disheartened. Simultaneously, illogically, I also resented being reminded of all the babies other people managed to have.

Another door opened and a pleasant-looking young woman with brown hair drawn back in a short pony tail, and a suit, rather than a white coat, popped her head out. 'Mr and Mrs Bailey?'

I jumped up, dropping my bag and letting the *Woman's Own* slip to the floor.

The young woman – surely too young to have qualified – settled herself on the other side of a desk, as I sat down, feeling flustered.

'My name is Dr Hardy.' She put her hand out to shake.

'Mine's Dr Bailey.' She and Will locked eyes.

'Another doctor!' She didn't sound particularly pleased about it. 'I expect you know more about all this than I do.'

'Absolutely not,' Will reassured her.

Her pen flew over the page. Address. Profession. (Another raised eyebrow at that: 'We have a lot of ladies here with high-powered careers.') Daytime telephone number. Evening telephone number. Illnesses.

'Any previous pregnancies?'

We were into the system. It was like buying a parking permit, all waits and questions and documentation.

I asked her if I should modify my lifestyle, bracing myself for unwelcome recommendations in terms of food, sleep and stress-reduction. And they hadn't mentioned sex yet, which presumably was bound to come in at some point.

Dr Hardy smiled dismissively. 'We like to ask you to drink in moderation and to give up smoking. There isn't really anything else you can do.'

Not a holistic treatment, then. Her voice implied that my inability to have a baby was quite unconnected with any other part of my life, which was reassuring in one way, but made me feel that I had a disembodied womb. Perhaps I could go out partying and leave my reproductive organs behind to get on with their business.

'We don't like you to be on the fertility drugs for too long,' she explained, locking her fingers together and smiling like a bank manager. 'So I'll just prescribe you a three-month course.'

'I understand,' I thought I'd bring up the subject before she did, 'that sex every other day maximizes sperm potential.'

She looked slightly surprised, as if she'd forgotten sex existed. 'Yes, that's what we recommend.'

Every other day sounded quite hard enough work, but I couldn't help remembering something I'd read recently. 'But didn't that Danish study come out last year with the conclusion that although sperm counts did rise with abstinence and fall with daily sex, it didn't make any difference to pregnancy rates?'

The smile turned glacial. 'Well, of course, if you wish to disregard our advice, there's very little we can do about it. But I'm only telling you how we get our best results.'

I could see that independent thought was not going to be appreciated. Will nudged my foot gently under the table. After all, if he, the doctor, wasn't asking any questions, who was I to throw a spanner in the works?

We made arrangements for a laparoscopy in ten weeks' time. That was when the prodding about would really begin.

I promised myself to be very, very good about having sex every other day until then, in the hope that it would all prove unnecessary.

'One last thing I feel I should say.' Dr Hardy took off her glasses and laid them on her desk, an absurdly middle-aged gesture for such an apparently young woman. 'You've seen the statistics. You know what the success rate is.'

We nodded. It was highest at that particular clinic which is why we'd chosen to come here.

'So you know what your chances are statistically. This means we cannot guarantee that you have a baby. It's very important that everyone embarking on this programme knows that. Ultimately, the outcome is not under our control.'

If you don't get pregnant, in other words, it is not

our fault. I felt as if she was washing her hands of us already.

At 8.30 p.m., the house was so still that the click of the front door echoed softly behind us. I switched the lights on, and walked into the kitchen, tiredness scraping at my eyes and throbbing through my feet, weighing me down as if gravity had suddenly doubled and thickened into a leaden haze. The inside of the fridge was not appealing. Two or three mis-shapen vegetables had grown blue fur, to the extent that you couldn't tell whether they were tomatoes or peppers, and a lump of sweaty cheese glowed a stagnant yellow, almost radioactive in its malevolence. I shut the door, and briefly leant against it. One day I would clean the fridge out. Until then, perhaps it was best ignored. A brief vision of a fridge full of gleaming red, green and orange food for healthy children floated across my mind like a hallucination, and I dismissed it.

'That wasn't too bad in the end, was it?' Will pulled a bottle of white wine out of the fridge. 'Here's to sex every other day.' He raised the bottle in salute and ran the other hand down my back in a proprietorial way. I twitched away. It was all very well for him.

But I could see something distant and anxious in his eyes, and it occurred to me that even as a doctor, he might feel just as vulnerable as I did about this whole procedure. He'd been so irreverent and funny when we'd first met, so confident in his ability to challenge anyone. I wondered if I'd changed him, or life, or whether it was just this apparently hopeless quest to achieve something that any half-educated schoolgirl on a deprived council estate seemed to manage so effortlessly. Having a baby.

'Don't forget, we're not supposed to drink too much,' I reminded him.

'Give me a break.' But he said it quite nicely, wrinkling up his nose and pulling me affectionately towards him. He poured us both a glass and I drank it, disliking both myself and the sharp, vinegary back-bite of the wine. Why did we do it, I asked myself, when the bottle sat empty on the draining board a few hours later? There'd be another hangover tomorrow.

We were numb with the exhaustion of watching too much television because we were so tired. Will turned to me silently, drawing my head into his arms and leaning his cheek against my hair.

'Sh.' He held me firmly as I started awake, his jumper tinged faintly with that antiseptic smell of hospitals and surgeries, along with other city smells, such as the faintly metallic odour of the Underground and the lingering acrid notes of exhaust fumes. 'Sh.'

I don't know how long we rocked there gently, clinging together.

'It's time to go upstairs,' he whispered eventually. 'I'm sorry.'

I wondered what he was sorry about. Perhaps he felt as guilty as I did that we were having to embark on fertility treatment.

'It's too late,' I said. 'Too late.' I didn't know what I meant.

'I know,' he murmured. 'We're going to bed. I'll help you get undressed.' It had been a long time since someone suggested something like that. It was like having a parent again to help with homework. He pushed me upstairs, and ran a bath, undressing me and washing my back.

'There,' he said, pulling a stretchy T-shirt nightie over my head. 'All right now.'

'You rat,' I murmured. 'Setting Laura on me like that. She came for lunch today, you know.'

He lifted up the duvet for me to get in. 'I just didn't want you to be hurt.' The sheets felt cool and soft, and, as I slipped into sleep, I put my arms out towards him.

At some point in the middle of the night, we half-woke and moved together gently, in soft, damp and silky movements. Gliding and sighing, I shuddered quietly and sank off again to sleep, feeling his breath rise and fall evenly against my neck, and the warm solidity of his arm across mine.

8

I felt a great deal happier when I woke up the following morning. Perhaps the simple fact of going to the infertility clinic had signified a new level of commitment between us. It reassured me that we were, as we'd always been, on the same side, cupped into each other's bodies like spoons.

At work, however, I had to deal with yet another of my predecessor's bad decisions. She'd agreed to carry a series of supplements, starting with the September issue and running until December (for heaven's sake), sponsored by a company called Bellingham Glass. This was a company which specialized in making unspeakable glass goblets, hefty, over-elaborate glass vases and fantastically over-priced whisky tumblers, along with a great number of other outstandingly unnecessary items. Maeve (in her role as publisher and therefore chief-money-getter for *How?*) and I were booked in to visit the Bellingham Glass factory in Easbiton, a suburb a few miles outside the M25, and, frankly, I could have done without the journey. Apart from the appalling prospect of being yoked to Bellingham Glass for four interminable issues, it would mean the whole morning gone. The days until the May edition went to press had ticked away without my being able to make any real difference to the magazine. There was so much that, for one reason or another, I hadn't been able to change. It was frustrating.

'I'm not sure these supplements are a good idea,' I told Maeve in the train on the way down there.

'They'll be fine.' She patted my arm with a gloved hand. Gloves! I hadn't seen anyone wearing gloves, except as a brief, rather deliberate fashion statement, for years. Maeve, I was sure, wore gloves to protect her hands from anything unladylike, such as cold or wind. 'I'm sorry you've got to go through this, but I'm afraid we couldn't possibly afford to lose a spend the size of the Bellingham Glass account. Advertising and promotion money is hard enough to come by as it is.'

As we pulled into the station, I could see a sign on the side of a factory saying 'Bellingham Glass welcomes you to Easbiton'. Most of the buildings in Easbiton looked as if they'd been left there accidentally. Even the few Victorian terraces looked like unsuccessful samples for later, more elegant models, and the overwhelming impression was one of rubbish blowing across concrete or grey buildings with their backs turned. There were two ropey minicabs waiting outside a kiosk, and once we settled ourselves inside one, it smelled of cigarette smoke.

We were ushered into the boardroom to meet Dave Beckett, MD of Bellingham Glass, and his marketing department, which consisted of Alison someone and

Janet something, plus a young man with a pony tail, whose name I couldn't catch. Cases of glass, each more hideous than the last, were displayed on the walls.

'Bellingham Glass is known for its quality,' intoned Dave Beckett, after welcoming me fulsomely.

Just as well, really. It didn't, on first glance, appear to have much else to offer.

The company's problem was, apparently, that not only were fewer couples getting married, but those that did no longer automatically expected to receive an item of Bellingham Glass as a wedding present. Looking at the brightly coloured brochures Dave Beckett spread in front of me, packed busily with Bellingham Glass trophies and vases, many decorated with a few stiff carnations, I wondered whether anyone had ever chosen a piece of Bellingham Glass for themselves. Perhaps the whole company had survived for generations on making items that were thrust at people, then consigned to a dark cupboard.

However, Bellingham Glass owners apparently saw Bellingham as a way of life, according to Dave. The marketing team leant forward with the enthusiasm of Jehovah's Witnesses about to make a convert.

'Every milestone is marked with a piece of Bellingham Glass. Christenings, confirmations, graduations, gold and silver wedding anniversaries. We are the European leader in golfing trophies. We recently supplied presentation shields to the Far East for synchronized swimming competitions. Our marriage goblets are, of course, famous world-wide.' He unlocked a cabinet behind him and pulled out a piece of two-handled crystal, too big to drink out of and too wide-lipped and shallow for flower arranging. I wondered what people used it for. This was inscribed 'To celebrate the marriage of Mavis Dawkins and Henry Browne, 19 March 1952'. I wondered if Mavis or Henry had ever been unfaithful. Perhaps Bellingham could do a cut-glass condom on a stand and inscribe it to mark the event as a milestone.

As Dave mapped out the Bellingham Glass buyer in more detail, anything as disorganized as infidelity seemed increasingly unlikely. Instead they had fan clubs, newsletters and waiting lists for limited edition pieces.

By the time we'd been marched round all ten acres of the Bellingham Glass site, and introduced to every single glass-blower and packaging expert, been given goggles and ear defenders, a plastic helmet and a white coat, I was faint with despair. Maeve, who had seen it all before thousands of times, was impassive.

'What do you think of it all?' asked Dave Beckett triumphantly.

I murmured that I'd no idea that glass was so complicated to make.

'Not all glass,' said Dave Beckett proudly. 'We have no less than five extra stages in the making of Bellingham Glass.' I came out of the factory knowing even less about glass-making than when I went in. Information overload, I think they call it.

Bellingham Glass was a way of life for its employees too, many of whose families had worked for the company for three generations. For a hundred-odd years, all the workforce had regarded Bellingham as a part of the family. A benevolent uncle. Only Dave himself had come from 'the outside'.

'The board decided they wanted a fresh approach,' he explained. 'It was a big challenge. I hit the ground running.' He had come from a tractor manufacturer, and an animal foodstuffs' company before that. His role at Bellingham was to spearhead some big new investments, and he'd had to make a quarter of the workforce redundant. He spoke as if 'letting people go' was like lancing a boil. Painful, of course, but a great relief all round once it was done.

'Glass, tractors, washing machines . . .' he explained, with a wave of his hand. 'It's the marketing principles that matter. As products they're all the same.'

A coach drew up outside the 1950s porch at the front of the main office, and disgorged a party of women dressed like the Queen, sprinkled with a peppering of men who looked as if they were on their way to visit a War Memorial. Bellingham Glass buyers, explained Dave Beckett.

'The trouble is,' he added, in a rare moment of plain speaking once we were inside, 'that they're all dying off.'

The thought of Bellingham Glass Special Edition Bedpans or Hip Replacements flitted briefly through my mind.

'So,' he said, taking me by my elbow and guiding me into a claustrophobically small lift. 'We've been updating our designs. In the same Bellingham quality.'

The updated designs were fairly similar to the traditional ones, but with more rounded edges and less decorative detail. Not dissimilar, in fact, to the cut-glass condom of my fantasies. He waved a hand. 'We've got a new range of casual dining glass. Very innovative.' His tone placed 'casual dining glass' on a level with a cure for cancer. Or some new material discovered on the moon.

It turned out to be a range of quite nice coloured glass beakers, with solid bottoms and the famous purple tinge deepened to a rich hue.

'Lovely,' I said.

We sat back down at the boardroom table. 'You'll need new photographs,' I told him. Bellingham's past brochures were spread out on the boardroom table in all their lurid glory, packed with stiff photographs and busy detail. I visualized a soft focus, more romantic image in a cooler, cleaner, more contemporary background. Some glittering close-ups of glass shimmering temptingly from a whole page. I wondered what Fortune would make of the glass condom trophies. He was the only photographer we used who really could make anything look fashionable and glorious. And I had discovered that, in spite of his threats about *Vogue*, Fortune liked to work. He had an expensive habit. Perhaps Bellingham could appeal to the younger customer with a cut-glass cocaine tray, plus snorting spoon. Engraved with carnations, of course.

I took a grip on myself. This was business.

After a nod from Dave, Alison came to life. She began to sketch out what Bellingham Glass wanted from these supplements.

'A lifestyle approach. A day in the life theme.'

'Updated,' interjected Dave.

'Contemporary without being over-modern,' confirmed Alison.

'We're looking for a unique approach,' she continued. 'Although, care should be taken not to be too different.'

'Informative,' prompted Dave.

'Informative,' she agreed, 'but not wordy. Our research shows that ninety per cent of people don't read the words in our brochures. But the Bellingham customer is very literate. And discerning.'

They wittered on like this for a bit, but Dave Beckett seemed to be prepared to spend an enormous amount of money on the supplements. Which was lovely, but I couldn't help wondering if there was really any point in trying to convince a world in which one in four babies were born out of wedlock that a marriage goblet was a must-have item. Wouldn't it be better to make something that people did want?

Back in the office, that afternoon, I decided to go through ideas for the supplements with the staff. Much as I hated the whole concept, it had to be as good as we could make it.

After a more or less successful series of sessions, I finally reached Ginny, the fashion editor, a stringy-haired blonde dressed from head-to-Patrick Cox-clad-toe in swathes of baggy beige. Camilla and Mimi, tired of a morning of sitting down, perked up at the thought of talking about clothes.

Ginny's ideas were always good. She ran through September, October and November as we nodded our heads in agreement. Then she tossed a scarf over her shoulder and proceeded to map out her plan for the Christmas 'Touch of Glass' supplement, currently full of ideas for sparkling recipes for festive drinks in which I suspected the horrible Bellingham Glass punchbowl might have to feature. We planned to have it so festooned in decorations that it was scarcely visible.

'I thought we could shoot the Christmas party evening wear on musicians from an orchestra,' explained Ginny. 'Provided that we picked the good-looking ones. All black and white, stark and graphic, with some crumbling gilt backdrops, and glittering glass chandeliers.' Her eyes shone at the thought of it. Bellingham Glass did, fortunately, have a chandelier which would look very nice provided it was photo-graphed out of focus with lots of twinkle everywhere.

I liked the idea. She had a pile of cards with photographs of the musicians. A really stunning flautist. Two ethereal violinists, as alike as twins. A statuesque cellist ('useful for the over-16 fashion' interjected Ginny, 'and most of the cellulite will be hidden behind the cello anyway'). Finally, she tossed down the last card.

'And we need a pianist, of course.'

Of course. I picked up the photo, a flutter of tension in my stomach telling me what I would see before my eyes spotted the cascade of curls, and the sculpted, almost mannish face. It was Saffron. I looked at it hard, to give myself time to think, and reflected that it must have been taken several years ago. I had heard almost nothing of her career for years – she never seemed to make a record, or be playing at the ENO, or appear on even the most arty late-night television programme. But it was a world I knew nothing about, so I presumed that she had been quietly going from strength to strength somehow. Occasionally I wondered if she'd ever lived up to her early promise, but felt rather ashamed of wishing her ill in this way. It was no skin off my nose whether she was successful or not. It wasn't ability or fame that had drawn Will to her. At least, I didn't think so.

'She looks fab.' Ginny filled the silence, obviously anxious that I might, for some mad reason known only to myself, turn down the perfect model for Christmas party fashion.

I put the card down. 'She won't do it. She's not very keen on publicity. I went on holiday in Provence with her once. She told me that she didn't like appearing in magazines.' That hadn't been quite what she'd said, but never mind.

'Oh, but she will.' Ginny sounded relieved to have got that sorted out. 'I sounded her out, and she said she was an old friend of yours and would do it as a special favour.' She looked at me, and the set of her mouth told me that she was determined to have that cascade of hair tumbling down the V of some backless evening dress.

Camilla picked up the card. 'Amazing face. Really strong. And fantastic hair.' She passed it to Mimi.

'Mm.' Mimi, for some reason, turned the card on its side, and then over again. 'She'll look great in clothes. As slim as a model.'

I took the card back. 'You know that this is quite an old photo. She's in her mid-forties now.' This was only a slight exaggeration – I thought she was probably around forty-three.

'Really?' Mimi's face lit up. 'That's brilliant! The others are all so young, we need a bit of balance.'

'She still looks great,' added Ginny. 'I met her at a party. That's what gave me the idea for the feature.'

Really? How convenient. I wondered if Saffron had actually suggested it all herself to seep even more pervasively into my life. I had to remind myself that, as far as I could see, Saffron barely considered me as more than a boring addendum to Will. It was even quite possible that she did consider herself my friend, yoked as I was under the label 'Will-and-Leonie'.

There would be weeks of sulking if I deprived

Ginny of her vision. I had imagined, somehow, that leaders were in charge. Instead I felt inadequate.

And I realized that everyone was looking at me. Camilla had stopped lounging back in her seat, and was watching my face. I knew that jealousy was an emotion that could destroy you, and I'd vowed to suppress it in myself. There was no need to feel threatened by Saffron. Will and I were a unit, more closely bonded with each passing year. I was imagining things, as I had before, by thinking that Saffron appearing in the magazine might somehow take something away from me.

And it wasn't fair on Ginny to make her waste time looking for someone else simply because of my own private, groundless imaginings. She'd worked hard to pull the ideas together. Mimi was anxiously playing piggy in the middle, ready to jump either way. She obviously thought Saffron would look good in the feature – she would, after all – but, out of all of them, she was the only one who would simply accept a 'no' without anything stronger than passing irritation. But Camilla, I realized for the first time, had both a nose for a story, and the perception to see that something had disturbed me, and that it was personal.

I shrugged. 'I just thought she was a bit old that's all. And I do know she's very keen on her privacy.' Hang on, I told myself. Try not to offer them so many excuses that even Mimi spots a door creaking closed on a secret. I forced the next words out, like a final squeeze of an empty toothpaste tube. 'If you really think you can make it work, go ahead.' I threw the card back into the pile, but misjudged it, and they all scattered to the floor.

There was a silence and everyone looked at me. Lucy knelt down and gathered the cards up, reaching under the desks to get them all. No one helped her.

I couldn't leave Lucy trying to clear up my mess so I bent down and picked up a few cards that had slipped under the chair. I turned one over in my hand, and Saffron smiled out at me from the black-and-white photograph. She looked remote and enigmatic, yet somehow triumphant. It reminded me of the way she'd looked in France.

9

I had never admitted to anyone – and barely even to myself – how uneasy that holiday in Provence had made me.

The journey out had been fine, just a hectic scramble of tickets and taxis, queues and duty-free purchases.

We'd shuffled slowly towards the desk at Check-in. 'Those jeans are a disgrace on someone your age,' I'd told Will fondly, pointing out the bleached, bare areas where his bony knees were almost poking through.

He'd looked down at them as if he'd never seen them before, and his face had cracked into a grin. 'I'll have you know that people spend weeks trying to get jeans to look this worn. These are the real thing. They're probably worth a fortune.'

'Better sell them, then,' I'd advised, but I rather liked him shabby.

He'd kissed the tip of my nose, and our eyes had locked, bewitched with the pleasure of finding each other at last. We hadn't heard the Check-in staff ask for our tickets and the girl had had to repeat her request, smiling indulgently. Once through Passport Control, he'd laughed. 'Next time we do this, we'll be married.' He kissed the palm of my hand, before dragging me towards Duty Free. He'd suggested that I bought gin and he purchased a really good malt whisky as our contributions.

There were more queues for the car hire at the French end and some rather bad-tempered exchanges due to the fact that my map reading and Will's driving never quite synchronized. My head had ached with the panic of waking up four times during the night to check that we hadn't overslept.

As soon as we arrived, he seemed different under the sun, more urbane and glossier, but distanced from me. Exotic somehow, as if he belonged here and I didn't. The warmth in his eyes was hidden by sunglasses and a battered Panama hat. But, even with the torn jeans, an old cotton shirt and sandals, there was a solidity about him that made me feel I had come home. My heart lifted. This, I had decided, was my future. It was the one I had chosen.

As we drove into the valley, and saw the sunflower fields spread on either side, and the dusty pink paint of the villa appear as a speck nestling amongst the trees, I could feel that I'd lost his attention. Perhaps he was concentrating on driving on the right-hand side of the road.

There was silence between us by the time we drove up the short gravel drive to the villa. As soon as he cut the engine, a petite dark-haired girl came rushing out, squeaking with excitement, and hurled herself into Will's arms. A man in shorts followed with more restraint, shaking our hands and patting Will on the arm. Jo and Jonathan, I gathered.

'We've been here for simply ages. At least four hours,' burbled Jo. 'It's simply heaven. Look, we'll take your cases in, go right down to the pool. Saffron's sunbathing.'

We walked round the villa and across a short, scrubby lawn. The pool was hidden behind some trees, flanked with a built-in barbecue, a dark ever-green hedge and a row of sun loungers. On the nearest one stretched the utterly still form of an almost-naked girl, with a cascade of auburn corkscrew curls and the whitest skin I've ever seen. She wore nothing but a huge pair of sunglasses and the tiniest triangle of metallic fabric as a bikini bottom. She lay motionless, although she must have heard us coming.

'Saffron?' Will stood over her, sounding remarkably unsure of his welcome. I hung back.

She took off her sunglasses with one hand and continued to lie there. 'William.' I'd never heard him called that before. Then she appeared to notice me, and swung her long slim legs over the side of the lounger. As she stood up, the creamy breasts plopped down into the horizontal, small and neat with surprisingly big nipples. Like loganberries.

She kissed Will demurely, one of the breasts grazing the light-gold hair of his arm. 'And you must be William's bride-to-be. The one who's finally snapped him up. At last!' She had the kind of thighs that don't meet at the top, and her stomach was taut between

jutting hipbones. Her face wasn't particularly pretty –
it was too strong – but she was incredibly narrow, and,
with masses of chestnut hair bubbling and twizzling
down to her waist, you didn't notice the almost masculine shape of her nose and jaw.

'Hello.' I extended my hand, wondering if her
remark meant that I was the latest in a long line of
popsies who had tried to ensnare Will, or whether
he'd been lingering on the shelf for so long that he'd
been considered thoroughly dusty in marital terms.

'I do hope you don't burn,' I added anxiously,
mindful of all the warnings about sun we printed in
the magazine. I was features editor of *Penny*, and we
were always trying to stop teenagers from frying
themselves into early melanoma. 'Would you like to
borrow some sun protection?'

'That's absolutely sweet of you, but I'm fine,' she
said, putting the sunglasses back and lying down again.
Will and I hovered uncertainly. I decided not to leave
him alone with Lady Godiva.

'Shall we get unpacked, darling?'

He shrugged. 'In a minute. I'm just going to relax
after the drive.' He lay down on the next sun lounger,
rustling his newspaper in a way that I might have
called nervous, if I'd ever seen him nervous. Feeling
obscurely dismissed, I trailed back to the house, wondering why the heat was so exhausting. Well, if Saffron
went on lying there much longer, she'd fry. And skin
like that would be flayed alive. Still, I'd warned her.

Of course, she never got sunburned. I did, in spite

of my tubes of Sun Protection Factor 15, hat, T-shirt, and sarong.

'What on earth have you come as?' Will had asked, when he first saw me by the pool encased in seventeen layers of cotton and greasing myself in great dollops of white gunge. I mumbled something about burning.

'Well,' Jonathan had said genially, 'I don't think you ought to be in any of the holiday snapshots. You're wearing so many clothes that everyone back home will think the weather was cold.' But I still got painful burns and decided to leave the poolside to Saffron, Will and occasionally Jo, who was as brown as a berry within minutes. Jonathan and James played tennis, and I stayed inside the cool darkness of the villa, brewing up salad dressings and making garlic bread.

'I can see why you're marrying Leonie,' said James, after one particularly good meal. Will merely smiled and patted my knee.

'Oh, Leonie'll be the perfect wife for William. Now that he's decided it's time to settle down and have lots of lovely bambinos,' said Saffron, showing a small, even, pearly set of teeth in what purported to be a smile. 'Isn't that true, darling?' This could have been addressed to either Will or James, and made the perfect wife sound just slightly more exciting than the perfect antacid tablet. She obviously thought that Will was only marrying me because he thought it was time to settle down. I raised my chin slightly. I was not just a brood mare, a suitable companion. I would be his wife. Saffron ignored me, and turned to James, tickling him and laughing.

He slopped his wine. 'Stop it, you monster.' But he laughed, and put aside his last forkful of food.

And sometimes Will was the last to go to bed, I noticed, staying up into the small hours long after I was dropping with tiredness. I just couldn't keep up, particularly in the early days when the accumulated exhaustion of having worked long hours for months on end began to drop off my aching shoulders. It wasn't as if he was always with Saffron, though, sometimes James and Jonathan, or even Jo, joined them. But it was rarely just the two of us, and I missed the easy intimacy we'd grown used to. Once I'd shaken off the initial languor of the holiday, I did feel like staying up one night. It was the only evening that Will, just as James had poured me a Grand Marnier, made his excuses and left, mumbling something about too many late nights. I looked up at him to see if he wanted me to come with him, but he'd already gone, and when I'd finished my drink, he was already asleep.

Saffron rarely addressed me directly. I can remember almost the only time she actually volunteered information. She wandered into the kitchen when I was alone in there chopping something. She stretched, yawned, and said, 'I must have a bath.' As an opening gambit, it was hardly an earth-shattering confidence. And she didn't seem to expect a reply to it.

Once, quite early on, she rifled through the drinks cabinet and laughed, 'William, you angel, you're so

clever to find my fave Laphroaig at the Duty Free.'
She poured herself a huge slug. 'Be an absolute saviour
and get some ice.' Will disappeared and she started
rummaging again. 'What else is there? God, gin, how
suburban!'

I murmured something about having bought it,
and she put her hand on my arm. 'Oh, my God, I'm
so sorry,' she cried, as if she really meant it. 'I hadn't
realized you'd brought it. I'm really, really sorry.' She
went on and on about it, apologizing in everyone's
hearing, and telling everyone how tactless and stupid
she'd been. So I could hardly hold it against her.

Occasionally, I tried to talk to her about concerts
and recordings, but she usually said something like,
'My agent says it's important for me to avoid being
too commercial too soon. I don't want to attract the
wrong sort of attention.' As I knew nothing about
the world of classical music, I couldn't think of the
appropriate response.

'You ought to write an article about Saffron,' offered
Jo, who was incredibly enthusiastic about everything.

'I'm a very private person,' replied Saffron, with
one of her enigmatic smiles. 'Ever since the *Harpers*
piece, I've had to be very firm about personal publicity.'

'Why?' I wasn't sure that I bought the Garbo act.
After all, it had been a delightful piece, and I'd have
thought that anyone in their right mind would
have been eternally grateful.

Saffron just looked at me as if I was several sandwiches short of a picnic, and Will said, 'She doesn't want any distractions. Anyway, darling,' he looked at me as if I was about to bring down half the paparazzi of France on Saffron's back, 'she wouldn't really want to be in *Penny*, would she?' He squeezed my knee under the table to take the sting out of his words. I was beginning to realize that Will always stuck up for the underdog, but I couldn't understand why he thought that, in this case, it was Saffron. *Penny* was hardly a doorstepping tabloid, even if it was true that most people didn't much want to be in it, sandwiched between articles about teenage angst, spots and boyfriends.

I could have pointed out that this appalling violation of Saffron's personal privacy had not been my suggestion, but I knew it would sound like whining. I did try a bit of a grumble when we had a few minutes alone together in the car on the way to the market. Will implied that criticism would be petty. 'Saffron has a very special talent,' he said, quoting the *Harpers* article, I later discovered. Then he added, 'Women often find her . . .' he paused, as if looking for the right word . . . 'difficult – because she's so attractive.'

I know loads of incredibly attractive women who have real girlfriends and are generally very popular with other women. Saffron was not turning out to be one of them, but as she was an old girlfriend of Will's, I decided to keep quiet. 'Actually, I think she's very nice,' I said stiffly, because lying did not come easily to me.

Will put his arm round my shoulders briefly and kissed me, keeping his eyes on the road, murmuring, 'Good. I thought you'd be different,' rather absent-mindedly.

In fact, I enjoyed most of the holiday. The pungent cheeses, the fragrant patisserie and the glossy greens and purples of the vegetables in the market. The chance to sleep and swim whenever I wanted to. I liked cooking. I loved reading novels all day. James, Jo, and Jonathan were all terribly nice, although I had the sensation of having arrived at a party when it was all over. They all knew each other so incredibly well. One lunch time, they all started talking about a previous holiday. Jo reminded them of some old Greek man and his wife in the market, something about a misunderstanding, and James kindly filled me in on the story. It was impossible to understand, especially as he kept spluttering with laughter. By the end, Saffron was gasping hysterically behind her hand, her nose crinkled up with mirth, apparently unaware of a thin trail of peach juice trickling down her arm, Jo was choking into her napkin and wiping away tears, while the three men were slapping the table and guffawing. My jaw ached from smiling politely, straining with the effort of sharing the joke. I felt like someone who didn't speak English.

'You must think we're all mad,' laughed Jonathan. 'Do you know what you're taking on?'

I smiled politely, and scraped up the tangy salad dressing with the fresh crusty bread. 'I think so.' For a moment, everyone stopped laughing, looked at me, and the bread scraped painfully down my throat as I swallowed. It seemed, somehow, as if they knew something I didn't.

Will threw his arm round my shoulders, and I tried to unstiffen and melt into his chest, not very successfully. 'Leonie's a lion. She can cope with anything.'

In fact, I wasn't at all sure.

But I told myself that Will and I weren't arguing. It was just that from time to time, very briefly, we didn't seem to be on the same wavelength. Admittedly, we weren't all over each other, hugging and touching the whole time, the way we'd been in London, but I told myself that our relationship had reached a new maturity.

And, after a conversation around the pool late one evening, I stopped regarding Saffron as a potential rival, and viewed her as merely a temporary irritation. Jo and I were talking about when we planned to have children, how many years it would seem sensible to wait, whether our men were really ready. Jo said, 'I envy Saffron, I suppose, in a way. At least she doesn't have these debates.'

'Why not?' Saffron seemed sure of herself, but surely no woman could really be so self-confident as to take the baby element of life for granted.

'Oh, she doesn't want children.' This was a surprise to me. Neither Jo nor I could imagine a woman who didn't, and had both agreed that we ourselves desperately did. But I could see what Jo meant. It would be lovely not to agonize over it, to have already decided how you were going to manage that chunk of your life and simply shut the door on it.

'Perhaps she'll change her mind. When she gets a bit older, and the biological clock begins to tick more loudly.'

Jo looked amused. 'She's older than we are as it is. She's thirty-five now, so she hasn't got all that long for a re-think.' Jo herself was only twenty-five at the time, and obviously thought that thirty-five was practically antique. 'And to be honest,' she added thoughtfully, 'I think there's some medical problem. Anyway Saffron doesn't often change her mind. Except about men.'

I was interested. Saffron was, indeed, older than I'd thought, and I was innocent enough to think that being younger automatically earned you points as a woman. And she didn't want children. Will had made it quite clear to me that he did. 'If I didn't have children,' he'd once said, 'I think I'd regard my life as wasted.' I realized that his affair with Saffron couldn't have been all that serious, because Will would never have married an older woman who couldn't – or wouldn't – have children. I knew him well enough to know that.

On our last evening Saffron came into the kitchen wearing a short, backless, sleeveless metallic-silver dress that flared out around her thighs. She asked Will to do up a necklace at the back.

'This is okay without a bra, isn't it?' she asked him, twirling provocatively in front of him. Will, Jonathan and I stopped what we were doing and looked at the small firm breasts rippling under the silver fabric. The loganberry nipples bobbed pertly.

'Or do you think this black one would be better?' She had a strappy little cotton shift over her arm. Apparently unselfconsciously, she whipped the silver dress off over her head and threw it on to a chair, and, almost in a single movement, slipped the black dress on. There was a flash of very white cotton briefs. Oddly enough, she had acquired a light, honey-coloured tan, something I'd thought would hardly be possible with that creamy red-head complexion. I saw a flash of raw desire flare up in the eyes of both Jonathan and Will, as they reacted to the simple white cotton briefs against the pale gold skin. There was something about their crisp cleanliness that made them far sexier than all Saffron's skimpy leopardskin bikini bottoms.

'Which one?' She twirled again. James came into the kitchen. 'Oh God, it's James, he gets awfully cross when I keep taking my clothes off.' For a moment, she looked quite frightened. I thought, fleetingly, that she was really scared as James gazed at her hungrily, and then looked at the other two men. For a second I wondered if he was capable of real violence, and, if so, what Saffron was up to, egging him on in this way. Suddenly James's face slid back to its normal, civilized expression, with a half-smile that told us he didn't take anything seriously, not even Saffron. He tapped her possessively on the bottom. 'Out.'

I turned away, chopping up and de-seeding tomatoes for a side salad for our last lunch the following day. I wondered what Jo thought of Saffron undressing in front of her husband, but as they'd been friends for such a long time, I couldn't ask her. Jo herself was very modest, and usually stumped around the villa in shorts and a white Aertex shirt, her stocky, brown legs twinkling without the least hint of seduction. She was friendly and sympathetic, and I planned for her to be a great friend.

Somehow the men sorted out Saffron's wardrobe for her, and Jo appeared too, looking like a pretty gipsy in brightly coloured flounces and a huge necklace.

'You look great,' I told her. I hadn't realized how attractive she was – beside Saffron's exotic fragility, Jo always seemed like a sturdy peasant, just as I felt insipid, yet at the same time rather too solid, not to mention pale and freckly to boot. Mere prettiness – and both Jo and I could lay claim to the adjective on our better days – could not compete. We set off for the restaurant.

There was something urgent and impersonal in the way Will reached for me in bed that evening. I could have been anyone, I thought, as I lay awake afterwards looking at the moonlight and listening to an owl. As his breathing deepened, and the room grew quiet I heard other noises. The rhythmic creaking was unmistakable. Will was not the only man who had gone to bed with only one thing on his mind. But underneath it, I could hear sharp bursts of whimpering that were scarcely human. There was a screech as the owl dived on its prey outside, a shout from another room, and a soft, sobbing noise. It was impossible to tell which noises came from the bedrooms on either side of me, and which were the natural noises of the killing fields outside. Probably all of them came from the fields and woods outside except for the shout. But I couldn't shake off the feeling that Jonathan, Will and James had each, in their own way, made love to Saffron that night. That Jo and I had been no more than recipients. But that's the kind of thing you think at three o'clock in the morning after too much to drink. I pulled the thin sheet up over my head and curled into a ball. The thought of Saffron upstaging me at my wedding flitted briefly across my consciousness.

However, she didn't come. She wrote to say how sorry she was that she'd be on a tour of sixty-seven cities with something like the Leeds & Bradford City Orchestra at the time, and sent a telegram which was read out to roars of laughter. And, anyway, the minute we landed back at Heathrow, Will came out of his dream and began to play the part of loving, attentive fiancé. Everyone envied me. I began to think I'd imagined it all.

A copy of the June issue of my new, glossier-than-glossy *How?* arrived on my doorstep in early May, thumping through the letterbox with a satisfyingly dull thud. As editors, we had it posted to our homes in order to keep track of whether subscribers were getting their copies delivered in time. I seized it and tore it open, longing for the first impression as it emerged from the plastic packaging.

It glowed at me, bright, sparkling, good, I thought. I flicked through it as if I was starved of its contents, although I'd pored over them enough in the process of producing it. Yes, on the whole, it looked the way I'd hoped it would. A few quibbles here and there, one feature that could have been better, but, all-in-all, a triumph.

'Look,' I waved it proudly at Will, who was eating a piece of toast standing up.

'Hm.' He spread it over the pale, slightly marked wood of our kitchen work surface, scattering tiny specks of jam and the odd crumb over the pages in the process. 'Looks great. Well done.'

He stopped flicking through it when he came to the fashion shoot at Rosse Manor. 'I recognize that.'

I smiled at the memory. 'Yes, so did I. Amazing

coincidence, isn't it? I don't suppose we could go back there, could we?' I wanted to share my success with him, toast the future in his eyes.

He swallowed the last of a chunk of bread, and wiped his fingers on a tea-towel. 'When we win the lottery.' He flicked quickly to the end. 'These models are a bit anorexic.'

Those who work on glossy magazines get completely fed up with being told that they use anorexic models. We use very thin models because that's what makes the public buy magazines. And what did Will know about it anyway?

He grinned. 'Like you, I see anorexics in the course of duty.'

That made me very cross. 'And I suppose they all saw one copy of *Vogue* with thin models and just stopped eating?'

He pulled his coat on, his mind already half out the door. 'It's a very complex disorder. Like any kind of addiction or phobia.'

'Hang on, I'm ready to go too.' I grabbed my huge bottomless bag, stuffed with proofs and articles, that I dragged round with me. It wasn't chic and it gave me backache, but it was the only way to stay on top of work.

'It's all very well your seeing the odd anorexic or phobic in the surgery,' I said, determined to win this argument for some reason, 'but I bet you've never really known one.' We'd had about six anorexics at my boarding schools, spread over the years, although each and every one of them had stringently denied any question of starvation, maintaining that they were grossly overweight until the day they were carted off to hospital.

'Well,' Will still sounded equable. Why was I arguing over a syndrome that meant little to either of us? 'That's where you're wrong. Saffron was anorexic for a while.'

'Saffron?' I was rocked. It completely altered my perception of her. Mind you, I bet, I absolutely bet, she was putting it on. Just to gain attention and look romantically in decline. Like all those Georgian heroines who used to waste away.

He strode on. 'Mm. For years. Not very badly, though. Except for . . .' He trailed off, raising his hand to his head to check if it was raining.

'You never told me that.'

Will didn't reply for a moment. 'You've never had much time for her.'

I burned with the unfairness of this. 'She's never had much time for me. I've tried quite hard, actually.'

He smiled and squeezed my shoulder, as we waited to cross at the lights, partly but not wholly, acknowledging some truth in this. 'I know.'

I was determined to prove my point. 'She hardly spoke to me when we all went on holiday in France. But I kept trying.'

'Yes,' he said. 'You did.'

The ensuing silence accused me of not having tried since.

'I mean,' I persevered, 'she never even says hello to me when she phones up. She just asks for you.'

'She's quite shy, you know. That's why she behaves badly with new people.' The pedestrian light switched to green and he picked up my heavy bag before I could. 'And you can be quite frightening sometimes. You seem so in control.'

Me? Frightening? To Saffron? I snorted. 'We're all shy. Do you think I'm not shy? And the way to deal with shyness is to think about other people rather than yourself.' Didn't she ever read the problem pages of women's magazines, packed as they were with nannyish advice to ask people about themselves?

Will refrained from answering. I was silent with indignation, not wanting to mention reading the problem pages in case he said that Saffron was also dyslexic.

After five minutes I could no longer bear the sense of injustice and added, 'Anyway, if you'd told me she was anorexic I might have had more sympathy for her.'

He raised one eyebrow. 'Would you? I don't see that it would have made any difference.'

Only a man could say that. Whatever you believed about anorexia, whether you thought it was attention-seeking and self-inflicted, caused by a mechanical problem like zinc deficiency or an illness, there was one thing that every woman knew. When an anorexic looks in the mirror they see a fat, distorted image of imperfection. I had always carelessly assumed that

Saffron flaunted her narrow, long limbs and flat stomach out of pride rather than insecurity. I had always thought that to look in the mirror at those small, perfect breasts, the incredibly slim hips and almost flesh-free thighs must have afforded her considerable satisfaction. I had visualized her shopping, running her hands impatiently along the size 10 rails then leaving a pile of clothes on the floor in the changing room as she stalked out, telling the shop assistant they were all far too baggy. I had believed that she despised my more generous flesh while eating what she pleased. Realizing that she also believed herself imperfect, fat and greedy did make her seem more human. Not that I believed we could ever have cosily talked about it together, but still, there was something.

I wondered why. It took me a few more minutes to puzzle it out. I had never before believed that Saffron could suffer. She seemed to have everything – a slender, beautiful body, musical talent, men hanging on every word, a small but secure private income. She had seemed like a porcelain figurine in a glass case, untouchable. But with the word 'anorexia', the glass case had shattered, leaving the figure inside still exquisite, but, if you looked closely, there were now hairline cracks and tiny chips.

'Anyway,' said Will, 'it's all pretty much under control now. I don't think she's been really bad for years. Since long before you knew her.'

I remembered the bleached-out heat of the afternoons at the villa in France. While Saffron's territory had been the pool, mine had been the cool, dark, cavernous kitchen, with its gleaming stone flags and ancient, cracked blue-and-white tiles. There was always someone here, leaning on the scrubbed wooden table – Jonathan or James pouring themselves a lager and lingering; Jo helping me chop glossy outsize red peppers; or Will, talking about life, ribbing me gently, even making me blush. Until Saffron would come wandering through, wrapped in a sarong and idly nibbling at a few walnuts I'd meant to use in the salad. My conversation would falter, in the face of her massive indifference to me.

'Darling,' she'd say to James, winding herself round him. He'd draw aside the thick red hair with one hand and kiss the back of her neck. She'd turn round and hold his gaze, or if he was lounging against the window, standing up to drink the lager out of a can, she'd stretch ballerina-like on her toes to kiss him on the tip of the nose before drifting out again. 'Must change,' she'd murmur. A few minutes later, he'd follow her, jokes forgotten.

Or she'd open the fridge to pour herself a long, cool glass of iced Evian water. 'Will, darling,' she might say. 'This bottle cap's too stiff for me to turn. Would you?' She'd flash him a secret, conspiratorial smile. 'You are an angel.'

An anorexic and a doctor. Does that sound dangerous?

*

We walked to the Tube station in silence after that, Will's face focused on the day ahead, mine on what he'd left behind. I was still completely disconcerted by the time we reached the parting of the ways, the Tube station, already packed with milling, sleepy workers trying to get to places on time.

Will's mind was obviously on work as we kissed goodbye, but even he must have noticed something odd about me.

'Are you all right?'

I didn't want to go into it. I didn't want to be late for a meeting.

'Fine. Just thinking about the fertility programme, wondering if there'd be any side effects.' This was partly true. I had begun my first three months of a pill to stimulate my ovaries. I felt like a bomb about to explode. I assessed myself constantly for possible side effects. It seemed barking mad to be about to embark on a pill I didn't need to take, in order to achieve something that ought to be achieved naturally.

'Oh, I shouldn't worry about that. The side effects don't cause many problems. And it's only for three months, after all.' He lingered for a moment. 'Dearest. Please don't worry. It's going to be fine. I promise you that.' He searched my face with concern. 'Trust in Dr Bailey? Okay?'

My eyes stung unexpectedly with tears. Probably the worry about having a baby, I told myself, making me over-emotional. Or something. I resolved to pull myself together.

But a lingering feeling of unease niggled as I sat at my desk later, checking the proofs of an article on Feng Shui we were running in the September issue. It was about four different people who'd put their lives right by re-arranging their furniture, and hanging the odd windchime in a hallway.

If only life were that simple. Still. I looked up. Lucy had left her desk, and Camilla wasn't back yet. I was alone. I ran my finger under the name of the Feng Shui practitioner, and, feeling an awful fool, booked an appointment for the next time Will had an early surgery. After all, if I was going to be running the feature, I might as well find out what it was really about.

I opened the front door the following Tuesday morning, expecting to see the milkman with a bill or the postman with a registered letter. Instead I found two men, both looking rather concerned. One had something like a compass in his hand, and the other was peering up and down the road with a furrowed brow. Perhaps they were estate agents who'd come to the wrong house. Although they were wearing knitted woollen jumpers under their jackets, which didn't seem quite right.

They introduced themselves as Philip Brookes and Nigel Smith, the Feng Shui people. After the usual shaking hands and wiping feet routine, they settled at the kitchen table and Nigel looked at me.

'Now what are you hoping to achieve?'

It was the kind of question I find very difficult to answer, and one of the reasons why I hate filling out forms. Were we talking cosmically? Long life? Happiness? Astronomical sales figures for *How?*? Or did he mean something more practical like a sensible place to keep saucepans? Or a baby? I thought of Saffron but didn't think she was likely to be expunged by moving a few tables and chairs. Anyway I certainly wasn't going to mention her to two people I'd never met before. After our initial flurry of workmen, plans and architects we'd never quite completed everything we'd wanted to do to 37 Branworth Terrace so there was plenty to go on at the saucepan-hanging level. I looked around wildly.

'Well, er.' Why had I got myself into this situation?

They looked at me kindly, and waited.

I surprised myself by saying that both Will and I were facing a number of challenges – at work, I added.

They nodded. 'And you want to create a harmonious space in order to encourage your full potential?'

I hadn't thought of it quite like that, but it seemed as good an answer as any, so I seized upon it.

There was a short silence, which made it clear that they knew I wasn't telling them something. Or possibly that I wasn't telling them anything.

'Can we look around?'

They walked round the house, occasionally making notes, and waving a small electrical gadget at the beds.

'Have you got a basement?'

We hadn't. It was a source of irritation to Will, who

muttered occasionally about a 'proper cellar', although what he planned to keep in it I couldn't imagine. I'd never met a man so incapable of coping with a tool-box.

'Loft?'

'Only a tiny one. We keep suitcases up there.'

Philip's eyebrows shot up. 'Full ones?'

'Quite full, yes. Summer clothes, stuff that might be useful one day. Old books.' I wondered if this was good or bad.

They exchanged glances and made more notes. I looked at my watch. This was going to turn out to be a waste of time and money.

'Have you ever been really happy in this house?' Nigel sounded merely curious, as if it was highly unlikely but that he'd better check anyway.

I was about to say, yes, of course, happier than I'd ever been in my life. I had, really, in the early years when Will and I had so much hope. However, looking back on it, perhaps it hadn't been the present we'd really enjoyed, more the prospect of what the future held. But it occurred to me that that future, so far, simply hadn't turned up. It made me wonder whether the happiness had been real either, or whether we had both just been living two separate dreams which had happened to intersect at that point.

Nigel didn't ask again. They began telling me about the chi, the life force or energy that flows through everything, and which shouldn't be blocked or rushed. I'd read about it in the *How?* article. It all seemed incredibly complicated and involved adding up birthdays, and heaven knows what.

We walked round the house again while they told me that almost everything was wrong. We were sleeping in an 'energy river' and needed to move the bed. I should put silver foil behind the bedhead ('the bedsprings are charged up'). Still, it would be nice if all our fertility problems could be sorted out with a bit of Alcanfoil around the bed base. They suggested I remove the mirrors from the bedroom ('energy is bouncing from one to the other – no one could possibly sleep well in here'). I thought of Will's tired, drawn face and decided that anything was worth trying. Then they pointed out that the chi was very stagnant in the guest bathroom. This was, I suspected, due to the fact that Zack and Phoebe had been round again, and gone for 'one last piddle' without flushing the loo. I hastily did so and opened a window, under their impassive stares. Various sofas were to be shifted – not a bad idea, I thought, and the coffee table moved away from the centre of the room, which would be a relief because I was always barking my shins on it.

'But there are two things that are really important. Firstly, you'll never settle in this house unless you do something about the front.'

The front? No wonder they had been looking worried when I opened the door.

'There's a tree directly opposite the front door.'

It was the neighbour's cherry tree – very pretty in spring, I thought.

'Pretty or not, it's blocking you.'

They mapped out the cure, which was to have properly polished door furniture or a Feng Shui mirror. Well, it would be nice to have a shiny knocker instead of the rather dismal plastic doorbell that we'd always meant to change.

'And you must clear the loft.'

They could see by my face that 'yes, of course' meant 'not in a million years'. Loft clean-outs, like cupboard clearing, were strictly for when I had the time. A retirement project. I began to shoo them out the front door, murmuring my thanks.

'The loft,' said Philip, holding out his right hand to shake goodbye, 'represents your future. And it's full of clutter from your past. Think about it.'

I wrote out an enormous cheque, and handed it to Nigel.

'And clutter,' Nigel added, as he ran his eye over the cheque in a practised fashion, 'is anything you don't need. It weighs you down. Get rid of it.'

'I will,' I promised, determined not to.

I leant against the wall and sighed as the door shut behind them. I was having trouble believing that Will and I might be at risk of splitting up because we had hung a mirror in our relationship corner, or that he'd failed to become a consultant because he always left the loo seat up.

But somehow I found myself going upstairs, pulling down the loft hatch, mounting its extendable ladder, and edging my head and shoulders up into the cob-webby triangular space beneath the eaves of the house. As usual, I checked it out as a possible loft extension, hoping that it might somehow have grown since I last looked at it. No way. A four-year-old child would have had trouble standing upright at the highest point.

There were about four suitcases, a trunk and three boxes of books. It doesn't sound a lot, but it took me three-quarters of an hour just to heave it all out, ending up with a dusty heap of jumble on the top landing, and a couple of broken boxes. A real tip.

I got a roll of black dustbin bags and began to sort through things with the feverishness of someone looking for a lost will. Old summer clothes, slightly stained or crumpled, that I'd always meant to mend. A sweater with dried-up pieces of heather tangled up in it. It could go. Out. So could dated copies of magazines. A broken teapot. Some freebies. Old party invitations (although they triggered off reminders of great parties). Out, out, out. I paused over a dog-eared photograph of Will and myself, outside a picturesque Cotswold pub, both looking unbelievably young. Laughing and drinking cider. So we had been happy. It hadn't been a dream, after all. I felt a flicker of warmth deep down inside, and tucked the photograph into my handbag.

Anyone who wants to 'find themselves' doesn't need to go trekking in Nepal or backpacking over Asia. Your real self, I guarantee, will be at the back of a cupboard in Solihull or Streatham, buried amongst the newspaper cuttings (why a four-page feature on vegetable gardening?), the old shoes, the too-tight, unfashionable jumpers, eaten away by moths but still echoing with the smoke of that jazz pub everyone used to visit on Sunday lunch times. I even found a book of 1950s love poetry in a faded two-tone cover that an old boyfriend had bought me. I smiled at it, and put it aside to take downstairs, feeling my spirits rise at this evidence that I, too, had a past, and that it didn't interfere with my love for Will.

I stuffed lots more clutter into the bags, speeding up the sorting and lugging six black dustbin bags down to the bins in triumph.

The last suitcase was full of Will's things, and I hesitated before going through them. I told myself that he couldn't have put anything important away in a torn leather carry-all. Old tennis racquets, tracksuit bottoms with holes in, shirts that were now too small but which he thought might do for painting or gardening. Not that he ever did either. One trainer. One trainer? I chucked that out without remorse, but decided to set the other things aside for his say-so.

At the bottom of the case was a yellow tie. I'd forgotten all about it, but as soon as I saw its vivid, jazzy pattern, I saw Will, looking unnaturally clean and nervous, standing beside me at the altar, his voice hoarse as he murmured our wedding vows.

It had given me a shock, seeing him in that tie as I lifted my veil and faced him for the first time that day. Saffron had given it to him – quite openly – as a wedding present. She had given me a pink chiffon scarf at the same time, an impossibly small, but obviously expensive, square that could only have been tied around the slenderest neck. Both had been beautifully wrapped in luxurious Bond Street boxes, and addressed in her sloping, exuberant script. I always thought of hers as an autograph signature – a big bold S dominating an elegant trail of letters, a confident slash of self-expression. Quite unlike my rounded, careful writing. I saw that inscription again in my mind. 'To darling William from Saffron' she had written, as if signing a charter, claiming her territory, the words burning themselves into the thick, expensively creamy card. William. She had a private name for him, I'd noticed, that no one else used. It would have sounded formal if anyone else had called him William, but in her writing it just seemed like a lingering caress. 'William,' she'd say, at her most engaging, drawing out the three syllables for maximum effect. 'William, you are absurd.' And he'd grin, acknowledging her.

I, along with everyone else, called him Will.

'I thought,' she'd said in her low, laughing voice, as she handed him both his and my present, 'that, as you haven't moved into your home together yet, I wouldn't know what your taste would be. So I got you both something to wear.'

It was the sort of thing that made people say how clever Saffron was, and how original. Personally I didn't see why she couldn't go for the wedding list like everyone else.

I'd been so shocked at seeing the yellow tie there on Will's neck in our little family church that I'd stumbled in the marriage vows, but by the third hymn I'd convinced myself that he was wearing it because it was a great tie. It was. It stopped just short of loud, but even I had to admit that it was stylish and witty. After all, everyone always commented on it. There really was no reason why he shouldn't have worn it. Although I never even tried the pink scarf on.

I'd managed a quiet word with Lindsey at the reception, and had asked her what she thought.

Lindsey had stroked my sleeve. 'I wouldn't worry about it. It's just a tie. He's probably forgotten where it came from. You look fabulous.' She'd given me a quick hug. 'Now enjoy your day.'

Eight years later I sat on the landing holding the yellow tie in my hand, and wondering if I would be wrong to throw it out. I was pleased he'd put it away – that flicker of warmth again – but one day he might ask me where it was. Not throwing away your partner's things is a bit like not opening his post. A mark of basic respect in the over-crowded shared space of marriage.

But I didn't want the tie in our house. I took a deep breath and stuffed it in the last dustbin bag. It gave me courage to do something I swore I'd never do. I went downstairs and opened up our wardrobe, pulling out his spare suit and two or three jackets and searched his pockets. Then I rummaged around for his sports bag and an old briefcase, felt down the linings, shook them and turned them over. Nothing. Feeling ashamed of my suspicions – and astonished that they had suddenly popped up in this way without any real reason for them – I went back upstairs for the black dustbin bag, knotted up the neck and propped the bag against the over-flowing bins.

Later, I regretted it. It was childish behaviour and I didn't want to have to own up to throwing away his tie. That might turn it into something more than it was. When I got home that evening, I intended to rescue it, but the dustmen had been and everything was gone.

Still, at least I could feel that I'd done something to get Saffron out of the attic and therefore out of our future. If you believe all that crap.

I I

Of course, it meant I was late for work. Several hours late, and, equally naturally, it happened to be the one morning I'd completely forgotten about a meeting booked in with Peter Rennie.

It didn't look as if moving the dustbins out of my 'career area' at the front of the house – another of Nigel's Feng Shui suggestions – was working. Maybe it took a few hours for the luck to shift. Perhaps it was like sending e-mail – a supposedly instantaneous process, but something that, in reality, spent a bit of time in the ether before settling down at its new spot.

Camilla had answered the phone to Peter three times, she stressed. 'As you weren't in, and Lucy's at the dentist.' Camilla being helpful enough to answer a telephone? I was amazed. She usually left other people's telephones ringing unanswered and could be quite difficult about answering her own. On this occasion she must have had a sort of sixth sense that flashed up 'managing director' in her mind as it rang, rather than 'irate reader' or 'public relations company trying to fix up factory visit to Huddersfield'. I had to admit that she did have her talents, after all. It was just a pity we weren't on the same side.

'I told him that I'd no idea where you were,' she

added, making it clear from the tone of her voice that she thought communication in this office was non-existent. 'There was nothing in the book.'

I thought of about three first-class rejoinders as the lift ascended to the eighteenth floor. Any of them would have been better than going bright red under her dismissive gaze.

'I'm sorry I wasn't there when you called – I . . .' I had, by the time I settled in Peter Rennie's smoked-glass eyrie, worked out a dignified way of explaining my absence without stooping to sounding as if I was making excuses. But Peter just waved it aside with irritation, and proceeded to discuss staffing levels.

As he waded through reams of facts and figures from management research in the US – loads of stuff about profit bases, cost per head and where Maglife stood in relation to similar companies, I became uneasily aware that he'd already murmured about reducing staff and making redundancies when I accepted the job. It occurred to me that this was another area in which I simply hadn't asked enough of the right questions, or possibly hadn't listened carefully enough to the answers. In the thrill of getting the job, it hadn't really dawned on me that words like 'rationalisation' and 'natural wastage' meant that perfectly nice women might be made redundant, and that I was going to have to do it. I was beginning to wonder how anyone as naïve as I'd obviously been had been appointed in the first place. I could kick myself, I really could.

Sadly, kicking myself wasn't going to achieve anything practical.

Peter drew to an end, and suddenly barked, 'So I thought we should implement it all as soon as possible. You'll find that staff are upset for a day or two, but after that things should settle down quite quickly.'

'Oh, yes,' I said, hastily adding, 'but I'd like a day or so to consider everything before we make a final decision.'

He looked displeased at the 'we', and I restrained myself from saying 'No, no, don't worry, I'll just grovel at your feet and do as I'm told', which was what the dutiful schoolgirl inside me was hissing. But I suspected that there were several women working for *How?* who were going to mind a lot unless I could learn to stand up for myself and them.

I waited for the heavens to open. They stayed closed.

'Well. I'm sure we can reach an agreement. Making staff changes is a completely normal part of a management role, and you should, of course, be prepared to hire and fire at any point.' He pushed a piece of paper over. 'These are my suggestions, based on salaries and ability.'

Mimi, as art director, was earning too much. He wanted her replaced with a younger, less expensive model. And, I had to admit, she didn't have the sparkle I was looking for.

'I don't think we should make her redundant just because of her age.' I was taken aback to discover that ageism started at thirty-five or thirty-six, which was the most Mimi could possibly be.

'No, no, of course not. But, I think you may find that a younger art director might have a more contemporary feel,' he said smoothly.

I thought he was probably right – I'd found myself thinking that *How?* wasn't the right job for her about twice a day, but I did wonder if he could find her another within the group. He promised to look into it. Then he mentioned Mary Elliott, another woman whose sullen refusal to co-operate with me in any way whatsoever exasperated me. Every time I asked her to do something she responded with: 'Martina always said . . .' or 'Martina never . . .'

I agreed with him, hoping that I wasn't making someone redundant just because I disliked her. I noticed that he'd marked out Jackie, the most junior sub-editor for redundancy – yet she was a bright, capable girl who stayed late every night to catch up on things, and often offered suggestions about articles she might write. She was the kind of cheerful, hard-working, generous person who should go far.

'She's the most recent to join,' explained Peter. 'Last in, first out.'

There seemed to be a different principle behind each dismissal.

'So who would you suggest?' He seemed to resent my involvement in what was, after all, my own staff.

'Well, the person whose work is least good, I suppose.' I thought about it. Sadly, there was only one candidate, Sandra, a delightful, motherly woman I liked very much but who was, quite simply, hopeless at her job. I thought she'd probably only hung on so long because she was clearly such a nice person.

'So.' I thought I saw a certain amount of relish in his eyes. 'I'll leave that decision to you, shall I? Jackie or Sandra.'

I went on to tell him how, in the last few weeks, I'd been very impressed with Kate, the deputy homes editor, but had found Deirdre, the homes editor, lacking in vision, with dull, predictable work. I mentioned this.

'Ah,' he said, closing the file. 'Deirdre's just had a baby.'

'I know. But she'll be coming back after maternity leave, and frankly her work isn't up to it. If she was made redundant we could leave both Jackie and Sandra in place.'

'I don't think you quite see my point. We've had a number of quite difficult court cases in recent years over making pregnant women redundant, and we have decided, after discussion at board level, that it probably is wise, at such an emotional time, to give women the benefit of the doubt.' He looked levelly at me. 'It's part of our ongoing programme of caring for our employees.'

A hands-off policy, in other words. Belinda Bracken had mentioned something about this, but I'd thought she was joking. She'd said that someone had had three babies in three years just to keep her job.

'But,' I protested, 'if someone was brilliant at her work, and she was pregnant, I'd promote her.'

'I'm sure you would.' He smiled. 'After all, we're very proud of our equal opportunities policy here.'

'So, why are pregnant women treated differently when their work isn't up to scratch? That's just discrimination of a different kind.'

'Mm? Well, we shall see.' He obviously had no intention of giving me a proper answer. 'Mind you,' he added, 'her husband is very successful, I understand. Isn't he?'

I couldn't help looking blank. 'I've no idea.'

He gathered up his papers and gave me a wolfish smile. 'I think you'll find that when a woman has a baby, her commitment to work often drops off over the following few years if she has a wealthy husband. I expect this particular problem will sort itself out in time.'

I was so shocked that I temporarily lost my thread, and found that he was standing up and extending a hand to shake in dismissal. I resolved to settle one issue at any rate. I gathered up every last bit of determination, and ploughed on, although I could see that he wanted me out of that door. Fast.

'Camilla . . .'

He cut me off. 'If you can rely on her enough to represent you at a major lunch like the House of Commons one last month – which I was most disappointed not to see you at, by the way – I really don't feel that you have a great deal to complain about.

Now, I have another meeting. I know this is always hard for an editor, but I'm sure you can cope.' He bared his teeth in a smile. 'As always.' As if by magic the door opened, and his secretary, Ingrid, appeared. 'Elaine, for you, Peter.'

'Elaine, my dear . . .' He rose to meet her, clasping one of her hands in both of his, as my mouth opened and shut like a goldfish trapped silently behind the glass wall of his determination not to hear any more.

I got back to the office to find one of *Home Life*'s staff – a very pregnant one – holding court in *How?*'s open-plan office.

'The great thing about pregnancy,' she explained to a circle of listeners, 'is that you have to go to the toilet a lot. I'd no idea how much gossip you can pick up that way.'

I did hope this wasn't going to cause a rash of pregnancies amongst staff. They were going to be angry enough about the numbers being cut from fifteen to twelve without much of a corresponding drop in workload. Adding in a couple more maternity leaves without proper cover could cause a riot.

'Do tell us.' I must have spoken more loudly than I intended. I didn't really mean to make everyone jump, because I still thought of myself as 'one of the girls'. It still came as an ugly shock to find myself 'the headmistress'. Mimi went slightly pink and everyone scuttled back to their desks.

'Oh, I didn't see you there. I've got the final proofs of the cover – look.' Mimi seemed anxious to avoid my hearing the enthralling saga of the ladies-room gossip so I let it go. It was probably better not repeated anyway. My management training scheme had emphasized how important it was to create a climate of trust and openness amongst the staff, which was quite a challenge with Camilla slinking around hissing insurrection at anyone who would listen.

Camilla herself seemed innocently clear of this particular group, though. I could hear her singing under her breath as she pored over the latest transparencies of handbags on the light box in the art department. She stopped as Mimi joined her. 'Prada,' she murmured in a reverential chant. 'Gucci. Prada, Gucci, Patrick Cox, Anya Hindmarch.' They could have been the names of saints, and she the high priestess of a devotional sect.

It occurred to me that Tuesday was rubbish collection day. The refuse collectors would have been to 37 Branworth Terrace and might have unwittingly returned the empty dustbins straight back to my career area. I was sure that that sort of cosmic fiddling about would do one's life no good at all.

And it wasn't fair to say that women's commitment diminished after having babies if their husbands were rich. Sandy White earned squillions and Lindsey had never slowed up for one moment.

Will didn't really grasp my dilemma that evening.

'That's what being a boss is about. Redundancy. Difficult decisions. Hiring and firing.'

I was irritated. 'It's all very well for you to say that. You don't have the responsibility for fifteen lives hanging on your decisions.'

I could have worded that better. He raised an eyebrow, and refilled his glass. 'On the contrary, I have the responsibility for about 25,000 lives hanging on my decisions.'

'Oh, sorry.' I was contrite. 'But you know what I mean. People's jobs are absolutely fundamental to their well-being.'

'And their health isn't, I suppose?'

We just weren't getting anywhere. Perhaps, I thought, he minded my earning more than him. It was only about £2,000 a year more, anyway, not enough to feel superior about. But I decided to soothe any fractious feelings by asking for his advice. 'So should I make Jackie, who's young, keen and bright, redundant, or Sandra, who's incompetent, nice and vulnerable?'

He sighed and stretched, topping up the glass of wine again. 'Christ, I'm tired.'

I felt a stab of concern. 'All I can say,' I muttered crossly, 'is that we're supposed to have rampant sex tonight, and you're hardly being very romantic.'

He looked at me as if from the bottom of a deep, dark well. 'Sex? You must be joking. I can hardly keep my eyelids up, let alone anything else.'

Then he added the final insult: 'Sorry, darling.'

Sorry! Sorry indeed. Bruised, and burning with

indignation, I trooped up to bed to spend a restless night alternately feeling furious with him and worrying about Mimi, Jackie and Sandra.

The following morning I knew I'd have to focus on the redundancies. I'd promised Peter Rennie, and, anyway, I couldn't concentrate on anything else until I'd got it all over and done with. I thought about Dave Beckett, making 300 people redundant and saying 'it's like lancing a boil'. To me, it seemed a much sharper, more cutting pain, but I suspected that the Dave Becketts of this world would call this 'inexperience'.

Elaine Brown stepped into the shining steel lift beside me, along with a tired-looking blonde with straggly hair. The blonde closed her eyes as the lift doors shut, leant back against the gleaming walls, and sighed.

'How's the week going?' I felt I had to say something to Elaine, as a fellow editor.

'Wild,' said Elaine. 'Really.' She shook her immaculately dishevelled auburn crop, as if overwhelmed by the number of parties given by famous and beautiful people that she had had to attend. She never had followed up her invitation to lunch, and when I'd left a couple of messages, feeling that I should be friendly, she hadn't returned them.

The lift clicked neatly open at the third floor. After a bit of half-hearted 'after-you-ing' Elaine and

I stepped out. The blonde's eyelids flickered open briefly and she extended a weary-looking arm to press the button for another floor above.

'You can always tell the working mothers round here,' commented Elaine. 'They look exhausted.'

This was true.

Elaine cast a quick look at my waist, which had expanded by about two inches since coming to Maglife, due to the enormous number of meetings editors were expected to sit through. Our bottoms became completely chair-shaped by the end of the day, and if I wasn't careful I'd be a size 16 soon.

'You must be thinking of sprogging soon,' she said, more as a statement of fact than anything else. As she had never asked me any questions about myself, this was astonishingly personal. Worryingly so, as I couldn't think of any rumour that would deprive me of management support more quickly. I wouldn't even put it past Elaine not to circulate it just to make life difficult for me. I suspected that the 'hands-off' policy might not extend to editors, and particularly not to brand-new editors.

'Certainly not,' I said, firmly. 'No chance.' I wondered whether to go on the offensive by asking after her own two children, aged five and three, who were safely tucked away with nannies who rotated on shifts like airline pilots. Someone had told me, admittedly with a gleam of malice, that Elaine often made it clear that the term 'working mother' was a contradiction in terms. Certainly I'd noticed that she treated any implication that she might belong in this category – such as a reference to school holidays – as a direct attack. If you were lucky, you got a tight-lipped 'I always keep my family life private'. I decided not to antagonize her, so we merely smiled at each other briskly before stepping into our separate open-plan offices.

I was just bracing myself to talk to Mimi, Sandra and Mary when Laura rang.

'I'm sorry,' she said huffily, although I hadn't said anything, 'but there's a piece in the paper you ought to read.' Laura is the sort of person who explains rocket science to rocket scientists.

'It's about getting pregnant,' she informed me briskly.

Great. I was about to be treated to one of her half-baked enthusiasms for vitamins or Thai Chi. They never lasted, but for a brief, irritating period they were pressed upon us at every opportunity as the cure-all to everything.

'Hello? Hello?' she shouted into the receiver, under the impression that she'd been cut off.

'Yes?' I replied wearily, hoping she'd take the hint.

Laura is not a one for hints. You basically have to sit a response in a Sherman tank and drive it directly at her before she'll pick it up (and then she'll complain that you're over-reacting).

There was a rustling as she opened a newspaper. 'It's here. The chances of conceiving are higher after female orgasm.' She gabbled through the story. Scientists, who had always wondered what the evolutionary reason for the female orgasm was, had established – God knows how – that at the point of orgasm something, she thought it was probably the cervix, tipped up and drew sperm in. It accounted, apparently, for the reason why women were more likely to get pregnant if they were having an affair than with their regular partner. Because they were more likely to have an orgasm.

'For God's sake.' I could see the staff pulling up their chairs around my desk for the next meeting.

'Well,' she notched up the aggression in her voice a degree or two, 'I'm sorry, but if that's the attitude you take, it's not surprising you don't get pregnant.'

'I can't talk about this now,' I hissed back.

Laura chirruped on, oblivious. 'Really, though,' she added, clearly on a mission to improve my sex life. 'That's why natural contraception doesn't work. Because women always want sex most when they're likely to get pregnant. There hasn't been enough work on the effect of female sexuality on fertility.'

I don't usually tell Laura anything. It's just asking for trouble. Particularly not my immediate response which was that it was bad enough having to have all that sex without feeling obliged to enjoy it as well. Was there no corner of one's life that could not be penetrated and re-arranged after some study on 156 Danish farmers or 19,000 US nurses? If only these nurses and farmers could keep their sex lives and butter-eating habits to themselves the rest of us could get on with our lives.

'Well, perhaps you ought to get a research grant and do something on it,' I told her, just to get rid of her.

'There's no need to be like that. You ought to know about these things. You really ought. I'm surprised, in your job, that you don't.'

Aargh. 'Laura . . .' I began, desperately hoping that we could bring this conversation to a close.

She swept on in tones that could probably be heard halfway across the office. 'It's absolutely nothing to do with swinging from chandeliers or funny positions with cushions tucked under your hips.' She sighed, presumably at remembered passion. 'There's a certain kind of baby bonk.'

I didn't want to hear any more. 'Look, I really have got to go now.'

Laura is unstoppable. 'Why not treat yourselves to a romantic weekend? Something really relaxing.'

I inspected the idea in my head after I'd finally disentangled myself from the conversation – it had been a bit like getting something sticky off your fingers without it spreading to your silk shirt – and I wondered why I didn't hold out much hope for it. Will and I poring over the *Joy of Sex* together, somewhere like Paris or Rome, somewhere that didn't have any memories for either of us, where slivers of the past didn't suddenly stab us in the back. I don't think there is such a place.

But I thought that – if only to stop Laura from setting out on one of her campaigns – perhaps it was time for me to try for IVF. If the three months of fertility pills didn't work, that is.

For us to try IVF, I corrected myself. I wondered why this mission to get pregnant seemed to be mine rather than ours. It was almost as if Will didn't have anything to do with it, and was just a spectator waiting in anticipation of a victory. A sort of football club supporter.

I returned to the issue of the redundancies, which currently loomed much larger in my life than babies.

On the other hand, if she was right about the importance of female orgasms in getting pregnant, perhaps it wouldn't be necessary. I thought with pleasure of the night after we'd been to the clinic, and felt, for the first time in years, a sense of delicious anticipation. This time, there was a good chance everything might have worked.

I'd been offered a private meeting room to carry out my butchery.

I decided to start in order of seniority. I reminded myself that Mimi really didn't do her job properly – the covers, for example, the most expensive and crucial element of any magazine, had to be re-shot so often that we might as well simply open the huge smoked-glass windows and let the budget blow out in the riverfront gales. Not, of course, that the Maintenance Department would have allowed that. Opening a window, in the world of air-conditioned offices, is now a subversive act.

Mimi settled herself in front of me and smiled confidently, crossing a shapely pair of legs in blue velvet pedal-pushers.

I hated the thought of what this conversation would do to her. It would crucify her. She'd pick herself up – there was always a market for good freelances, and the pay-off would mean that she'd be cushioned financially for a while – but some people never forgot being made redundant. Why did it have to happen to nice people like Mimi, while the Camillas of this world remained a protected species? I took a deep breath.

Mimi opened her mouth first, while I was still searching for a tactful, dignity-enhancing way to say one of the most terrible things a boss can tell an employee.

'I just wanted to say that I'm having a baby.' She glowed with happiness. 'In November.' Six months to go.

It knocked the air out of me.

After a moment I managed to congratulate her.

'So what did you want to see me about?' She looked at me brightly.

'Er.' I thought of my conversation with Peter, and rallied. 'I just wanted to discuss your future. I'd wondered what you were planning.' This was hardly a lie, after all.

We wittered on about maternity leave for a while, and I looked at her departing back with a massive twinge of regret. Never me. And never would be, if Will went on behaving like a bad-tempered bear about to hibernate. Unless, of course, Laura was right.

I reminded myself of the fertility pills, felt tons better, and rang Peter Rennie to tell him about Mimi.

'For God's sake,' he said. 'What have you got in the water down there?'

'Well, this is the first pregnancy announced since I took over.'

He forbore to point out that this had been barely two months, but he sighed. 'At least the other two can't spring anything like that on us.'

I wasn't so sure. I had told him that I'd decided that Sandra had to go, rather than Jackie. Lovely, gentle Sandra, who flapped about ensuring that whichever pages she worked on were the last down to the printers, and always leaving about a dozen mistakes unchecked. I'd decided that my responsibility was to the team, not to individuals, and that I'd be letting everyone else down if I made the more able person redundant on the grounds that she'd survive better outside. But even saying that out loud didn't make me like myself any better.

'Hm.' I thought that either Sandra or Mary Elliott, who both wore swathes of grey/brown wool and might have been any age from thirty-five upwards, could have hidden anything under their voluminous garments, from a twin pregnancy to a personal computer.

*

Sandra came in first, with her usual sweet-faced smile.

'Sandra,' I hated myself. 'I'm really, really sorry, but we've had to make cuts and . . .'

Her faced paled and she watched me, sitting very still.

' . . . please believe me, it's nothing personal,' I concluded after talking for much longer than I intended and making far too many excuses. As if whether it was personal or not would make any difference to her.

She bit her lip. 'I quite understand.'

'Will you be all right?' It was a stupid question. Of course, she wouldn't be. I thought of all those articles about people who found themselves through redundancy, setting up small businesses doing what they really wanted to do.

She nodded bravely. 'It's just that my husband was made redundant too ten months ago, and hasn't found anything. But don't worry,' the sweet-faced smile again, 'we can sell the house.'

This was terrible, much worse than I'd imagined.

'It must be so awful for you,' she added, putting a hand on mine. 'I'm so sorry you had to do it. I think you've been a very good editor so far.'

It took me about fifteen minutes to compose myself enough to call Mary down.

She plumped down and crossed her arms, staring me straight in the eyes, her wispy hair drooping down to her shoulders like a reproach.

I managed this message a lot more briskly. It was like walking on a tightrope across a river gorge; just focus on the end result, I told myself, and don't look down.

Her face flushed angrily at the end of my pre-prepared speech. 'You shitty little cow.' She virtually spat the words out.

'I . . .'

She cut me off. 'You think you're so clever with your management-speak you've just learned out of a book, and your pathetic new ideas that we've all tried before and found didn't work.' Her voice rose to a shout. 'We all laugh at you down there, you know. Laugh. Because you replaced a really good editor they got rid of because she was too old, and too expensive, and too bloody good for them.'

She rose up and looked down at me, coming so close that I could smell her, a stale, acrid waft with undertones of poor food. 'And do you know why she was made redundant?'

I opened my mouth to point to falling sales, but she cut across me.

'Because she took two lots of maternity leave. In quick succession. They don't like editors having families. They think they'll be less dedicated.' Her eyes flicked dismissively over my stomach, an unpleasant, knowing look that made me cringe. 'And they'll do the same to you. Sooner or later. And if you don't show at least a tiny fraction of Martina's talent, at some point, it'll be sooner.'

She turned back at the door. 'I can't wait,' she said viciously. 'I really can't.'

I had never come across such naked hatred before. And she was right about the management-speak. What else had she been right about? I lifted the phone with a shaking hand and asked Personnel if they could come down and make sure that Mary Elliott left the building quietly and as soon as possible. When I got back to the office a hush fell as I went into the room, and everyone bent over their work. Mary was throwing things into a bag with snorts of anger, and Sandra was nowhere to be seen. I found her sobbing in the Ladies, being comforted, ironically, by Jackie.

'Is there anything I can do?' I asked.

They both looked up in amazement. Of course there wasn't.

I rang Will and, amazingly, got through between patients.

'It's been awful. Worse than I imagined.' I told him I'd done the redundancies. 'Could we go out to dinner tonight? The local cheapie? I desperately need to get away, even just for a meal.'

He sighed deeply. 'I was hoping for an early night. I'm really bushed.'

'You're a doctor,' I said crossly. 'Can't you find out why you're so tired all the time and do something about it?'

There was an edge of steel in his voice. 'I do have a very demanding job.'

'So do I.' Trying not to cry made me aggressive. 'It's not easy making people redundant, you know.'

'Well, it can't be quite as bad as being on the receiving end,' he pointed out, being infuriatingly fair to the underdog as usual. 'Sweetheart, I'm really sorry, but all I can face this evening is a quiet vegetate in front of the box. We can talk then.'

He was right, of course. He'd never made anyone redundant in his life, but he does have to try to pick up some of the pieces afterwards when they come into his surgery with depression or alcoholism or whatever.

It was impossible. I refrained from slamming the phone down on him because I knew it was counter-productive, and simply said a small, hurt goodbye to try to make him feel at least slightly guilty.

13

Two weeks later, I popped my pill, took my temperature, widdled over something like a popsicle stick and, feeling like a witch doctor reading the entrails of a slaughtered chicken, told Will that today was a good day to get pregnant. We were, however, in danger of missing out if we didn't go for it today or tomorrow, as the cycle was slipping by.

It was a nuisance because I was supposed to leave early for a breakfast meeting, and I knew the milkman was likely to start ringing the doorbell to be paid at any moment. Not to mention the postman, and the gas meter reader. Laura had not been right about the 'baby bonk', or, if she had been right, it didn't apply to me. The gentle, genuine night we'd spent together after we'd first gone to the clinic hadn't achieved anything. Perhaps I was impregnable. It was a daunting, bleak thought. On the other hand, we'd hardly begun with the fertility pills. Even reluctant sex does bring you closer together and I felt miles away from Will these days, as if Planet Maglife was my real home.

I eyed him without enthusiasm. He smiled and stretched out a hand. 'I'm ordering you back in bed under the doctor.'

It wasn't a very good joke, but it cheered me up slightly.

'Can't you fantasize or something?' he asked.

I nearly said 'Like you thinking of Saffron?' but changed it to 'Like you thinking of Claudia Schiffer' at the last moment.

He looked irritated. 'I wish you didn't put yourself down all the time. Why should I want to fantasize about Claudia Schiffer?'

I could think of several reasons, mainly related to cellulite and spare tyres. 'Look,' I said, because this wasn't getting us anywhere. 'You just lie back and think of anything sexy and I'll seduce you.' That would get it over and done with fairly quickly.

He looked surprised. 'That's a nice idea.'

I got through it by pretending it was just a very intimate form of aerobic exercise.

'But you didn't have an orgasm,' he commented when we had finished.

'Orgasm,' I repeated crossly, as I headed off to the shower. 'It's bad enough having to have all this sex when one doesn't feel like it without having to enjoy it as well.'

A wooden look came across his face. I'd been joking, but it hadn't come out that way. I went back to him, mentally cursing myself for being careless, and wasting even more time.

'I'm sorry. I didn't mean it. I was trying to be funny.'

He smiled briefly, and squeezed my hand. 'I know. I understand.'

Did he? I hoped not. I wasn't particularly proud of myself. Something – perhaps it was the job – seemed to be turning me into a complete cow. On the Tube, I read two stories about women and sex. One was about a female teacher who had been sacked for having an affair with one of her male pupils, although he was seventeen and therefore over the age of consent. The other was a survey stating that many women prefer a bacon sandwich to a night of passion. In my early days with Will my heart – and my body – would have understood the teacher. Now my sympathies lay with the bacon-sandwich eaters. This is the price you pay for infertility.

At least work was really beginning to sparkle. The first issue that could remotely have been ascribed to my editorship came out two months after I had joined, and its sales figures in the first week showed a small but perceptible upturn. As sales for the previous six issues had all shown a drop, this was quite a victory, and I opened a bottle of indifferent white Chardonnay and poured it out in paper cups to celebrate with the staff. Camilla wrinkled her nose, and said 'Yech,' but quite nicely. Even she seemed to be thawing out.

After a few days of murmuring – resentful groups had formed and re-formed around the photocopier and the coffee machine, dispersing as soon as I rounded the corner – people had quickly forgotten about the two redundancies. Sandra had been so hopeless at her job that it was almost easier not to have her muddling around, and Mary had worked on a section we had genuinely decided to get rid of. There was almost a lightness of spirit among the staff, which I put down to the uplifting effect of having survived the typhoon of redundancy. It was, I now suspected, with a lingering sense of guilt and regret, down to Sandra's and Mary's families and friends – not to mention their GPs, probably – to pick up the pieces. At Maglife the ripples caused by their departure had entirely died away.

Mimi, who had maintained an enviable slenderness while her pregnancy stayed secret, had blossomed out into an earth mother once she went public, cultivating a duck-footed waddle and wearing a Lycra tube that showed off the beginnings of her bump in a way that could not be ignored. I tried not to be critical, knowing that it stemmed from my increasingly intense desire to have a bump myself, although I didn't think Lycra was going to be particularly life-enhancing in my case. I had quite strong opinions about what I would wear for pregnancy and found it almost impossible to read the small ads in magazines without mentally noting the names of good mail-order pregnancy-wear companies. It was the mental equivalent of all dressed up and ready to go, then having to stay in after all.

The only really irritating thing that day was having to read the interviews that accompanied the 'Musicians in Fashion' piece for the Bellingham Glass supplement. We had had to promise their agents that we would treat the musicians as serious artists before they would allow their clients anywhere near our photographer, so each picture was accompanied by a 'lifestyle' interview and a few credits for their next concert or record.

I flicked quickly to Saffron's story. 'Life is what you make it,' Saffron had explained to the interviewer. 'I discovered a lump in my breast a few years ago, and although it was benign, it made me realize you have to make every day count. Everyone is someone.' I could imagine her leaning forward earnestly and tossing a hank of the red-gold curls behind her, then fixing the writer with an impassioned look. 'You owe it to yourself to find out who that someone is.'

I tried to decide whether this was complete bilge-water or whether the readers of *How?* would feel touched and comforted to know that even a woman with 34-inch hips and waist-length hair really believed that everyone was someone.

I passed it over to Camilla, the acid test in more ways than one.

She read it. 'She's awfully brave, isn't she? I mean, she's so real. I couldn't be that calm if I'd found a lump in my breast.' She handed it back.

If Camilla swallowed it, the readers would lap it up. I have to say that Camilla does have her finger on the popular pulse. My own opinion, which was that Saffron was completely unreal, was doubtless based on sheer jealousy, and, as such, should be suppressed.

It's no good being obsessed by feuds, they only eat you up in the end.

Telling myself that penny philosophizing was obviously infectious, I passed the page to the sub-editors with a scribbled comment 'find out what she's doing now'. This wasn't, I hasten to add, because I wanted to know. But the writer had become so fascinated with Saffron's diet ('I used to eat junk food, but since the breast-cancer scare, I really look after myself and mainly stick to raw fruit and vegetables with a piece of grilled fish in the evening') and her wardrobe ('just jeans and things I've picked up in Oxfam shops, my favourite is a lovely Issey Miyake in dark green') that she had omitted all mention of her career. Mind you, anyone who can find Issey Miyake in Oxfam shops probably doesn't need a career. I was relieved that we weren't hearing about her home – I'd never been to the tiny studio she had occasionally described as 'my very private place', but I didn't think I could have stood having to look at stylish photographs accompanied by the information that Saffron had picked up all the good pieces in skips and junk shops.

I found it difficult to concentrate on the other musicians, and probably let hundreds of mistakes go through. I couldn't help remembering the night that Saffron's breast-cancer scare had started.

The phone had trilled at 10 p.m. on a Sunday evening, just as I was sinking down into my pillows for an early night. Will's light had still been on, and he'd been reading copies of the *BMJ*, although I'd warned him that working late would affect his sleep. I wished he didn't have to live his job twenty-four hours a day. Still, that's dedication for you.

The phone is on my side of the bed, so I'd picked it up. At first I hadn't recognized Saffron's voice. The throatiness had deteriorated to a hoarse whisper and she'd sounded panicky.

'Saffron!' I'd exclaimed. 'Are you all right?'

Will had stopped reading and looked over the *BMJ* at me.

She'd ignored me. 'Could I speak to William, please? It's urgent.'

I'd handed it over to him with a sigh, and slid down the bedclothes, trying simultaneously to get to sleep and work out what they were talking about.

It hadn't been difficult to grasp. The telephone had twittered like a budgerigar, as Will tried to get a word in edgeways.

Eventually he'd said, 'Listen. Calm down. Nine out of ten lumps are benign.'

There'd been more chirruping from the phone as I'd stared at the ceiling. Oh God. Saffron with possible breast cancer. I'd instantly felt fantastically guilty about all the times I'd wished her swept away in some tidal wave. In fact, I'd told myself, I'd never wanted her to be ill, just abroad, indefinitely, preferably somewhere too difficult to visit. Ulan Bator, perhaps, or an obscure town in the Mid-West.

They'd gone on talking for over an hour, and every so often I'd wondered whether I'd prefer it if Will took the telephone into another room. Then I'd decided that perhaps I wouldn't. This, I'd told myself, was just the problem with being married to a doctor. Even if Saffron hadn't been an ex-girlfriend, she'd probably have rung him. People did.

Will had told her to go to her GP in the morning – several times – but eventually he'd said, 'Look, do you want to come round and stay here tonight? I don't think you should be alone in that state.'

I had just been slipping into sleep and my eyelids had jerked awake.

Saffron round here, probably wanting Will to feel her breasts? My better self had reminded my nasty, mean, jealous self that one of those breasts might well be harbouring a killer disease. My nasty, mean, jealous self had said that it didn't care, breast-feeling was breast-feeling and Saffron's small pert ones were an awful lot nicer than my boring old droopy ones that he saw every night.

Will must have seen my eyeballs goggling over the top of the duvet because he'd put out a reassuring hand and squeezed me. 'Leonie agrees, don't you, darling?'

This was the best thing he could have said because Saffron was reminded of my existence. Perhaps she thought I'd stand over any bare-breasted women with a lamp, like a vengeful Florence Nightingale. Anyway, the upshot was, after an awful lot more chirruping, that she'd decided not to come.

As Will had finally put the phone down, I'd looked

at the clock. It was eleven forty p.m., not late as in LATE, but it had still wiped out our early night.

'Poor Saffron,' I'd said, determined to be magnanimous and also light-headed with relief that she wasn't going to be lying on our spare bed with Will palpating her chest.

He'd shaken his head. 'I've never heard her in such a state. God, some people just have such rotten luck.'

I wasn't sure about this. I didn't think Saffron's life was that disastrous, and I thought she probably manufactured many of her problems herself, even if she could hardly be held responsible for this latest scare. But I'd thought it wiser not to say that.

'I asked her how she was, and she didn't even bother to reply,' I'd observed grumpily.

Will had tried to reassure me. 'I'm sure she didn't mean it. If you had a lump in your breast, you might forget a few social niceties, don't you think?'

He'd been absolutely right, of course. I would. I'd felt selfish and horrible, and even worse that I'd displayed this selfish horribleness to him. How could he possibly love a woman who only thought about herself when someone rang up to worry about breast cancer?

I hadn't slept at all well that night.

The progress of the breast lump had dominated our answering-machine messages for about three weeks, ensuring that Will spent more time talking to Saffron on the telephone than to me in person. He'd driven her to hospital for the biopsy – she was temporarily between boyfriends – and picked her up afterwards. She'd actually been so shaken by the experience that she'd even addressed a few words to me on occasions, usually to tell me how wonderful 'William' was. However, it all ended relatively calmly with the news that it was, indeed, benign and that there really was no cause to worry. We'd subsequently had a brief period of witnessing Saffron's spiritual re-awakening, as she went on a course to learn a healing process called Reiki, which she proposed to inflict on the inhabitants of Notting Hill Gate in return for cash as an addition to the piano lessons she gave. Even Will's brow had furrowed and he'd murmured something about it being high time Saffron focused on what she wanted out of life instead of trying a new fad every time she didn't have a concert coming up. Then she'd vanished from our radar screens completely. We did hear some rumour about a German composer in her life. I'd prayed he was based somewhere in the middle of Germany – Holzminden, for example – so that it would require several changes of train to get there, which would save us from even considering going for the weekend. But, in fact, she never got in touch. One thing you can say for her is that she only bothers with us when she's temporarily lost or broken all her other toys.

I don't mean to be such a bitch. But, four years on from the breast-cancer scare, sitting at my desk in *How?*'s offices, facing the prospect of yet another evening in her company – 27 May was less than a week away – I was beginning to wonder if I should talk to Will about it. Be honest. Actually admit to not liking her. Point out that she obviously doesn't rate me. In essence, ask Will to choose.

It was going to sound pretty silly, though, asking him to give up a friendship with someone he hadn't actually seen for eighteen months, and whose only communication in that time – to my knowledge – had been a telephone conversation about the location of a stop tap. The other option was to admit, finally, that this whole Saffron business was in my own head, and that, although she was a silly, irritating woman, I had this sneaking feeling that the shadow she cast over our marriage was not entirely about her. Or, more accurately, about her and Will. Perhaps she'd become some kind of symbol for our inability to produce a baby.

This was a cosy line of thought and one which cheered me greatly. Saffron as a symbol of something else I could cope with. I thought that I might consider going to a counsellor and talking all these feelings through – without Will, of course – and coming to terms with it all.

I wrenched my mind back to the offices of *How?*, as Lucy passed over the most enormous stiff card invitation I'd ever seen in my life. It had been delivered by motorcycle messenger and was hand-made from watermelon paper, according to the accompanying press release. Grown on the banks of some Chinese river, harvested by virgins, made with a previously-lost centuries-old process, then inscribed with gold calligraphy. Well, you know, something along those lines. Basically it said that 27 May was the biggest, most important perfume launch this century, and the makers would like to fly me to Paris to be part of it.

I gazed at it in horror for a few minutes and then pulled myself together. Firstly, this invitation came from a major advertiser, and consequently there would be a three-line whip from both management and the advertising department for editors to attend. Pleading previous family engagements or that it was a Sunday evening, would not, of course, lose me my job, but it would be a big black mark against me, particularly on top of my non-appearance at the House of Commons lunch. Sending Camilla in my place would be dangerous. If I was to ask myself, honestly, who could do more damage to my life, Camilla or Saffron, the answer had to be Camilla, although I had to admit that she had recently been positively helpful occasionally.

This was another very cheering thought, surprisingly. It shrank Saffron down to size. It wasn't as if I expected Will to run off with Saffron, because he could have done that at any time. If she'd wanted to marry him, she would have done so, presumably, before we met. He married me. And if she'd really wanted Will on a permanent basis, surely she'd have tried a bit harder? As far as I could see, she used him as a shoulder to cry on when there weren't any better shoulders about. That hardly constituted a grand passion.

In a way, I told myself, this invitation was a blessing because it had forced me to focus on what I really feared about Saffron. And the answer was quite possibly that it was all more about my own sense of inadequacy than her power.

It was time to grow up. I trusted Will. He could go alone, and I would go to the perfume launch.

And that's what happened. I went to the launch of Affair, and he started an affair of his own.

14

As I stood in the gloomy hallway at 7.45 a.m. on 28 May, flicking idly through some post, Will's key in the latch surprised me. He must have gone out to get some milk.

Someone walking through a door the wrong way at the wrong time doesn't have to mean that life flips over on to its B side in a few seconds. There is no reason why it should spell betrayal and upheaval. It shouldn't mean that you can never, ever have a baby. And, of course, that's not what it means. There is always a reasonable explanation.

He gazed at me in complete amazement, and shut the door behind him. White-faced, terribly tired, hollow-eyed and unshaven, he just went on staring. I couldn't have looked much better – last night's extravaganza had ended with fireworks overlooking a lake at 1 a.m. My eyes felt like sandpaper, and my skin was dry and prickly. My stomach lurched sickeningly, as I tried to make sense of the scene: 'Have you been out to get the papers?'

'No.' One bleak word.

'Or the milk? Couldn't you sleep?' I knew I sounded desperate, so I threw him a lifeline. 'Were you on call?'

He was too honest to take it. 'I'm sorry.'

Sorry is the saddest sound. He wasn't going to give me a way out. He wasn't going to pretend any more. I just looked at him in horror, furious at the realization that the hand holding the letter was shaking and that he'd noticed. I placed the letter down carefully and put my hands in my pockets.

'It didn't mean anything,' he added.

'What . . .' I tried to stop my voice trembling . . . 'what didn't mean anything?' I already knew, of course, exactly what it was, but I needed to hear him say it. Otherwise I just wouldn't be able to believe it.

'I've been with Saffron, but that doesn't mean . . .'

'Don't try to tell me that you spent the night with her without anything happening!' I knew I sounded shrill and shrewish, and hated myself for it. Why couldn't I be calm, confident, cool Leonie, able to understand, forgive, dismiss? Perhaps, though, he had come home just to get his things. He might be leaving for ever. It was like seeing a chasm open up in front of my feet, threatening to topple me over and into the blackness.

'No, I can't tell you that. We . . .'

The 'we' cut sharp and deep. I leant against the wall, trying to breathe calmly, while I waited for him to choose the next words. They mattered. Would he say 'made love'? 'had sex'? 'fucked'?

'We shouldn't have done it.' Then he added quietly, 'But we did.'

The small logical bit of my brain, the one that keeps

calculating no matter how frantic the rest of my thoughts are, popped up with the reminder that if Will went, I would probably never have a baby. I wouldn't have time to meet someone else, get back in the queue for the clinic . . . I scrabbled to regain my dignity, retrieve the situation.

'I see.'

'It won't happen again. It was . . .'

I felt the sparks of anger ignite, engulfing the fear, and I began to walk past him. If I stayed I would say terrible things, so it would be better if I just went to work and forgot about it.

He tried to stop me. 'Please, Leonie. I'm sorry.'

I shook his arm off impatiently. We both stared at the ground for a bit. I noticed that my shoes needed cleaning. So did his.

He took my hand and I snatched it away.

He spoke softly. 'Think about what we have together.'

What did we have together? A few snatched moments, the occasional dispute over the allocation of housework, two jobs that didn't intersect at any point, and those tired, tired times at the end of the day. And his ex-girlfriend hanging over us like a long, dark shadow. My eyes filled with tears, remembering the excitement of discovering each other and then the gentle quiet times when we'd lounged around together in companionable silence, reading, resting an arm or a leg against the other's warmth. Those times would never return. I could never take him for granted again.

Whatever happened now, the Will I'd known had gone for ever.

'Sometimes,' he sounded despairing, 'it seems impossible to talk to you.'

'I think,' I tried to steady my voice, 'that we should talk later. When I come home.'

And I staggered out of the house, blinking in the sunlight, running like a wounded animal for the safety of cover. The office.

I got lost on the way in, accidentally getting on the wrong Tube train, noticing too late, getting off again and on to another wrong train. I finished up in Finsbury Park. Finsbury Park! I'd never been to Finsbury Park in my life, and I couldn't see, from looking at the Tube map, exactly how I'd got there this time. People pressed against me, stepping on my toes and swamping me in smells that ranged from aftershave to dank, unwashed hair. I shuffled in the packed crowd towards another train, and eventually, hours late, trudged into the office.

I went into the Ladies to wash my face, which looked swollen and blotched with tiredness. The room was empty, and I leant against the towel dispenser, relishing a moment of privacy. There was nowhere safe to cry any more.

Maeve came in, acknowledging me with a brief 'Hello'. We'd become reasonably friendly for an editor-publisher relationship, nothing more. I forced my face into the rictus of a bright smile.

She looked at me in the mirror while she was washing her hands, and pulled a make-up bag out.

'Do borrow some. I think it might help.'

I looked at myself. It might. I told her that I'd come out in a hurry and left mine behind. I muttered something – regrettably all too accurate – about period pains to account for my wild-eyed, sleep-deprived look.

Her wise eyes told me she understood. As she left, she touched me briefly on the shoulder, the simple contact communicating a surprising depth of warmth and sympathy. 'Lunch today?'

I nodded. When the going gets tough, the tough go out to lunch.

And that was how we came to be together, eating lunch in All Thai'd Up, and it was then I first realized that I wasn't going insane. Maeve, whose only knowledge of Saffron came from picking up the page proof on my desk, reading it, and asking me how and where we'd found her ('An old girlfriend of my husband's,' I'd said), understood when I told her what had happened. I didn't feel I had to explain the background. Trying to describe the situation would have been like picking up a set of children's wax crayons and trying to draw an Old Master. You knew where the lines and edges should be, you knew how powerful and vibrant the colours ought to be, and how deeply the picture in your mind affected you, but all you would see, there on the paper, would be a scrawled mess.

15

The best thing about work is that it rumbles on relentlessly, no matter what happens to any individual. It's like having the Russian army roll its tanks over any finer feelings you might have.

As soon as I'd sat down, gazing blankly at the pile of letters Lucy had managed to do for me, and which I knew would be peppered with mistakes, one of the sub-editors, a pretty, tired-looking woman called Polly, sidled up and asked for a chat about her future.

She wanted to job-share, in order to see more of her three children, aged seven, five and two. She proposed working a three-day week, and she'd found another former sub-editor, with the best possible CV, who wanted to work the other two days. They'd worked out how much each would earn, and how they'd communicate. She'd got a clear policy on holidays and sick leave, and even what might happen in the event of a bonus, overtime or redundancy.

I congratulated her on working it all out so thoroughly.

She looked pleased and expectant.

'But . . .' I spoke reluctantly, 'I'm afraid it's not quite that simple.' I had discussed flexible working in general with Peter Rennie and he'd been evasive. I suspected it wasn't going to get any easier once we got specific.

'There's an editors' meeting later on this afternoon,' I promised. 'I'll bring it up then.' I wouldn't ordinarily discuss a staffing matter in a general meeting, but I thought I'd get more support that way as most of the editors were women.

Once in the meeting, I realized I was wrong. Everybody exchanged glances, as if to say 'this old chestnut'.

'We've always said we should try it again if the right situation came up,' murmured Belinda Bracken, who seemed cautiously sympathetic as the gentle, balanced editor of *Home Life*. 'Perhaps if Leonie feels like trailblazing, this is a good opportunity.'

'Really,' this was Elaine Brown, glitzy in her go-getting *My Life* role, 'if the girl isn't committed enough at least to come in every day, you ought to give the job to someone else. There are plenty of people out there looking for work.'

Edward Taylor mumbled something about redundancy and part-timers. No one took any notice.

Peter Rennie leant back in his chair with an air of exasperation. 'I'll be frank with you, Leonie. Personally, I don't care if your staff come in at midnight and work standing on their heads as long as the magazine comes out and is as successful as it can possibly be. But the main point is that the employees you are responsible for do care. They feel very, very uneasy about certain sectors being given special privileges, merely because they're mothers. It's caused a great deal of unrest and instability in the past.'

There was a murmur of assent around the table.

'I can't tell you what trouble I have with the child-care allowances,' explained Belinda, referring to the £100 extra every month that Maglife paid mothers for childcare in place of a workplace creche. 'Quite a few of the younger girls simply don't accept that the person sitting next to them doing exactly the same job for exactly the same hours should earn an extra £25 a week merely because she's got a child. They feel that having a baby is a matter of individual choice, like buying a sports car, so it's up to the individual to deal with the consequences. What they say to me,' she paused with a sigh and replaced her reading glasses, 'is that there's no other area of your private life which you would expect the company to subsidize.'

If you have it, you look after it and you pay for it. I had, I suppose, grown up with the generation of feminists who believed that the route to female happiness was equal opportunities, broken glass ceilings and subsidized daycare, and while I'd expected to fight my corner with men, it had never occurred to me that other women might not agree. Or that the resistance to flexible working did not come from bosses but from the rank and file. I suppose that to a twenty-year-old girl, the whole concept of being thirty-something and a mother is just too distant to contemplate.

I wasn't prepared to give up that easily, however. 'Polly's not asking for subsidies or special privileges.

She'd be earning proportionately less, and she says she can guarantee that the same amount of work – if not more – will be done. She did say,' I thought this was a strong point, 'that if she has more time with her children overall, she'd feel more able to work late, and that she knew the other job-sharer would too, so she thought we'd actually get more hours out of them for the same money.'

Everyone grinned cynically at this.

'After all,' whined Loulou Steel, editor of *Night Life*, picking at her purple nail varnish, 'Peter's told me an editor can't work part-time or job-share, so why should any of my staff have privileges that I can't have?'

I felt like asking her if she usually insisted that her own and her staff's privileges be necessarily the same in all respects, but I wasn't going to get anywhere antagonizing everyone. I wondered why I, to whom motherhood seemed very remote indeed, was taking the side of the working mother. It was hardly Lindsey's influence – she believed maternity leave was far too long as it was and placed a completely unnecessary burden on industry, while Laura's aggressive 'mothers at home' stance meant that, were she Prime Minister, she'd forbid mothers of children under five to work, and would pay them a salary to stay at home. Luckily for the nation's coffers, Laura was unlikely to achieve this position. Perhaps the only reason why I still believed that there was a middle way, a correct, fair, middle way, one that supported the next generation without over-taxing this one, was that, without a baby,

I hadn't the faintest idea what I was talking about. I shivered. Laura's perpetual cry – 'you don't understand' – rang in my ears like a reproach.

'I can understand your reservations,' I told them, 'and you are all probably right. However, I'd be very grateful, Peter, if you could let me go ahead this once, on a strictly trial basis, just to see if it could be made to work.'

Although he looked extremely reluctant, he agreed. 'But I would remind you, Leonie, that we have over 400 women employed in this building. If they all want to job-share or go part-time, there'll be absolute chaos, and I'm simply not prepared to countenance that.'

Belinda quietly congratulated me afterwards in the Ladies. 'I hope it succeeds,' she said, 'although I'm very much afraid that it won't.'

I was about to point out that job-shares and part-timing were both considered quite ordinary in some industries, when Camilla walked in, not bothering to greet anyone. She rarely did, unless someone important was around, and neither I nor Belinda really counted in her view. Out of the corner of my eye, I looked at her in the mirror, tall and dark, with her pale skin and sleek, dark bob. As usual she was dressed meticulously in the latest fashions, as only a twenty-six-year-old with a private income can. Someone with the time and money to change her clothes – and the accessories – six or seven times before leaving the house, and then repeat the ritual in the evening. She carefully drew her lipstick on, puckering up her full lips, blotting them, and working the lipstick in. Then she stepped back and frowned, totally engrossed. I'd seen this before several times, and she always seemed unaware of the chattering behind her, or of anyone else wanting to use the basin. What she saw in the mirror was never perfect. She'd return to even out the shade, add a few more layers of mascara on her dark, almond-shaped eyes, turn and check her back view for stray hairs or dandruff. Eventually, after flicking a few imaginary motes of dust off her shoulders, she'd stride out through the door, often knocking someone flying in the process. I didn't think I'd ever heard her say 'Sorry', but perhaps I'm being unfair.

Belinda and I had stopped talking while she was beside us, but after she left we both finished tidying up our hair and rummaging in battered, capacious bags. She smiled at me conspiratorially, and I knew she felt much the same about Camilla as I did.

It had all taken my mind off the molten lava of pain at the core of my being.

I had to go home at last, though. I'd put it off by checking pages, I'd sliced my pen through over-long, gushing articles and insisted on re-wording letters until Lucy began to look so desperate that I let her go. Then I had a skirmish with Mimi and Camilla over the shopping pages.

I called her over. 'Mimi, I really don't think anyone's going to pay £89.50 for a loo-roll holder. Can you find another pic?' Mimi picked up the glass and peered at the transparency I was pointing at.

'It's a lamp not a loo-roll holder.' Camilla's tone implied that I was an eighty-year-old great-aunt up in town for the day from Shropshire. 'Look. That's a lampshade not a lavatory roll, and there's the flex.'

I was annoyed. Blurred photographs at funny angles were great for the Bellingham Glass catalogue, but recently I'd mistaken a grainy close-up of the inside of a sock drawer for a pile of sofa cushions.

'Can't we have photography that shows what things actually are?'

'Well!' Mimi was huffy. 'If you want it to look like a catalogue . . .'

'No,' I snapped. 'I don't want it to look like a catalogue. And I don't want it to look like a mess either.'

Mimi took the offending layout away looking martyred, and Camilla answered her phone. Actually answered it herself. I was beginning to notice that things were settling down round here. Camilla did occasionally lift a finger to help out.

Up to a point. 'Bunny?' she drawled. 'Yah, well. I'm not sure, I might be busy.' She yawned. 'Who else is coming?' I sometimes wondered if her friends minded having to issue a full guest list before she accepted an invitation. She had swung her chair away from the desk, and extended her long, elegant legs, clad in tight silk 'clam-digger' trousers that ended at mid-calf. Occasionally the fashion department eyed them enviously. They photographed, priced and wrote about the top designers, but mostly had to fold the clothes neatly up in tissue paper and send them back to the fashion companies. Camilla actually shopped for things priced at £657.

'Can I be frightfully rude and let you know nearer the time?' It seemed as if the guest list had not, after all, come up to scratch. I could hear some tinny squeaking in reply.

She finally put down the phone and swivelled round. 'What about a piece on Gardening as the New Sex?'

I shook my head. 'Been done. Food as the New Sex. Done. Interior Decorating as the New Sex. Done.'

'What about Accessorizing as the New Sex?'

Polly marched past with a pile of papers. 'I think washing up is the new sex. It's the only thing that brings me closer to my husband and makes me feel all warm and drooly about him.'

Camilla just looked at Polly as if she was several sponge fingers short of a trifle, and said, 'Accessorizing as the New Sex, then, do you agree, Leonie?'

I thought I might as well. I wondered what she'd say if I told her that some of us – not me necessarily – were still engaging in the old sex, and with all the wrong people. She'd think it terminally un-hip, worse than carrying the wrong handbag.

Perhaps that's what I'd tell Will. Accuse him of being outdated. Tell him that if he wanted to be a really modern man he should have been trying to decide whether this season's Gucci loafers were more important than Patrick Cox footwear, rather than rolling around with an ex-girlfriend. Frankly, I knew he wouldn't care. I don't think he's bought any new shoes since his last pair of wellingtons. He was, I realized with a fresh stab of pain, my lifeline to reality. Whenever I started to get too wound up – usually about something trivial such as whether to have tulips or roses on the cover – he'd listen and ask questions until I'd talked myself into what was always the right decision. I'd often wondered how people stayed sane without an invisible steadying hand behind them. Now I was probably about to find out.

Camilla looked at Polly's departing back. 'Honestly, I used to want to swan up the aisle in a white meringue, but judging by you lot, it seems very over-rated.'

I stopped reading a dull article about a couple who had renovated a wrecked house.

'Except you, Leonie.'

I just stared at her. Was she greasing up to the boss? And, if so, why?

'Your husband's a real hunk. Dead sexy.'

That was all I needed. Camilla pronouncing Will sexy. Was he? I tried to remember sexy, old or new style. All I could see was his pale, unshaven face and the dead look in his eyes when he walked in that morning. All I could feel was a huge, cold crater where he had once been.

The last article I had to read that evening danced in front of me in a meaningless squiggle. 'It is hard to believe that just three years ago this house was almost derelict,' the writer burbled. 'Friends said that Amanda and Jolyon were mad to take on such a wreck.' I read on with mounting irritation. Raven-haired Amanda, whose willowy outline apparently belied her strength, was determined to create the atmosphere of a country kitchen, although they were in the middle of town. Amanda tinkled with laughter as she passed on her renovation tips and by the end of the piece, I'd had enough of hearing how to re-create a rural manor in a moderate suburban terraced house. But everyone needs dreams. At least Amanda's and Jolyon's could be satisfied by a painted pine kitchen and a collection of hanging baskets.

With a sigh, I realized I couldn't go on avoiding the shattered remains of my own dreams. I still hadn't worked out what to do. Would we tear each other apart, listing the failings that had driven him to seek out Saffron? Would I be playing 'Stand By Your Man' while he hummed along to 'Twenty-Four Hours from Tulsa?' I re-wrote the song in my mind – twenty-four minutes from Tulse Hill, I muttered hysterically, and a night away from my arms, and suddenly neither of us could ever, ever come home again. Perhaps it would be better to be stiff-lipped about it, and brush it all under the carpet the way people used to before divorce was a reality?

But divorce was a reality now.

Part of me prayed for a divisional meeting or even a patient crisis, so that Will would be late home again.

But he was there, cooking a pasta sauce.

I was flummoxed. Was I going mad? First he sleeps with his ex-girlfriend, next thing he's started chopping onions.

'I thought I'd cook for a change,' he said, kissing me on the cheek. 'To give you a break.'

I thought of saying that I didn't do the cooking, Mr Marks or Mr Spencer did it most nights, along with Pizza Pueblo and the Local Curry House.

I took my coat off and hung it up without comment. Then, because I didn't want to seem sulky, I went back into the kitchen and said, 'Well! This is a lovely treat!' My voice came out all false and high, but he appeared not to notice.

But I had to admit to myself that it smelt delicious and that the prospect of eating something that hadn't come out of a silver foil container was very appealing.

'I even got a starter. I went to Soho.'

It seemed a worryingly louche place to go after a night of infidelity.

'Where did you park?'

He gave me a quizzical half-smile. 'Anyone else would ask "What did you get?"'

I raised an eyebrow. 'I know what you got if you went to Soho.' Parma ham, focaccia bread, gleaming roasted vegetables in oil.

I wondered if the rest of my life was going to be like this, asking off-the-wall questions in the hope of tripping him up every time he did something even slightly unusual.

'I went by Tube.' The tone of his voice was even, conversational and bland. The edge underneath it said, 'I'm trying to defuse this situation. Don't strike a match.'

In fact, I was frantically calculating whether one could easily get from Soho to Saffron's very private place in Notting Hill Gate. I rather thought one could.

I smiled. 'Brilliant. Just what I feel like.' I moved carefully around the kitchen, determined to be the one who unwrapped the packet. I knew the difference between the carrier bag from Lina's Stores in Soho and Tom Conran's in Notting Hill Gate. You could get focaccia and parma hams at both.

It was Lina's Stores. I laid the succulent hams out in a neat pattern and nibbled a fiery slice of peppery salami. God, this adultery business was exhausting. For the person cheated on, at least, constantly having to add up figures and times in their mind, working out if five minutes had been stolen here or there. Checking the logos on carrier bags. I supposed I'd have to start searching pockets for give-away receipts.

We went on dancing politely around each other for a bit, jumping to be the first to lay the table or answer the telephone. Laura rang to ask Will about some pregnancy scare. He spoke gently and carefully to her, and I wished the words of reassurance were meant for me.

I put a candle on the table and lit it.

'A candle!' He made it sound as if I'd introduced

full *son et lumière* into the house, complete with orchestra and fireworks.

'Why not?' I shrugged.

We sat down eventually and for about ten minutes it was like one of those French art films, just the sound of the clock ticking and forks scraping against plates, with long silences between relatively pointless remarks.

'I think . . .'

'I'm . . .'

We both spoke together, and then said, 'Sorry, you first' in unison.

I looked at him with a sense of mounting dread.

'I'm sorry,' he said, again. 'I never meant to hurt you.'

'It's not just last night,' I said. 'It's the whole picture.'

'It is just last night. I promise you that.'

I suppressed my anger. Last night was enough. I reminded myself that nothing could be gained from losing my temper. It was my – our – whole life together that was at stake. I thought of cancelling the next appointment at the fertility clinic. But I didn't want to do that. I just wanted to hurt myself in some way to take the edge off the pain I was going through.

'Why did it happen?'

For a moment I didn't think he was going to answer. I knew that if he blamed me, if he tried to protect Saffron, that really would be it. But if not . . . could I live with it?

'It was an accident. It was late. I was tired, I'd drunk

too much . . .' I could see that each word was agony as it was pulled out of him, so I didn't point out that being drunk and tired didn't have us falling into each other's arms in the usual way of things.

'It just happened. It was a one-night stand. One night. That's all it was. All it'll ever be.'

'But why?' It hurt me to repeat myself, even to think about it. My heart wanted to bury everything without mentioning any of it ever again. My mind couldn't leave it alone, growling and worrying at the events of the past twenty-four hours like a dog with a bone. 'Why did it have to happen at all?'

'She needed me.'

I didn't want to ask the question, in case something else got broken and another fragile fragment of our life splintered into tiny pieces. But I couldn't help it. 'And I don't?' I whispered.

He looked at me, as if thinking it through for the first time. 'No,' he said. 'You don't.'

'Needing you,' I tried to speak carefully, 'doesn't have to mean desperate calls at midnight trying to find a stop tap, or running to you with every single problem.'

'She doesn't run to me with every single problem,' he pointed out. This may have been strictly accurate, but hearing him defend her made me so furious that I couldn't tell him outright that I needed him too. Desperately. Even passionately.

I merely folded my arms. 'So. Where do we go from here?'

'Go?' He sounded surprised. 'I don't want to "go" anywhere, as you put it. It isn't as if Saffron is someone new,' he added. 'I slept with her long before I even met you. It's hardly as if anything's changed in that respect.'

'So you think we can just leave it here? Go on as if this had never happened?'

He was silent. 'Perhaps not. But I'm willing to try if you are.'

Willing. Trying. Sensible, sound words for sensible, responsible people. Parent-like people, who plan things. People like us.

But then again, I didn't want to probe too deeply. I didn't want to make anything final. Not at this stage. There was too much at stake.

There was another silence.

He walked to the French windows and looked outside. You could see a few stars, in spite of the green London glow. 'Did you know,' he asked, 'that there are more stars in the sky than there are grains of sand on earth?' He leant against the window, and I thought he might stay there for ever, counting them. 'One night,' he added, 'is like one grain of sand if you think about the whole of our life together.'

I thought of pointing out that a grain of sand could be very, very irritating if you got it caught in your sock on a long walk. But I was beginning to learn to keep my thoughts to myself. If everything was to be prevented from falling apart, I suspected I might have to get very good at that.

I noticed another conically wrapped package on the top of the dresser. 'What's that?'

'For you,' he said, crossing the room and lifting it towards me. It was a tied posy of roses – not stiff, regimented guilt-buy roses from a garage, but blush-pink puffballs, heavy with scent. 'Because I'm sorry with all my heart. Truly.'

When he held them out to me I knew what he was offering. A return to a normal life.

'We ought to talk.' I knew, from advice offered by marriage guidance counsellors in magazines, how vital it was to tell all, to air problems in a marriage. It was the emotional equivalent of turning your mattress and clearing out your cupboards. Or servicing your car. It guaranteed that you weren't suddenly going to find your immaculate, beautifully cut designer relationship was full of moth-holes just when you were counting on it for a special occasion.

But I didn't really want to talk any more. And neither did he. Perhaps we were both afraid of what we might say.

'Just tell me one thing.' I took a deep breath, ashamed of my cowardice in not taking it all further, but determined to make this one show of courage. 'Can you promise never to see Saffron again?'

There was a perceptible pause. 'Yes. It's over. That's all you need to know. I promise you that.'

I didn't remind him of the promise he'd already broken, the one to 'forsake all others, until death do us part'. Instead I took a deep breath, got up and pulled a vase out of the cupboard, a perfect cut-glass bowl, clear and simple. Just right. The flowers hardly needed arranging – they were so wild and beautiful, yet so artfully marshalled. The Soho market stalls must have come up in the world a bit since I used to work in the area. Really up to Notting Hill Gate standards, in fact.

'Fine.' I could see no other option. I wasn't going to bring the whole carefully constructed edifice of our lives crashing around our ears just because of one night. I don't know why I ever thought I could. There were, after all, far more frightening things than infidelity. Never being able to have a baby was one of them.

Will topped up our glasses and lifted his towards me. 'To us.'

'To us,' I echoed, forcing a bright smile on to my face as if I meant it. I told myself that pretending wasn't deceit. Or, if it was, one deceit deserves another.

Later that evening, when I went upstairs, I thought he was pretending to be asleep.

Incredulously I crept right up to his face, and touched him on the shoulder, listening to his breathing. He really was asleep. I didn't know how he could. But then, of course, he hadn't had much sleep the night before. I hunched away from him and tried to concentrate on a novel. I hadn't had much sleep myself, but I knew that if I closed my eyes everything would go whirling round my head in a sick, dizzy, incredibly painful vortex.

If he could sleep like that, it obviously really hadn't meant that much to him. And I would make sure that it didn't mean that much to me either. We're a modern couple. No one is perfect. We would make it work.

But we hadn't talked about one important thing. We hadn't talked about love.

I hardened my heart and turned over. Everything would look different in the morning. It was only one night, just one.

16

I slept surprisingly deeply, and woke up slowly, as if I'd been drugged.

Will brought me a cup of tea in bed. This caring, sharing behaviour made me feel rather lonely, as if I'd woken up in bed with an extremely polite stranger. And, as we made our arrangements for the evening, it was like making a first date. Nervous, over-anxious not to be misunderstood, carefully considerate of each other's needs. Exhausting in other words. I already missed the easy, absent-minded man I'd lived with for so long. But, I reminded myself, this is how we can make a new, a better, life.

As soon as I got to the office, I called Lindsey. She must have heard something in my voice because she re-shuffled a few meetings and cancelled her lunch to meet me. Our communication was usually muffled by the ever-increasing layers that now surrounded her – husband, children and secretary, as well as an assistant, a housekeeper and a succession of nannies and committees, all wrapped around what seemed to me to be an ever-diminishing core. But she was meticulous in keeping the thread between us intact. She – or rather her secretary – solemnly booked us into a new, talked-about restaurant and there she was, pinned to her smart seat as neatly as the brooch on her suit lapel, hardly glancing at the menu.

'The salad and the fish,' she told the waiter, handing the menu back to him almost immediately. She never wasted time on unnecessary luxuries like spoiling herself.

I hastily picked the first two dishes I saw, before she could accuse me of time-wasting or dawdling (echoes of 'Come on, Leonie!' still reverberated from our childhood), and looked around. Lindsey's eyes assessed the tables – not too close together, the discreet meldings of greys and beiges on the walls and the crisp, white linen cloths, nodding approvingly to herself. She liked restaurants that looked like First Class airport lounges from the 1970s. They appealed to her sense of order. Out-sized tin plates sat solemnly in their places in front of us, flanked by cutlery and asserting themselves as fashionable must-haves. The menu further reassured us that a big-name chef was in charge. There was nothing to frighten anyone away, and even the odd famous face to boast about. You could even – very unusual this – hear what your companion was saying without having to shout. She relaxed slightly. As part of her big City job, she lunched out constantly, and she liked to use our lunches as a way of checking out new places before she brought clients along. It made having lunch with me work on two levels – family and business. No wonder she looked older than forty-three.

'So how're things?' When Lindsey asked this kind

of question, I knew that she wasn't just being polite – she actually wanted to know. I suddenly wasn't sure I should tell her. Perhaps it was disloyal to Will.

So I told her about my fight to get a job-share for Polly instead. She'd been a woman in management for much longer, after all.

She listened carefully. 'It's much easier in an all-male office,' she commented. 'The thing is that being all men, they'd much rather not have paternity leave or get home in time to bath the baby, so they don't see it as a privilege. As for part-time work or a job-share, well, it's completely irrelevant. They just don't give a stuff. If you want to commit professional suicide by working part-time, why not? They're all quite happy to agree. They'll try to shaft you, but they'd have tried to do that anyway.' I wondered briefly why, in that case, Lindsey – or other City women I knew – hadn't decided to take the part-time option, when she added, 'The trouble is that you need to be there full-time in order to see off even a fraction of the shafting.'

'Anyway,' she changed the subject, 'what's up?'

I shrugged. 'What do you think of Laura's news?' It was a safe way of diverting attention away from myself.

Lindsey sighed. 'She's so scatty. Always was. Another child will be an absolute disaster for them.' The waiters, having decided that we'd contemplated the tin plates for long enough to absorb their message, whisked them away, replacing them with two salads.

'You've got three children.' I had always wondered

why. Producing two — a girl and a boy — seemed quite enough of a triumph when you work as hard as she does, and going any further seemed out of character.

'I'm different,' said Lindsey. 'I've got more money. It's still been quite a leap, even so.' She looked distantly at the salad, and pushed a fried oyster under a mint-green frond of some fashionable leaf. If she got any thinner, she'd be transparent, I thought. We'd been about the same build once, but while I was aware of thickening, she seemed to be melting away.

'Did you mean to have Daisy?' Oliver was a couple of years younger than Ella, but Daisy trailed far behind them, and was only five. I'd never quite dared ask if she had been a mistake.

Her eyes gleamed with an emotion I couldn't quite identify. Perhaps it was amusement. 'Oh, yes. Maybe I just wanted to mess things up a bit. It was all too perfect. A boy and a girl. So tidy and balanced. It didn't seem real, somehow.'

If one of the statues in the British Museum had declared itself ready to boogie I couldn't have been more astonished. And I wasn't sure that she was telling me the whole truth. There had to be more to it than that.

'Did it work?'

'Well, there she is. Very solidly there, in fact. At the drop of a hat. Or perhaps at the drop of a contraceptive pill.'

I flushed. I did not wish to discuss my inability to conceive with any member of my family. It was my business, and I didn't want it picked over, with every detail humming down the telephone wires, and all the ramifications and possible solutions dissected and agonized over. I was getting tired of being sent clippings from newspapers about the efficacy of certain vitamins on fertility, and so on. 'What I meant was, did it untidy your life?'

''Fraid not. It just made all the tidy bits even more vital. Sometimes I feel like the captain of a boat in a squall, just chugging on over the most enormous waves.'

It was also very unlike Lindsey even to suggest that she wasn't in total control, but then, she was a bit like a captain of a boat, maintaining perfect discipline among the crew and keeping everything stowed away neatly and properly battened down.

'At least it's a very luxurious boat,' I said. 'A real gin palace.'

She screwed up her face. 'Give me a break. A luxury yacht perhaps.'

'So how is life on board?'

'Well, at least the new nanny's working out.' Her life was punctuated by childcare crises, and I couldn't help wondering if she was a difficult employer. Nannies departed at anything from three days' to three weeks' notice to look after ill parents, join boyfriends in Australia, go to Australia to get away from boyfriends, have babies or abortions, train to be Montessori teachers, or, the most recent one, join the police force. One had even propositioned Sandy, which Lindsey had professed to find hugely amusing. The latest, a bland blonde called Vicky, rarely seemed to speak, and lived a mouse-like existence in her loft bedroom. Perhaps Lindsey liked her because she was so invisible and lacking in personality.

'Isn't Ella getting a bit old for a nanny?'

Lindsey shrugged. 'No other option. Anyway she still needs someone to make her tea and let her in after school.' She thought for a bit. 'She's just reaching the difficult age. I don't know what to do with her.'

It all sounded a bit bleak, so I let it drop. Though I imagined that Ella being 'difficult' was hardly a big deal. She was such a sweet, gentle girl, smiling shyly and always offering to help out. Lindsey probably just found the slightest stirrings of independence threatening.

She swatted away a waiter who had come to ask us if 'everything was all right'. 'Fine, thanks.' He retreated hastily. 'Now then,' she resumed. 'What about you?'

'If you mean . . .' I headed the question off, 'isn't it time I was having a baby myself. Yes, you're right. But things don't always happen exactly when you want them to, you know.'

Lindsey looked at me shrewdly. 'Actually I wasn't going to ask you that. But it'll do.'

Suddenly, I realized that there was very little point in fighting off her sympathy. I might as well tell her about Will, because, if anyone had a clear view of it all, she would.

So I told her.

She listened intently. 'I see,' she said at the end of my speech. 'I must say, I always thought Saffron was one of life's great takers. A parasite.'

This was a bit strong, if entirely what I wanted to hear. 'I'd forgotten you'd met her.'

'She came round to your house for Sunday lunch, remember, a couple of years ago. She'd just got back from Goa or somewhere like that. She was padding around with bare feet, wearing exotic shawls and being very sincere. You remember.'

I did. Saffron was one of those irritating women who could wear a shawl without looking like a refugee or an impersonation of the Virgin Mary. Whenever I tried to follow the advice on shawls dished out so frequently and liberally by our fashion department I usually looked like someone who had just been rescued from a sinking ship. Saffron had declared – several times – that her pashmina was almost the only thing she'd taken on her round-the-world trip. 'If you have one of these, you can really travel light. I've even used it as a blanket when I had to spend the night on a station in the Indian hills,' she'd told Lindsey. Lindsey, who liked to take outfits for every occasion and always packed them neatly divided into two separate suitcases so that she'd always have a spare pair of knickers in case the airline lost one case, had merely replied, 'Goodness. How terribly brave of you.'

Saffron had smirked.

Laura had fought back, however, by telling Saffron bossily about a new, even finer, goat hair that made pashmina shawls look like army blankets. Saffron had dealt with her simply by repeating the Hill Station story, and refusing to acknowledge the existence of a superior goat hair. Laura had reluctantly conceded that round.

And I'd been so pleased when I'd originally heard that she was going to travel round the world. I thought there was a fair chance that she might fall in love with some hunky Australian singer while she was about it. And a year sounded for ever. It had never occurred to me that she'd come back, unchanged except that she was inclined to inform everyone that seeing the poverty in some parts of the world really made you think. She also had several heart-warming tales of locals who only had a bowl of soup and a loaf of bread but who'd invited her into their homes to share them with more natural grace than you'd find at any London dinner party. She'd shown Will several photographs of herself in saris, or with garlands of flowers round her neck, or in ponchos (depending on where she was in the world), arms linked with grinning people of various ethnic shapes, sizes and colours. If you were a traveller, rather than a tourist, you got to meet the people, she explained, and the language of music was global. Lindsey and I had retired defeated, but Laura continued to make a stand, however, occasionally saying things like: 'I'm sorry, Saffron, but that part of the world isn't really poor. Not starving, in the real sense of the word.'

But I was glad Lindsey'd had the chance to meet her and form an opinion.

She now considered the matter carefully. 'You're sure he hasn't been sleeping with her all along?' I examined the crumbs on the white cloth. 'It's just a feeling. I suppose that I think . . .' I paused. 'That I do still trust him to tell the truth. He's never lied to me.'

The statement lay on the table between us, the first time I'd really articulated why I was staying.

'Well,' said Lindsey. 'So you do have something going for you. Now then.' She leaned forward and I could see that she was going to analyse the situation as if I was a multi-billion-pound bank. 'You've told me the down side of the relationship. What else would you list on the up side?'

I couldn't help smiling at the thought of Saffron being pigeonholed so neatly under the 'Loss' column of a Profit-and-Loss chart. It contained her somehow, made her seem smaller and less painful. 'The good things?' I thought for a bit. They'd seemed a bit thin on the ground recently. 'Firstly, he's my best friend.'

Lindsey looked perplexed. 'Is he?' Her face conveyed that friendship was not necessarily what you needed from a husband. Perhaps all husbands could be divided into Heroes or Friends. I remembered that Sandy, amazingly, had been the romantic hero when she'd married him. Twenty years ago, he'd had everything young girls were taught to admire – he was ten years older than her, but tall and fit, with fine blond hair – although it would soon recede – and a tipped-for-the-top career. All this, added to the family money that helped him afford sports cars and romantic holidays, made him seem glittering and irresistible, a conquering prince with his perfect young princess. All Lindsey had known about men until then had been garnered from a few broke students as hesitant and inexperienced as herself. Sandy had dazzled her. Yet he'd matured into a king – demanding, autocratic and pompous – and Lindsey seemed more like his formal consort than his friend. And however successful she became, the age gap was still there, along with the unspoken assumption that she played the little girl to his masterful male. Personally, I was not sure that this really suited Lindsey's temperament, while it would have been perfect for Laura, whose constant complaints about Paul were, I thought, rooted in disappointment that he hadn't been able to play the role of extended sugar-daddy. I'd married a Friend, which had been what I'd always thought I'd wanted. Lindsey had married a Hero, when she really needed a Friend, and Laura had chosen a Friend when she was temperamentally better suited to a Hero. In that case, why was it my marriage that was tottering?

'Friend?' repeated Lindsey, unusually lost for words.

'Well, you know, we have fun together. Sometimes . . .' I trailed off. I didn't think fun figured highly in the Lucas-White establishment. It hadn't, after all, exactly been first and foremost in the Bailey household for the last few months. But until then . . . I squinted into the distance to remember . . . until then, we had

had fun. Curled up on the sofa on a Sunday evening, eating ice cream straight out of the packet and baked beans with a spoon from a tin. We didn't have to pretend in front of each other.

'Good, good.' Lindsey recovered herself, and allowed fun to be included in the list of positives. 'And what else?'

'We both want a family.'

'Both?' I could see that she regarded this as the crux of the matter. Everyone in the family generally agreed – they always had – that Will would make a wonderful father, and the unspoken assumption had been that only my career stood between him and the fulfilment of his life's dream in this respect. All my fault, was the general view, particularly as the one time I'd revealed some of our tests publicly it had been to exonerate Will entirely by confirming that his sperm count was absolutely normal. As Lindsey, and then Laura, had popped their babies out with so little trouble, I felt accused of being unco-operative. Defensively, I would look into the eyes of each new baby with a brittle laugh, muttering things like 'rather you than me'. Deep down inside, below my ribcage, I craved one of my own.

'Both of us,' I repeated firmly.

'In that case,' she waved for the bill, and the triple diamond Sandy had given her on their engagement twinkled in the light, 'you have a deadline ahead of you. It doesn't get any easier after forty, you know. Or even after thirty-eight.'

I wished people wouldn't keep on about it. I know the facts about fertility perfectly well, but it just doesn't help to have them re-iterated like a stuck record.

I decided to fight back. 'Well, would you have had Ella and Oliver – or Daisy – if Sandy had had a one-night stand?'

She leant forward. 'I've never told anyone this. But not long after Oliver was born, he did. Twice. A girl in the office, and then an air hostess. Of all things! It took a long time – and a lot of work – to get us properly back together afterwards. In fact, Daisy was really a reconciliation baby in a way.'

Aha, the truth, at last. But the trouble with Lindsey is that she's always got to beat me. At everything. If Will has a one-night stand, Sandy has to have half a dozen. Even so, my stomach lurched at the thought that her carefully orchestrated marriage wasn't quite as smooth and harmonious as I'd always assumed it was. I wanted other people's marriages to be perfect. It was proof that mine could be one day. Apart from anything else, I'd always imagined that Sandy White, with his now jowly face and seven-months-pregnant paunch would be too busy counting his lucky stars in having captured neat, efficient Lindsey even to start looking at other women. And it was fairly shattering to think of other women wanting him. He would look like a plucked chicken naked, I thought, all white, saggy and bristly. Frankly, if either Sandy or Lindsey had one-night stands, that meant everyone in the world probably did at some point. Perhaps I was making too much of a fuss about it.

'What do you mean by "a lot of work"?' I asked cautiously, wondering if this meant spreading another layer of appointments on to our lives. Therapists always talk about 'working' at your marriage and I'm not quite sure what they mean. If it's sitting in carefully anonymous rooms saying what you really mean, or tiptoeing indefinitely round each other's feelings, like this morning, I wasn't sure that I was capable of it.

Lindsey smiled faintly. 'I gave him a choice. Stop mucking about or else.'

'Or else?'

'I'd not only divorce him but employ very expensive lawyers to take him to the cleaners. I told him he needn't think I wouldn't notice chunks of money hidden away in Switzerland or the off-shore accounts, because I'm very good at all that sort of thing.' My eyes watered at the thought of being pursued by Lindsey's lawyers and accountants to the ends of the earth. Not pleasant, even if Sandy did deserve it. But it didn't sound like a very romantic reconciliation. 'No counselling, nothing else?'

'Counselling!' She snorted. 'You wouldn't get Sandy to go to counselling.'

Well, no, you wouldn't. I could see that. I suspected that when it came to it, you wouldn't get Will to counselling either. That was the sort of thing his patients did. Anyway I didn't relish the thought of him sitting there telling the counsellor that he'd never been able to forget Saffron. And we didn't have any off-shore accounts I could threaten him with.

I was taken aback, faced with depths of steeliness in Lindsey that even I hadn't suspected.

Lindsey continued. 'Worked like a dream. Now we're back together more solidly than ever.' She smiled, as she scribbled her signature on the American Express form. 'Very much in love, you could say.'

I peered at her. Was she being ironic?

She was looking positively business-like as she leant towards me, having stowed her credit card back in her small, elegant handbag. 'Your problems are different, though. Even if this . . .' she searched for the word . . . 'this one-night stand does ultimately spell the end of your marriage . . .'

I flinched at the baldness of this statement. I didn't want it to be the end. But I didn't know what I did want now.

Lindsey continued, 'This may be your last chance of children. If you want them, that is. If you leave him now, it may be too late by the time you find someone else. It puts you in rather a weak position.'

That's why big companies pay Lindsey huge sums of money. She can sum up a complicated, sensitive situation in a few short words. It makes their dealings so much easier.

'Don't look so shocked,' she added. 'I know several women who stood by their men, in similar circumstances, until they had two children. Then they made their decision.'

What had shocked me was that I wasn't shocked. I hadn't liked to admit that, although the first terrible blow about the night with Saffron had gone straight to my heart, the second one had equally directly landed on my head. I had had very clear, concise thoughts about what a split could do to my chances of having a family. My first coherent thought had been 'What about the fertility treatment?' I'd been aware of a massive crushing pain in my chest that gripped me with the words 'Perhaps you'll never have a baby now.' That was why, when Will had declined to talk about it, I'd agreed so readily.

I knew that treating a man as a sperm-donor is wrong, but what choice did I have?

'Sometimes it's very difficult to get all the cherries to line up in the Great Fruit Machine of Life,' added Lindsey, being extraordinarily poetic for her. 'You might have to decide which cherry you really want.'

The image reverberated in my brain as we stepped back through the restaurant, noticing two or three vaguely famous, *Sunday Times* Style Section-type faces on the way out.

'That was a nice place.' Lindsey kissed me on the cheek. 'I'll definitely take clients there in future.'

I wasn't sure. It seemed a bit soulless to me.

'Lindsey?' She turned to me, one hand raised for a taxi. Magically, one slid to a halt beside her.

'What do you think I should do? Would it do any good to talk to Saffron myself?'

She turned as she stepped in. 'I think you should

just forget all about this little incident. Put it out of your mind completely. One day you'll look back on it all as a bad dream.'

Lindsey was right, of course. My niggling conviction that Saffron was determined to stay in our lives was not based on anything remotely like fact or evidence. It was just an emotional reaction.

17

Will and I went on being very, very nice to each other as I was swept on by the relentless schedule of fertility treatment. Every evening I asked him about his day. He asked me about mine. We offered each other cups of tea, glasses of wine or, politely, requested the butter, the salt or *The Times* – 'if you've finished with it, of course'.

Then there were the things we couldn't mention. It was like treading on eggshells, but I began to think that, on the whole, we were getting quite good at it all. Occasionally I looked at us both sitting formally at the table with a special meal that one or the other had cooked and congratulated myself on how well we were doing. How hard we were trying. That, in itself, must mean something.

And, of course, I seemed to be eternally padding down lino-ed corridors and being greeted with professional breezy cheerfulness by neat receptionists. The laparoscopy was the next stage. I had thought, for a brief, muddled moment, that Will's one-night stand with Saffron might have jeopardized this operation. That we'd have to go back to square one in some way. I thought, I suppose, that Will being unfaithful would bring our lives to a complete halt.

In fact, eventually, after a few days of this unnatural politeness, things started to drift back to normal, and I felt that our lives had simply washed over the event, leaving just the tip of it above the waves, crudely blunt, an iceberg of pain.

I feared – and other women whispered to me – that if you were honest about hiccups in your life – a nice touch, calling Saffron a 'hiccup', I think – you could easily go back to the beginning of the waiting list. Then, when it comes to being accepted for IVF, you might have to fight even harder to convince everyone that you really do want a baby, that you're a good candidate, both steady and solid as rocks. Hesitation, prevarication, excuses, one-night stands . . . well, they're hardly evidence of commitment. We couldn't afford to be seen to waver, not at this point. It was, I thought, rather like having second thoughts before a wedding once the dress was hanging up on the outside of your wardrobe in its immaculate tissue paper, and the marquee had been erected. There's a point at which you can't express reservations, can't slow things down, can't prevent them from hurtling forwards, not unless you want everything to stop entirely with a sickening jolt.

And I didn't want that. Lindsey's advice rang in my ears. An infertile late-thirty-something doesn't have that many options.

In fact, I'd decided the whole thing was more like getting your first job after leaving school. Nobody wanted to employ you because you didn't have experience, and you couldn't get experience because you hadn't got a job. We couldn't turn into a family until we had a child, and we couldn't have a child until we gave a very good impression of being a family.

All in all, being anaesthetized might be rather a relief. Quite pleasant, really.

So, early one morning, before all the traffic was properly awake and while a pale turquoise dawn glittered on the empty streets, we trooped into an anonymous-looking hospital with linoleum-smelling floors and determinedly cheerful artwork on the walls. Will looked serious, but constantly cracked bad jokes in order not to worry me, squeezing my hand as we ascended in a capacious but rickety lift, which kept almost stopping between floors.

I was welcomed and docketed, gowned and injected, then, after an interminable wait while Will and I played noughts and crosses and swopped tabloid newspapers, whisked along a corridor in a trolley, and told to count to ten. The world swam away in a dizzy circle and almost immediately came back again. I woke up, feeling furry-mouthed and finding it difficult to focus.

'You'll be glad to know that we didn't find anything wrong,' barked the surgeon. 'No reason at all why you shouldn't have a baby quite successfully.' He made a note on the chart. 'Bit of a mystery, really.' He swept off while I tried to work out where I was and what it all meant.

As Will put it later, when I was feeling sober enough to take it all in, 'The good news is that there doesn't seem to be anything wrong with you.'

'The bad news,' I pointed out, 'is that if there is, they couldn't find it, so they don't know how to put it right.'

'But there isn't,' he added, squeezing my hand. 'All you need to do is to recover from this. Come home with me, and it'll all be all right.' He drew his chair – an ugly modern contraption with those synthetic knitted covers – near the bed, so that he could go on holding my hand until I slept.

I could hear someone in the next room weeping, as the door opened and closed on her, and the rhythmic padding of students' and nurses' feet following the surgeon's slightly heavier shoes out. A few voices echoed in the corridor, murmuring. I wondered what he'd told her, and whether there was anyone with her. But I closed my eyes, and slept, still holding Will's dry, strong hand in mine. I didn't have the energy to get involved in anyone else's problems.

I felt rather sick at work the following day in an editorial meeting.

'We must feature these new home fragrances. You can spray your bedroom with the scent of fresh linen,' Kate, the deputy homes editor waved a number of sinister-looking, if stylish, canisters in the air with the fervour of a religious convert, 'and your kitchen with the smell of home cooking. There's a choice of fresh bread, real coffee and curry.'

'Curry?'

'It's the smell that goes with the East Meets West look. Very hot now,' Camilla explained.

I supposed it would be. 'What's the fresh linen one?'

'It's the scent of laundered sheets.' Kate sprayed something sharply lemony into the air, reminiscent of washing powder.

I waved it away. 'What's wrong with just washing your sheets?'

Everyone exchanged glances, as if I was going into my dotage.

'People don't have the time these days.' Camilla spoke slowly, as if to a child.

The desk went murkily out of focus.

'Are you all right?' She sounded genuinely concerned. 'Shall I get you a glass of water?'

I'm surprised I didn't faint after all. Camilla had never offered to get me anything before.

Perhaps I was still under the anaesthetic and hallucinating.

A glass was placed in front of me and everyone looked worried.

I pulled myself together, and we moved on to whether we were going to cover the trend of Baby As Must-Have Accessory.

'Everyone's doing it now,' explained Ginny, the fashion editor. She listed off the models who had babies. 'It'd look fab.'

Saffron looking sultry in the Bellingham Glass brochure was one thing. Pages and pages of fulfilled-looking size 10s with endless legs and perfect complexions talking about having discovered the real meaning of life and how they and baby lived happily on liquidized raw vegetables was quite another.

'No,' I said. 'Let's invent a new trend. Dogs To Die For. A Cat is a Girl's Best Friend.' I stopped before I could suggest hamsters for your handbag.

Camilla leant forward enthusiastically. 'That's a great idea. Tonny Simpkins-Steering has two gorgeous Persians, and India's got a beautiful Seal Point Burmese.'

It occurred to me that Camilla had got a lot better since I stopped being collegial. She'd never suggested her friends for a feature before. Or perhaps cats were the secret to her personality. I asked her if she had one. Her eyes shone in a way they never did when we told her some latest man was on the phone. 'Boggins. He's not much to look at . . .' she implied that she was just being modest, 'but he's got a wonderful personality.'

Cats it was. With Camilla in charge. Ginny, who clearly didn't relish having to sweet-talk a dozen hysterical moggies down from the roof of a photographic studio, looked mildly distraught, but I reminded her that babies were just as bad.

Mimi, looking increasingly like a drainpipe with a football stuck halfway down, waddled in with a copy of the *Evening Standard*.

'You'll never guess . . .' she wheezed. A few people looked up, expecting a revelation about a new shoe shop or style of handbag.

'Elaine has walked out of *My Life*! To spend more time with her family!'

There was a general hubbub as everyone tried to read the paper at once. A whole double-page spread was devoted to her, with a headline that screamed: 'The sacrifice of a powerful woman'. It was accompanied by a beautifully styled photograph of Elaine in profile, lifting her three-year-old daughter up in the air so that they were laughing nose to nose.

'I had the best job in the world,' Elaine gushed to the *Standard*. 'And I gave it all up. I was working twenty hours a day.'

'Twenty hours?' we shrieked collectively.

'I should coco,' muttered Camilla.

'I can't see,' complained Kate.

Camilla started reading out loud: 'And what for? To pay my taxi fares, my cleaner, the person who irons my clothes and my nanny . . .'

'Surely that should be nannies in the plural,' I interjected, remembering a brief conversation I'd had with her on the subject.

'And some,' added Camilla, beginning to camp it up. 'When I come through the door, exhausted, my children cling to me and cry. Every day, the sound of their tears follows me as I close the front door. A man can have photos of his children on his desk, but when a woman goes to work, she's considered unprofessional if she even mentions her children. A childcare crisis or attending sports day is considered a dereliction of duty.'

'Well!' Polly sounded put out. 'I asked her about her children once and she cut me dead!'

'Now we come to the sexy bits.' Camilla ran her finger down the page, skimming over a few more paragraphs about Elaine's dinner-party caterers and gardeners, who all had to be 'co-ordinated'. ('Probably means they had to wear the same outfits,' I muttered.)

Camilla raised her voice. 'Time alone with my husband is a distant memory. Our relationship is on the rocks, and we have sex once a month if that.'

Everyone looked impressed with the upfront quality of this admission, except for Polly who grumbled that she was boasting again. 'Nobody with small children has sex as often as once a month.'

Camilla giggled, and added, 'Lucky you having an excuse. Us singletons are expected to bonk constantly, even when we'd much rather be in bed with a book.' She continued reading. 'My husband and I have talked about this move for some time. We both now agree that a woman's place is in the home, supporting her husband and children, no matter what the personal sacrifice is to herself.'

I tried to equate the hard-boiled, ambitious Elaine with this model of selfless devotion.

'Well,' said Polly, 'if Elaine can't hack it, I don't know who can.'

There was a silence while we all digested this radical

new concept of Elaine, and re-read bits that Camilla had missed out or that we hadn't managed to read over everyone else's shoulders earlier. Maeve rang.

'Have you heard the news? Peter Rennie's absolutely hopping mad. And there's a camera crew outside the building, interviewing working mothers on how unfairly they're treated.'

Maglife's Press Office were on the other line. 'Can you send Polly up? We're offering interviews with women in the company to show how flexible we can be when a mother wants a job-share and to spend more time with her children.'

I put down the phone. 'I smell humbug,' I muttered.

Camilla caught my eye and giggled. 'Overwhelming, I'd say.' She tapped her teeth with her ballpoint pen. 'I wonder if Daddy would know anything about what's going on?'

I raised my eyebrows. When Daddy was Brian Carstairs, advertising supremo, whose budgets made our budgets work, it was more than possible that rumours and theories might hit him before they hit us.

'You try Daddy,' I suggested. 'I'll try the editor grapevine. We'll pool our information.'

A wicked pair of dimples appeared in Camilla's cheeks, as she reached for her phone. 'You're on.'

Perhaps we could be a team, after all. I just hoped it wasn't the alliance of the childless against mothers. I was beginning to think that there was a guerilla war being waged, and I feared that I might be changing sides. I thought of dear, innocent Ella, and even the runny noses of Phoebe and Zack, and suppressed a giant pang of regret.

Later that evening, an indignant Lindsey rang me. 'Who is this bloody woman who's letting the side down? Do you know her? And why's she on *Newsnight*?'

'*Newsnight*?' You'd have thought Elaine was a Cabinet Minister or the head of a small African state. I couldn't see why her domestic problems were being splayed all over the headlines. I switched on the television and was fascinated by finding her on screen almost instantly, looking warm and sympathetic with softly cut brown hair (the elaborate tousle I'd last seen had obviously been changed for a gentler, more sympathetic outline), and barely-there make-up. One elegantly French-manicured hand was pressed to her chest.

'Please don't get me wrong,' she said, fluttering her eyelashes. 'I'm not trying to tell other women how to live their lives.'

Well, that was a change, I thought. *My Life* was nothing if not dictatorial on what kind of shoe you should be wearing, what restaurants were now social death, and what smart people were reading. Occasionally its wings spread a little wider and it told its readers that they had to have a non-executive directorship or that everybody was going back to college, taking up organic farming or going into therapy.

'I think every woman has to make her own choices,' she breathed, looking earnestly into the camera. 'I just know I couldn't have carried on living what was essentially a double life any longer, although, of course, I feel desperately guilty at letting *My Life* down. I do know how difficult it's going to be to find a top editor of the right calibre to replace me, and I can quite understand why Peter Rennie, the managing director, is upset.'

There was a short flash of Peter Rennie pushing past photographers, muttering 'No comment' as a pack of reporters shrieked questions like: 'Is it true you're victimizing working mothers?' and 'Do you still maintain that Maglife has family-friendly policies?'

'Some things,' concluded Elaine, her voice flowing like rich treacle, 'are just more important than a job. One's children must come first.'

I had the phone in one hand and the remote control for the television in the other. Lindsey was still squawking down the line as I clicked the TV off.

'Every time a senior woman does this,' she fumed, 'I get weeks of teasing from The Suits, I get told that that's why women don't break the glass ceiling, and I get to be sniped at rather than included on deals. It could even affect my chances of promotion. I don't mind her resigning, but why does she have to do it so publicly? It's all the Press's fault.'

I'd never heard Lindsey so angry. 'Now that fox-hunting's so unfashionable,' she added, 'people get their sport from hounding working mothers.'

I was still trying to work out what Elaine was up to myself. It all seemed so out of character. She had always worn the right labels, and had often indicated that the one marked 'mother' was scarcely considered smart. And she didn't see women as sisters, either, refusing to join Women In Journalism on the grounds that she'd already made it to the top and didn't need them. The concept of bonding with other women was clearly anathema to her. I just couldn't imagine her swopping her kitten heels for a pair of JP Tod's loafers and hanging around at the school gate chatting to other mothers about the PTA tombola.

'I don't think that was actually *Newsnight*,' was all I could say in reply.

Almost as soon as I put the phone down, it rang again. It was Laura.

'Did you see that girl on *Panorama*?' she demanded.

'Girl? *Panorama*?'

'The one who's realized that you just can't combine a career and children.'

'*Panorama*? Surely not. They make that weeks in advance.'

'One of those programmes, anyway. An important one. It just shows.'

'Shows what?'

'I told you so.' Laura sounded smug. 'Now perhaps you'll believe me.'

Was Laura on some kind of sponsored cliché marathon?

'Laura, I never . . .'

'Well, I'm sorry, Leonie, but I've been made to feel completely inadequate until this Eleanor girl spoke up . . .'

'You'd feel a lot more inadequate if you met her, I can assure you,' I growled. 'And she's called Elaine.'

'Whatever. She looked terribly nice. You see she's discovered that it just wasn't possible to be a good mother and work all those hours at her job. She was only earning to pay the nanny and the cleaning lady. And she was absolutely knackered all the time.'

Laura always likes to tell you what you know already, dishing it up in tones of wonderment, as if she'd made a new discovery. 'You'll find out it just isn't that easy, you know, Leonie. I know you think you can manage everything, but it doesn't work that way. You don't understand.'

I counted to ten, trying to decide why she was so determined to convince me that her way of life was best. 'How are you, Laura? Is everything going fine?'

'Fine? What do you mean fine?' She gave a mighty sigh. 'We've all got nits from Phoebe's school. Do you know, I spent an hour last night with conditioner and a comb, and out crawled some of the biggest head lice I've ever seen. Then Zack was sick on the sofa. I don't know how I'm going to get the stain out.'

I felt a certain amount of post-anaesthetic nausea myself, as dinner congealed unpleasantly in my stomach at this account. Conversations with Laura never strayed far from sick, what with two children, a dog with a dodgy digestion and her own recurrent pregnancies. But I persevered in an attempt to have a normal conversation with her. 'Have you spoken to Mum recently?'

'The wheels on the bus go round and round,' she sang in a bright, inconsequential voice.

I was just trying to work out if this was a new philosophy for living, borrowed from the *Daily Mail*, when she added, 'Sorry, Zack's on my lap now.'

'I'd better fly.'

'Before you go, can I speak to Will?'

I handed the phone to him with a muttered goodbye. Doubtless she wanted to discuss swollen ankles or piles, or whether water births were over-rated.

He was always very gentle with her, saying 'Hello, how are you, Laura?' as if he really meant it. Will is a genuinely nice man. But sometimes he drives me mad.

'I can't understand the fuss about this Elaine person either,' he agreed, sweeping our foil containers into the dustbin, after he'd put the phone down on Laura with a comment like 'It's natural to worry a bit at this point. Just try to get a bit more rest.'

More rest! Huh. I always considered that Laura had more rest than anyone I'd ever met, flopping about on sofas at Mum's like a beached whale, and taking to her bed at the oddest hours of the day.

I passed the last foil container to Will with an indignant rattle, wondering why I felt so cross with him. The fact that the Local Curry House had not, in fact, been quite up to standard that evening was hardly his fault. I reminded myself that it was nice to have the authentic East Meets West aroma without having to spray it from an aerosol or light a candle costing £10.

'I mean, we've got several doctors in the practice,' he continued, 'who work three days a week, mostly to fit in with childcare. One of the men does a three-day week so that he can look after his children for the two days when his wife does supply teaching. It all works rather well.' He dropped the rubbish bin lid with a noise that made me start.

I was absolutely fed up with hearing about people who'd got their lives worked out perfectly. I glared at him.

'Perhaps that's what you'd like? For me to get pregnant, so you could work part-time?'

He stopped. 'I hadn't thought about it . . .'

'Well, you can jolly well stop starting to think about it.' I didn't know why I was incoherent with rage. It just seemed like . . . like . . . oh, I don't know what it was like. He was just being impossible.

I stood up from the sofa and pointed the remote control at the TV like a lethal weapon. It burst into life, and I plumped back down with a thump.

Will picked up the remote control, and suppressed the noise. 'Leonie? What is wrong?'

I looked at him in amazement. What was wrong? What was wrong? Well, what did he think was wrong? I certainly wasn't going to risk that sort of a conversation. 'Nothing.' I turned the television back on again.

He dropped down beside me. 'Look, has this Elaine thing upset you in some way? Do you want to talk about it?'

'No,' I gritted my teeth, and snatched my hand out of his. 'I do not want to talk about it. I'm sick of people talking about Elaine and her bloody sacrifice. I've had a hard day, and I do not want to talk. Is that okay?' I was aware that a part of me was testing the limits of this new, formal friendship that existed between us.

'Fine.' He seemed very calm, not hurt at all, and straightened up. 'Coffee? Herbal tea? Wee dram?'

I looked at him with dislike. It was as if he didn't care. Nothing touched him.

I stalked up to bed, fuming. You just couldn't get away from the issue of children, could you? Not even in *Newsnight* or on a fashion shoot.

It all made me very, very cross. I hurled myself down amongst the clutter in the spare room and told him, when he followed me up ten minutes later, that I was still recovering from the anaesthetic and wanted to sleep on my own that night.

He hovered anxiously at the door, with the expression of someone who knows that whatever he does will be wrong. 'Well, if you're sure . . .'

'Absolutely.' I bared my teeth in a grin. 'Don't worry about me, darling.'

As soon as I closed my eyes the slightly synthetic

scent of Fresh Linen swirled over me, drumming through my head. I'd sprayed some in the spare room to test it out, and I wished I hadn't.

I tried to tell myself, with the greatest authority that I could muster, that it was over, and that Saffron was now powerless to hurt us, but the memory of my sudden burst of irritation continued to drift into my mind as I slipped off to sleep. Something somewhere was not right. Apart from anything else, there is absolutely no point in taking fertility pills if you don't have sex. Two weeks had gone by since 27 May, and I was horribly aware that the three allocated months were slipping by.

Anger does this to you. Its white heat is like a soldering iron, distorting everything until you can no longer think straight. And when you cool down your view is set solid, permanently misshapen.

18

I'd been aware of the phone ringing as I dozed off, but Will didn't shout up to me. Probably some medical emergency, although he wasn't on call.

It wasn't. As we were tearing about in opposite directions the following morning, he yelled through a faceful of shaving foam.

'You'll never guess who rang last night.'

Probably not. 'I haven't got time to play guessing games.' I was down the stairs and had opened the front door before he finished the sentence. 'Either tell me or don't.'

He came to the top of the stairs, clutching a white towel around his waist and waving a razor. 'James.'

'James?' I couldn't think who he meant.

He lowered the razor. 'For God's sake. James.'

'Oh, that James.' From the holiday in France. One of Will's old drinking buddies. For years Mike, Will and James and a few others had all been fixtures in the pub, buying each other pints and – probably – joshing each other about women. Occasionally they'd done daft things, like drop their trousers in a row outside a posh restaurant, scandalizing (or cheering up, depending on whose account you believe) the wealthy matrons inside. One by one, marriage, careers and children had claimed them and now they hardly bothered to stay in touch. Men just don't seem to.

'What did James want?' I shouted back, surprising myself by the brief pleasure I took in observing the lean, oblong outline of Will's torso silhouetted against the landing window. A nice torso for a husband. Very nice. For a moment, I wondered what would happen if I went back up the stairs and wrapped myself round it.

My smart suit would get covered in shaving foam, that's what. Anyway it wasn't likely to be a fertile time.

Will's voice cut through my daydream. 'They're buying a flat in London so he thought it'd be good to meet up again.' There was a fractional pause. 'I asked them to dinner. A week on Friday.'

'Fine.' A gust of wind seized the door from my hand as I dismissed naked male torsos from my mind and left the house. It crashed shut behind me. I walked briskly to the Tube station, already calculating headlines and budgets in my head.

At work everyone was crowding over a newspaper, with Camilla at the hub.

'God!' She pointed to the paper. 'Read this! It's absolutely absurd.'

It was a huge double-page spread on the lack of childcare provision in Britain, with a photo of Elaine at its centre, helping her pretty five-year-old daughter down a slide, with a toddler on her hip. She smiled caringly into the camera, and was wearing a divine leather jacket, I noticed. The caption said: 'Britain is losing billions of pounds worth of talent and expertise as women like Elaine Brown leave high-powered jobs in order to look after their children.'

I was puzzled. 'But Elaine had childcare provision coming out of her ears. Didn't she have two nannies?'

Camilla nodded, following the story with a lilac-painted fingernail. 'Just for starters. There was a Croatian au pair as well, not to mention a babysitting team about the size of the chorus at Covent Garden. The husband earns pots and pots of money.'

I was surprised at how much she knew.

'I belong to the same health club as she does,' Camilla added. 'She can't bear to lose at tennis.'

'That's what makes this whole thing so odd,' I mused. 'Some people are genuinely torn between work and children.' I looked up and saw Polly, ashen-faced and lank-haired, hunched over her work. She looked exhausted. 'But Elaine really didn't seem like that. Far too competitive. Perhaps one can just never tell.'

'Hm.' Camilla shut the paper with a rustle, and our eyes met in complicity.

A week on Friday raced towards me, leaving me no time to plan dinner, although I'd managed to ask Laura and Paul as well to make up numbers. I thought that Lindsey would be too frightening for someone like Jennifer, who'd apparently spent the last seven years bringing up children in Northamptonshire.

Laura, on the other hand, would enjoy grumbling about the dirt, crime and general unsuitability of London for children, darting sharp looks at Paul to reproach him for making his family live in such a place.

Recipes divide into two categories. There are those which are a great deal of work to prepare in advance, but leave you lots of 'time with your guests' as the books put it, and those which you throw together at the last minute, getting red and sticky and spattering half the ingredients over your dress. I'd been defeated by the former, sallying into the supermarket armed with a shopping list for a recipe, only to be successively beaten back by the enormous amount of choice there seemed to be. There were hundreds of different options for every ingredient, none of which ever exactly matched those in the recipe.

After wading through several yards of creme fraiche, low fat creme fraiche, single and double cream in organic, ordinary, low fat and uht versions, in single person mini-cartons and family size buckets, and various creams that had other ingredients beaten into them, I couldn't find whipping cream, and couldn't decide which of the hundreds of other variations was nearest to it. That was followed by a series of questions on whether to buy organic, Fair Trade, recyclable, new and improved, low fat, low calorie or fibre enriched. Decisions, decisions. I'd been making them all day. No wonder I hardly ever cooked any more. Cookbooks were so bossy these days. 'Don't use ordinary sponge fingers,' said one recipe for trifle, 'only Savoi-ardes from Italy.' The shelves, which had about twenty-seven different varieties of rice on them, didn't have the only risotto rice really worth buying, ac-cording to another recipe. As for the choice of olive oil, well, it was worse than choosing a red wine for Christmas dinner. I'd struggled home, getting in just twenty minutes before everyone was due to arrive, with several carrier bags full of things that I thought I remembered were needed for another recipe labelled 'Fast'.

This had suddenly and inexplicably announced that it needed half a pint of walnut oil, and that it should have been marinating overnight, when Will came back, laden with wine and beer.

'I haven't seen James since . . . oh . . . years,' he said happily as he unloaded them on to the wine rack. 'We didn't manage to make their wedding, did we?' The two men had finally lost touch when James split up with Saffron, a few months after our French holiday. Not long after our wedding, she'd publicly pro-nounced James 'such a bore', having apparently told everyone from the start that 'James would never do'. I wondered if she'd ever thought that Will 'would do'.

'No. It was in Scotland. Too far and too expensive to get there. As we hadn't met Jennifer.'

I wasn't particularly looking forward to this trip down Will's memory lane, but I did long to know how Jennifer had coped with the Saffron factor. Whether James got urgent calls late at night to discuss the latest offer from an orchestra, or requests to find the stop tap in her flat on a Saturday afternoon. I wanted to know if it was just us. And perhaps, I thought, I could find the clues to the future by re-tracing the past. Finding out exactly where it had all gone wrong. Or if it had ever been right. I still felt, you see, that I should actually do something about Saffron, or she would seep back into our lives the way she'd done before. Perhaps Jennifer could offer some clues.

On a more practical level, I decided to miss out on all the sauces and marinades, and go for completely plain, grilled salmon with salad and new potatoes. I pressed a few cartons of 'Fresh Soup' into the refrigerator, hoping that they'd cool down in time, and vowing to do croutons. First, get changed.

Our latest issue had informed readers that a brighter, more intense lipstick would make them look more confident. I applied a fiery red meticulously to my mouth, and stood back, hoping to face a confident image in the mirror. It made me look like a middle-aged chorus girl auditioning for her old job at the Moulin Rouge.

I wiped it off as the doorbell went.

'Merchant banker, very good at tennis' had just about summed James up on that holiday, a perfect description for an athletic-looking, tanned man with a conventional army haircut and a selection of polo shirts in pastel colours. Now, seeing him standing on our doorstep eight years later in a pin-striped suit, I got the impression that life had somehow shrunk him slightly in the wash.

'Leonie,' he peered at me. 'How nice to see you again. You've cut your hair.'

'Several years ago actually.' I'd had long, straight mousy-blonde hair in those days, but had recently had it cut in a short, layered style to look more serious and professional. 'We can't have seen you for ages.'

'Someone told me you've got a frightfully smart job now,' he said, handing his coat to Will.

'Editor of *How?* magazine.'

'Not my usual reading matter, har, har. This is Jennifer.' This was followed by more forced joviality as he and Will slapped each other on the abdomen, grunting competitively over the sizes of their girths. Not that either of them had a paunch – Will had, if anything, grown more gaunt, and only I could detect the slightest softening at his middle. James seemed almost shrivelled. With drink, I suspected, looking at his mottled complexion.

Jennifer looked like a sofa – square and chintzy, with frills around her neck, and contrasting braid on her collar and cuffs. She smiled, showing traces of the lipstick on her teeth. But, worst of all, was the protruding dome of her belly. Very, very pregnant. I reminded myself that I had got quite expert at suppressing pangs of envy by now. They simmered just under the surface, only occasionally boiling up and foaming over into hatred.

As they hovered in the narrow hall, bobbing first

one way and then the other – 'In here?' – I removed a bottle of Rioja and Jennifer's coat, ushering her into the sitting room.

Jennifer turned to me. 'Do you have children?'

This was now the first thing people asked me. I shook my head.

'But, of course, you're a career woman, James tells me.' That was usually the second conversational gambit. I murmured a brief explanation of my job, wishing I could get one of those signs that lollipop ladies use for crossing roads, with 'No, I haven't got children' on one side and 'Yes, I do have a career' on the other. I could come into dinner parties showing the 'No, I haven't got children' side, and then turn it round before the questioning started.

'My friend, Dodo, is a career woman and she . . .' Jennifer was off on an interminable story about some friend of hers. I followed it carefully, looking for signposts, reasons why this story should be thrust at me. I couldn't find any, so Jennifer issued another monologue on the subject of school runs, having three children, and homework, flattening me with the volume and length of her speech rather than with anything she'd actually said.

'Janey's going to school next year, but then I'll have . . .' She trailed off.

'God, I'd better check the soup.' In fact, I just wanted a rest from the tidal wave of words that was threatening to wash me away.

'Can I help?' She followed me into the kitchen,

leaving Will and James head-to-head on digital broadcasting and rugby. In a way, this suited me – what I wanted from Jennifer was an insight on how she'd coped with Saffron. I had a number of opening gambits lined up, involving asking her how long she had been married, and thence, circuitously and subtly, round to Saffron. Or so I thought.

I did quite well at first. They had, she said, been together for seven years. I did a quick mental calculation, while she gave me a detailed account of everywhere they'd lived in that time, as James changed jobs and climbed corporate ladders. James couldn't have spent long grieving for Saffron. Months, or possibly even just weeks. Lucky Jennifer. She'd obviously swept in and obliterated her completely, possibly by suffocating her memory in an avalanche of talk.

'Not long after the villa holiday when I met James, then?'

Jennifer peered at me as I hurled a plateful of croutons into a sizzling pan. These 'easy finishing touches' we always include in *How?* finish off me rather than the dish. I made a mental note to stop the cookery department suggesting such garnishes – they were particularly hot on deep-fried radish flowers and freshly toasted nuts at the moment. As I concentrated on swirling the crumbs round the pan, she commented, 'James says you're a very good cook.' I wondered what else James had said about us. And how he ever got a word in edgeways.

'Well . . . I cooked quite a bit on that villa holiday.'

I was determined to keep the conversation on the rails.

'Damn! Is that my mobile? Probably the babysitter.' She was off, leaving me in the kitchen.

But I still longed to know whether Jennifer had had to fight. Whether it had been difficult to wipe clean the imprints of Saffron's narrow, angular body and the small, creamy breasts that must have burned themselves into James's memory. Or the sight of that wispy triangle of cotton stretched across her pelvis, so infinitely more alluring than the average over-washed M&S briefs. I imagined Saffron offering all kinds of sexual delights, like a houri, bending and twisting her whip-slender body into enticing, unforgettable positions. Exactly what these positions might be was foggy in my mind, but I always imagined that someone like Saffron would know. How could a Jennifer fight her? And had she had to change James in order to do it?

She reappeared, stuffing the mobile back again. 'Sorry about that. Janey always insists on an extra goodnight when we're out. Now where were we? Can I help?'

I squinted at her, as if to try and find something she could possibly do, and felt guilty because she was trying to be nice. Still, it was time to persevere with the conversation: 'There was a couple called Jo and Jonathan on the holiday. Do you ever see them?' I had my head inside a cupboard by this time. 'Dill mustard. Dill mustard.' I slammed the cupboard door shut and opened another. 'Will never puts things away in the right places. There!' I looked at it. 'Bother! Almost all gone. Never mind.'

'Jo's an old schoolfriend of mine. I went up to stay with them about eight years ago, and James was there. That's how we met.'

'So you know Saffron?'

Jennifer shrugged. 'Saffron Perry? James's old girl-friend? I'm afraid we've rather given up on her. I feel terribly guilty about it.'

The idea of simply 'giving up on' Saffron was so deliciously revolutionary that I grinned at her.

'She's not exactly easy to stay in touch with,' Jennifer continued. 'She was in New York for a bit recently with a German composer, but, of course, that didn't last, and she'd turned down a really good recording contract to go with him. Frankly, I think her problem is that she's such a terrible judge of men. She gives up everything for them, and they just don't commit back.'

I blinked at her.

'Except for James, of course.' Jennifer turned her attention to the kitchen. 'You ought to open this out a bit more. It would make a lovely family room.'

In spite of my fascination at this new, flawed view of Saffron, I was irritated. 'We're going to, one day.'

'James doesn't say much about it, but I think he always felt that Saffron was letting him tag along until someone more interesting came along. She's got this obsession about having to go out with someone in the music world, and, frankly, a poor old banker just didn't cut the mustard. I think he got really upset about it at one point.'

'Will went out with her too.' The words came out in a croak.

Jennifer stopped running her finger along my admittedly sticky work surface. 'Really? So you know what I mean.'

I didn't. I had got so used to thinking of Saffron in total control that I had never considered her to have weaknesses.

There was a raucous, pub-style laugh from Will and James. Jennifer raised her head sharply and moved back towards the sitting room, possibly to prevent James from enjoying himself too much. 'Well, if you're sure I can't help . . .'

I stopped grappling with the croutons for a moment and watched her splay-footed waddle. I don't know why the protruding dome of her belly should hurt so much more than all the other domes I'd seen in the last few years, but it did. Perhaps it was because it underlined how long it had been since that villa holiday, and how much everyone else had done in that time.

I stood in the doorway of the sitting room and looked at them all quietly for a moment. I was struck, once again, by how different James seemed. Like Will, he'd be in his early forties now. Eight years ago, he'd been compact and unformed – a young, good-looking man with dark hair and even features. Nearly a decade had turned him into the person he was always going to become. The aquiline nose and sharp chin had made him ferret-faced. Had Will changed too? I looked at him with new eyes. He had faded – the honey-coloured hair was now sandy, and his broad, strong shoulders had rounded with years of trying to sort out the health of people whose real problem was fungus on their ceiling or sub-standard housing. No wonder he didn't laugh as much as he used to.

Laura and Paul arrived. She was wearing a navy tent printed with a design that resembled bird-droppings, and gave a cry of recognition at Jennifer's bump. They plumped down on the sofa together with every sign of turning into each other's new best friend.

'So, where do you live?' Laura loved to place people geographically.

'We moved out of London, you know, and I've never regretted it. Theodore and Janey just race about in the garden all day, and Charlie does too. Of course, we've only got twenty-seven acres, so it's not masses of land, but I feel quite safe about sending them bicycling down the lanes on their own. You couldn't do that in a city,' she concluded triumphantly.

Laura agreed that she couldn't, but opened her mouth to make a counter-claim on behalf of Wandsworth Common.

Jennifer swept on. 'James gets back in the evening about 9.30 and has a swim, and the day just falls off him.'

'Nine thirty? Paul is back at 6.30. We're only twenty-five minutes on the train from the City.'

'It's only an hour and three-quarters commute.' Jennifer was clearly determined to ignore the advantages of Earlsfield's railway links. 'Each way. Then you're in real countryside. And it's so wonderful not to have to use public swimming pools any longer. I always tried to swim right round men with moustaches, but, you know, it isn't always possible.'

'Men with moustaches?' Even Laura, with her advantage of membership in the motherhood club, was lost on that one.

Jennifer lowered her voice. 'You know. Men with moustaches. Gay.' She looked at our blank faces, and hissed, 'Aids!'

I tried to explain that Aids could not be transmitted through swimming-pool water, but got nowhere.

'After all, that's more or less what they said about BSE, and look what happened.'

I was staggered into silence while she and Laura rabbited on for a while about school runs and the awfulness of pushy parents, each informing the other of her own views in definite, confident voices.

On the other side, I could hear James telling Will and Paul how seriously rich he was now.

It was time to go into the dining room end of our double room to eat chilled soup and grill-hardened salmon.

'I'll tell you this – and this is really funny – where we live has a real village feeling.' I'd lost track of where this particular conversation was going, but

Laura always sensibly pointed out jokes to people beforehand so that they knew when to laugh.

'In our place,' Jennifer obviously didn't think that where you lived was a laughing matter, 'people drop in with home-made pies when you're ill.'

This triggered off a competitive round as to who had the nicer neighbours, which Jennifer won because Laura did really want to move out of town eventually and was therefore arguing against herself. Not that that usually worried her.

In fact, after a remark from Will she switched sides. 'Well, I'm sorry, Will, but I don't want my children growing up having to walk past drug pushers on every street corner.'

'Plenty of drug pushers in Northamptonshire,' asserted James, who'd got the wrong end of the stick and whose own competitiveness had been alerted by the thought we were boasting about how easy it was to buy illicit drugs in inner London. 'In fact, a national survey recently identified us as one of the leading counties in . . .'

'Darling!' Jennifer glared at him. 'Not in our part of Northamptonshire.'

He pulled himself together, helping himself from the wine bottle on the table. 'No, not ours, of course. We have policemen on bicycles.'

None of us quite knew how to take this statement, and even Laura couldn't top it, so Paul told me that the soup was delicious.

'Mm, lovely,' echoed Laura. 'Was it Sainsbury's or

the Covent Garden Soup Company? What brings you down to town, James?'

James focused unsteadily on her. 'We've just bought a flat in London, too. For shagging.'

'For James to stay after late meetings at work,' Jennifer beamed at the rest of us.

'Are you moving back permanently?' Will hesitated fractionally before re-filling James's glass.

James shuddered. 'I wouldn't come back here to live.' He looked round at our perfectly pleasant yellow-painted dining room end of the room, punctuated with fabric-covered dining chairs and liberally dotted with silver photograph frames, and added that he couldn't imagine how people could bear to exist like this.

'Like what?' Will affected not to know what he was talking about.

James waved at the security grille on the windows and the winking red eye in the corner, which we'd had to install to protect a couple of rather fed-up looking oil paintings Will had inherited. Personally I'd be only too glad if the burglars took them, except that Will had so little from his childhood that they had assumed the status of heirlooms. His Victorian great-aunt glared disapprovingly at him – or perhaps at the security precautions – out of her gilt frame.

'Life behind bars,' James continued. 'This whole dirty, city thing. But I'm taking over the European division, which means more entertaining in town, so we've bought a flat for me to doss in.' He looked at me. 'I shall want to shag all your friends. I shall be relying on you.' He peered into his glass as if he was looking for a contact lens, then swallowed it back in one gulp, re-filling it himself.

Jennifer beamed. 'The thing is,' one of her hands dived into her cleavage, rummaged around for a bit, then hauled up a greyish bra strap, 'there's such a wonderful community spirit in the country. People will be popping in and making sure I'm not lonely.'

Laura counter-attacked with a long story about the thriving mother-and-toddler group in Earlsfield. Will helped me clear the soup plates away. 'I think he's about to fall asleep,' he muttered in the kitchen. 'For God's sake, don't do anything to wake him up.'

Laura and Jennifer started to talk about Elaine Brown.

'She's my heroine,' offered Laura. 'At last someone's spoken up for mothers at home.'

I started to say that I thought that the debate between working and staying at home had been in the forefront of women's issues for at least quarter of a century.

'But from someone so high profile, it means more,' explained Jennifer, ignoring the fact that you could scarcely be at home spooning baked beans into your child's mouth and be high profile at the same time. The word 'humbug' was just forming on my lips when Laura interrupted me.

'Oh, Leonie thinks we all ought to go out to work.'

'I don't, I . . .'

'What did you do before you had children?' Laura was more interested in Jennifer than in my opinions, which she could hear any time if she chose to.

Jennifer had worked in an advertising office. 'I hated it. I couldn't wait to give it up,' she said, with satisfaction.

She didn't ask Laura what she'd done, but I thought Laura looked wistful. She used to grumble about it, but in reality she'd adored her job in a smart Fulham Road boutique, and she'd been good at bossing customers into styles that really suited them. But it didn't pay. Once they'd worked out that after childcare she'd have £6,000 a year left over, much of which would be eaten up in fares, lunches and smart clothes for work, Laura had taken up this aggressive 'mothers should be at home' stance. She really believed it now. It was all a million miles away from the situation of someone wealthy like Elaine, whose dry-cleaning bills alone probably came to more than £6,000. And it was all a pity, because although Laura wasn't very academic she was brilliant at selling. Now the only sales targets she had to meet were for the raffle tickets at the school's Christmas Fair. Last year she'd told us, her eyes sparkling, that she'd outsold all the other mothers by about two to one. But with the new baby, she thought she'd even have to give up the book club sales she'd just started.

I noticed James wilting over his plate and hoped he'd finish it before his head landed in the carrots. Will and I whisked the second course out and replaced it with a chocolate whisky bombe from the patisserie Konditor & Cook.

The sugar hit seemed to wake James up and he started reminiscing about France.

'Do you remember that amazing tarte tatin from the patisserie in the market place?' he asked no one in particular.

I did. Saffron had never cooked, but every so often she'd drifted down to the patisserie and impressed everyone with her grasp of conversational French. After quizzing the proprietor in a charming accent on his children, grandchildren, and the weather, she'd usually bought a tarte tatin and a couple of French sticks, and retreated with kisses on both cheeks, and a flurry of '*au revoir*' and '*bon apetit*'. (Personally I noted that her interest in families or the weather never seemed to extend to Jo or me, but kept the observation to myself.) The morning sun would glint on her red hair, and the boys from the Tabac would sit up, alert as hunting dogs, as she swung past, arms laden. She'd very rarely had to carry the packages all the way to the car. Once she'd flicked her hair towards Jo with a half-smile: 'I'm so sorry about all this attention I get,' she'd said. Jo had been too startled to reply.

James, amazingly, was still talking about the tarte tatin when my attention came back to the dinner party. 'Do you ever see Saffron nowadays?' he concluded.

I wanted to say 'Funnily enough, Will slept with her only the other day' but, darting a look at Will, didn't dare. Pity really. The evening could have done with some livening up.

Jennifer sliced herself an extra tiny sliver of cake and ate it with her fingers. 'I hadn't realized that Will was also an old boyfriend of Saffron's.' She sounded amused. 'Do you suppose there's a man in London who hasn't slept with Saffron Perry?'

'She was bloody awful in bed,' asserted James. 'For a stunner like that.'

The table froze.

'Mind you, if she doesn't settle down soon, she'll be a Blanche Dubois type.' James picked up the wine bottle and waved it at Will as if he was in a restaurant. 'Beautiful women like that go all scrawny. Is there anything to drink round here? This end of the table is damned dry.' Will extracted another bottle from the sideboard, as James asked us if we knew the difference between a golf ball and a clitoris.

'What *is* the difference between a golf ball and a clitoris?' we chorused, relieved to be on less personal ground.

'A chap can find a clitoris.' James sniggered into his wine, while Jennifer leant forward earnestly.

'No, darling, you've got that wrong. A chap can find a golf ball. That was the original joke.'

James waved her away. 'Whatever.'

'I gather Saffron's father died a few months ago,' she added, clearly not having picked up on the undertow of tension at the mention of her name. I shot a look at Will, but he appeared to be concentrating on his food.

'I don't suppose she noticed,' replied James. He waggled his wine glass at Jennifer. 'Girl had an awful childhood.' Jennifer and Laura looked interested.

Will maintained a discreet silence, and I certainly wasn't going to tell anyone anything.

'Well?' asked Laura, who relished a good tragedy.

'Her mother was some sort of a hippy, and died when she was ten of some overdose.'

'So that's why she's called Saffron. It seems such a funny name for someone of our age,' chirped Laura. I felt like saying that she wasn't really our age, she was a bit older.

Saffron's interesting, tragic childhood irritated me. It seemed to let her off being practical in any way. People always said, 'Poor Saffron, of course, she's never really had a home as such.' Her father had been quite a famous jazz musician in his day, which was presumably where her musical talent came from. But he'd been married so often that Saffron, along with various other half-siblings and step-siblings, had been mislaid all over the world. She, I suspected, had spent rather more time than she admitted to with an extremely nice aunt in Tunbridge Wells, so there was absolutely no reason why she shouldn't know exactly what washing up was.

I never voiced this opinion because I knew it didn't sound very '*simpatico*', a word that Saffron had once used about me. 'Leonie, of course, is so *simpatico*,' she'd said once, and I now felt sentenced to being permanently, irredeemably nice in her presence.

We picked over the issue of absentee families for a bit, and Jennifer expressed the view that you got fewer broken marriages in the country.

There was a silence, and I tuned into the sounds of the terraced houses around us.

'Hit me again, you Arab bitch,' floated through the air of the summer evening, accompanied by the dull rumble of the traffic and a roar as an aeroplane flew overhead. James, who'd dozed off again, woke with a start, looking interested.

'There's a house full of tarts at number 24,' I explained, looking at the green-tinged city sky outside, and getting up to close the curtains.

'Is there?' asked James, struggling to his feet.

'Well, we must be off.' Jennifer got up, and began to say her goodbyes, with James weaving unsteadily behind her. Laura, too, mumbling about babysitters and early nights, got Paul to fetch her coat.

While we stood in the sitting room, as Will waved James and Jennifer off, Laura touched my arm in concern.

'Is everything all right? You and Will hardly seem to be speaking to each other.'

'Well, you can't when you've got guests,' I pointed out. 'There hasn't been time, that's all.' It was rich coming from her. She never let up on Paul – in her view, he was always either working too hard or not earning enough, or occasionally – heinous crime, this – reading a paper when he could have been changing a nappy.

But it was kind of her to ask. I squeezed her arm back and tried to smile. 'Everything's fine. We both just get so tired, that's all.'

I watched Paul help Laura on with her coat, and the way she turned to him. There was trust and closeness there, I thought, and in spite of the snapping, love. I think it works for them. I hope so. Perhaps we shouldn't be so afraid of having arguments.

'God, James hasn't changed a bit.' Will shook his head as he piled the plates into the dishwasher. 'Although Jennifer's obviously got him under control.'

I thought James was totally different from the pleasant, ordinary banker who'd played tennis and drunk red wine in the hot sun of France. Either that or Will had changed much more than I'd realized. Perhaps we'd all changed. Too much.

But he – and Jennifer – had presented a revolutionary view of Saffron, one that I had never conceived of, and one that justified Will's assertion that she was 'vulnerable'. I remembered our conversation about Saffron being anorexic and thought about the dead hippy mother. It seemed, perhaps, that Saffron did not have – maybe had never had – the dice loaded on her side in quite the way I'd imagined.

Oddly enough it made me feel more threatened, not less. This Saffron had obviously had to learn to fight for survival. She could be ready to compromise, to give up her quest for composers and conductors and record-label moguls. And she might well be beginning to consider that Will, dear loyal Will who'd always been there for her, might be her knight on a white charger. I didn't think, somehow, that she'd allow my existence to get in her way.

And I could no longer ignore the fact that there was a terrible emptiness in our relationship because I hadn't been able to have a baby. That was what we really needed to turn us into a family.

But turning us into a family wasn't going to be that easy, though. And the complications weren't purely medical. I suddenly remembered one of Elaine's many interviews in the press after her resignation. 'I was the only senior woman with children,' she'd declared. 'All the other editors and directors were either men or they were childless.'

Technically that was true, I realized, mentally scanning the senior Maglife team. Even Belinda Bracken, for all her gentle sympathy, only had two grown-up stepchildren. But I was sure that that was a coincidence. As Lindsey – and several other women I knew – had already proved, there were women with children at the top everywhere these days.

I didn't know which was worse, having to choose between work and motherhood or not having the choice.

Actually I did. Not having the choice. That's definitely worse. It was time to move across to the other side of the bed, to touch Will where she had touched him, to break through the sheet of ice that separated us.

I extended my hand tentatively, and he moved towards me.

'Hello,' he kissed my forehead. 'I've missed you.'

And it was all right. Not earth-shattering, not like being carried away on a wave of bliss or attaining a peak or reaching up for the stars. Just all right, pleasantly familiar, an act in which we both knew our places and our movements and which we knew too well to risk changing anything. We each moved in a pre-arranged, satisfactory – and satisfying – way, because anything different might raise the question 'Why?' and the answer might have echoes of another night in another house. But it had warmth and gentleness, and, even, I thought, love. It drew another veil over that night with Saffron, and I knew that if we went on covering that memory with gossamer-fine ones of our own, we would soon bury it completely. Warmed from the inside, I slipped into sleep.

19

There were now only days until I was to swallow the last fertility pill. There had been three packs for three months, all too quickly over. We had returned, patiently, to charting sex, writing it in our diaries along with lunches, dinner parties, work appointments and reminders to pick up the dry cleaning. Occasionally I'd felt feverishly hormonal, ranging from snapping at Will, to weeping quietly to myself, or suddenly deciding to paint the bathroom bright pink. He maintained a dignified, male, doctorly response based on careful consideration and understanding. Sometimes I fantasized about shooting him – anything to ruffle his calm, gentle air of control. Every so often I'd felt a high, sharp pain quickly stabbing my abdomen, and wondered what it meant.

It meant nothing, I was told. It might, I was assured, even be imaginary. It was getting difficult to sort out illusion from fact when it came to sensations anyway – before I'd lost faith in it all, I'd imagined that every tiny pain, ache or dizziness was a symptom of pregnancy, and had twice convinced myself thoroughly of success in what had turned out to be complete false alarms. These highs and lows also meant I could blame any residual anger about Saffron on my intake of fake hormones, which conveniently erased any further need to think about her, or that night they'd spent together. I no longer trusted my own feelings.

The office, after nearly four months, had become more of a home than home, although after the elation of the rise in the first sales figures, I suddenly hit a rather choppy time. On the minus side, Bellingham Glass, having approved everything we'd sent to them without comment, suddenly came back only days before the first supplement went to press, and told me the 'tone' wasn't right. On the plus side, the sales of the July issue – the second one I could truly call mine – rose again, but only fractionally, although Peter Rennie was warmly encouraging ('A great achievement in the current climate, Leonie'). But back to the bad news again – Maeve called me to her office to tell me that Brian Carstairs' group had cut its advertising in *How?* by thirty per cent.

Why couldn't anything go smoothly? I wondered if this had been due to Camilla's carping, whether he'd lost faith in the magazine because she'd been talking it down. Although things had been much better recently.

Maeve shook her head. 'I very much doubt it. Carstairs is an out-and-out pro, and he's also an old-fashioned chauvinist. Frankly, he gives the impression that his daughter is just playing with her career until she marries someone eminently suitable and has babies.'

I felt a spasm of sympathy for Camilla. Whatever

else you could say about her, she did passionately love magazines and wanted to succeed, even if getting in at 10.30 a.m. every day and spending an hour on the phone discussing last night's party wasn't necessarily the best way to go about it.

'No,' continued Maeve. 'The word is out that there's another recession coming.'

'Another? We haven't finished the last one yet.'

Maeve shrugged. She had a timeless quality, as if she had seen the boom-and-bust cycle so many times that it made no difference to her. But it terrified me. Recessions were scary, particularly with IVF looming up, costing £2,000 a throw. And that, I had discovered with a shock, didn't include the drugs that prepared you beforehand.

I returned from Maeve's lavishly appointed rabbit hutch to the open spaces of the editorial office.

Camilla waved a newspaper at me. 'Read this.'

My least favourite paper – nicknamed the Daily Moan – informed me that I could read its new star columnist, Elaine Brown, every Tuesday in a ground-breaking column called 'Mother's Home!'

'Puh-lease!' Camilla rolled her eyes.

'Pass the sickbag,' said Polly, relatively briskly for her, adding, 'Do you know, I had a fairly decent night's sleep last night? I'd forgotten what it felt like to be a human being, as opposed to a sleep-deprived zombie.'

The Daily Moan's half a million readers, I learned, would hear from the new front line – The Home –

from where their intrepid correspondent would file reports that opened up new frontiers. 'Hear it like it really is!' shrieked the blurb.

'But if she's to find out how it really is,' Polly put her head on one side, 'she'll have to get home somehow between chat-show appearances. At least for a few minutes. How do you think she'll manage it?'

'Her husband has a chauffeur,' Camilla informed us crisply.

'Wow! Really like it is,' murmured Polly, burying herself in her work with a sigh of irritation.

Kate, who was standing in for Deirdre while she was on maternity leave and clearly wasn't enjoying the idea of going back to her subservient role as assistant homes editor, sidled up and asked if we could 'discuss her future'. I checked my watch. Two meetings before lunch and three afterwards.

'Would tomorrow do?'

Clearly not, by the expression on her face, so I agreed to stay late and talk to her after everyone had gone home. I suspected she would have stayed all night, if necessary.

I wondered if there was anything in the budget for her – a small salary rise and a slightly more exciting title to compensate perhaps – and popped round to Maeve again.

She sighed. 'There's always trouble after maternity leave. The stand-ins don't like standing down, and the first thing that the returner does is grumble about how the job's been done in her absence. They come marching in here and complain about the filing. The filing! I ask you!'

'Well, the human race has to reproduce somehow,' I commented, secretly wishing that you could just order babies in the required size and sex from John Lewis.

'Hm.' Maeve looked as if she'd like to have all her staff compulsorily sterilized.

'After all,' I added, thinking hopefully of my chances of successful treatment and wanting her to be on my side, 'there won't be anyone to pay for our hip replacements in twenty years' time unless we produce lots of little worker bees who'll all pay taxes.' Maeve didn't like that, possibly because she's in the Hip Replacement Years already, and prefers not to be reminded of the fact. Come to think of it, I'm not far from the start of the Hip Replacement Years myself. In fact, to be honest, I'm as near to them as to the age when most women begin the Head Lice Years, as Laura calls having small children. Almost, anyway. What a frightening thought.

On Friday morning, Bellingham Glass insisted on a meeting. As soon as possible. Monday, for example. They made it clear that the 'tone' had to be discussed urgently or they'd pull their money out of the supplements. At this late stage, we'd be liable for the production costs, which were considerable.

The IVF clinic said they had a cancellation on

Monday, and that, once I'd seen the consultant, I could start the programme immediately. If I couldn't make the Monday appointment, the next available one was in five weeks' time. Five weeks doesn't sound very long, but I was beginning to realize how quickly the months – and years – slipped by waiting for test results or being ready for the next stage. Now that I'd finally decided to go ahead, I didn't want to wait any longer.

Peter Rennie demanded to see me as soon as possible, phoning from his car on his way down from the Midlands. 'On Monday.'

'Peter,' I said desperately. 'Everything is happening on Monday. Bellingham are kicking up stink about some idiotic problem they think they've spotted.' I tried to think about something else important enough to turn the MD down for. 'And I've got to go to a funeral at 11.30,' I lied, feeling dreadfully, dreadfully wicked. Lies like that have a habit of rebounding badly.

'Oh!' He sounded startled, but, with typical British reserve, didn't ask who had died. 'I'm sorry to hear that.' He paused and added, 'What about a breakfast meeting?'

So Monday's diary read: 8 a.m. Peter Rennie (mental note: remember to wear black), 11.30 a.m. funeral (mental note: code for IVF appointment), 2 p.m. Bellingham Glass in Easbiton. There were various other appointments in there too, some of which I asked Lucy to re-distribute to Camilla. Her eyes lit up. Trying to edge me out, or grateful for an opportunity to have some responsibility? I was too frantic to worry about it.

My eyes scraped past sandpaper every time I blinked, and my brain was screaming for sleep on Monday morning, when Peter Rennie amazed me by offering me the editorship of *My Life*.

'Why?' I was too shocked to act like a top executive. Lindsey would have simply moved in for the kill.

'You've done a very good job on *How?*.' Peter sounded too smooth to be true.

I wasn't going to point out that two tiny sales rises – all I had to show for my four months – were scarcely anything to shout about. Although we had been nominated for an award, and people were saying good things to my face, some of which, at least, might be true.

'But surely you need me to consolidate *How?* before moving on to anything else?'

'Look,' he sounded impatient. 'This is the best job in the group. Do you want it or not?'

'Of course I want it,' I countered. 'But I . . .'

'Think about it.' He hustled me out of the door. 'I'd like to hear your decision soon. It's important that *My Life* isn't seen to flounder.'

I was almost in the corridor before he said, 'Oh, and Leonie, it's quite a bit more money than you're earning at the moment.'

That was the meeting in a nutshell as I explained it later to Will, although, to be fair to Peter, we'd talked a bit more about it than that. He had, in fact, gone through plans and budgets, and made me feel genuinely wanted.

It still simply didn't make sense. Except for the bit about *My Life* not being seen to flounder. Perhaps this was damage limitation after Elaine's defection.

Will wasn't really listening. He'd had trouble getting out of his Monday morning surgery, and was feeling alternately irritated and guilty. It was the busiest morning of the week, and when he'd told Sally, the receptionist, of his putative dental appointment she had, I gathered, pursed her lips in disapproval. He was letting people down, he felt.

The IVF consultant ran forty minutes late, but this clinic was more luxurious than the last. Beigey-pink moquette chairs, the legs sinking into deep-pile carpet, were grouped round coffee tables. A few other couples flicked through magazines, avoiding our eyes. In the corner a woman sat, propped motionless like a tailor's dummy, her face silently streaming with tears while the man next to her passed her tissues. Everyone pretended not to notice her. We knew we couldn't help her. We knew she didn't want stories of couples who'd tried and tried to have a baby, despaired, relaxed, and suddenly found themselves pregnant. And that's about all anyone seems able to offer in the way of comfort. Even Will, caring, conscientious Will, raised his magazine high so that he couldn't see anyone, his shoulders hunched in tension. It was like being finalists in a desperate competition. We knew that only twenty per cent of us – or whatever the individual figure was – were going to succeed. Our eyes were on the finishing post, not the other competitors.

The clock moved towards the time of my train to Bellingham Glass with maddening speed. I thought you only got lateness on the National Health.

Eventually a nurse appeared from a door and called our name. We hurried in.

'Sorry about this.' He didn't sound at all sorry. 'My name's Dr Grant.' We all shook hands. He ignored any indication that Will, too, was a doctor.

He sketched out the programme.

'We put you into a false menopause for around ten days, and then get your ovaries working in overdrive. We'll scan you every two days and when the eggs are ripe for harvesting we'll make you ovulate, so that we can take them out to fertilize. This egg collection is done under a light anaesthetic, although you can opt merely for sedation. You won't need to go under when the fertilized eggs are re-implanted two days later.'

Under where, I felt like asking. I was dizzy with the terminology alone.

'There's a choice of drugs,' he clattered on, having been through this too many times. 'Recently, we've been having the greatest success with this one . . .' he indicated a leaflet on his desk, 'but these two are options as well. It all depends on stocks and what you can get where.'

'Can't we get them here?' I was taken aback, I'd

expected them to choose and provide the drugs, not turn the decision straight back to us.

'Oh, yes.' He pulled out a few more leaflets. 'Sometimes anyway. If we're out of stock, you can usually find a chemist who's got some. Well, usually. If you're lucky. Some people can get their GPs to prescribe them.'

I looked at Will, who shook his head. 'Not in our district. The guidelines are quite clear. The NHS won't stump up.'

'If this drug is the most successful . . .' I pulled out the top leaflet and stared it, so that we'd remember which one to get, 'why do people bother with the others?'

'Hm? Oh, cost, mainly. That one's very expensive. It'll add, let me see, £800 to £900 to the cost of your cycle. Approximately, that is. Maybe more. Mind you, you can often ring round the chemists and see who has the best price.'

I tried to visualize phoning round chemists to check prices of fertility drugs in my open-plan office, with Lucy and Camilla listening to every word. I didn't think it was an option, unless it made a big difference to the price. I asked him.

'It might save £50 to £100 a cycle. If you're lucky. But I don't handle the money myself.' He flashed a cursory smile, washing his hands of anything as mundane as finance.

Then he added, more gently, 'Sometimes the whole consultation is taken up with discussing the financial side, and, frankly, that's not what I'm here for.'

Eight or nine hundred pounds is a lot of money. Even if you're both professionals. That means that IVF costs around £3,000 a cycle. And the success rate is around one in five. I'd never been good at maths, but even I could see that it added up to an average of around £18,000 to achieve one baby. We might save a bit of money with the less effective drugs, but only a few hundred pounds a cycle. A few thousand in all, perhaps. Anyway, of course, we wanted the best drugs. The odds were stacked against us as it was.

'A typical series of cycles, one that might quite reasonably end up with a baby, can cost around £20,000.' He obviously thought we couldn't calculate.

The price had gone up by £2,000 in less than a minute. I had a feeling that that was what it would be like from now on. Never mind. We could take out a larger mortgage on the house. It would be worth it. If we succeeded.

'Do the drugs have any side effects?'

'It's all in the leaflets. Of course, if your ovaries get over-stimulated we can usually correct that now.'

'Now?' I wondered what an over-stimulated ovary did. It didn't sound comfortable, at any rate.

'Women used to have to come off the programme if their ovaries were over-stimulated. But, on the whole, that doesn't happen so often these days.'

'And then the eggs are collected . . .'

'Not always,' he interrupted. 'There are no guarantees.'

I was alarmed. 'You mean I could go through all that, and wake up after the anaesthetic to find out that I hadn't got anywhere after all?'

He nodded. 'I'm afraid that can happen at any stage.'

No wonder there was always someone sobbing in the waiting rooms.

It was quite difficult to take in, to assess what it all really meant to us, and to our lives. I mentioned, tentatively, that I'd been offered a great new job, but was worried about taking on extra responsibility at this time.

Dr Grant looked incredulous. 'It's up to you.' He steepled his hands and leaned back in his chair. 'But it's only fair to warn you that you can't choose your appointments, particularly your scanning slots, so you'll have to be available every two days, possibly at unpredictable times. This clinic is exceptionally successful . . .' (which was why we had chosen it, after all), 'so demand for scans is high. We can't guarantee to see someone first thing in the morning or last appointment in the evening. This can be a strain for some people.'

For some people. For pretty much everyone, I'd have thought.

'And, of course, as I'm sure you've been told, we can't offer you any guarantee of success,' added Dr Grant. 'Your chances, let me see . . . dum, dum,

dum – ' he traced a finger down a graph ' – are quite good, compared to some people, but I wouldn't put them higher than around, say, thirty per cent. Perhaps less.'

It's a meaningless statistic, like when the weather report tells you there's a thirty per cent chance of rain. Either it's going to rain or it isn't, as far as I'm concerned.

'Less than 50/50,' I told Will glumly as we left the office. 'I'm surprised they don't make "We Can't Guarantee Anything" their official slogan.'

'No,' he said. 'Look at it like this. The usual success rate is one in five. If your chances are thirty per cent that means you could get pregnant nearly twice in five cycles instead of once.'

It made my head swim. 'I don't think statistics work like that.'

'How do they work then?'

'Oh, I don't know,' I admitted. 'But not in our favour anyway.'

He dug his hands deeper into his jacket pockets and shrugged. 'You don't have to do this, you know.'

I wondered why he hadn't said 'we'. Perhaps it was because it was me who would be having an injection every night (the alternative was sniffing something every four hours which would be impossible to remember, let alone carry out under the collective eyes of Peter Rennie, Maeve and Camilla, all of whom would privately disapprove of my trying to become A Mother). It would be me whose legs were in metal stirrups, who felt sick, who would have needles slicing through my flesh and cold metallic instruments invading my body. All he had to do was wank into a test tube.

I tried to tell myself I was being unfair. He was concerned, that's all. 'Don't worry,' I reassured him. 'It'll be fine.'

We walked on a bit further, still scanning the crowded, baking July streets for a taxi.

'The only thing is . . .'

Will obviously thought that I wanted to pull out after all. His face tensed up. 'What?'

'Do you think that, as it's all going to cost so much, I ought to take the *My Life* job, then?'

A taxi screeched to a halt. I had exactly seventeen minutes to get to the station to catch the train.

'It's your choice,' he said. 'Honestly.'

'What will you do?'

He looked at his watch. 'The Duke of Boots isn't far. Might pop in for a pint. Just for old times' sake.' He kissed me, his face clearing at the thought.

I leant back in the taxi. I should just about make it. We passed the Duke of Boots, and, for a moment, I wished I was in there, sitting on a round pub stool waiting for Will before an afternoon of strolling down the King's Road. All we'd had to do in those carefree days was think about what we were going to have for dinner.

The taxi turned another corner and I caught a flash

of a pale face and red hair as we sped past. I looked back and saw the familiar corkscrew cascade and the impossibly slender waist under a belted fawn mac. She was heading towards the Duke of Boots.

I tapped on the glass dividing me from the taxi driver. 'Please,' I said. 'Can you turn round?'

He shook his head. 'One way system, Miss.'

'Well, could you wait here for me?'

He looked doubtful.

'Please.'

He stopped with a sign, and I tore out of the door as soon as the red light on the door winked off, feeling the most awful fool. What was I going to do if I did find them both drinking in the Duke of Boots? I raced round the corner but the girl had gone. She'd been striding very fast and she had a long gait. I hurried to the pub.

Will looked astonished to see me. 'Hello?' He was just going in.

'I, er, forgot to ask you when you'd be home tonight.' I peered into the darkness of the pub. There was no girl there. 'Are you meeting anyone?'

'No,' he sounded surprised. 'I've only just decided to come.' He looked at me a little more closely. 'Are you all right?'

'Fine.' I tucked my hair behind my ears nervously. 'Fine. Just a bit late, that's all. Must fly.' I saw him looking after me, bewildered.

Of course, I missed my train.

*

Bellingham Glass were completely horrible.

'Mr Beckett's a busy man,' the receptionist told me spitefully. 'You're late. You'll just have to wait.'

'I know, I'm sorry, the train was delayed,' I lied. She looked unconvinced and returned smugly to her switchboard. 'Bellingham Glass, how-can-I-help-you?' she sang out.

I sat there for forty minutes, tapping my feet, and thinking of the work piling up on my desk. It was utterly idiotic to allow this night with Saffron to turn into an obsession. I had been a fool to get out of the cab, and if anything ever happened like that again, well, I must just sit tight, then ask Will in the evening. A lot of this was just an over-active imagination, stimulated by hormones to create fantastical visions around every corner.

My over-stimulated imagination remained leadenly convinced that I was missing something. I just hadn't quite worked out what.

Eventually a pallid girl in a limp, black cardigan and skirt appeared and greeted me with tension. 'Mr Beckett will see you now.'

She teetered ahead of me on high heels, directing me into an empty boardroom and left me to wait for another five minutes. The man was impossible.

Eventually he lumbered in, followed by the usual duck's tail of acolytes. 'These supplements just aren't upmarket enough,' he explained, swinging back in his chair and putting his feet on the boardroom table.

'In what sense?' I was taken aback. Considering

that they had been put together by the *How?* team –
the one that Dave Beckett had professed to admire
so much – with all the attention to detail and creativity
as anything else in the magazine, then carefully
checked and re-worked by every department, it was
amazing that they should turn round at this stage and
claim that they wouldn't do. Perhaps he was having
an early male menopause or something. Or his wife
had left him.

'Well, in every sense, really. Take the December supplement front cover of a table laid for Christmas, shot
in soft focus through one glass bauble. It's very con-
fusing. Bellingham doesn't make Christmas tree balls.
We can't have a situation where thousands of people
are ringing up trying to buy something we don't make.'

I could see his point – although it did occur to me
that Christmas tree balls might find more of a market
than golfing trophies – but I didn't think he needed
to worry. 'The bauble would be almost completely
clear. It's just a symbol of glass and . . .'

He cut across me. 'But that's quite a minor problem
compared to the rest of it. There's no real understanding of the Bellingham philosophy.' I pointed out
that my understanding was that they wanted new,
fresh ideas, and a different approach.

'Up to a point, of course, but we can't disenfranchise
the traditional Bellingham buyer totally. The tone
is very important, and the tone of these is frankly
popularist.' He looked at me to see if I agreed, and
added, in translation, 'Too down-market.'

I was so outraged that I was completely silenced. What did Bellingham Glass think they were? Royal Warrant holders? Frankly, the vulgarity of some of the objects I'd seen the day I'd toured the factory was breathtaking.

'On the kitchen pages, for example,' his tone was silky, 'you talk about "worktops". The Bellingham buyer uses "work surfaces". There's a bit here talking about "friends for supper". Bellingham people have "guests for dinner". And there are other examples like that.'

'For example?'

He waved me away. 'No, I really don't want to sound petty. I think we'd better move on to the larger picture.' The argument went round in circles and I tried to listen hard to find out what he really wanted. If he knew himself. Eventually he came to the Christmas supplement and the evening-wear pages, 'Musicians in Fashion'. 'This,' he held the pages aloft so that everyone could see, 'now this is the sort of approach we'd hoped for.' I gazed at the image of Saffron, preening herself in two-dimensional gloss, casting a provocative, victorious smile over a strappy black velvet number.

'In fact,' his eyes lit up briefly, 'we should put that lass on the cover. Now there's class. Much more like it.'

I tried to work out why it differed from the other pages. 'You mean you'd like more real people, more minor celebs . . .?'

He gave me a withering look. 'No, that's hardly the point.'

'So,' I leant back, exhausted. 'Perhaps you'd like to be more explicit about exactly what you do want.'

He gave me a self-satisfied smile, like a cat with cream. 'I really don't think it's wise to hire a dog and bark yourself, do you, Leonie? We're spending this money in exchange for your ideas and expertise. I would really hope,' he paused for effect, 'that the next draft might manifest a more professional approach.'

Draft? We were just days away from press day. He rose and extended a dead-haddock hand for me to shake. 'I hope you don't mind my being frank, but we just can't have work like this, and it's so much easier all round if one's direct from the start.'

I opened my mouth to mention something about schedules, deadlines and the amount of time they'd sat on the material we'd sent them, but he interrupted. 'Don't worry. Together I'm sure we can come up with something.' And, with a steely smile, he left the room.

I knew that a man who saw no real difference between tractors and glass was not going to have rational opinions on whether something was upmarket enough or what the importance of 'tone' was.

Only Jenny, his assistant, remained, with two spots of high colour in her cheeks. She didn't meet my eyes. 'I'll show you down to the door.'

'I'm sorry it didn't work out,' she said, offering a hand to shake. 'But the tone really is very important.'

She was obviously anxious that I should forget how much she had originally said she liked it all.

I was shaken. If I couldn't pull together a brochure for a tasteless glass company, what hope did I have of editing *My Life*?

I told myself not to be silly, and trudged wearily back to the office to pull together some new last-minute ideas for the Bellingham stuff, and to get someone to find a bit more time in the schedule. Saffron, it seemed, was beginning to creep into our lives again. But this time it would be purely business. I told the over-active imagination to be quiet.

What I really wanted to do that evening was to talk to Will about the offer from Peter Rennie. Should I do it? It was a terrific, prestigious job, and we needed the extra money. But I was under no illusions about how much work it would entail, and how difficult it would be to jump in a taxi for scans at the drop of a hat. And what if the IVF succeeded? Could I lose the baby through overwork? No one ever seemed to know any answers to these sort of questions, although when I'd asked them in the past, nurses were cautiously optimistic that, on the whole, women could work and be pregnant without either suffering. One reason why I'd stayed eight long years at *Penny* was because I'd been expecting to get pregnant any minute for much of it. Looking back, I think that was a mistake.

On the other hand, no one could accuse you of

putting your life on hold when you've only been in a job four months. It wasn't the same thing at all, not at all.

When I finally got home, at 10 that evening, having seen the Bellingham supplements halfway through their redesigned versions, Will had been back for hours, waiting for me with the TV remote control in one hand, and an empty beer can beside the sofa.

'For God's sake,' I couldn't help being impatient. 'You know we're not supposed to drink much.'

'It's only my second.' There was a pause as I divested myself of coat, bags, folders and files. 'Bad afternoon?'

'Bloody.' I hurled a file across the room. 'Bloody Bellingham Glass.' I brooded on them as I buttered some toast, crashing the plate and knife down.

He got up. 'You can talk to me about it, you know.'

I leant against him, as some of the tension went out of me. 'Sorry. Yes, I know. But I really want to talk to you about something else. About taking on this other great challenge.'

He obviously thought I was mad even to consider a new job. 'For God's sake,' he said impatiently, 'you've only been there five minutes. Of course you don't have to accept a new editorship.'

'Why do you think they've offered it to me, though?'

'Did you ask them?' He wasn't being sarcastic, just curious, but he tore the top off another beer absent-mindedly. There wasn't any point, I screamed inside, in my doing all this if he was going to decimate his sperm count with drinking. 'Are you having another one?' I tried, unsuccessfully, to keep the sharpness out of my voice.

He closed his eyes, then opened them again with exaggerated patience. 'I'm having one more, all right?'

'But shall I take *My Life*?' I persevered.

'I don't want to hold you back,' he replied.

'So you don't want me to take it?'

'That's not what I said.'

I looked at him, then leant against the wall, my head in my hands. 'What's happening to us?'

He met my gaze and there was a stillness between us. For one terrible second, I thought he was going to say something. Then his shoulders dropped and he sighed.

'Come on, sit down.' He pulled me down to the sofa, and put his arm around my shoulders. 'Nothing's happening between us. I promise. Everything is fine. Just fine. If you want to take the job,' he took my chin in his hand, so that I had to look at him, 'I promise I'll be behind you.'

I thought of what more delays might mean to us. Whatever he said, I couldn't put the brakes on the IVF now. The endless waiting and delays were the worst of it, I thought. I opened my mouth to say this.

He silenced me. 'But I don't have to tell you that a new job is always harder work than a familiar one, even after only four months, and that *My Life* is clearly a more demanding magazine than *How?*. As a doctor, and as your husband, I'm worried about what that'll do to you if you combine it with IVF treatment.'

I was irritated. So he didn't want me to take the job and didn't want to say so. I felt sulky as I gazed at my hands. So I didn't really have a choice. This time the treatment had to come first. We both agreed. It was a joint decision. There'll always – well, probably – be another big career move one day. As they say, no one ever died wishing they'd spent more time in the office. And all that.

20

The false menopause was fun. If that sort of thing amuses you. I spent ten days putting my handbag in the fridge, leaving fragile things like lettuces on chairs and then sitting on them, and I went absolutely scarlet when I told Peter Rennie I couldn't accept his offer.

It was like being baked in a furnace. The flames crept up my neck as I stammered out my desire to establish *How?* more securely before moving on. Mind you, I'd only taken a day's worth of hormones at that stage, so perhaps it isn't fair to blame them. He looked at me curiously.

'I'm disappointed in you, Leonie. I'd have expected you to take an opportunity and make the most of it.'

'I do usually, it's just that . . .' I rifled through my addled brain for anything that would make sense. 'Personal reasons,' I concluded.

'Ah.' He looked surprised. 'Personal reasons.'

'Temporary personal reasons,' I added. I wished I could have discussed it with him, but confiding one's fertility plans to the average managing director, combined with the company's hands-off policy on pregnancy and its famously paranoiac attitude towards working mothers, made this the career equivalent of trying to defuse a landmine with a safety pin.

'I hope you don't regret it,' he murmured.

I was already regretting it.

I sent Camilla down to Bellingham Glass with the new layouts and text. That would give them class, I thought. They were rendered completely speechless by her endless legs, tiny skirt and cut-glass tones.

'Pussycats,' was her verdict when she returned. 'Although that man with the sideburns kept stroking my knee.'

'Dave Beckett.' Maeve and I exchanged glances, and agreed that there were considerable advantages to growing older.

'Mind you,' added Camilla blithely, 'I felt it was my duty to *How?* to make sure that he spent more time looking at my knees than at the layouts.' She giggled. 'He just went "fine, fine, fine", grope, grope, grope.'

It was hardly feminism, but it merited a bottle of champagne in a wine bar, where Camilla got hopelessly tiddly – because I was sipping very carefully and slowly – and told me how much she wanted to be like me.

'Like me?' I was taken aback. Giving her all those extra appointments and responsibility seemed to have had a surprisingly good effect. 'Why me?'

'Well, you've done it, haven't you? Top job, fanciable husband – he's awfully nice, too, by the way. You've got a life.'

She hadn't mentioned children. I wondered if she was softening me up for something. And she didn't seem to have the superior image of herself that I'd always seen reflected in the mirror in the Ladies. 'You've got a life too.' I was incredulous that I needed to point it out. She had looks, money and a job that most twenty-six-year-olds would love.

'My life.' She sneered into her glass of champagne. 'Men and night clubs.'

'Well,' I pointed out, thinking that men and night clubs didn't sound too awful to me, 'you could cut down on night clubs during the week, and start coming into work on time, for a change. That way I could give you more responsibility, and you'd be ready for promotion sooner.'

'Really?' She looked surprised, as if someone had recommended some new, unlikely herbal remedy. 'Do you think that would help?'

'It would help me,' I said firmly. 'And this is the stage, when you're in your twenties, that you can work really hard, make the career gains, and be fairly senior by the time you get married and have children.'

She thought about this for a second. 'Why didn't you ever have children?'

Ever. The word clanged in my mind like a heavy steel door closing behind me. I could feel my hand beginning to shake. I pulled myself together.

'Oh you know,' I made my voice sound bright and carefree, 'no time, really. The years just flew by.'

Anyone older, like Maeve, would have seen through my casual tone, but Camilla, who had no interest in children and was only too relieved not to work for someone who wanted to take their holidays in August, let it go.

I thought I might try to take advantage of this relative friendliness. 'Did you know that "Daddy" has cut down on our advertising?'

'The shit. Well, it's no good me talking to him. He never listens to me. He just thinks I'm an airhead. He got me the job here because he thought women's magazines were a soft option.'

'Well, as you may have noticed, they're not.' I decided to stop being collegial. 'And if you treat the office as if it was just a way of filling in time before you go to a party, you'll never get to the top. You've got talent, Camilla. Don't throw it away fulfilling your father's prediction that he's got an airhead for a daughter.'

She flushed. 'I don't behave as if it was all a party.'

I regretted being so direct. We'd only just started to work together properly, and I'd thrown it all away being authoritarian.

She suddenly smiled. 'Okay. It's a deal.' We walked back to the office in a relatively companionable silence. The loss of that advertising was worrying. So was the thought of having to drop everything to have a scan every two days.

When we got back to the office, it was buzzing.

Belinda Bracken had been made editor of *My Life*.

'It's a very odd choice.' I thought about her sensible tweed suits and neat little blouses, the perfect counterparts to the homely little tips that formed the back-bone of *Home Life*, Belinda's current magazine. You couldn't find a greater contrast between that and Elaine's sophisticated, raffish style, matched to the hard-edged cosmopolitan gloss of *My Life*. Well, perhaps *My Life* needed a few more ideas about what to do with leftover curry or ways of getting stains out of suede and fewer articles about oral sex titled 'Should you swallow?'

Belinda had apparently said that *My Life* was a great magazine and a wonderful challenge, and that she was delighted to be following in the footsteps of so many great editors. Tremendously nice and tactful. It was quite unlike Elaine's pronouncement, which I remembered from a year earlier when she'd been appointed. 'I'm going to put some buzz back into this title,' she'd declared publicly.

I went to see what Maeve had to say about it all. She was engrossed in some early sales figures. As a director she got them for all the magazines in the group.

She was wearing her sparkly rhinestone glasses to read them and was frowning.

'Is anything wrong?'

'Hm?' She folded them away hastily, and took her glasses off. 'Nothing.'

I took a seat by her desk.

'Still,' she added, 'you might as well know. Don't tell anyone else though.' She handed the paper over to me.

It takes me a great deal of concentration to read figures, and I couldn't believe these. *My Life*, the flagship title, had dropped astronomically since Elaine took over. Every month the figures had fallen.

'Surely that can't be right?'

Maeve sighed. 'I'm afraid it is.'

'So Elaine was sacked. She didn't walk out to spend more time with her family after all?'

'It looks like that. Most likely, to be honest, she jumped just before she was pushed.'

It all made perfect sense. I couldn't help giggling. 'No wonder Peter Rennie was furious. He'd hardly want to tell the whole world why she was really going because it would reflect so badly on *My Life*. She really trumped his ace.'

'She did. No wonder he's been so desperate to plug that gap at all costs. Elaine was going round town damaging *My Life*'s reputation terribly, and there just wasn't anyone there to contradict the things she was saying. He had to appoint Belinda in a terrible hurry.' Maeve sighed. 'I have to say it'll be a long time before he hires a working mother as an editor again. And I can't say I blame him.'

This was outrageously unfair. 'But Elaine's behaviour has nothing to do with her being a mother! Her children were just a convenient excuse. I don't think she sees them for one moment more than she used to when she was working here. She's hired an office near her house, apparently, and installed two secretaries in there. That's what she calls "working from home". And there are lots of working mothers at the tops of corporations everywhere, who work incredibly hard.'

'And most of them give up when the going gets tough. And that lets people down.' Maeve shook herself. 'I'm sorry. I shouldn't be talking to you like this. I know it's not exactly . . .' she searched for the words, 'politically correct. But it's what I think.'

I was really shaken. If I'd told Maeve that I'd refused the top job at *My Life* because I had embarked on fertility treatment, would she have called it 'getting out when the going got tough'? I suspected she would. If I'd mapped out Laura's predicament in being unable to go back to work because her salary barely covered her childcare costs, would she think that Laura had taken the easy option? I hardly even needed to ask myself the question.

And did I think Laura and I had both ducked out? There is a tiny, niggling, resentful little bit of me that does, I'm afraid. And I suspect that some of the resentment in Laura's eyes is fear that she'll never ever work again. But I don't see what else we could have done.

At least I could put forward Lindsey to Maeve. 'My elder sister has a very senior job in the City,' I told her. 'And she's got three lovely children. She never lets anyone down.'

'Really?' Maeve looked amused. 'Good for her.'

21

Mind you, Lindsey is easier to cope with when she's an abstract concept, such as A Successful Working Mother, than she is in the flesh. I like to hold her up as a shining example of what women can achieve, but I have to admit that I do sometimes find her a bit smug.

'Oh, you know that MBE I mentioned?' This was on the telephone one evening a few days later.

It was typical of her to be so off-hand about her achievements, as if to stress that getting an MBE in the last Honours list was the sort of thing that just about anybody could do if they put a mind to it. 'Yes, why?'

'I've got the date for the investiture.' At last, she allowed herself to sound pleased. Obviously all those committees she sat on were paying off. Lindsey was clearly heading towards becoming one of the Great and the Good. 'I thought you and Laura might like to come with me to the Palace,' she continued. 'I can only take two guests.'

'What about Sandy?'

'Oh God, I can't take Sandy, he's far too busy,' said Lindsey, managing to imply that my schedule was so much less important than his.

'What about Ella?'

She snorted, apparently in disgust, then added, 'Well, do you want to come or not?'

I assured her that I'd love to.

'Speaking of Ella, she has something she'd like to ask you,' she added. 'But I've told her she mustn't bother you for too long. And if it's too much trouble you must say so.'

'Ella!' I heard her call up the stairs in ringing tones. 'Now! Why can't you answer when I call you? You knew I was phoning Aunt Leonie.' Lindsey, I was beginning to think, really had it in for Ella. Why couldn't she just leave the poor girl alone for five minutes? Go and deal another two thousand million Brazilian rials or something to let us all catch our breath? I tucked the phone under one hunched shoulder in order to slice an onion and talk simultaneously. A great many new and wonderful resolutions had accompanied the intake of artificial hormones. With the fake menopause over, and another lot of drugs stimulating yet a different kind of follicle, I'd resolved on a life filled with spinach and broccoli, fish and health-giving stir-fries. It did at least make finding my way through the forest of supermarket choices so much easier – I could just head for anything marked 'organic'. And on one level, I did feel better for it, although hormones were swamping my body, and virtually taking it over. I felt chained to an out-of-control helter-skelter.

There was a scuffle and some hissed muttering in

the background, and eventually I heard Ella's clear, high voice. She still sounded like a well-brought up ten-year-old.

'Aunt Leonie? How are you?'

'I'm fine.' I heard the warmth creep into my voice. 'How can I help?'

Ella's tones lurched into self-conscious teenager mode. 'Uh, well.'

I waited.

'Like, er, the school wants us to do work experience next term. Can I, er . . .' She trailed off.

'Work for me? Of course. I'll look forward to it. When do you want to come?'

Her voice brightened. 'Really? That'd be cool. No one else is going anywhere half as good.' This was more like the Ella of old. I asked her where her friends were going to do their work experience.

She lapsed back into monosyllables. 'Er . . . Like banks.'

I couldn't really think of a way to spin the conversation out after untangling the exact dates of her arrival, which seemed to involve me guessing when she might need to come and her grunting negatively or positively ('Half-term?' 'First half of term?' 'Oh, I see, the first week of term?'). As I put the phone down I reminded myself that I didn't want to be a responsible grown-up who pointed out how much better a career she could have if she went into banking.

Ella in an office! I couldn't imagine it. It seemed only weeks since Lindsey brought her home in a frilled

Moses basket from her high-tech hospital birth, a starched and efficient maternity nurse hovering in a uniform at her elbow, whisking Ella off every time her nappy needed changing.

This reminded me that it was only a few months before Laura was due to pop. She was planning to do it in a vast paddling pool already hired for the purpose, which was currently stowed, folded up, behind their sofa. The only floor that would be strong enough to take it when it was filled with gallons of water was their kitchen-cum-dining room which doubled up as the children's playroom.

As I put the phone down on Lindsey and Ella, murmuring more congratulations, I thought I'd better call Laura, and see if she was okay.

She answered with her mouth full.

'Mm?'

I gave her a moment to swallow, and asked if she'd heard from Lindsey. I hoped she wasn't going to be churlish and defensive about the achievement.

'Mmm. Good news, isn't it?'

Whew. She wasn't. Presumably because an MBE was so far away from anything either of us would ever achieve that there was no point in getting jealous about it.

'She wants to take us both to the Palace instead of Sandy.'

'I know. I don't think I'll go though, I'll be too busy with the baby.'

I was startled. Giving up a few hours with a small baby to support her sister on her special day didn't seem much of a sacrifice. Whatever her faults, Lindsey was always there for us, always included us in her parties, rang us up regularly, and frequently connived to pick up a bill without anyone feeling in debt to her. What sort of care did babies need anyway? I felt a twinge of fear.

And if Lindsey wanted us there, I just assumed we should move heaven and earth to go.

I wondered whether Laura had thought it through. 'Don't you think it matters to her to have us there? You know, to support her?'

'She's got plenty of people to show off to. She doesn't need us.' There was no malice in Laura's tone. As far as she was concerned, Lindsey was her elder sister, and, as such, it was her job to pick up the pieces — or the bills. It had clearly never occurred to Laura that she might have anything to offer in return.

I wondered if it was worth trying to change her mind. 'Couldn't you find someone to look after the baby? It's only a morning, you know. Plus lunch. Knowing Lindsey she'd stump up for a very good lunch.'

Laura sighed. 'Honestly, Leonie, you don't understand. At that age, very small babies need their mothers constantly. I can hardly just leave him or her for something as frivolous as a lunch, however good, and I can hardly take a baby to the Palace, can I?'

Probably not. 'Oh well,' I left it there. 'I presume you're right. How's it all going anyway?'

We discussed the birthing pool for a bit, and I asked Laura if she minded giving birth in a room that people would wander in and out of, making cups of tea and slices of toast while she grunted away.

'I'm sorry,' she'd told me, 'but birth is a perfectly natural process, you know. I want to share it with Phoebe and Zack. Make the baby part of the family from the start.'

I hoped it wouldn't traumatize either of them, and wondered how Paul and the midwife would cope if the arrival of the baby's head coincided with one of Zack's fiendish tantrums. But perhaps the children would be overawed by the majesty and wonder of birth, like it says in the books. I really did hope that Will and I weren't going to get hauled in on the experience. It would be just like Laura, what with Will being a doctor, and her constant desire to make me 'understand'. It was going to require some courage just to visit her in the first few weeks, and be made to hold the tiny, wrinkled being, let alone be present at the birth.

Later, as I rifled through the post, I found a card from James and Jennifer, announcing the arrival of 'Amelia Daisy weighing 7lb 6oz. Born at home'. I tossed it into the bin. I couldn't think why, but I'd reckoned Jennifer for a Caesarian type myself. She just didn't seem like a warm paddling-pool kind of person.

I told myself, very firmly, that this baby business was turning me into a complete and utter bitch, and if I started classifying my fellow woman by the kind of birth she had, I would very shortly go mad.

The next two weeks passed in a blur of discomfort and waiting. I faded away under an anaesthetic again, and came round to hear that I had passed the first test. There were 'good' eggs. I felt irrationally optimistic, but, once they had been fertilized and uncomfortably re-implanted, I became obsessed with time. Meetings seemed to stretch to hours, measured out in promises of rewards to myself if I could manage, for one hour – or even five minutes – not to think about whether it had all been successful. The words 'pregnant? not pregnant?' ticked away implacably in my brain like a timebomb waiting to go off. And then, of course, the whole fortnight was shrouded in the oppressive fog of failure once the daily injections stopped and it was immediately clear that the fertilized eggs, implanted with such optimism, had simply slipped out again without even attempting to 'take'.

'Ah, well,' we said to each other. 'The first attempt never works. We'll have better luck next time.' But I felt terribly afraid that I would never, ever succeed. I hid this from Will, furtively, as if it was a dirty secret.

But as the summer sped by, and I apprehensively started the whole cycle all over again, writing out the huge cheques and worrying about how long we really could carry on at this rate, I looked forward to seeing Ella on her own as an emergent adult, instead of flanked by Lindsey, who never stopped adjusting her collar, straightening her clothes or commanding her to get her hair off her face.

One morning, in early September, she trailed into the offices at *How?*, sidling in against the walls for as long as she could (there's not much protection in an open-plan office) and blushing every time anyone spoke to her.

'Hello, Leonie.' She drooped self-consciously over my desk, having been told by both Lindsey and me to drop the 'aunt' title. She never used it all that much anyway.

She had two silver rings through her top lip. I tried not to stare at them. After all, I was a sophisticated magazine editor, not someone from the Dark Ages.

'Does . . . er . . . Lindsey know about that?'

She looked innocent. 'What?'

'Your, um, lip thingies.'

Ella shrugged. 'Dunno.'

'Oh, well.' I sounded rather too bright and breezy, even to my ears. But piercing was fine on royalty and the trendy middle-aged. On one's own sweet little niece, well . . . And wasn't fourteen really seriously a bit young for all that?

'I expect you'd like to know how magazines work?'

She fiddled with a toggle on her bag. 'If you like.' But I could see her eyes gleaming with interest.

'A call for you,' Lucy gesticulated. 'Peter Rennie.'

'Sorry,' I mouthed, taking the phone and indicating that Lucy should introduce Ella to Camilla, feeling relieved that at least I had one member of staff with a pierced navel to make her feel at home. It was, I reminded myself, not the immediate prelude to sex, drugs and rock 'n' roll. Or was it?

I felt rather queasy, as Camilla bore her off ruthlessly to the toppling pile of envelopes known as the incoming post tray. It took about two hours to sort every morning, and was guaranteed to see off any student who was less than one thousand per cent committed to being a journalist.

Queasy! Perhaps I was pregnant. My heart leapt for a second. But no, a pregnancy at this stage was not possible, according to the scans I was now having every two or three days. I was so monitored now that I knew exactly what was going on in my body, and any element of surprise – except for the constant possibility of bad news about over- or under-stimu-lated follicles – had been completely erased from my life. No, the wobbly sensation around my knees was because having a cold sore or a cracked lip was painful enough without inflicting anything on oneself in the name of fashion. What did the school say about it? And hadn't I read something about tongue cancer and tongue studs in *The Times*? I felt anxiously aware that I was responsible for Ella's well-being this week, and that perhaps I had a responsibility to prevent her from getting oral cancers in my office.

'Is Ella all right?' I inquired worriedly of Camilla

later on that morning, suddenly remembering my aunt-like responsibilities.

'Ella?' Camilla looked surprised. 'Seems fine. She's going into the fashion cupboard after the post.'

Ella spent the rest of the morning photocopying ear-rings, and wrapping up and marking pairs of shoes to be sent to a photographic studio. She did seem fine. Just a bit quiet. I reminded myself that tongue studs and lip rings were perfectly normal these days and that I mustn't be judgemental. After all, couldn't I remember how much fuss there'd been over ear-piercing when I was fourteen? Things had just moved on a bit, that's all.

There was a phone call from Dave Beckett, this time to Camilla, and all worries about studs and rings, cancerous or no, flew right out of my head.

Camilla put the phone down. 'He wants a party. On the day the Christmas Bellingham Glass supplement comes out. He said business gets done at parties these days. He thinks a joint event between *How?* and Bellingham Glass would be good for both of us.'

'Would it indeed?' I wasn't so sure about that.

'He'll pick up the tab. All we have to do is find somewhere stylish.'

This, alas, was a more serious proposition. Prestigious parties were good for business. They made people believe in you.

'And he wants to invite all the musicians. Especially Saffron Perry.'

I felt a finger of colour creep up my neck.

'You don't like her, do you?' Camilla leant forward confidingly.

Camilla and I had got a lot closer, but not that close. I saw Ella hovering nervously over me.

'Yes, Ella?' It saved me having to answer.

'I just wondered what I should do now?'

I realized I hadn't explained the workings of magazines to her. 'Sit down,' I indicated the chair in front of me. 'I'll tell you what happens and how we put the magazine together.'

Her eyes lit up with a sparkle I remembered from childhood. She'd been so sweet and enthusiastic, full of hugs and stories. Perhaps, if we really spent some time together I could resurrect that generous personality and its innocent pleasure in life. She couldn't have got totally cynical quite so soon, could she? Not in Sandy's and Lindsey's over-protected, plumped-up, sanitized household.

As she sat down, I glanced at my watch. 'Shit!'

'Sorry?'

'God, I'm really really sorry, but I'll have to fly.' I could hardly say that I had just under twenty-five minutes to get to the hospital for a scan.

Lucy and Camilla looked surprised. 'There's nothing in your diary,' said Lucy, trying to be helpful. 'Unless you're thinking of the editors' lunch upstairs, but that isn't for another hour.'

'I'm not thinking of the editors' lunch.' I pulled my coat on. 'It's an emergency dental appointment. Pain came on during the night.'

Lucy and Camilla were both obviously still puzzled, I could see, as I shot towards the door, shouting at Lucy to let Peter Rennie know I might be late. I was beginning to run out of excuses. Perhaps this dental treatment had better get a bit more complicated. But I did hate lying.

Ella seemed resigned. She had grown up with adults rushing off to mysterious appointments.

'Here,' I heard Camilla say kindly to her. 'Why don't you go through this pile of newspapers and magazines and look for stories about women you think might be worth featuring?'

It took ages to find a taxi and I was ten minutes late for my appointment. Which didn't, in the end, matter because when I got there, panting with anxiety and the effort of running up three flights of stairs, I found that the clinic itself was running twenty-five minutes late. All of which added up, what with taxis in the lunch hour being scarcer than faithful Cabinet Ministers, to my subsequently being three-quarters of an hour late for the editors' lunch. Peter Rennie glared at me, and even Maeve, who was not very punctual her-self, looked disapproving. I tried to look sufficiently like someone who'd been to the dentist, getting instantly and perilously entangled in sympathetic questions from Belinda Bracken about root-canal work.

None of which mattered even the tiniest bit, I

thought, as I virtually flew back to 37 Branworth Terrace that evening.

'The day after tomorrow!' I shrieked, wrapping myself round Will as he came in the door half an hour later. 'The day after tomorrow!'

He kissed me briefly and got a handkerchief out of his pocket, blowing his nose loudly.

'Good.' He knew what I meant. Egg collection. He blew his nose again, more thoroughly this time.

I stood back. 'Have you got a cold?' I couldn't keep the sharpness out of my voice. A virus could play havoc on his sperm count. We had been told, by a doctor friend of Will's over a Sunday lunch, of a man whose sperm count had been absolutely normal at the start of treatment, but that when it came to Egg Collection Day, it had dropped to zero, simply because of a bout of flu. What I hadn't asked, and didn't know, was how long it had taken to reach wipeout. Days? Months? Could this cold affect the day after tomorrow? Or would it mean a zilch sperm count for a cycle in three months' time? Panic gripped my insides, bloated as they were with drugs.

I asked Will.

'I don't know.' His voice was tired and thick, spelling out the onset of a real shocker of a cold. He dropped his briefcase with a thud in the hall and opened the door under the stairs to hang up his coat.

With the greatest self-control I suppressed the desire to scream, 'Why don't you know? You're a doctor.'

It was all I could do just to turn away, and start slicing vegetables, trying not to cry. I had to be stuffed full of different kinds of injections, and be probed, tagged and anaesthetized. He merely had to stay healthy. Even a doctor should be able to manage that.

I knew I was being unfair. Life's unfair.

'It's only a cold,' said Will, turning the television on. 'It won't matter.'

The following morning, still worried about the possible onset of flu, I reminded him to book himself out for Wednesday.

Will looked, if anything, worse than he had the night before. 'Christ!' he said. 'I hadn't thought about that. This bug is flying round the doctors and the patients. There's only me and old Brodie on at the moment, and the waiting room is crammed.'

'This is,' I pointed out with some restraint, 'the bit that concerns you. You know, fertilization? Your chance to shine?' I wished I didn't sound so sarcastic, but I was frightened. It all seemed to be slipping away again, after all these weeks of effort.

'I know, I know.' He sounded resigned, as if conceiving our baby was just another chore. 'Okay, I'll sort it somehow. Just don't worry about it.' We now seemed to have got ourselves into a kind of old-fashioned doctor-patient relationship with this – I felt helpless and out of control, and looked to him for all the answers. He, meanwhile, never seemed to tell me anything, and appeared to be trying to wrap me in cotton wool.

He paused for a second before he closed the door. 'I promise, sweetheart, I will do everything I can. But please don't expect miracles.' He gave a ghost of a smile. 'They take a little longer.'

Well, did he think it was easy for me, constantly lying about dentists and trying to account for my movements every other day? But I knew that he saw his job as important, and mine as relatively frivolous. It didn't really matter, in his view, if a meeting about the latest trend in shoes got delayed to another day, but you couldn't turn your back on a surgery full of desperate mothers and sick children, one of whom might easily have meningitis or asthma or something else really serious.

And he was right, of course. At the heart of it all, he was right.

But it didn't make it any easier. All-day root-canal work? Another funeral? I was having to get more inventive by the day.

In the end I opted simply to take a day off, then another day off on Friday. It seemed the easiest option, although Camilla, Lucy, Polly and Deirdre were all baffled.

'Why don't you take Thursday and Friday off?' suggested Camilla, smoothing a microscopic suede skirt over her bottom, 'and have a nice long weekend?'

I muttered something about things that had to be done on Wednesday.

'It seems a bit of a waste to come in on the Thursday,' suggested Polly, pushing a straggle of unwashed blonde hair behind her ears. 'Why don't you take three days off?'

'Because there's too much to do,' I snapped. Couldn't I even take a holiday without having to explain it to everyone from the postboy to Peter Rennie?

'Peter for you,' said Lucy, holding out a phone.

I tried to fight off a suggestion from Peter that I join a focus group on Friday afternoon, scheduled to go over recent issues of the magazine and tell us which features were most liked. However, Friday's re-implantation – always assuming that I had any eggs this time and that Will's sperm hadn't been decimated – wasn't under anaesthetic. The clinic had said before that I could go back to work afterwards, and that, once in, fertilized eggs didn't drop out. Personally I couldn't believe this, and was determined to take myself to bed with a soppy novel, drinking gallons of tea and relaxing. It was going to be the treat I'd promised myself for getting through the experience for the second time.

Still, what with Will's cold and everything, it seemed quite likely there might not be a re-implantation so I settled, therefore, for the whole of Wednesday off, plus Friday morning. It was clearly the oddest holiday timing any of them had ever heard of. I faced a row of perplexed faces, muttered about gas meter readers and having chairs upholstered, and then decided that they could mind their own businesses.

I heard Lucy stammering as she moved my appointments. 'I'm terribly sorry, but Leonie won't be in that day,' she told a prominent advertiser.

His secretary obviously gave her a hard time because I heard her say, 'Oh, I really am sorry. I'm afraid it's all my fault. She's been booked out for weeks, and she just can't change her flight. Will you tell him she was very angry with me for messing up this appointment?'

I was touched. Lucy had no idea why or where I was going, but she was still prepared to lie for me. Rather convincingly, too, by the sound of it.

22

Wednesday morning sparkled against a brilliant autumn dawn, as Will and I trooped off to the Tube station, silent with nerves and scuffing our feet against a drift of brown and red leaves that had fallen from the prolific lime trees which lined the street in a higgledy-piggledy way.

The tall, grey slab of the hospital building now seemed familiar, almost homely even. Once we strode through the great glass double doors, my heart suddenly lifted, and I felt a sense of liberation and purpose. This was it. The beginning of the end. I headed confidently down the left-hand corridor. Will hung back, still needing to check the signposts to ensure we were heading in the right direction.

'Don't worry,' I tugged his arm. 'I know where everything is.' It was now my territory, and I exchanged comfortable 'hellos' with the two receptionists and, later, with the usual radiographer. There were several men waiting nervously round one coffee table, reading magazines and avoiding everyone's eye. I nudged Will. 'That door,' I whispered, pointing to a door beside them. 'Since last time they've changed where you go to . . . you know.'

His face crinkled in amusement, as he took in

the three furtive-looking men trying to pretend they weren't queuing to jerk off into test tubes. Everyone knew what that room was for. One of them looked at his watch. A few seconds later, so did the other two, casting anxious glances at the door, and sighing.

'Looks like some poor bugger can't quite manage it,' he whispered back. I hid a smile, as the door opened, and a man in a pin-striped suit scuttled out, looking at the ground. A chap in jeans and a fleece stood up, said, 'Cheers, mate,' and swaggered in before the door could close. Pin Stripe Suit swerved nervously away from him and bolted out into the hallway.

A motorcycle messenger appeared at reception. 'Delivery from Sweizer Bank.' He took his helmet off and proffered a chart for the receptionist to sign.

'Oh, yes,' said the blonde one, who I knew as Patty, 'that'll be Mr Elliott's sperm.' She turned to the Indian receptionist, Bindu. 'He's always on some takeover bid or something, and never has time to come in.'

Bindu smiled and whisked it off to the lab. The motorcycle messenger looked horrified. 'Jesus!' he said. 'Is that what I've been carrying?' He slammed his helmet back on, and strode out.

Will and I, holding hands, suppressed a giggle. 'I think he reckons that ferrying fresh sperm across London is more or less a homosexual act,' murmured Will.

'I expect he'll need counselling,' I whispered back, wondering about Mrs Elliott, and how she felt about her husband's absence. Presumably he earned squillions and she spent it, probably on IVF treatments, and that was their deal. It seemed bleak. The phrase 'never has time to come in' seemed ominous too. Mrs Elliott, whoever she was, was clearly one of the unsuccessful statistics.

Will's hand was wrapped protectively round mine. Even his cold seemed better. Perhaps everything would be fine this time, after all. A ray of sunshine struggled through the grimy windows of the hospital and stretched out towards us.

'I'm afraid I can't be here on Friday, for the re-implantation,' he said. 'I'm really sorry.'

'Oh, no!' I gazed at him appalled. 'Why not?'

He squeezed my hand. 'Seriously, I would if I could. But technically I'm not needed, and I simply can't take any more time off.'

'But I have to take time off.'

'I know.' He squeezed my hand again, and I snatched it away. 'But you can and I can't. My surgery is only open between certain hours, and sick people have to be helped. I can't go on letting them down. You can catch up after hours if necessary.'

My eyes filled with tears, as much at the reminder of the backlog of work that kept piling up at the office as at the thought that Will couldn't, after all, be with me all the way, as he'd promised.

It was easier to complain about the work. 'Yes, but I keep trying to catch up and it's swamping me. There's so much, all the time, everybody needs something from me. And now you're not going to be here.' This incoherent outburst finished up slightly louder than I'd intended and everyone looked up. They looked down again immediately, anxious to avoid our eyes. They each, in different ways, doubtless had quite enough to deal with in their own lives. They didn't need any second-hand drama. The glossy pages of magazines rustled in the silence like wind through a forest. In spite of my distress at thinking that Will wasn't coming with me on Friday, I couldn't help craning my head to see if any of them were reading *How?*. They weren't, although I could see several copies of *My Life*, and one *Home Life*.

'Anyway,' he tried to appease me, 'I promise that if either of the two sick doctors come back, or if we can find another locum, I will come. That's the best I can do.'

I knew that they'd never find another locum just for a Friday morning, and that the two doctors who were off were really quite ill. And I also knew that I could go through the re-implantation process perfectly well on my own. It was only selfishness wanting Will to be there, but I did want to be selfish. Just a bit. I wanted him to hold my hand, and to see the miracle of the little divided cells, magnified 100 times on screen, before they were re-implanted.

Mind you, I was getting ahead of myself. As I knew so well, there might not be enough good eggs to go ahead with the re-implantation anyway. Will's sperm might have been decimated by his cold. The eggs might not fertilize. Once fertilized they might begin to break up. There were, as the experts so assiduously told me at every possible opportunity, no guarantees. I started to feel nervous again. Please, God, I don't mind Will not being here as long as there are eggs. And sperm. I couldn't pray much further ahead. I took another article about a house out of my bag to take my mind off everything. It was about a couple who'd created their entire kitchen out of recycled motorbike parts. Will read an old copy of the *Spectator*.

There's something slightly creepy about walking into an operating theatre and getting up on the slab yourself. It underlines the fact that you are about to have the kind of operation that, for most people, would be deemed quite unnecessary. It makes it feel frivolous – no, not quite that, indulgent, perhaps. A rich woman's operation. A bit like cosmetic surgery. I lay down and winced as the anaesthetist jammed a drip into the vein of my hand.

But all operations mean giving up responsibility for yourself for a while. I handed my consciousness over to the operating team with a sigh of relief.

I couldn't quite understand what they were saying when I came round, but Will was smiling and squeezed my hand as I slipped back to sleep again.

When I sat up again, quite efficiently this time, Will had disappeared.

For a second, I panicked and suddenly felt sick and dizzy.

He came back. 'Oh hello, you're awake. I was just in the loo.'

'Well?'

'Fine. Nine eggs.'

'Nine! Brilliant.' I lay back. That was better than last time. Surely, from now on, it was plain sailing.

Except for the sperm. I shot up again. 'What about you?'

'All fine. We haven't had the results yet, but they didn't seem to think a cold would make much difference. You need a good bout of real flu to decimate sperm.'

Do you? Well, I presumed he'd know. I was beginning to find out that there were still whole chunks of science and medicine that still couldn't quite be quantified. It was reassuring in a way, as if fate, rather than man, was still in control.

It almost seemed too easy. There were so many problems that could have tripped us up again.

'How was it for you, darling?' I tried a joke. 'Did the *Spectator* make the earth move?'

His face clouded over. 'It was fine.' His voice was final.

Oh dear. I could see that pin-striped bankers might have a problem with admitting to having sex with a test tube. You'd have thought a doctor could be a bit more down-to-earth about it all. Still, it was clearly no laughing matter.

We got home in time for Will to nip back to the

surgery and do the afternoon slot after all. I sat in bed, feeling slightly depressed, a complete fraud and wondering if I felt too wobbly to go into the office.

I didn't have to bother. Camilla rang.

'It's Dave Beckett,' she announced. 'He demands to know if we've fixed a date and venue for this party yet.'

I thought about the way tufts of hair sprouted from his ears, and shuddered.

'He wants to make sure it's oopmarket enough,' added Camilla maliciously. 'Classy like. And most of all he wants us to make sure it's a date that Saffron Perry can make.'

I had almost forgotten about her. Really.

'Well, he'll have to take pot luck,' I told Camilla briskly, 'because I'm not organizing this party round Saffron's availability.'

We fixed on early November, and Camilla agreed to get Lucy to book a room at either the Savoy or the Ritz.

'Shall I get Saffron's number off the fashion department?' Camilla inquired, sounding deceptively innocent. 'Or would you like to give it to me?'

I thought for a moment. I'd had a few words about Bellingham Glass with Maeve, and she'd made it quite clear that, in the current climate, we desperately needed big spenders like Dave Beckett. Many of the major advertisers came through Brian Carstairs' company, but we had direct access to Bellingham Glass, and that was invaluable.

'Oh, God, never mind.' I lumbered to my feet, feeling very slightly dizzy as I stood up. 'I'll get her bloody number. And don't go to enormous lengths, but you might as well find out if there are any evenings both she and the Ritz have free in early November.' With any luck, I thought, she'd be off with the German composer again.

One thing was certain, however. Will was not, definitely not, going to be invited to this party.

23

Saffron was utterly charming to Lucy on the telephone on Thursday afternoon.

'She's awfully nice, isn't she?' Lucy replaced the phone. She often had to put up with unbelievable stick from women who thought they were too important to be polite to secretaries. 'She said she'd be delighted to come,' Lucy continued. 'She asked if we wanted her to wear the same dress as she wore on the cover of the supplement.'

'How sweet of her.' My voice dripped acid. 'I expect Dave Beckett would have an instant orgasm.'

Lucy looked hurt. I reminded myself that she wasn't responsible for the situation. What I really hated about Saffron was how she always brought out the worst in me. After any kind of Saffron encounter I felt spiritually, emotionally and physically lumpen. Unattractive. Unpleasant. Mean-minded. All those things.

Camilla watched me with interest. I was dreading this party. Really dreading it. What would I say to Saffron? 'Hands off my husband'? As far as I could see, she had given up. But it niggled me that I'd never told him about her role in the Bellingham Glass supplements.

I tried to reason the niggle away, reassuring myself,

firstly, that I never usually told him everything that happened in my day. I hadn't discussed Bellingham Glass – why should I? It was too small a part of my workload. That's what I'd told myself when Saffron's involvement was first discussed, when I hadn't expected it to be more than one picture buried in an easy-to-discard supplement. And, secondly, that it was perfectly sensible not to start discussing it just because Dave Beckett wanted her on the cover. It would have meant a reminder of that one night. Admittedly, I'd visualized myself telling Will casually over dinner, but somehow the moment had never come up. That didn't matter. There was no reason why it should.

Now Dave Beckett wanted a party, with Saffron virtually as guest of honour. Was her involvement beginning to lie between Will and me like a dirty secret? Of course not. After all, I was hardly ashamed of myself. In fact, I thought I'd done pretty well to override my personal feelings about Saffron for professional reasons. This party would be my best chance to prove – to myself, if no one else – that the Saffron issue was no longer important in my – our – life.

I wasn't quite sure of my own logic, though. The niggle wouldn't quite go away, like a grain of sand in your shoe. You can usually persuade yourself that you don't feel it for a few minutes after giving your foot a good shake, but it inevitably works its way back into the middle of your consciousness again. I could feel Saffron there under my foot, a small, sharp grain in a sensitive spot.

I thought about this for a bit, and suddenly realized something. Apart from anything else, the fact that Will still didn't know was proof that he hadn't been seeing Saffron. There was no way, if he'd spoken to her, that she wouldn't have told him about Bellingham Glass.

I thought a bit more. On the other hand, if she had told him, he could hardly talk to me about it because it would have been proof that he had seen her.

Suspicion, dormant for the past few weeks, began to fester again. The trust between us, I thought sadly, was still so fragile that the slightest thing – such as Saffron in the Bellingham Glass brochure – could shatter it.

I shook myself, and decided to worry about something else. Like who should be invited to this party, and what form it should take. Parties are big business now. You need the right people. Between us, Lucy, Dave Beckett, Camilla and I fixed on 6 November. Coincidentally, it was the day Laura's baby was due. I had to admit that given the choice between paddling around the edge of a birthing pool in Earlsfield, trying to subdue Phoebe and Zack, and sipping champagne at the Ritz with Saffron, I might even, for the first time in my life, prefer the Saffron alternative.

Thinking about Laura reminded me of Ella. I'd hardly had time to pay attention to her, and the week was almost up.

'How's Ella?' I asked Lucy.

'Fine. She's been at the studio with Fashion. I think

she's been on the New Cosy shoot. In front of the camera.'

This was a bombshell. Lindsey would kill me if Ella started modelling. I had visions of her being whisked off to catwalks in Paris and Milan. Sandy and Lindsey were propelling her towards Oxford or Cambridge, and anything that 'took her eye off the ball', as Lindsey put it, was strictly off limits.

'Don't worry,' said Camilla, who had got remarkably adept at reading my mind. 'She was just that black blur that you have to have on sofas in photographs these days. You know, a person moving so much that you can't really see them, dressed in a black T-shirt. Just a feeling of life rather than a person.'

I relaxed. It would give her a thrill without suggesting any ideas about catwalks.

But I had still failed in my duty to explain to her how magazines worked, and ask her what she wanted to know.

'Ella,' I called, as she came back in. 'Sit down. How was the shoot?'

'Well,' she said cautiously, 'I didn't think those suede cube things were all that cosy.'

'I don't suppose they were.' The point of the New Cosy was that it wasn't. You sort of perched on things, and appreciated textures.

I leaned forwards to explain this to her, and our eyes met, gleaming in complicity. She thought it was funny too. Suddenly I looked forward to the day, when this awkward phase was over, when we could open a bottle of wine together and laugh the way we used to, but as equals. It would come. It would definitely come, if only we could keep a line of communication open while she struggled to find out who she was going to be.

I picked up a dummy issue of the magazine from my desk, to show Ella how it was all put together, and the phone rang.

'It's for you.' Lucy punched it through. 'Peter Rennie about tomorrow's focus group.'

It seemed to have been a very long time since I last finished a sentence. Laura always complained that you could never do anything with small children underfoot. I was beginning to think much the same about managing directors.

When I finished the conversation, Ella had gone, because she had to be back by six. Lindsey would have gone ballistic otherwise.

I woke up on Friday morning and turned to look at Will.

'Sorry, hon,' he mumbled. 'I couldn't swing it. I'll be thinking of you.'

I didn't say anything and swung out of bed to have a shower. Later, he stopped me. 'Listen, I do really want to come, you know. I'm not ducking out. It's important to me, too.'

I put my arms round him. 'I know.' I did know. I just felt angry, that's all. I wanted to come first, not at the end of a line of patients and Saffron.

I gave myself a firm ticking off on the way to the hospital. Saffron was no longer relevant, and, as for the patients, they didn't want to be in line either, coughing and sneezing, and almost definitely feeling worse than I was. Think of poor Mrs Elliott, the banker's wife, with her husband's sperm being ferried all over town by motorbike messenger. She obviously saw even less of him than I did of Will. Women like me and Mrs Elliott had to remember that real life wasn't like a fairy story, that our princes couldn't just get on a white horse and gallop over everyone else to be at our side.

I'd almost cheered myself up by the time I arrived. Then I sat in the queue for an extra twenty minutes waiting for the implantation. When I'd gone through this before I'd expected it to feel meaningful. The beginning of a new life.

This time I knew it was going to be too uncomfortable to allow any real emotions, because they asked me to have a full bladder before inserting a speculum, which was followed by the cannula containing the little clusters of cells, a long tube slipped up me, replacing them safely where they were supposed to be. It didn't really hurt, but it made me feel edgy, and I didn't dare go to the loo for at least half an hour afterwards in case the three little clusters of cells I'd gazed at so worriedly on the screen fell out.

'They won't,' the nurse reassured me.

'But how do you know?' I pressed her. The failure rate of sixty per cent might be entirely due to women going to the loo too soon afterwards. You'd never find out.

I saw the nurse bite her lip. 'Just take it from me,' she said firmly. 'We do know they don't drop out.'

It seemed to be the only thing that anyone was prepared to give me a one hundred per cent guarantee on. I didn't trust it.

The next two weeks stretched ahead of me in an agony of waiting. I felt like a child who has been told that Father Christmas probably won't be coming this year, but who still feverishly counts down the days in the desperate hope that it will turn out well after all.

One evening, when I was tense with worry, Will sided with the nurses in an all-medics-together stance.

'If they say the fertilized eggs won't drop out, then they won't. If you knew the science behind it, you wouldn't worry.' He poured himself a glass of wine in celebration, briefly hovering over my glass before I put my hand over the rim. Better not drink if I was pregnant. Might be pregnant. Once again, we were on a different agenda. But I really should tell him about Saffron and the party.

'You know the Bellingham Glass supplements . . .'

He looked at me, worn out. 'Not really.'

'Well, it's a company which . . .' I began.

He began flicking through the paper absent-mindedly. 'There's a load of rubbish on tonight.'

'Are you listening?' I tried not to sound sharp.

'Yes, you're talking about a glass company.' He

made a gallant attempt to look extremely attentive. 'What sort of glass company?'

'Oh, a horrid, vulgar one run by a funny little man who used to be in animal foodstuffs. We've done a series of supplements with them and . . .'

His eyes had drifted over to the papers again.

It was pointless. I could, of course, get his attention by barking Saffron's name at him, but I wasn't sure that would actually achieve anything.

Oh well, he wasn't likely to come to the party anyway, or even hear that Saffron was there. It was just that if he did, he was going to wonder why I hadn't told him all about it.

'Sorry, darling, you were saying?' I could see he was longing to switch on the news.

'Never mind.'

'Really?' He pulled me down and squeezed me close. It felt safe. Much better than the New Cosy. I didn't really want a conversation about Saffron, not when things were beginning to feel good again.

I had thought that the second lot of waiting would be easier than the first. That, having experienced it, I might have come to terms with it. Someone once told me that there are two kinds of ways of reacting to this period – either you take to your bed and lie there worrying and watching the clock, or you cram the day with as much activity as possible to try to distract your mind. Much as I hated to conform to a stereotype, I fell, partly through necessity, into the latter. But my mind, although functioning perfectly well on a practical level, simply refused to be distracted at this more fundamental one, and I found myself avoiding the cracks of paving stones, waving at single magpies, and stepping away from any ladders in a desperate desire to propitiate any ancient gods of fertility that might, or might not, be watching over me. I wasted precious minutes scouring horoscopes in the vain hope that one of them might say something as concrete as 'expect the imminent announcement of a pregnancy' but I was left trying to read something meaningful into the usual tantalizing 'the new Moon offers fresh opportunities' or 'with Venus changing signs, you feel a sense of security that helps you come to terms with difficulties'.

The days inched by until the first morning I was allowed to do a pregnancy test. I was shaking as I peered at the blue line, re-checking the instructions to make sure I was doing it right. That one line meant the test was working, a second line one minute later spelt pregnancy.

I turned away and counted, forcing myself not to turn back until the clock told me I could.

And the most wonderful, extraordinary thing happened. I was pregnant. Exactly two weeks after implantation. The sight of the second thin blue line in the window of the pregnancy test kit completely obliterated thoughts of Saffron. The whole topic dwindled in importance down to the size of a pinhead.

There was, after all, no longer any need for worrying

about secrets. It had all been solved by the battery of drugs, the stimulation of follicles, the long, tense waits on the beige moquette chairs. Passion had been put in its place – diminished to a purely recreational trivial pursuit. It made that one-night stand just seem like the silly mistake Will had always told me it had been. It was time to put everything behind us and go on ahead to make a family.

I could hardly wait. 'Will,' I said, trying to sound off-hand, as I buttered some toast.

He bundled everything into his briefcase, and looked up with a furrow of anxiety across his face, and started to say something himself. 'Darling. I wanted to talk about . . .'

It could wait. I told him.

Will looked overwhelmed. 'Are you feeling all right?'

'Fine, fine,' I said feverishly. 'Wonderful, in fact.' My slice of toast heaved and curdled of its own volition, and I surreptitiously slipped it into the bin.

He held me tight. 'I knew we'd get there in the end.'

We pored over our diaries, delightedly picking out a day in July. 'The Second.' He circled it triumphantly.

It seemed a long way off.

'Plenty of time to get the kitchen turned into a proper family room.' The thought of a baby had obviously woken Will's dormant practicality. 'Can you get some brochures in?' He made another note in his diary. 'And I'll speak to a good architect.'

He kissed me, then left, closing the door with a soft click. The satisfaction of having finally given him what he really wanted crept through me, warming my veins with pleasure. I gazed at our small patch of garden. In my mind's eye, I saw a plump baby sitting on a tartan rug in the middle of the lawn. Our baby.

On the way in, on the Tube, I couldn't resist a look at the horoscopes, to see what star sign it would be. Cancer. Unless it was very, very late, which first babies often are, apparently, when it might just be a little Leo.

I rang Laura, because Lindsey would be in a meeting and Mum did the Red Cross on Friday mornings.

There was a short silence.

'Are you telling people already?' she demanded. 'Don't you know that over thirty per cent of pregnancies end in miscarriage?'

'I'm not telling people, Laura. I'm telling you. You're my sister, in case you'd forgotten.'

'I'm just warning you to be careful, that's all.' She sounded aggrieved.

'Thirty per cent of your pregnancies haven't ended in miscarriage, have they?'

'Well, no, but . . .'

'And my telling you isn't going to make the slightest difference as to whether I have a miscarriage or not.'

'I never told anyone until thirteen weeks.' Much as I love my sister, she does have to bring every conversation round to herself eventually. We put the phone down on each other shortly afterwards, presumably both feeling misunderstood.

Mum, when I finally got her, was surprised. 'Darling! Are you sure it's what you wanted?' We hadn't told any of them about the IVF treatment, as I'd decided I'd prefer to be on the end of the mild disapproval meted out to the intentionally childless rather than the cloying sympathy and constant questioning that I'd be subjected to if the family knew we were 'trying'.

'Yes, why shouldn't I have a baby?'

'I don't know, dear, I'd just assumed you'd decided to be a career woman.'

I ground my teeth. 'As, indeed, I shall be.'

'Very young children do need their mothers, you know.'

I was regularly treated to this diatribe when discussing Lindsey, although my mother occasionally switched sides – just to keep me on my toes – and criticized Laura for not getting a job: 'I really think those children would be better behaved if she got a good nanny.' Until now, I had murmured sympathetically in agreement with her in either case. After all, Lindsey's children clearly did need to see more of her, and Laura's children would undoubtedly be improved by a dose of boot camp. I'd tentatively discussed Mum's attitude with Lindsey once, who had replied crisply, 'A mother's place is in the wrong.' Well, it was up to me to get it right.

Lindsey was brisk and congratulatory. 'That's terrific, sis. Just don't let The Suits at work get the faintest idea until you're about to pop.' She had concealed all three of her pregnancies from higher management behind stiffly tailored outfits until she was seven months, thus ensuring that she got her fair share of various bonuses and promotions. I had once met a colleague of Lindsey's at a party who hadn't realized she'd got children, so apparently brief had been all her pregnancies and maternity leaves.

It wasn't so much The Suits I needed to watch out for, because Maglife was famously reluctant to get involved in any kind of litigation or redundancy that might be related to pregnancy, but Camilla. All these conversations were hissed down the phone when she left her desk to gossip in the art department or re-arrange her clothing yet again in the Ladies loo. Camilla had made it clear that she regarded pregnancy as 'sweet', and obviously assumed that it rotted your brain from Day One. I had sometimes overheard her talking to Mimi rather as nurses talk to elderly patients with dementia. And she was very much in with all the younger, single girls, who deeply resented the fact that pregnant colleagues could have four months off simply because they were having a baby (three weeks, surely, would be quite enough, they'd just be on a great, long, unnecessary paid holiday for the rest of the time).

But Camilla was obsessed with a press party we'd both been invited to.

'What are you going to wear?' she asked happily. 'John Rocha or Armani?'

Nothing too tight, I thought with joy. Surprisingly, my body already felt as if it was beginning to tingle and swell.

24

Five weeks later, I woke up on the morning of the party and pulled open the curtains with a flourish. A sparkling, crystalline frost dusted the row of small front gardens along the street with icing-sugar festivity. The thin November sun cast long shadows over groups of women and children. I watched a small, spindly-legged boy drag his satchel along the ground reluctantly. His mother bundled him into an apparently full car: 'Come on,' I heard her shout. 'I haven't got all day, you know.' For a few moments I watched them drive away, my breath clouding up the window. The day had begun.

'I've got a meeting at the Royal Society,' said Will unexpectedly. 'So I'll be up in town. We could go out to dinner.'

I hesitated feeling, as usual, slightly nauseous. 'There's a party. For Bellingham Glass. Very dull.'

'Don't worry.' He opened his wardrobe and pulled out the sweater I'd bought him for our first Christmas together and started to pull it over his head. 'I don't mind hanging around until it ends.'

'You don't have to.' I picked up a cornflower-blue pot of skin cream and read the ingredients several times over to give myself time to think. It had borage oil and would repair free radical damage. Well, I thought, as I rubbed it in. Just right for tonight. If I wasn't careful there could be some pretty radical damage looming, although it would take more than beta-carotene and vitamin E to deal with it. I replaced the lid. 'Liz Earle', it proclaimed, in sloping writing. My hands smelt faintly of sandalwood.

He was still standing there, waiting to go. 'So where and when?'

I looked at the ends of his sleeves. That jumper ought to be thrown away. Did it really matter? Probably not. I made a final effort to stave off the inevitable. 'I might be feeling a bit too tired to go out later.'

'In that case, we can come home together, and I'll make you beans on toast at home.' I felt guilty. He was trying to be so nice. It was just rather difficult not to snap his head off. What I wanted to say was that bloody Saffron was going to bloody well be there.

What I actually said was, 'It's at The Regency Strand.' I hoped I was doing the right thing. The party was from 6 p.m. to 8 p.m, so if Will appeared at 8.30 there'd be no excuse for him to come in. And Saffron would have gone. He'd never know she was there. But perhaps I ought to mention it anyway. My head began to ache. The timing would require the precision of an air-traffic controller.

He looked in the mirror and didn't seem to notice the state of the sweater.

'Bugger! I'm late again. Sally will have my guts for garters.'

And with a quick, affectionate kiss, he was off.

I spent the last hour of the afternoon reading articles and proofs in the marble splendour of the Charles Worthington salon at the Dorchester, having my business-like bob turned into a suitably festive shape, nibbling a biscuit cautiously to steady the constant nausea. The salon was deep below ground, hidden away from the rest of the hotel. Everything was hushed and the day's bustle slowed to a gentle padding. As the minutes ticked by I felt less and less inclined to leave its safety.

When I eventually stepped out of the Dorchester, I thought, for a moment, that something terrible had happened. In the brief hour I'd spent there, the atmosphere over London had changed completely. A viscous yellow sky, almost like the old winter fogs of the 1950s, smothered Hyde Park and tendrils of thick, heavy cloud wound around my head, suffocating me. The air was leaden and clammy, a damp, seeping mist that caught at the back of my throat, and was surprisingly sharp.

'There's a terrible fog,' said the doorman, raising a hand for a taxi. 'Be careful, now.'

I thanked him, and as I sank back into the taxi, I thought about all the people who used to just walk into the fog and never come back. Some of the disappearances must have been intentional, they must have been waiting for a day like this.

The sense of foreboding continued to thicken, without actually turning into a storm, making us all wrap our coats tighter around our bodies as we set out for the party. We hadn't, in the end, managed to get any of the glittery hotels like the Ritz or even the cool ones like The Metropolitan or One Aldwych, but Dave Beckett seemed more than pleased when we ended up with some reasonably smart place with a name like The Regency Strand. Dressed in the tried and trusted black suit, I stepped confidently through its revolving glass doors at exactly five minutes to six, flanked by Camilla in a fluted column of silk by Amanda Wakely and Lucy in a slightly unsatisfactory jumper and skirt.

The room echoed nervously to our voices.

'Do you think everyone will come?' Lucy sounded anxious. 'There are a couple of other big parties on tonight.'

Camilla shot across the room to bully the staff about not pouring out too much white wine in case it got warm, and then chivvied a waiter, somewhat contradictorily, to be on standby with a tray of full glasses by the door.

The first, rather lost-looking, person drifted through the door at 6 p.m.

I extended a hand for him to shake: 'And you are . . .?'

With a gust of halitosis reminiscent of my mother's

compost heap he explained that he was one of Bellingham's major stockists. Unable to cope with the gusts, I introduced him to Camilla. She quickly offloaded him on to someone else.

It was a slow start, and we'd all introduced Compost Breath to each other several times before a few other guests, looking tentatively about them for more important people, began to trickle in. Eventually, the hum rose to successful levels, like the Kings Road on a Saturday afternoon. A top TV personality did a 'walk-through', arriving, signing in, and working her way from one end of the room to the other before, presumably, going on to one of the other big parties that night. It all seemed pleasantly smooth going. The face of a Cabinet Minister popped up at the door. A Cabinet Minister! He did a quick round of the room and disappeared. I supposed Maeve had invited him.

'Leonie,' said Maeve, who had been patrolling the room and collaring VIPs, and was now gripping my elbow and dragging me over to a richly carved marble fireplace, 'you must meet Clavering Briggs. Did you both see John Hay? You know, the Cabinet Minister?'

Clavering Briggs was a possible American advertiser, 'real innerested in what you're doing here in Yurrup. There's a lot of innovation going on.'

'Innovation,' I repeated, nodding wisely. Around me I could hear people discussing their books.

'My book sold 90,000 copies,' stated a tiny bouffant brunette, teetering on high heels.

'Mine sold 200,000,' countered a statuesque bottle blonde in a trailing designer cardigan.

Clavering Briggs told me that he had always wanted to write a book, so I introduced him to them. I turned to Maeve. 'It was good to get John Hay, wasn't it?'

'At the wrong party,' she whispered. 'Doesn't matter. No one knows.'

Peter Rennie appeared by my side, immaculate in a grey suit and with an Old Boy tie nestling smugly under his lean, craggy face. I introduced him to Dave Beckett.

'We're right pleased with the supplements,' said Dave, scratching his polyester shirt around his middle. 'Once we'd sorted a few things out, eh Leonie?' He winked at me.

I tried to smile back.

'Reckon this magazine business is a licence to print money,' he told Peter Rennie, who looked inscrutable and bowed slightly.

'Indeed, I wish it were.'

'You want a few marketing techniques, you do,' explained Dave. 'Tractors, glass, magazines . . . they're all the same, you know. Cut the costs and the profits go up. Get rid of all the arty-farty fiddling about, and show people what work really is. I could come on board and give you a hand if you liked.'

I froze. I'd seen enough of Dave Beckett's bulk to last me a lifetime.

'How kind.' Peter flashed him a vulpine smile.

There was a commotion by the door, and Dave stiffened. 'Will you excuse me? I've just seen someone I'd like to meet.'

They shook hands, and when he'd disappeared, Peter turned back to me, and raised an eyebrow. 'Tractors indeed.'

I relaxed and grinned at him.

'What's the company really like?'

I hesitated. 'I don't know how it keeps going, to be honest. They seem to sell completely unnecessary things.'

He gave a wry smile. 'I expect people could say that about us. Still, these are tricky times.' We watched Camilla darting in and out of groups, deftly moving in on anyone well known, charming them, passing them on to someone else. She had such confidence.

Peter indicated her with a nod of his head. 'I know everyone thought I brought her on board to please Carstairs, but I think she's got something. And you're doing a very good job of bringing it out. All that desk business was insecurity, you know.'

Possibly. I was warming to Camilla, and almost prepared to give her the benefit of the doubt. The combination of a quick intelligence and an encyclopedic knowledge of accessories had to be a winner in the world of magazines, and things were certainly a lot easier now.

'You're a good manager. I thought you would be. You've got the confidence to give her some responsibility. Some of the others won't.'

I didn't like to tell him that these management techniques he so admired were not so much due to confidence as to the necessity of having scans every other day.

The movement around Dave Beckett intensified into a minor scuffle. Someone was making an entrance.

I knew only one person who could cause that sort of fuss merely going through a door.

Saffron. I caught a toss of the corkscrew curls, and saw her slim, white hand extended to shake his. She sparkled at him for a few moments and turned her head, as if looking for someone. The photographer's flashbulb illuminated her briefly, preventing her from being able to see across the crowd.

But I could see her quite clearly, and I was taken aback. I hadn't seen her for a couple of years, admittedly – perhaps not since the lunch party after the world trip. She had aged. She would always be striking, and the cascade of red hair still tumbled down her back, but the mannish face had plumped out and the slender body had thickened. Bright red lipstick was painted in a hard line around her mouth, and her skin looked powdery. She wasn't wearing the strappy little number from the fashion shoot. Instead something deliciously expensive (where did she get her money from?) was swathed round her in floaty layers. Saffron certainly looked older, and, for the first time ever, almost stocky. Statuesque, perhaps, would be a kinder way to put it, if you were feeling kind, which I wasn't.

'Are you all right?'

I became aware of Peter Rennie looking at me in concern, and pulled myself together. 'Absolutely fine.'

I supposed it must be middle age. The pale skin obviously needed make-up to subdue a few red veins. The thicker middle required cunningly cut layers to deceive the eye. Saffron must be, what? Forty-three or forty-four? Something like that, anyway. I was old enough myself to realize that this didn't really mean anything as far as Will and I were concerned, because she probably had looked like that five months ago, and they'd still slipped into bed together. She looked different from the photographs taken for the Christmas issue, but of course, good lighting and make-up can do almost anything. But it was interesting that James had been wrong about her getting scrawny with age. The extra weight had improved her looks in some ways. The easy victory of a young woman over an older one was not to be taken for granted, however many trophy wives get down-graded every year. But still, it changed something, at least in my own head.

Peter Rennie followed my gaze. Saffron played the part of celeb very well, charming Dave Beckett and his acolytes with the same glittering sympathy that she'd used so effectively in the patisserie in France all those years ago. She gazed at him as if his words were unique, interjecting with one or two soft, bubbling laughs. I watched her turn aside to thank a waiter with a direct gaze and a flattering smile. You'd have thought she was a visiting princess. Occasionally, she'd bring Dave's acolytes into the conversation or tell an amusing story about a performance she'd given. Not once did she look over Dave's shoulder in search of someone else, yet I knew she wouldn't bother with him long. Sure enough, minutes later I saw her at the centre of another group, with Camilla at her elbow, introducing her to Brian Carstairs. Dave Beckett looked after her wistfully, like a dog whose bone has been unexpectedly whisked away.

'Who's that?' Peter Rennie, standing beside me, arms folded, surveyed the party to check whether there was anyone important he needed to talk to.

Camilla popped up beside us. She was very nippy at parties, I'd noticed. 'Saffron Perry. A pianist. She was on the cover of the Bellingham Glass Christmas supplement.'

He nodded. 'Interesting face. Belinda Bracken wants to bring a few good-looking older women on to the pages of *My Life*. I think she might be interested.'

'I'll get her.' Within seconds, Camilla was threading her way expertly through the crowd, touching an arm here, exchanging air kisses there.

I began to prepare my retreat, but Peter caught sight of someone he wanted me to meet, 'As big as Carstairs in his own field,' he murmured in an undertone.

I'd just been treated to chapter and verse on how 'big' the man's company was when Camilla reappeared looking triumphant. I couldn't help wondering if she'd orchestrated this – her eyes darted from me to Saffron and back again, bright with malice. Or perhaps it was just curiosity.

Close up, Saffron looked better. In spite of the changes she was, for her age, very much more striking than she'd been at thirty when beautiful women are ten-a-penny. I could see why she would go down better as an older star than she would as a younger starlet.

'Do you know our editor, Leonie Lucas?' Peter bowed over Saffron's hand.

Her eyes glinted with mischief. 'Of course. I'm an old friend of her husband's. We go back a long way.' She drew out the 'long', and Camilla's eyes sharpened with interest.

'Really?' she drawled. 'And do you still keep in touch?'

Saffron's eyes never left my face. 'Of course. Don't we, Leonie?'

I smiled, keeping as calm as I could, hoping that my rising colour wasn't going to betray me. 'Well, Will and I are so busy these days,' I murmured.

Our eyes met. Her gaze slid away, and she looked expectantly at Peter.

'There's someone I'd like you to meet . . .' He drew Saffron away. 'Excuse us a moment, Leonie?'

I nodded.

She twinkled her hand at me. 'I'll be in touch. Soon.' She blew an air kiss.

Really? I wouldn't be so sure.

Peter, towing Saffron behind him, set off to penetrate the group, hardly noticing the guests parting respectfully as he walked past them.

I didn't care. She was a long way away from everything I had at 37 Branworth Terrace.

About an hour later, Camilla tottered towards me again, looking slightly drunk, and hanging on to Will's arm.

'Look what I've found. Your gorgeous husband.'

He'd put a jacket over the holey jumper.

'I do love shabby chic,' she said, stroking him as if he were made of cashmere and reduced in Harvey Nicks sale. 'So masculine.'

He grinned down at her, and reached towards me. She reluctantly let him go.

I kissed him, and Camilla moved off in search of easier prey. 'Have you been here long?' I tried to look round to see if Saffron had gone, but the room was still too crowded to see easily.

He was just about to tell me when Saffron came dancing towards us. Everybody looked at her.

'William! Darling!'

I smiled. Everyone is called 'darling' in my world. She couldn't claim him as hers with that word.

When she was a few feet away from us, she swirled the soft shawl around her, re-arranging it in an attention-seeking rustle. I remembered these gestures, the way she'd toss her hair back so that it streamed out behind her, the way she could take up the maximum amount of space around herself. This movement, though, was less graceful than usual. Briefly, I was reminded of a carthorse in a tutu, until the shawl was draped and re-draped to her exact satisfaction, and she presented herself with the elegance of a ballerina again. Once a drama queen, always a drama queen, I thought sourly.

'Isn't this a surprise?' The cat's eyes were on Will.

I remembered how she had always loved to flaunt her body, but it had been strange to see the flirtatious gestures on her new, chunky shape.

Will did not reply.

Saffron re-wrapped the pashmina shawl around herself again, and snuggled down into it in a rich-girl gesture, instantly restoring the illusion of slenderness. 'Dave is taking me to Pharmacy.' She twinkled her fingers at us. 'Bye darlings.' She turned her head slightly and I saw the curious hazel eyes narrow. 'Thank you so much, Leonie. You've no idea how much I've looked forward to this evening. I hope we'll see much more of each other in future.' She paused. 'I've been talking to dear Peter about doing some magazine work. Writing, perhaps, as well as modelling. And I've met the most lovely agent, who thinks he'll probably get a six-figure deal on my little novel.'

She had so rarely spoken to me directly that it came as a shock. I'd always thought she'd dismissed me as being of little or no consequence. Will's dreary little wife. But now I knew.

Saffron really hated me. It was an acknowledgement of sorts. I raised my chin in a salute and watched her slender ankles cross in front of each other as she exited the room as if she was walking down a catwalk. She still had wonderful legs. Dave bustled after her, the loose grey fabric of his trousers flapping, reminding me of an elephant in pursuit of a gazelle. So Saffron was writing a novel. That was just about all I needed.

I gazed after them both for a few moments and turned to Will. His face had set, and there was a small muscle twitching in the corner of his cheek. I felt a flutter of panic, and laid a hand on his arm.

'Are you all right?'

He looked into the middle distance, as if calculating something. 'Don't fuss.'

Camilla swooped down. 'Fab party. I'm off to the Ivy.' I could see some young, anonymous man hovering behind her, whose face had not yet been imprinted by life. He was youthful and arrogant, I could see. He knew nothing.

'Let's go.' Will strode past Peter Rennie and Maeve without saying goodbye, and was standing outside the door waiting for me when I caught him up.

'That was rude.'

'I had to get some air. I don't know how you stand those parties.' He stamped his feet and his breath plumed in the cold, mingling with the fog. 'They're stifling.' He was angry.

We'd run an article recently on feelings. It was important to address them, the reader had been informed, quite firmly. I addressed this one and ignored the dig at media parties.

'I did mean to tell you Saffron would be there, but somehow there was never the time.'

'No. That just about sums it up, doesn't it? No time.'

'That's not fair.' I had to skip every few paces to keep up with him. 'Where are we going?'

'In here.' He propelled me into a steel-and-glass shed, roaring with a level of noise that nearly rocked me off my feet. 'Your magazine said that this restaurant was the place.'

That didn't mean I had to be dragged there. I could see a row of chefs in what looked like a stainless steel cage, banging pans at each other and roaring at invisible assistants. A pianist competed with them in a corner and everyone was shouting to make themselves heard. There were hard surfaces everywhere – slate and steel, stone and glass. The lighting, starry and theatrical, hurt my eyes.

What with the digs about the party, and making me go to what was clearly a horrible restaurant, anyone would think that my job was the problem. Perhaps it was. I decided to address a few more feelings.

'Is this all about being jealous of my job?'

'Please!' He looked up in exasperation. 'Don't be fatuous.' He ran his finger down the menu and added, much more kindly, 'And spare me the psycho-babble from your latest articles.'

He ordered us drinks, but didn't say anything for a

full five minutes after that, hiding his face behind the menu. He laid it on the table when the waiter arrived, ordering the first options at the top of each course, carelessly, as if he couldn't care what he ate.

I broke up a small piece of bread into tiny crumbs and arranged them in a geometrical pattern on the table. It was unlike Will to sulk, just because I hadn't told him Saffron was coming. 'Do you want to talk about seeing Saffron?'

'No. I'd just like to forget all about her.'

But you're not succeeding. I didn't say it.

He put his hand gently on mine. 'I'm sorry. You're the one who matters now.'

It sounded like a poor script borrowed from a cheap Hollywood movie. And so unlike Will that I couldn't really be expected to believe it. I dug a fork into a steaming pile of soothing pasta. Comfort food, even if the surroundings weren't all that comfortable.

The pasta was greasy, heavy and leaden. Inside me, something imperceptible hardened, like the beginnings of a crust. It had been just over five months since that fateful night with Saffron, and in that time we had been carefully re-building our life together, with willingness and kindness, if not, perhaps, with passion. Each brick had been laid with consideration, with gentleness; sometimes, on my side, I thought, with a little anger. Occasionally I'd felt that we'd become closer than ever, mostly I thought it was a truce, a healing time, a chance to re-trench. Until I got pregnant, it had been a period of waiting for something to happen. For something to drive us forward, or blow us apart for ever. We had been holding our breath, I thought, for too long. It was time to exhale.

We ate in silence, one of those couples you always laugh at when you see them at other tables, gazing into their plates as if they'd dropped something in the soup, occasionally sighing and making a remark about the decor. Will's mind was elsewhere. Possibly in Pharmacy.

After half a plateful, I put my fork down. 'I'm sorry. I'm beginning to feel rather sick.'

He looked surprised. 'Really? Do you want something else?'

'No. I'd just like to go home. I'll wait outside. It's too hot and noisy in here.'

I left Will trying to pay and shovelling in the last of his food as I gazed at my reflection in the glass of the restaurant window. He came out looking worried.

But not wholly about me, I suspect. The careful, polished security of the past few weeks, when it really seemed as if we were making something together, seemed tarnished.

There was a cracking noise and the sky seemed to heave, finally tearing itself apart and releasing a torrent of rain so intense that it was almost impossible to breathe. People began to scurry away, into doorways, and under the roof of the bus shelter.

'Shit!' Will held a newspaper over my head to shield me. 'We'll never get a taxi now. We'd better run for it.' He grabbed my hand, and we half walked, half ran to the Tube station, drenched and freezing. By the time we got there, the storm had blown over, and the rain had stopped.

Will shook his coat, shedding droplets. 'We should have stayed at the restaurant.'

'I told you I'd be too tired to come out afterwards. I said don't come to the party.'

'I'm not blaming you.' He bought himself a ticket, and I slipped my season pass through the barriers.

We sat there all the way home, opposite each other, soaking wet, cold, and silent, while the train rattled along the tunnels far too fast.

25

Just to prove that you absolutely shouldn't judge a woman by the way she gives birth (at least if you listen to Laura's friends, you'd think that's how women judge themselves), Laura produced Hero the following day, without fuss and with the greatest efficiency.

We had all expected the same kind of twenty-two-hour forceps-and-stitches drama that had resulted in Phoebe, or the meaningful, eighteen-hour odyssey, punctuated with yoga breathing, aromatherapy oils, TENS machines and active participation from Paul that had introduced Zack to the world. In fact, Laura was almost off-hand, having gone into labour in Sainsbury's.

'Once my waters broke, I thought I'd better pop out to the supermarket because we're a bit low on things like tea and bread,' she explained on the telephone. 'But by the time I got there I could tell things were moving a bit. There was a special offer on teacakes, though, so I thought I'd better hang on.'

She'd driven home, which struck me as wildly irresponsible. 'It was only ten minutes,' she pointed out. 'And pains were coming every fifteen minutes, so I did it between contractions.' This seemed remarkably clear-sighted of her, and more like Lindsey than Laura, who usually dithered and flapped at the slightest challenge.

'And then there she was,' she concluded. Both Laura's previous births have been described in blow-by-blow detail. This abridged account, with its emphasis on teacakes and special offers at Sainsbury's, reminded me of a censored film. It was almost frustrating – I longed to immerse myself in birth plans, but didn't quite dare to yet.

She briefly went on to explain that the baby's head had been nearly there not long after the return from Sainsbury's, but that the midwife and Paul had arrived in time to sort out the final bits, and that there had been no complications whatsoever.

'It hurt a bit,' she added. 'But then it always does.'

'Was the birthing pool a help?' I finally gave in and allowed myself to plan. After all I was now nine weeks pregnant.

She sighed, sounding more like herself than the efficient Madonna I'd been talking to for the last five minutes. 'You don't understand. There wasn't time for the birthing pool.'

'It sounds to me like your best birth so far.' I waited for her to tick me off, and tell me that Zack's gloriously orchestrated introduction to the world had been the most meaningful event in her life.

'Mm,' she said. 'Probably. And it means I'll be able to do that book fair next week after all. I thought I'd have to cancel if I was going to be late.'

'Is she a sweet little baby?' I thought we were rather

forgetting Hero in all this. Phoebe and Zack had always had central roles in their births, each assuming the status of the Baby Jesus from the moment they appeared.

'Sort of,' said Laura cautiously. 'A bit crumpled. But when she irons out, she's obviously going to be quite pretty. I think so, anyway.'

I thought I might leave my introduction to crumpled, pretty Hero for a few days. I was waiting, almost obsessively until the magic thirteen weeks. New mothers have a nasty habit of propelling tiny, fragile little babies into the arms of the childless, which I wasn't quite ready for yet.

I didn't think I could cope with Hero and Saffron in the same week. I left Laura bemoaning the fact that although Hero was huge (8lb 8oz), she didn't feel any thinner.

I wonder if Hero's generation will all call their children things like Mary, Jane and Peter. Bet they do.

26

I arrived at the office an hour late the following morning because I was still spending rather more time than I might have liked gazing around the inside of a lavatory pan, reading the words 'Ideal Standard' over and over again, and wondering if I'd ever feel well enough to step on to something as sick-making as a swaying Tube carriage. But I was even pleased about that, as the innumerable health surveys that came into the office always stressed that women with acute morning sickness were eighty per cent less likely to miscarry.

'Congratulations!' said the receptionist to me. I stepped into the lift just as Belinda Bracken was getting out. I goggled at her.

'Yes,' said Belinda, smiling at me. 'Well done. You know, I do think the secret is to stop relying on sex. Apart from anything else, it's become so unfashionable. It just isn't sexy any more. Ha, ha.' She sounded pleased with her little joke. 'I mean, really,' she stood back slightly so that I could take in her new, honed, more sophisticated look, her flatties replaced by discreet high heels, the tweedy suits reproduced in a lighter, more expensively sheer fabric and the glitter of jewellery at her throat and ears. 'Really,' she repeated.

'Take *My Life*, for example. Our readers, who are at the cutting edge, would be embarrassed to admit they were still doing it. It's like having a Fendi baguette handbag from 1998 rather than this year's model. Frankly, you know, I've had to change so much in *My Life* that was almost halfway to the printers. We managed to substitute "Twenty Ways to Turn Him On" with "The New Bedlinen, Soft, Sensual and Just for You". Luckily we could use much of the same photography, we just changed the headline and captions.'

I blinked at her. In 1998 the only baguettes she'd had any contact with were stuffed with twenty different kinds of mince. I started to feel slightly sick again.

'My God, my taxi. Must fly, darling.' And she dived into a waiting limousine. Was I going completely mad or was Belinda, although not exactly talking and looking like Elaine, now a million miles away from the gentle smiles, stain removers and better-baking tips of a few weeks ago? And how on earth did she know so much about my life?

And how had everyone found out? More importantly, what did Peter Rennie think of it? I hadn't been here long enough to feel protected in pregnancy.

'Great news, isn't it?' exclaimed Camilla.

'Well, it is, of course,' I admitted reluctantly. 'I mean, we've been waiting so long, and to be honest, it's all worried me much more than I ever admitted. But how does everybody know?' This was meant to be a dig at Camilla, who was prime candidate for Chief Earwigger.

She picked up a piece of paper. 'Peter Rennie sent out a memo to all staff.'

What?

I read it. '*How?* Magazine a Sellout!' trumpeted the headline.

'I'd like to congratulate Leonie Lucas and her team at *How?* on a record-breaking issue. The Christmas issue has sold out completely in less than ten days, and there are no stocks left in the warehouse. As you all know, success has its frustrations, and this exceptional performance means that there won't be any copies of *How?* on the news-stands until the January issue is published on 10 December. Well done, everybody!'

I gulped. Thank goodness I hadn't said anything. Although being the golden girl might make it a lot easier to admit to a pregnancy. On the other hand, it would definitely tarnish the gilt a bit if I admitted to planning the heinous crime of motherhood at this stage. The Lindsey option – up-and-down straight-jacketed suits with a loose scarf distracting the eye over the bump – was definitely the safest bet in career terms, and could, depending on your shape, get you up to seven months' remission.

It took me a few moments to recover and take in the real message. *How?* was a sellout. The Christmas issue, Bellingham Glass supplement and all, had gone down a storm. It was beyond my wildest dreams.

Lucy waved a phone at me. 'It's the *Millie Roy* programme.'

A chat show! I visualized myself on a sofa in something bright and colourful, explaining that women today were looking for a better, more beautiful, more comfortable life. That they were now secure enough to take career success for granted and to enjoy the idea of going back to a beautiful home in the evening. 'We're realistic,' I imagined myself saying. 'We don't expect women to chop radish flowers or stir-fry pine nuts after a hard day at the office (we didn't, now that I'd sent strict instructions to the cookery department after my own dinner party), but we do show them how to achieve that level of lifestyle easily.'

'They want Saffron Perry's telephone number,' added Lucy.

Camilla looked at me sharply. 'Don't give it to them. Why should you do her a favour?'

Momentarily taken aback, I recovered enough to shake my head. 'They can have it, frankly. It's in my book, Lucy.' Lucy knocked several things over trying to find the book.

Who would have thought it? A throw-away supplement attached to a minor magazine, and suddenly television programmes wanted Saffron. I looked forward to hearing eventually that she'd told them reprovingly what a 'private person' she was. I had to smile. If Saffron thought I was giving her telephone number to television companies, I'd be treated to a lecture of great sweetness and understanding, as she explained to me that the dumbing-down of television meant that she simply couldn't afford to be seen anywhere near it. 'It could kill my career. I did the Bellingham Glass supplement absolutely as a personal favour, but I've learnt my lesson now, and I'll never do anything like that again.'

But of course the best thing about that one-night stand was that I no longer had to listen to her spouting forth. We had a watertight agreement. No more Saffron.

My heart soared. A baby, a brilliant magazine and no Saffron, whose image was no longer impossibly elegant and lissom, but flawed, scarred and lumpy. The time had come to leave her behind completely, and if I'd had any sense, I'd have done so earlier. She was only another woman.

Camilla passed me a newspaper with Elaine's page, folded to show the 'Mother's Home!' column. 'Staying at home is now the smart career move,' it told me. She explained how many friends of hers had chosen to leave their dream jobs and return home. 'The prejudice against stay-at-home mothers has reached record heights, but now women are rebelling. I found that many people thought I had been sacked. They couldn't believe I'd leave a wonderful career simply to return home. (I thought of *My Life's* disastrous sales figures and raised my eyebrows quietly to myself.) This is now the assumption – that any woman who doesn't work can't work. The 1980s and 1990s saw the first generation of women to break the glass ceiling. Now the new Millennium is ushering in a decade of real choice. And more and more women are feeling truly free to choose the home rather than being pressurized into staying in jobs for the sake of the outdated concept of a woman's right to have a career.'

Polly was hovering over my desk with a layout for me to check. 'I'm not working for an outdated concept,' she muttered through gritted teeth. 'I'm working for the money.'

'Elaine's friends are mostly married to bankers and partners in solicitors' firms,' added Camilla. 'They could maintain six wives at home if they wanted to.'

I quickly skimmed over the rest of the article, where Elaine explained how not working gave her so many opportunities that would have been denied her if she was tied to a nine-to-five existence.

'It gives you the chance to be on chat shows and write novels,' trilled Camilla.

'What?' I seized the paper back. 'Go to exhibitions and read great literature, you twit. Mind you, she doesn't say anything about spending time with her children.'

Camilla giggled. 'I should think she's forgotten she's got any. I saw their main nanny at the health club the other day, and they've still got a weekend nanny, too.'

The article concluded: 'I am enriched as a person by my new-found freedom of choice.' Polly snorted. 'I'd like to be enriched as a person. Preferably with a large cheque.'

'Your sister, Laura, on the phone,' interjected Lucy.

Laura was victorious. 'You see, even journalists think it's better for mothers to stay at home,' she said. 'Lucky you, though, you'll be able to write a few articles while the baby's asleep, so you can earn a bit of money without having to pay for childcare.'

'Laura!' I quickly glanced round the room. Everyone was out of earshot, poring over the fashion pictures on the light box. 'I love my job. I'm staying in it. The point about women having choice,' I hissed, 'is that we don't all have to do the same thing. You do what you think is right, and I'll do what I think is right.'

Laura laughed. 'You've got a nasty shock coming to you, that's all I can say. It won't be as easy as you think it's going to be. Just you wait and see.'

Roll on nasty shocks. I'd waited too long for this particular one. I picked up a piece about New Simplicity we'd commissioned for the April issue. It seemed rather complicated. Apparently the old simplicity was too plain and bare, so the new direction took the essence of simplicity and added things. An awful lot of things by the look of it. I waded through a list of items, shops and prices until my head swam. You needed to be Newly Rich to afford to be Newly Simple, I decided.

'Your husband,' Lucy punched the phone through.

He sounded strained. 'I'm going to be late again tonight, I'm afraid.'

'That's okay.' It didn't worry me. 'Guess what?' I told him the news about the sales.

'That's terrific.' I heard the warmth creep into his voice. 'Really wonderful. We'll have a double celebration soon.'

We agreed that he'd be back by around 8 p.m.

'Where are you going?' I asked. He usually said.

But he'd already put the phone down. Never mind. I'd find out soon enough.

'Camilla,' I put down the piece on New Simplicity. 'Do you feel sex is unfashionable?'

'Well.' She looked perplexed. 'We've all kinda been there and done that. Haven't we? All that three-in-a-bed, I made love with my father's mistress, twenty ways to turn him on, sex toys tried and tested, blah, blah, blah.'

We have? I felt as if I'd missed about two decades because all I did was work and get married.

She put her chin on her hands thoughtfully. 'So yes, in a way. A bit passé.'

'Wouldn't you think that sex would be a sort of eternal thing?'

Camilla looked even more puzzled.

'Classic.' I translated my words into accessories-speak. 'You know, like cashmere or the perfect white shirt.'

Her face cleared. 'Yes, I suppose so. You could say that, perhaps.' She pulled a layout towards her, and bent over it, checking it carefully for about five minutes.

'But you know.' She lifted her head again, wrinkling her cute little nose. 'This winter's not really a perfect-

'white-shirt sort of season.' She spoke in an un-conscious echo of Belinda Bracken. I shook my head.

So there you were. Sex officially declared dead. Camilla was not going to be seen in the wrong shoes, or last year's cardigan. I wondered if the sleek young men, anxiously adjusting their ties while they waited for her in reception, knew about this.

I was so amused I told Will when he got home, but he wasn't listening.

'What?'

'Camilla and Belinda Bracken both think sex has gone out of fashion.'

He gave an absent-minded half laugh, then recovered, focusing his eyes meaningfully at me to prove he really had heard what I'd said. 'Well, there're still plenty of sexually transmitted diseases in my surgery.'

I forbore to say there were still plenty of elasticated waists in the High Street shops, but that wasn't exactly what I was talking about. Instead I asked him where he'd been.

He hesitated. 'Nowhere. Why?'

'It's just that you're late back.'

'Late?' He turned away. 'Oh, late.'

I waited.

'I didn't go anywhere. We all stayed at the surgery. To discuss fund-holding.'

I was surprised. 'I thought that meeting was last week.'

'Oh, well it was, of course. It's just that we couldn't get everything sorted at once.'

I didn't care. It was all very dull. It was just that the way he'd talked about it on the phone had made me sure he was going somewhere, rather than staying in for a meeting. I briefly racked my brains, then forgot it all. This pregnancy seemed to have commandeered my body and taken it over completely for its own uses. I was getting very strong internal commands to go to bed now. This minute. Before supper. I toppled under the duvet, thinking happily about names. No Zacks or Heros for us, but something a bit different might be nice. What about Maud? Or Alice – except that there suddenly seemed to be more Alices about.

27

Even happiness, the glorious, all-enveloping, protectively warm duvet of total happiness, hadn't got me through these few weeks quite as easily as I'd hoped. What with feeling sick (intermittently rather than just in the mornings), tired (almost all the time) and absent-minded (chronically), it was very hard to pretend to be the Superwoman Editor. I simply pushed myself on by remembering that Lindsey had, at this stage of one of her pregnancies, worked through three consecutive all-night sittings when one of her companies had been taken over. During her second pregnancy she'd been sent on one of those absurd team-building exercises where the whole bank gets turfed out on to the Welsh hills with a bottle of water and a safety pin and is expected to get back by abseiling down mountain crags and building their own bridges. Even Laura had spent her first pregnancy on her feet for eight hours a day, although, admittedly, she'd been ten years younger at the time than I was now. I felt like a beached whale, and spent every spare moment alternately lingering over those magazine features on 'Your baby – week by week' and planning a perfect life for the little person growing inside me. I had the sensation of being on an adventure that concerned just us two. 'We're in this together,' I told it once, 'there's no point in making me feel any iller than you have to.' I seemed to have been pregnant for ever, yet its progress appeared to be agonizingly slow. Only nine weeks.

Looking back, I remember Will as quiet during that time. Quiet and watchful. I thought, perhaps, at times, that he was worried about something. But he denied it gently, stroking my hair and telling me that the hormones raging around my system were bound to make me over-anxious.

'I wish you'd slow down,' he said, more than once. 'I think you're doing too much.'

But I wasn't doing as much as either Lindsey or Laura had done in their first pregnancies, and, more importantly, I wasn't doing as much as I ought to do. Success creates much more work than failure. Every morning there was a fresh stack of demands for extra supplements, extra pages, extra radio-show appearances, extra meetings . . . the list was endless. I told the Bump that I'd take it easier once it began to show. 'Come on,' I murmured, stroking my slightly domed stomach. 'Grow as fast as you can.' Laura said that she always couldn't wait for the next stage to be over – potty training, or first day at school – and then she'd really regret it when the milestone was passed, and want her little baby back. Perhaps I'd look back on this stage of pregnancy that way.

One morning the week after the party I sat up feeling better. It was very early to feel better. Perhaps it was temporary. I threw open the window and warily tested the air. Fresh and clear, not filled with choking smoke the way it had often been recently. The ground under my feet felt firm and my limbs seemed more neatly joined together than usual. I felt perfectly well, hardly pregnant at all. It was going, I thought, to be all right.

Maeve and I were booked to go down to Easbiton to extract another large chunk of money from Dave Beckett. I couldn't believe it. I thought I'd seen the last of the flyblown, dusty, litter-filled suburb, and definitely the last of Dave Beckett throwing his weight around. It was deeply depressing.

'I'm afraid that high sales mean nothing without plenty of advertising,' Maeve told me regretfully, as she edged into the passenger seat of my car, and adjusted the silk bow at her neck. 'Carstairs may yet come back in with his old budgets, but we can't rely on it.' She flicked down the mirror behind the passenger sun visor and frowned disapprovingly at herself before taking out a compact and pressing more powder on to her already caked skin.

I'd offered to drive us because I didn't think I could stand the metallic stale-cigarette smell that permeated the outdated rolling stock carrying passengers to Easbiton. And I knew that the shuddering progress of the taxi from the station would definitely make me sick.

Will hadn't wanted me to drive, re-iterating his points about 'overdoing it' this morning when we woke up, but I'd over-ruled him, pointing out that pregnancy was not an illness. He wouldn't have told his patients not to drive, would he? He'd agreed that he wouldn't, but . . . I'd leant towards him, placing my finger on his lips to stop him talking, breathing in the early-morning male smell and snuggling into his arms.

'But, but, but.' I tapped him on the nose. 'You're a fusspot.'

He looked down at me. 'Perhaps a certain amount of exertion in pregnancy is essential.'

I giggled. Sex, however unfashionable, was slowly beginning to reclaim some of its old allure. It felt warm and happy, rather than hard and desperate. 'Come on, then.' I pulled him to me. 'Don't tell me you're all mouth and no trousers.'

'I don't think . . .' he murmured as he moved on top of me, 'that you've got that saying quite right. No trousers, perhaps, but . . .'

About halfway through the stop-start traffic of south east London, I began to think he was right. An hour and a half after we'd set out, we'd hardly travelled any distance. Maeve had fallen into silence. I felt drained. And there was the whole journey back to come, not to mention a teeth-grittingly irritating meeting with Dave Beckett.

Dave Beckett condescended to us all, telling everyone in the room that it was the Christmas Bellingham Glass supplement that had transformed the sales of the Christmas issue. The acolytes nodded. Maeve and I smiled as briefly as we could.

'I had the pleasure of dining with Saffron Perry,' he told me, as he ushered us back to the car. He was obviously in his 'upmarket' mode. He'd probably asked her to peruse the menu.

'Really?' I felt weary.

'She's a plucky little thing, all right. You've got to hand it to her.'

Aha. She'd been playing the role of fragile heroine under siege by the sound of it. She'd done that quite a bit during the breast-cancer scare. It all seemed so typically Saffron that I didn't bother to give it a second thought.

He shook his head. 'Brave. Very brave.' As he shut my car door, he said something else but I couldn't quite catch it. I waved to him. I didn't want the conversation started all over again. I was desperate to get home. The sensation of feeling better had evaporated, although I seemed to have stopped feeling sick.

'What was all that about?' Maeve shut her own door with a lady-like click and pulled the seat belt over her shoulder.

I shrugged. 'Dave Beckett took Saffron out to dinner after the party.'

Our eyes met and we smiled at each other. Conspirators.

'Well.' Maeve pulled the mirror down to check her make-up again. 'Well, well. I do hope they had a good time.' We smiled at each other again. I remembered the times when Saffron dated internationally known musicians and composers. Eight years ago she would never have looked at Dave Beckett. It seemed a lonely way to spend an evening. Poor Saffron.

'Poor Saffron,' I said, this time out loud.

After about five minutes I began to feel uneasy, somehow just not right. I realized I'd been feeling like that intermittently during the day. I accidentally took the wrong turning out of town and was on a motorway heading west before I was aware of it. The next exit was a tangle of minor roads, with signposts apparently placed so as to point equally to two roads each. Eventually I had to do a U-turn, reversing into a tree and smashing a brake light. By the time I got back on the motorway, facing in the right direction, I'd been driving for an hour.

Maeve looked worried. 'Can I help?' She couldn't drive.

I shook my head. My back was beginning to ache. I worried about the baby. Poor baby. I promised the little cluster of cells inside me that I would take it easier when I got home, just to give it a chance.

The drive was interminable and the ache in my back was joined by a low, frightening growling in my belly. Everything felt tight and tangled deep down inside. Just twinges as the womb expands, I told myself, as a sudden cramp took my breath away. It was getting difficult to concentrate. I began to shake. Terrified that something, somewhere was going wrong. I seemed, intermittently, to have a rock inside me, just where our baby should be.

'Hang on in there, poppet,' I begged silently. It usually comforted me to talk to the invisible presence. My little friend. 'Best little friend,' I added, hoping to be encouraging. A sense of reproach and a sharp pain was the only response.

'Do you think you ought to take a break?' asked Maeve, now looking anxious.

I gripped the steering wheel. 'Only another ten miles to London.' I spoke through gritted teeth.

Perhaps I ought to head straight for a casualty department. It seemed excessive, and the last thing I wanted to do was to alert Maeve to my pregnancy. I didn't want to let the side down.

But what was happening? I didn't know anything about pregnancy, except what I'd read in the four books I'd bought, plus *Having A Baby* and *Pregnancy & Birth* magazines. I'd pored over diagrams showing foetuses a few centimetres long, and counted the days anxiously until I could turn the page and point to a new, more exciting stage with fingers and toes. I'd read lists and made lists, and had all my telephone numbers ready. There had been no mention of rock-like feelings anywhere. But, equally, this could just be a natural stage, not worth worrying about, and if I did go to hospital, I'd have to sit there for hours on horribly uncomfortable chairs and I'd be home even later.

I dropped Maeve off at Victoria, where she hailed a taxi. Just as I thought things were getting better, a set of roadworks popped up, and filled me with despair. Suddenly I was in so much pain that stopping the car and re-starting it again felt like climbing Everest.

With shaking hands, I managed to dial Will on the mobile. Not there. Sally, the receptionist, said she didn't know where he was. That was unusual. Surely Tuesday afternoon was a normal surgery time? A knife-stab of worry managed to slash a hole in the screen of pain that had now cut me off from reality.

'Just tell him I need him,' I said. The traffic jam cleared and I could see the road ahead through a haze of exhaustion and guilt. It seemed best to ignore the mobile phone. I hadn't the spare energy to turn it off. It was time, I thought, to try the hospital.

Parking in the hospital car park was the worst — turning round in my seat to edge the car into the narrow space squeezed the rock in my pelvis almost unbearably. As I sat on a hard, plastic chair amongst the smelly drunks, the moaning children and listless pensioners, I felt tired, but the pain began to ebb a little. A man sat with his eyes closed, a bloody towel pressed to his head. A woman held her arm stiffly away from her. A tramp with a can of lager kept trying to engage me in conversation.

'Tisn't right? Tis it?' He waved the can.

I smiled weakly, and shielded my stomach. I wanted to protect it. My baby was in there. Hanging on, but too fragile for this big, ragged man.

'Not right a'all,' he shouted, staggering against me, stinking of urine. The rock hardened inside me again.

I was just about to look for a nurse to ask if there was anywhere to lie down when the doors flew open. Two trolleys, each surrounded by nurses and ambulance workers, carrying drips and murmuring urgently for us to whisk our feet and bags out of the way, were wheeled in, past, and out the doors at the other side. On them lay a woman and a small child, already plugged into drips and face masks. The woman looked terrifyingly still, but I caught a brief glimpse of a tiny childish hand curled up in pain, and a small, fair face waxen with shock. An ambulance man carrying a screaming baby covered in blood followed immediately afterwards. Everyone in Casualty looked at each other.

'Tisn't right,' hiccuped the tramp, throwing the lager can across the corridor. It tinkled as it hit the walls, scattering its last few drops on the cream paint. There was a smear of blood on the floor from the crash trolleys.

'Road Traffic Accident,' said one of the pensioners wisely. 'Poor little mites. There ought to be a law.'

I didn't have the energy to point out that there were several.

Amazingly enough, my name was called soon afterwards, just as the pain was beginning to fade.

Everything, according to the various people who examined me, with long waits in a bare cubicle in between, seemed fine. I was to be labelled a 'threatened miscarriage'.

'We could take you in and put you on a drip,' said the young female doctor sympathetically. 'But you might be more comfortable at home. It's up to you. There's nothing we – or you – can do to prevent anything from happening, so you might as well do what you like. We used to send women to bed, but that's now considered rather old-fashioned.' She scanned a few notes. 'The pain's gone? Well, I can't see any real reason for worry. Come in tomorrow and have a scan. The unit's closed now.'

'Isn't there any research? No guidelines?' I asked, unable to suppress the journalist in me.

She looked evasive. 'Well, there's a lot of experience to go on. Most women suffer a miscarriage at some point. Virtually all of them go on to have babies quite happily.'

Problem solved, in other words.

'But we've been trying to have a baby for six years.'

'Then you should feel very encouraged,' she replied, brightly. 'This shows that you can get pregnant, after all. And you may not lose this one, either. You're only bleeding a tiny bit.'

I didn't like the 'may', and decided not to bother to mention the IVF. The thought of home beckoned. I didn't want to spend the night on a drip, especially if it wasn't going to do any good. Deep down, I knew everything would be all right. This evening would be a bad dream one day.

'How did you get here?'

'I drove.'

'Well, then!' She sounded relieved. Things obviously weren't too bad, after all.

'Just one thing . . .' I decided to face the scary thought that had wormed its way into my conscience during the long journey down. 'Could . . . could this have been triggered by sex?'

She looked resigned.

'Were you using any sex toys? Candles, bottles, electric toothbrushes, sharp implements up you, douches, that sort of thing?' She rattled off the list very much as a waiter in a restaurant might recite the dishes of the day by the end of his shift. 'Unusual positions? Anything that seemed a strain?' I suddenly remembered a doctor friend saying that he had once retrieved a bust of Queen Victoria from up someone's bottom in his days in Casualty.

Shocked, I thought of our slow, gentle love-making. Who on earth would want a sharp implement up them? 'No. At the risk of sounding old-fashioned,' I said faintly, 'it was just an ordinary penis.' I mentally apologized to Will, who might not have cared for this description. But then, he wouldn't have liked being compared to a bust of Queen Victoria or an electric toothbrush either.

Her mind was already on her next patient, presumably someone who was really ill, and not with something as mundane as a threatened miscarriage. 'I don't think you need worry about that.' She spoke briskly as she was heading to the door. 'As I said, we know very little about the causes of spontaneous abortion. It's just a natural process. Nature's Way.'

I trailed out as the ambulance workers wheeled the crash trolleys, now empty and cleaned up, back to the waiting ambulance. I thought about the little family they'd brought in. The ambulance crew looked grim.

'He were only four,' I heard the driver say, with a break in his voice. 'He'd no chance at all. Only four. I've a grandson that age.' No one replied. They slammed the doors, and drove off.

I sobbed on the steering wheel. Only four. No chance at all. Then I blew my nose and wondered, how, if 'they' didn't know much about the causes of miscarriage, they could know what was natural and inevitable and what was not. Or whether sex, normal or aberrant, could affect it. Or champagne, or late nights, or overwork, or whatever I'd done to bring it on myself.

By the time I got home I was beginning to feel agitated about Will. Where was he?

He was standing in the hall, looking thunderous.

'Where the fuck have you been?' He never swore.

'In hospital.' I tried to reach into the back seat to get my briefcase and winced.

He wrenched it out of my hand. 'I'll take that.'

'And you weren't there. I called you and you weren't

there.' A part of my mind registered that this was hardly rational behaviour, but I thumped the hall wall with my fists and repeated, 'You're never there. When I need you.'

He put the briefcase down. 'What's all this about, Leonie?'

'I nearly lost our baby, and you weren't there.' By now I had lost track of what I was really upset about. Everything just seemed very urgent and desperate. And where had Will been?

'Where were you? Sally didn't know where you were.'

He looked bewildered. 'I was only out of the room for a moment. For God's sake, just tell me what happened.' He opened the sitting-room door and propelled me in and on to the sofa. 'And sit down first.'

'Why? What are you going to tell me?' A terrible sense of apprehension overwhelmed me.

'Just that I've been going off my head trying to get hold of you. Do you know how terrifying it is to get a message that just says that you need me, especially when you leave the mobile off the hook?' He took my wrists in his hands, and made me look at him. 'Listen.' He spelt it out very carefully. 'I . . . love . . . you. All right? Not Saffron or anyone else.'

I looked at him with the cunning of the mildly demented, although I could feel myself getting calmer. But I suddenly realized that I was really looking at him, and that there was something there, in those eyes, something more than worry and love. Something that had been there since the night of the Bellingham Glass party. I knew him so well now. It was, for a start, completely unlike him to come out with a declaration of love just because I was having a tantrum.

'But?'

'But nothing.' He dropped my wrists and looked away.

'You've been trying to tell me something.'

He didn't reply.

'Then tell me. I can cope with anything except lies.' It crossed my mind that he might have done something terrible, a terrifying, mad, wicked aberration. Perhaps he was about to be prosecuted or 'crossed off'.

'I wanted to leave this as late as possible. But I saw this clipping today . . .' He opened his fist and revealed a tightly scrumpled piece of newspaper.

I felt the icy fingers of horror taking a grip on my soul, as I tried to spread it out. A local supermarket opening. 'By the pianist, Saffron Perry, who is expecting her first child in three months' time. In the tradition of many actresses, she has refused to name the father.'

He swallowed. 'It's mine.'

Saffron flaunting her new, solid body instantly made sense. It wasn't age. It was pregnancy. At the chunky stage rather than the bulgy one, but still quite far advanced. I screamed, blotting out his reassurances that this didn't mean anything, his desperate desire that nothing would change between us, that Saffron would very definitely be a single mother, and that nothing mattered except me and our baby. For the first time in my life, I threw things. Photograph frames, books, letters, newspapers. He dodged them, and pinned me down, kissing my hair, wrapping his arms around me. 'Stop it. Just stop it. Listen.'

I wouldn't listen, and fought my way out of his embrace.

I locked myself in our bedroom. He tried to talk me down through the door. Eventually, at one in the morning, he went away to the spare room. 'I'll be just next door to you, Leonie. Call me if you need me.'

After five minutes, he came back again. 'Please believe me. I love you. You're my . . .'

I heard him sigh. His feet padded away again, and a wave of pain swept upwards from my pubic bone to my diaphragm. It lasted about forty seconds and disappeared. I lay down, curled up on my side. It was essential not to give in, not to let him help.

The wave came back with rhythmic and merciless determination.

I don't know if it was the long drive (should I have gone to Casualty earlier?), the brief, sneaked love-making, the chronic overwork, the shaking, shuddering rage that had swept through me on hearing about Saffron or, as a succession of nurses, sisters and friends continued to tell me afterwards, Nature's Way, but a small bloody sac slipped out in a spine-wrenching spasm at four in the morning. Was it my fault or his? Or was it just meant to be? The lavatory bowl bloomed with blood and I flushed it away, leaving only a faint raspberry tinge in the water. That was that. Then I slept.

28

I wondered why I felt so empty when I woke up. The sun was streaming under the curtains and I'd forgotten to set the alarm. 8.45 a.m. Then I remembered. I was on my own. No Will. No baby.

Shit! Important meeting at 10 a.m.

I hobbled across the room as the low grumbling in my belly continued to nag away. Two Nurofen and a cup of tea later, I was out of the house, having failed to make much impact on my ashen face and tousled hair. All I really wanted was to slide back under the duvet and stay there for the rest of the century.

Will had left a note: 'Darling, I hope you feel better. Please, please believe me, I never meant this to happen. Stay in bed. Don't go to work today, just look after yourself. We need to talk. Love you. XXX'

I scribbled underneath it: 'Lost the baby. Sorry. Not really up to talking at the moment.' I hesitated, and then added the kind of postscript you always regret later: 'PS I think it would be best if you moved out for a bit.' Then I thought about waiting and worrying for his telephone call if he did. My days of waiting for a man to ring were over, I resolved. In order to keep the ball firmly in my court, I added:

'Please don't try to contact me. I'll call you at the office.'

Well, that did it. I double-locked the door, determined not to turn back and tear up the note. I had effectively given in, and sent him to Saffron, because there was nowhere else he could go at short notice. And he had a ready-made family waiting for him there. Like the rest of the world, I didn't know much about miscarriage, but I did know that if you could get to nearly seven months of pregnancy, then the chances of the baby being born safely were very high indeed. Not like my little ten-week scrap. 'He'd no chance at all,' echoed in my brain, and I raised my copy of *The Times* in front of my face to hide the tears from the rest of the Underground.

The meeting, looking back on it, was hardly that important. It was about a new distribution strategy for the magazines in the group, and, if I'd trusted Camilla, I could have sent her. Even if I hadn't trusted her, I thought later, as I was trundled down the hospital corridors on a trolley, watching the ceiling lights fly past, there was a limit to the damage she could have done. Her eyes had widened when she saw me that morning: 'Are you all right?' Her concern had sounded genuine. Sympathy was the worst, and I had to swallow before answering.

'Fine.' I was aware of being brusque, but there we are. You can't do staff relations and pain together, they just don't mix. 'Thanks, anyway.' I murmured through gritted teeth.

Nobody else commented, although I saw Peter Rennie's brow furrowing every time he looked at me. Scrutinizing the rows of dates and figures I'd been handed was a marginal improvement on contemplating the wreckage of my life. I concentrated on reading the papers in front of me, ignoring both the pain and the meeting around me so as not to wince when the cramps got bad.

'If we follow this schedule,' I realized I was speaking out loud, 'we'll lose three days off the sales of our biggest issues in the Spring. It'll hit all our circulation figures.'

There was a silence while everyone traced their fingers down the seemingly endless rows of numbers.

'This schedule has been drawn up . . .' one of the directors began to bluster, but was cut off by Peter Rennie.

'She's right.' He threw the schedule back at him. 'Re-run it, please.' The man slipped it silently in his briefcase and I looked at the clock. Now could we go?

Peter cornered me on my way out. 'Well spotted. By the way, Brian Carstairs is coming in to discuss his overall advertising strategy later this week. I hope you can join us.'

I nodded.

'You're looking a bit pale. I hope everything's all right.'

'Fine,' I told him, clenching my jaw against a particularly sharp cramp. What was going on inside now? Surely everything had been lost by now.

'Well,' he said jocularly, 'I've had a record week for senior management telling me they're pregnant. Maureen Ellis is having twins.'

I glared at him. 'I can assure you that there's absolutely no question of my having one baby, let alone two.'

'Oh, er, yes.' He moved backwards. 'Of course.'

Still, it was a thought. Twins were so common with IVF. With a hope that one might not have been picked up on any of my scans and was still fluttering very faintly in my abdomen, I booked myself into the Early Pregnancy Unit, where they confirmed that I had indeed lost the baby but that various 'retained products of pregnancy' remained, and that a quick operation was necessary.

'You can go home tonight,' the doctor assured me brightly.

I must have looked appalled, because she added, 'But, of course, you're entitled to stay the night, and leave in the morning.'

So I never had to go back to 37 Branworth Terrace and face Will, and by the morning he was gone, his sock and underwear drawer half-cleared, a couple of suits missing from his wardrobe, and both his favourite sweaters, faded, patched with leather at the elbows, had gone. As if he'd died. I picked up the one he'd left behind, an expensive, pale blue one he rarely wore and pressed it to my face so that I could smell him, as if that could conjure him up out of the emptiness. It was just a sweater. I let it drop back into the drawer without folding it, and closed the door. He'd truly gone.

For a moment I almost picked up the phone to talk to him. I just wanted to hear the sound of his voice in the emptiness. But no. I pulled out all the telephones in the house. There would be no phone calls from anyone today, unless I wanted to make them.

The only comfort was that I knew I hadn't been going mad when I'd started to imagine Saffron around every corner. Deep down, I'd known that you can't have a one-night stand without some consequences, and this, even in a forty-three-year-old, had been perhaps the most obvious of all.

I had hoped that the doctors would give me clear, firm, copious instructions about rest, but they didn't seem particularly interested.

'Oh I should take it easy tomorrow,' one said, 'but after that things should be pretty much back to normal. See how you go. Sometimes people feel a bit tired after a general anaesthetic.'

With a pang of nostalgia for the days when doctors were doctors and patients were grateful to receive advice that could be followed to the letter, rather than expected to draw their own conclusions as fellow professionals, I decided to give in. I had seized up entirely. I simply couldn't make my legs get out of bed. I told Lucy I wasn't coming in, and hunkered down at home, alternately raging at the unfairness of life and fending off sympathy from the family. And they didn't know the half of it.

First, Lindsey arrived, at lunch time, a taxi purring outside in wait for her.

I was amazed. Lindsey never put family before work. She rarely made it to Speech Day, school concerts or the Carol Service. Parents' Evenings vanished in a haze of European division negotiations, and Ella had once told me that she was the only girl whose parents had never, ever taken her out of school a day early in order to go on holiday.

'How did you get away?'

'It's my lunch hour,' said Lindsey, frowning at her watch. 'Thank goodness you're very central.'

She handed over three novels. I glanced at the covers. 'A bleak and harrowing account . . .' 'Asks the ultimate question about love, hate and evil . . .' and 'One man's descent into madness after twenty years unjustly locked in an asylum . . .' Well, that should cheer me up. Various accolades such as 'brilliant', 'searing' and 'seminal' were spattered across the backs.

'I asked the assistant for today's hottest books.' Lindsey never reads novels herself, she can't see the point.

My throat tightened. I was incredibly touched.

After asking how I was feeling, Lindsey told me that Will must be devastated. 'I know how much he was looking forward to being a father.'

'Yes,' I said shortly. 'Well, he's away at the moment.'

'Still,' she continued, patting my hand, 'now you know you can get pregnant, you can always try again. I expect that this was Meant To Be.' There was the faintest extra intonation on the last three words. 'There was probably something wrong, and your body decided it was best to get rid of it.'

'That's what the doctors said,' I agreed. 'Not that they seemed to know.' I was only amazed that Lindsey hadn't got there ahead of me by having a couple of miscarriages herself, but perhaps that bordered on the inefficient. I thought I'd change the subject.

'How are things with you?'

Lindsey got up and stared out of the window. Eventually she spoke, reluctantly. 'The school says Ella's going to fail all her exams if she doesn't buck up.'

I was astonished. 'Ella? I thought she worked terribly hard.'

Lindsey sat down again. 'She did. I don't know what's happened. Of course, it's a difficult age . . .' She waved a hand to indicate the years between thirteen and eighteen, and sighed. 'I just don't know what to do about it. She looks at me as if she despises me, and she won't stay in the same room as Sandy. Just walks out when he comes in.' She leant back in her chair and closed her eyes. 'I'm so tired.'

I couldn't think what to say. If I woke up to life as an adolescent and found my father was Sandy White

I'd put as much space as possible between him and me too, but I could hardly tell Lindsey that. She purported still to love him. I thought of the puffy slab of his face, the eyes swivelling like an insect's antennae in search of someone to bully as he topped his glass up with the finest claret. He never let up. Lindsey was a useless housewife, Oliver would never become a man if he didn't get better at sport, Ella . . . well, he left the girls alone pretty much. He more or less ignored Ella and Daisy, except to explode at them if they left anything lying around.

The time was ripe for a good platitude. 'I expect she'll grow out of it.'

Lindsey brightened. 'I'm sure you're right. Must fly. There's a meeting about a takeover at 2.30.' She kissed the air around my face, and fluttered off, an iron butterfly returning to the wild wood of commerce.

Laura was more of a problem. Hero was just too close a reminder of what I'd lost, and I couldn't bear the thought of Laura turning up with mounds of equipment and a tiny baby in a car seat. I suspected that, if I said as much to her, it would be taken as a personal insult. But I could hardly not call her, so I braced myself, plugged in the telephone by the bed and dialled.

First, I had to wade through an infuriating conversation during which she pointed out that she had tried to warn me about the risk of miscarriage. 'But you wouldn't listen.'

I stammered out that I didn't feel up to seeing a newborn baby.

'Well!' She was temporarily silenced. 'I think that's extraordinary. I mean, you can hardly expect me to come and see you without Hero. She's far too little to be left behind, even if I had anyone to leave her with.'

'I don't expect you to come at all.' I sighed.

'That's ridiculous!' she retorted. 'You're my sister. Of course, I must visit you if you're ill. You must think I'm a very selfish person if you believe that I wouldn't bother.'

I tried not to cry. 'No. Of course, I don't think you're selfish . . .' Annoyingly, the sobs broke through.

Laura was not impressed. 'I don't know why you're crying. I'm the one with post-natal depression.'

'I can't take any more.' I gulped and blew my nose.

'Any more of what? Really, Leonie, do try to make sense. You don't understand. Small babies do need to be with their mothers, and I would have thought that seeing Hero might be quite comforting. After all, miracles can happen.'

I wondered whether Laura had merely wandered into cliché-speak again or if this was just a reflection on how very unlikely she thought it was that I'd ever have a baby.

Suddenly, I took in what Laura was saying. 'What's all this about post-natal depression?'

'Oh, this is no time to talk about that. You're the one who matters now.'

I'd heard that before somewhere. Oh, yes, Will, on the night of the Bellingham Glass party. No wonder he'd been so distracted. With his medical knowledge, not to mention his knowledge of Saffron's body – I winced at the thought – he must have realized that she was pregnant immediately.

The rest of the conversation with Laura continued like a fencing match. I eventually put down the phone feeling punctured in several places. Her final words sounded kindly.

'Do look after yourself. And better luck next time – I'm sure that if you just get pregnant again as soon as possible, it will all work out.'

I didn't want the next one. I wanted this one. Anyway, I couldn't have another, probably. Not in the time left to me; and without Will.

The phone rang again immediately. Camilla.

'Have you got flu?' she demanded.

I explained that it was just a headache and that I'd be in tomorrow.

'Good. Because everyone's being completely unreasonable about Christmas leave. Honestly, all the mothers say they want to take the whole break with their children. They don't seem to think the rest of us should get a look in.' It transpired that she wanted to go ski-ing, and had had a particularly delicious invitation from a gorgeous man to join him and a party at his chalet from Boxing Day onwards. Even for Camilla, it was the invitation of a lifetime. 'I'll never be asked again,' she wailed. 'He'll take some other girl, and I'll have lost my chance.' What it meant, however, was that there was nobody prepared to work between Christmas and New Year except for Kate, the deputy homes editor, 'and she's had an invitation to join her brother in Northumberland. She didn't get much of a summer holiday because she was covering Deirdre's maternity leave, so she was rather hoping to go.' Camilla went on to list, in giddying detail, everyone's claim to take the whole stretch off. Each case seemed worthier than the last. 'And then there are the mothers,' she concluded with disdain. 'They all always want time off, of course.'

To get her off the phone I told her to accept her ski-ing invitation, and that I'd deal with everyone else when I got back. I had a feeling that the Cold War between mothers and non-mothers was beginning to flare up into real resentment, and that this was just the start of the border skirmishes. My role as the United Nations peacekeeper was less than alluring.

I wondered if I felt well enough to get into the car and go out to buy some books. Delicious, soppy novels to whisk me into another world. Happy endings and handsome heroes. Just pure fantasy. That's what I wanted. There was a little bookshop on the Common that I loved, and it wouldn't take ten minutes to drive there. By the time I returned, and was about to park the car, I felt distinctly wobbly.

There was a loud bang from behind. A woman I knew slightly from across the road had shot out from nowhere and into the back of me.

We both got out in the pouring rain.

'Just a little scratch on your bumper,' she told me crisply. 'Hardly anything really. Mind you, you shouldn't have been turning left like that.'

Like what? I peered at what was definitely a bent wing. 'Er. It was my right of way . . .'

She snorted. 'My husband's a barrister.' She handed me her card, and got into her car without saying goodbye.

I closed the door behind me and stood in a dripping puddle, wishing Will would call. But I'd told him not to, and besides, there wasn't anything to say. Except to arrange the division of property and money, and I didn't feel strong enough for that. The hardest thing to accept was that I no longer had first claim on him.

There was no longer any reason to live a healthy life so I had two stiff gins, half a bottle of wine and some sleeping pills. It all seemed terribly quiet. The emptiness inside me threatened to swallow me up entirely. I had nothing left.

29

Many years ago, Will and I had sheltered from the rain outside an art gallery showing nineteenth-century South American religious paintings. We'd peered through the glass at a painting of the Virgin Mary, a crude creation in cobalt and gilt, depicting a simpering Madonna, her arms folded almost complacently across her breast. Yet she had been stabbed by seven daggers, plunged into her voluminous robes in seven different places, and the contrast between the tranquillity of her pose and the agony of the knives struck me forcibly. In pain and yet serene, the ultimate woman.

'Ah,' Will had said knowledgeably, 'the Virgin of the Seven Sorrows. Not a very good example.' And he'd turned round, losing interest. 'The rain's stopped.' But I'd pulled back for a moment, trying to count the seven sorrows. Jesus on the Cross was one of them, but weren't the others the burdens of the world she'd taken upon herself? I'd given up. I didn't know enough about it all.

I thought of the Virgin of the Seven Sorrows when I woke up the following day, with darts of pain stabbing my consciousness as soon as I opened my eyes. It was up to me to be as serene, as capable, as unruffled as the woman in the painting with the folded arms and the seven knife wounds. But I knew, from the way I hadn't been able to find a comfortable position all night, that I wouldn't be able to concentrate on anything until I'd rung Will. His departure could only be equated to having my right arm ripped away without an anaesthetic, leaving an aching, throbbing gap where he had been. Sometimes I was truly amazed to look down and see that I still had all the familiar limbs: two arms, two legs. Because things had been so bad for so long, I was surprised that I hurt this much.

I looked out of the window. It was still dark and drizzling with rain. The only movements under the yellow street lights were a man scurrying past with a lighted cigarette, and a mangy dog nosing around the dustbins. It might even have been an urban fox.

How?'s offices didn't officially open until 10 a.m., and Will was usually at his desk at the surgery by 8.30, so there was a chance to call him in privacy, and get it over and done with before having to adjudicate in the massive Mothers v. Non-Mothers row over holiday time.

At 8.25 a.m. Sally punched me through, and he picked up the phone immediately. 'Will?'

'Yes?' He sounded anxious. 'How are you?'

Suddenly I couldn't speak.

'Are you all right? I've been calling you. Is there a fault on the line?'

I had resolved to keep the conversation strictly practical, and swallowed the lump in my throat. 'No fault,' I told him. 'I just wanted to sleep without being disturbed.' See what he thought about that. I was determined to prove that I didn't need him, and that I didn't care.

'I'm only calling,' I stressed, 'because I just thought I should get a number for you, and an address for sending on post. And we probably need to discuss . . .' I swallowed again, 'practicalities.'

'Oh.' He sounded careful, leaving me to talk as much – or as little – as I wanted to, perhaps. 'Yes, I suppose so.'

I waited for him to mention the baby, my knuckles white with tension around the telephone handset. If he said anything, anything at all, I'd slam the phone down on him. He needn't think he could make it better just by saying sorry.

'Sorry,' he said. 'I was just looking for the number. I don't know it in my head yet.'

Perhaps he wasn't with Saffron after all. My heart suddenly lifted, absurdly.

'Yes, here it is.' It had an unfamiliar prefix, not Notting Hill Gate at all. The address was 11b something Gardens.

'What?'

He spelt it out for me, and added, 'W3'.

'W3?' I was astonished. 'Where's that?' Perhaps Saffron, expecting a baby, had moved to have more space.

'Acton.'

What on earth was he doing in Acton?

'I'm staying in James's flat.'

I couldn't help smiling. 'Didn't James imply that it was in Covent Garden or Chelsea or somewhere like that?'

'Well, he didn't exactly say so, but I must admit I got that impression too.'

Elated with the knowledge that at least he wasn't in Notting Hill Gate, I started to gabble. 'Until you got there. And how's the shagging?'

'Well,' Will lowered his voice conspiratorially, 'you must absolutely promise not to tell a soul – and particularly not Jennifer . . .'

'I promise.'

'But James goes to bed at about 10.30 every night. Alone.'

I burst out laughing and so did he. 'Poor James. Meanwhile I'm sure Jennifer has a procession of hunky farmers preventing her from feeling lonely down in the country.'

'I'm sure she has.'

We sobered up. For a moment, it was as if we'd been joking face to face, but suddenly the telephone line echoed like a stretch of desert between us. He felt very far away. As if he was on the dark side of the moon.

'Leonie? How are you? I'm so sorry about the baby.' I wondered if he'd add something about how he felt, but I know Will. He's a bit self-effacing on the tragedy front. This was the first of many burdens we'd each have to shoulder alone.

I tried to read things into his voice and failed. 'I'm fine,' I said, eventually. 'Absolutely fine.' There was nothing else you could say. I used to be pregnant, now I'm not. It's the nothingness of it all that gets you. No memories. No mourning period. Just over.

'Well, I'd better go,' he suddenly sounded business-like again, and I wondered if someone had come into his surgery. 'Is it all right if I come and collect some more things at the weekend?'

'Of course,' I knew my voice sounded stiff and harsh. He hadn't suggested meeting up to talk, just to collect more things. 'You've still got a key. I may not be there.' I didn't think I could bear to be there, in fact. And I didn't dare ask why he wasn't staying at Saffron's in case the answer was that the flat was too small but that they would be looking for something else soon.

He paused before putting the phone down. 'Leonie?'

'Yes?' Once again, my heart leaped – a mad, illogical skip of a beat that could be crudely labelled 'hope'.

'I'm sorry. So very, very sorry. From the bottom of my heart.'

His voice sounded final. The tone, as Bellingham Glass would doubtless have put it, just wasn't quite right for hope.

It was time to unpick the next row of stitches that held our marriage together. To go public.

The family, of course, came first.

'Oh, darling, I am sorry,' said Mum. 'Isn't it lucky you haven't got any children, after all? Losing the baby was obviously a blessing in disguise. It would have made it all so much more complicated. Still, you've got your work, that'll be a great help.' She then managed to imply, in her contradictory way, that, of course, it was probably my job that had both caused the miscarriage and undermined my marriage.

Next came Laura. 'This is terrible,' she wailed down the phone. 'I really love Will. I can't bear it. It's too awful. What happened?'

I muttered a few clichés about growing apart.

'Well, of course it can happen to anyone. With the way people work today,' she emphasized, making it clear that if you worked you only had yourself to blame for any misfortune that might befall you. 'I've told Paul that he should be around more. He never gets home on time, and always brings work home at weekends . . .' She was off, on the round I'd heard so many times before, delineating Paul's shortcomings as a husband. She concluded, 'So, you see, you're not the only one.' I decided that this was Laura's attempt at empathizing.

She returned implacably to the issue of blame. 'So what did Will do?'

I couldn't face telling her. 'It wasn't all his fault. He's just been very busy, that's all. He doesn't really talk about it,' I admitted.

'The bastard. How dare he treat you like that?'
Laura seemed to have forgotten how much she loved
Will.

'No, really,' I tried to say, 'this is about both of us.'

She snorted. 'Well make sure you get as much
money as you can out of the divorce, that's all I can
say.'

I flinched. I did not want to fleece Will.

Lindsey was silent for a moment when I told her
that Will had moved out.

'From the sound of your voice that isn't quite all.'
She didn't miss much. I briefly felt sorry for Ella, who
was presumably trying to grow up in privacy and was
probably getting irritatingly understood left, right and
centre.

'No.' I sketched out the Saffron situation.

'Ouch. Has he gone to her?'

'No,' I admitted. 'But that doesn't mean . . .'

'I know it doesn't mean anything. But I think you
should try to keep your options open.'

'I don't have any options.'

'Perhaps I didn't phrase that right. Keep an open
mind.'

I felt a quick, agonizing stab of hope, and suppressed it immediately. Perhaps one of the Virgin's
seven sorrows was hope. It could be just as painful as
grief. 'I don't think so.'

'I'm sorry.' Lindsey was sombre. 'If you need to
get away from home, you've got an open invitation
to stay here, you know.'

'Thanks.' It was kind of her, but Will and I knew what it was like spending any time at the Lucas-Whites. Every time either Lindsey or Sandy went out of the room, the remaining person hissed in irritation about the other's behaviour. No sooner had the door closed on Lindsey than Sandy would exclaim, 'I've told her that's pointless. But she won't listen. Never does!' Or if Sandy bumbled down to the cellar in search of more claret, Lindsey would look up from the pile of paperwork she always seemed to have in front of her and murmur, 'He's getting worse. Or is it just my imagination? What do you think?' Will and I would wriggle away, mumbling platitudes. As soon as the door closed on them both, we'd catch each other's eye and dissolve in fits of giggles. On my own it would be different.

By this time, the office was beginning to fill up and I could see people darting glances at me, and then at each other, each determined to get in first with their case. I could almost see the resentment boiling over.

Deirdre nobbled me first. Her mother-in-law, who was dying of cancer, had arranged for the whole family to take a series of adjacent cottages on a farm in Cornwall. 'She usually lives in Sydney, so this'll be the last chance for everyone to get together. And she hasn't seen the new baby yet.' Well, what can you say? Deirdre got her time off.

That left Kate, usually so easy-going, picking at her cuffs in a sulky fashion. 'My brother's moved to

Northumberland, and is having a huge party for friends. I split from my boyfriend earlier this year . . .' She made it clear that her social life, at rock bottom, required this party to jump-start it again. My head began to ache. I suggested that she make it a long weekend, and she agreed dully. 'But I haven't had a good long run of holiday off this year. Because of the maternity-leave cover,' she added, with obvious resentment.

Camilla didn't help, with little darting comments, usually against the Mothers. 'She thinks that having a baby excuses her from working late,' she said about one woman. This particular woman, admittedly, was always first out the door with her coat on. I suspected she'd always been like that, and that motherhood had made not the slightest difference. 'Why do they always have to take time off in the school holidays?' she said of another. 'You'd think they'd be glad of a bit of a change.'

And Deirdre, self-appointed queen of the other side, pointed out that single women like Camilla could hardly be expected to understand. 'All she has to do is earn a living and amuse herself.'

As my own Christmas plans had been blown out of the sky, I said that I would come in between Christmas and New Year along with one of the juniors, who muttered, 'Being Jewish and single, I know that that's what's expected of me.'

I couldn't help smiling. 'Well done.' Then Polly sidled up and said that she'd re-arrange her plans to come in after all. 'As I'm part-time, I feel I ought to make an extra effort.' I thanked her and told Camilla, who sniffed.

'She's probably dying to get away from the chaos of a house full of children. Leaving it to her husband.'

You couldn't win.

I threw a memo from Peter Rennie into the bin. It re-iterated the importance of making sure that the office was properly staffed between Christmas and New Year, and stated that it was essential that printing schedules were not allowed to fall behind. I gazed at it with numb pain. I felt like one of those earthquake or avalanche survivors you see on the television, unable to comprehend the scale of what had befallen me.

30

Christmas inched towards me, like a lone sniper crawling through a deserted battlezone, watching me through the sights of his gun. It was now only three weeks away. It was, I reminded myself, the time of peace and goodwill towards all men.

Lindsey fired the first shot.

The call, however, came from Mum.

'Darling,' she said, coming straight to the point, 'Your father and I are feeling tired.'

I wondered briefly – perhaps uncharitably – what a healthy, relatively well-off, retired couple in their mid-sixties had to be tired about. Perhaps there was a tiredness virus sweeping the planet, and it had even reached Horsham.

A sudden, terrible thought occurred to me. 'There isn't anything, you know, seriously wrong?' A series of visions of different kinds of cancer, heart disease and other more obscure illnesses popped up in front of me like dummies on a firing range, sliding out of view before I could really focus on them.

'Certainly not,' she replied, rather briskly for one who claimed to be tired. 'But I'm not – that is, we're not – getting any younger, you know.'

She gave me a few seconds for that to sink in before sweeping on. 'And I've been talking to Lindsey.'

I felt a stab of misgiving.

'And,' she continued, 'Lindsey has very kindly offered to do Christmas this year in Parson's Green. She's the only one who's got the space to have everybody, especially now that there seem to be more of us every year.'

I felt there were fewer of us this year. My baby was missing. And I didn't see how Laura's baby, however sweet, could possibly fill the hole that Will's departure had left. It would be at least a year before it left Laura's breast for long enough to be considered a separate human being in its own right. She believed in feeding on demand, and that breast was best until primary school. More or less, anyway.

Still, if that was what everyone wanted, I had no real objections. Going back to sleep alone in my old bedroom at my parents' house seemed a retrograde step by anyone's standards, and at least staying at Lindsey's would mean that I could return to my dusty, gloomy, empty home at any point that I wanted to. My experience of Christmasses with Phoebe and Zack indicated that even gloom and emptiness could potentially acquire a surprising degree of allure.

On the other hand, I did know that December was the time to get out for people in my situation, preferably to a ski resort, Caribbean beach or smart hotel filled with other people whose lives hadn't worked out. I visualized looking elegant and solitary for a day or two, then sipping cocktails with other people with unseasonally brick-red tans and white sleeveless dresses, sympathizing with them, making the odd new friend. Maybe I could manage an unsuitable love affair. Even if we didn't have much in common, it would be better than being the only single, childless spectre at the family feast.

However that option had to be dismissed thanks to my bank statement, stripped to the bone by the IVF treatments, and lurching ominously into the red even before I'd bought a mountain of brightly coloured plastic presents for all my nieces, nephews and godchildren. Not to mention the explosive situation over holiday time in the office.

I had already rung Crisis and a few other charities, hoping that I could give something back to the world in the midst of my unhappiness. Forget myself, Will and the baby by thinking of others. The image this time was of redemption through hard work, of laughter among the tears, and of realizing that so many people were much worse off than myself. There'd be merriment over rough red wine, I'd thought, and paper hats.

The world did not want anything I had to give, except a donation. Volunteers, apparently, have to book themselves in for good works even earlier than revellers do for ski resorts and Caribbean beaches, and there was a waiting list of selfless souls wanting to help others.

So Lindsey in Parson's Green it was. The only

comfort was that Will, who I'd feared might be spending his first family Christmas with Saffron, had rung me and said, 'I'm going up to James and Jennifer in Northamptonshire.' He couldn't get up to much there, even if Jennifer did tout him round proudly as a newly available bachelor. We'd arranged to meet for a Christmas drink beforehand. I hadn't been able to face seeing him in the three weeks since he left, but I was trying to persuade myself that a meeting would be part of the healing process. 'After all,' added Mum, breaking into my reverie. 'Lindsey'll do Christmas beautifully.'

She would, of course. Lindsey had a tree decorated by an interior designer, delivered exactly a week before Christmas. It was always bushy and beautifully balanced, swathed in tartan ribbon and colour coordinated in silver or gold (never both), with tasteful white lights. And it never dropped its needles. Underneath, artfully arranged by Consuela, rested a pile of professionally wrapped presents. Lindsey did not order presents in awkward shapes or with bits that poked out.

I asked Mum what she wanted for Christmas, and she told me that when you were older, things seemed less important and that all she really wanted was for us to be happy. Although she wouldn't mind some Chanel No. 5 if we were determined to give her a present.

The next call was from Laura, who was too cross to say hello properly.

'Have you heard?' she squawked. 'Lindsey's conned Mum into letting her do Christmas. Instead of going home and having a peaceful time, we'll have to go to that bloody great house and be grateful for doing lots of washing up because Consuela doesn't work on Christmas Day.'

'We'd have had to do washing up anyway at Mum's.' I couldn't quite understand Laura's objections. Lindsey organized the house so comfortably that, even without Consuela, it was bound to be more restful than cramming in hugger-mugger at home, with thirteen men, women and children sharing one bathroom with a temperamental water heater.

'Yes, but we wouldn't have had to be grateful to that horrid old lech, and have our bottoms felt while we were doing it.' She was talking about Sandy, who was, admittedly, a bit too touchy-feely for comfort.

'What I really mind about him,' added Laura, 'is that because he slides his horrible great hand over my bum, he can tell when I'm not wearing knickers.'

'Not wearing knickers?'

'I'm sorry, but I never wear knickers when I'm wearing tights,' Laura informed me in tones of great authority. 'I mean, what's the point?'

If she didn't know, I wasn't going to be the one to tell her. It was safer to return to the question of Mum and her tiredness, pointing out that at some time the older generation had to hand the baton over to the younger one.

'Yes, but not yet.' Laura was determined not to give

in. 'I bet Mum wasn't tired until Lindsey told her she was.'

This was entirely possible.

'I mean,' Laura warmed to her theme, 'if everyone just gave up when they were tired, the world would come to a complete stop and then where would we be?'

In absolute heaven, I felt like saying. The idea of everyone just giving up and the world coming to a stop sounded quite the nicest suggestion I'd heard for a long time. But I knew Laura would perceive this as a direct attack (don't ask me to spell out the exact logic, it's too boring – Laura takes almost everything personally).

Instead I agreed to have a word with Lindsey and Mum to see if this scheme for Christmas in Parson's Green was really set in stone.

'After all,' Laura was determined to make a final point to ensure that I realized the error of my ways in falling in with Lindsey's plan without a fight. 'You just don't understand. About Christmas. It shouldn't be an exquisitely tasteful designer experience. It's a family thing. If you had children, you'd be more supportive.'

I told myself – again – that Christmas was the time of peace and goodwill and refrained from roaring at her. She'd only have retired with hurt feelings and sulked about my aggressive behaviour for weeks.

I worded my conversation with Lindsey as carefully as I could, larding my tentative suggestion that we should have Christmas at home and find ways of helping Mum more, with murmurings that Laura was feeling post-natally fragile and that Christmas at home, with all its familiar ritual, might stabilize her. It sounded daft even to my ears, but it was better than saying 'Laura doesn't want to come to your house to be condescended to, then fingered by your husband', which was what it amounted to.

Lindsey saw through it immediately. 'Laura is so selfish,' she announced. 'She expects everyone to come to her all the time. If she's post-natally depressed, she needs a rest, and she'll get more of one at my house than at Mum's. And she won't have to travel so far. She can stay at home and just drive over for the day, if she wants to.'

'Laura wasn't suggesting that we go to her,' I pointed out.

'I'm speaking metaphorically,' countered Lindsey. 'You know perfectly well what I mean. Honestly, I'd have thought you'd have more sense than to encourage her demands. Anyone can see that Mum is absolutely knackered, and it's simply not fair for us all to land on her the way we always do. The least you could do is support me. I'm the one who's going to have to do all the hard work, after all.'

So Lindsey reinforced her saintly position of superiority, while Laura dug herself into her trench of inferiority more deeply. Both, for the time being, directed their fire at me for being unsupportive.

I wondered about taking out a bank loan and

heading for the Caribbean after all, but the bank was even more likely to tell me that I didn't understand than Lindsey or Laura had been, and I couldn't take another battle.

If Will had been there, we would have laughed about it. When I used to get caught in the cross-fire of sisterly argument, he'd put his arm round me and tell me he loved me. Then we'd make a joke about it, and, even down in my parents' house in Horsham, sneak off to bed in the middle of the afternoon. Ella and Oliver, as tiny children, had always been surprised to find our bedroom door locked at 3 p.m.

Three weeks to go. Faced with Lindsey's strictures on what was, and was not, suitable as a present for her children (I wanted to give Ella money, for example, but had been told that she must only have a book token, presumably so that she couldn't go out and spend it on unsuitable things), and Laura's expansive, but not very helpful, mutterings about 'anything vulgar and plastic will do', I decided to start my Christmas shopping one Saturday morning at Peter Jones.

I spent fifteen minutes in a completely stationary queue because a florid woman with dark hair, who looked vaguely familiar, insisted on having each of her packages directed to a different address.

'This one,' her tones carried clearly across the toy department and reminded me of someone, 'is for Scotland. These two for Northamptonshire, that for Gloucestershire and the small ones for Cheshire. This last one will be picked up from the Customer Collection Bay by a Lady,' she stressed the prefix, 'a Lady Cheal.' She looked at her pile with satisfaction while three assistants scurried round her packing them up and labelling them for different destinations.

'I'll just write a note for Lady Cheal.' She lingered over it, while a fourth assistant rang up her purchases and tried to swipe her card through.

'I must have been shopping an awful lot,' laughed the woman. 'My card's completely worn out.'

So was the assistant, by the looks of it, as she wearily tapped in the endless number. By this time the queue snaked round the Barbie doll shelves and prevented anyone from crossing the department from left to right. Another till was opened hastily, and I became the first customer.

There was a tinkly laugh from the woman as she wrote something out with the wrong date, and more fussing as she changed it. I could see her clearly now and realized with a shock that it was Jennifer, James's wife. I hadn't recognized her without her bump.

'Jennifer!'

She looked up, and her face darkened as she saw who I was. She almost turned away without answering, but I went bowling on, infected, I felt, with some kind of verbal diarrhoea. Possibly brought on by the relief that Will was not spending Christmas playing Happy Families with Saffron.

'How are you? I gather Will is spending Christmas with you. That's terribly kind of you.'

She looked mollified, as if she'd expected an insult. 'Well. I hope you don't think we're taking sides, but Will was our friend first, and I felt it was our duty to rally round.'

Taking sides? It wasn't any of her business why Will and I had split up. I certainly wasn't asking anyone to take sides, least of all someone I'd only met once. I merely smiled. 'Of course not.'

'Oh. I just thought you might have minded us inviting Saffron too.' She sounded quite put out that I hadn't.

The world swung upside down and righted itself again. I held on to the counter.

'Excuse me,' said the assistant. 'Excuse me. Could you sign this please?' She waved a scrap of paper at me. I wondered what it was. The bill, of course. I signed it numbly.

'It will be lovely for them to have a real country Christmas,' said Jennifer. 'A proper family atmosphere.' And she swanned off, leaving the assistants still marking and setting aside packages destined for shires all over Britain.

He hadn't said he was spending Christmas with Saffron. He obviously hadn't dared mention it.

I hadn't expected it to hurt so much. After all, it was what I'd thought would happen. It made perfect sense. But it was a terrible blow all the same. I resolved to get to the other side of the festive season without breaking down, and without thinking about it. But I made sure that Lucy telephoned Will to cancel our festive drink. She did so, looking alarmed. No one had dared mention the split to me, but I knew that it was a hot topic in the loo.

I read about the stresses and strains of Christmas in Elaine's 'Mother's Home!' column. 'It is a time of year,' she trilled, 'to link hands around the world. Christmas is not a dinner party to which guests must be specially selected for their interest or usefulness. (Her dinner parties sounded absolute hell, remind me never to go to one. I might get there and not feel useful enough.) 'No,' she continued victoriously, 'Christmas is a time when people of different races, colours, beliefs and strata of society come together. The old talk to the young and the deprived to the wealthy. (I thought of Laura seething over the way Lindsey could afford a different pair of shoes to match every single beige suit, and didn't think Christmas would necessarily bring them closer together.) Most of all, it's a time to think of others. If you can all, just once, stretch out into the dark and save one of your neighbours from loneliness, then this column will not have been written in vain. Our children have been deprived of their grandparents by an increasingly restless and mobile society, and our grandparents of their children. Bridge that gap! Invite an elderly or lonely person into your house today. I know from experience that you will be enriched by it.'

This was flagged 'From our award-winning columnist'. Elaine no longer told her readers that they 'must have' red in their wardrobes this winter, or that certain shoes were now 'fashion essentials'. Almost seamlessly she had switched to moral imperatives, and her usual column was based, sermon-like, around an incident at the school or the kitchen table, from which she drew the conclusion that we 'must have' more tolerance or that sincerity was one of this winter's 'essentials'. Occasionally I wondered if she'd simply hung on to her editor's letters at *My Life*, and used the 'search and replace' on her computer to find references to handbags, frocks and the Paris shows, substituting in their place qualities like honesty or love and places such as the school hall. Personally I found it creepy and formulaic, but according to the newspaper she wrote for, people were clamouring for a return to real values.

Even Lindsey seemed to have read it, I discovered later. It just shows you, you really can fool most of the people most of the time.

We all, in the end, assembled at her house on Christmas Eve. I had decided that waking up alone on Christmas Day was more than I could bear, and had opted instead for the sofabed in Sandy's study.

Lindsey's house is extraordinary. She bought it at the beginning of the 1980s, newly and expensively decorated in the style of 1979. It had been fully furnished, 'a turnkey' development, I think it's called.

And she hadn't changed a thing, unless it wore out. There was chocolate-brown carpeting everywhere, and terracotta hessian on the walls in the dining room. Big chocolate-brown velvet sofas sprawled comfortably around the room, and bottle-green velvet curtains hung severely at the huge windows. There were wall lights and a chandelier, all of which were kept on at full wattage all evening, which was deeply unflattering. The only other colour came from a row of dark-purple cushions ranged neatly along the sofa and two huge purple bean bags which lay in wait, ready to leave you inelegantly sprawled on your back like a cockroach. Occasionally people teased Lindsey about having a temple to 1970s design, but she looked so blank that the joke fell flat. If a room got too faded or bashed about, she simply dialled an interior decorator and had it done up, without really noticing the result: 'Just choose whatever you think,' she told one surprised decorator. 'But I'd like it to last. Nothing is more boring than constantly having to redecorate.'

So the best spare bedroom, converted three years ago from an au pair's room when Lindsey had stopped having an au pair as well as a nanny, was exactly mid-1990s in style, with red toile de jouy wallpaper, red and white checked Swedish painted chairs and an elegant polished wood lit bateau bed. The decorator had looked wistfully at the rest of the house, but Lindsey had told her that nothing else had worn out yet, and doing any more would simply be a waste.

This best spare bedroom was allocated to Mum and Dad, while Laura and Paul were allocated a smaller room, done up circa 1985, with a padded headboard, swatches of floral chintz pouring down from a coronet and over-swagged matching curtains, which Laura claimed made her sneeze, which left the study and sofabed for me. Phoebe and Zack were thrilled to hear they were having the pull-out beds in Daisy's and Oliver's rooms respectively.

Lindsey had forgotten the baby.

Mum and Dad instantly offered to swap rooms as there was masses of space for the carrycot in the main spare room. This was simultaneously shot down – before they'd even stopped talking – by both Laura and Lindsey. Laura insisted that Hero was still sleeping in their bed and didn't need a separate space of her own, although Paul did look slightly alarmed at that and tried to murmur something about 'not all night' above the hubbub. Lindsey suggested that the baby's carrycot go into Sandy's dressing room. Laura snapped that while Lindsey might abandon her newborn babies to strange dressing rooms and send them to boarding school as soon as possible, she, Laura, cared about her children. Lindsey pointed out, with pinched restraint, that neither Ella, Oliver nor Daisy had ever been sent to boarding school. Ella, sloping past on the stairs with her face concealed in her hair, muttered, 'Not for want of trying, bet I get sent away next year.' Sandy simply chuntered on about the necessity of being able to get into his dressing room at all times in case of an emergency, and what if the baby was sick on his Lobb's shoes? I suggested that everyone calm down and talk one at a time, so everyone rounded on me and told me variously to mind my own business, that I didn't understand, and that it was all very well for me, not having children.

Ella melted away upstairs and I took myself off to the drawing room, where a roaring fire (the very expensive gas log variety with fake ashes below) was framed by a glossy dark green garland, arranged along the mantelpiece by the florist who'd done the Christmas tree, interleaved with cinnamon sticks, oranges and thick white church candles. The candle-light flickered bleakly under the 100-watt overhead brilliance of the chandeliers, and a bottle of champagne was standing open in a cooler, surrounded by an elegant circle of cut-glass crystal. Sandy trundled in. 'Help yourself, help yourself, good, good, you have.' He poured himself a glass. 'Absolute chaos, absolute chaos. Impossible woman, Lindsey. Can't organize her way out of a paper bag. Was she like this when you were all young?'

Fortunately, this was a rhetorical – and, considering Lindsey's life, an extraordinarily inappropriate – question, and Sandy chuntered out again, muttering something about opening the wine to let it breathe.

It was a serene and peaceful scene, and made me feel slightly unreal, as if I was living in a magazine, albeit one from around twenty years ago. I poured myself another glass, sank down on to a comfortable velvet sofa, and compared it with last Christmas. Will and I had had Christmas Eve together, lingering over a special treat supper with champagne and smoked salmon before packing to go down to Horsham first thing in the morning. If we'd done that this year, we'd both have finished up working late (I hadn't left the office until 7 p.m.) and I could visualize us gulping down the smoked salmon and slightly warm champagne standing up, as we frantically wrapped presents and packed suitcases. By the time it was all finished, we'd be too tired to speak, let alone listen to each other, and we'd collapse into bed without doing the washing up. I'd got to know our life so very well that I didn't have to live it. I could imagine it.

At least, this year, I didn't have to worry about Boxing Day. We usually drive off to his mother, and toy with limp, overcooked turkey in the institutional dining room of her nursing home, while she struggles to remember who we are. I wondered what she would make of Saffron and her bump.

The door opened again, and Ella came in, fixing her eyes on the floor.

'How's my favourite niece?' I jumped up. She went scarlet and mumbled something.

'Would you like, an, er . . .?' I looked at the drinks tray. Were fourteen-year-olds allowed champagne? Should one offer? What would Lindsey say? I felt nostalgic for the days when Lindsey and Laura bickered over whether fruit juice was healthy or just a way of destroying your teeth. 'Er . . . a Coke?' Better safe than sorry.

She hovered tentatively while I poured one and racked my brains for a good topic of conversation. 'Have you been to lots of good Christmas parties?'

She looked at me as if I'd taken leave of my senses. 'We've only just broken up.'

'Heavens that's late, isn't it?'

Ella shrugged and stared at the floor again. Teenagers can make you feel as if you were a complete idiot. 'I'm going to a party on New Year's Eve,' she volunteered eventually.

I tried to think of something intelligent to ask. 'With boys?'

She went rather pink. 'Fiona's brothers probably have some friends.' She clearly didn't want to pursue the subject. I swallowed my champagne rather too fast, and wished she was still young enough to climb on my lap for a cuddle. Now I couldn't even put an arm round her bony shoulders, although I ached for human contact. It would make me feel less lonely, but I didn't have that kind of relationship with any of the younger ones.

By the time the room began to fill up with my family – Mum exclaiming over the cost of champagne and Dad countering Sandy's bonhomie with his own clubby banter, Paul wearing a strained smile and Laura a resentful frown, the littles looking expectantly overexcited before they were packed off with their stockings, Lindsey tense with list-making, and hissing,

'Sandy's being quite impossible, don't you think?' to me over the pop of another champagne bottle – everyone was looking bruised but separately triumphant. I'd had two glasses and decided not to find out who was sleeping where. 'Do you think, Lindsey,' I murmured, noting how much older and tireder everyone looked under bright light, 'that we might turn the top light off?'

She looked startled. 'If you think it's necessary.'

'Yes, please, darling,' said Mum.

We all shuffled through to the dining room, which felt less like an archaeological record of its time than any other part of the house. Formal dining-room fashion has not changed so very much in three hundred years, and this held no surprises: a big, long, highly polished dark wood table, laid with lashings of silverware and cut crystal and decorated with tight, scentless roses in a posy in the middle, rich red walls and Sandy's fake ancestral portraits. Sandy's father had owned a chain of garages, and had spent many of his millions on trying to convince the world that there were ephemeral dukes, barons, or even minor clergymen in the family tree.

We were all arranged in a carefully thought-through table plan, although I could see Lindsey's discomfort at being unequal numbers. Nobody had mentioned Will at all, but the prospect of having two women sitting together left both Mum and Lindsey distinctly uneasy. I almost expected one of them to say that while it was very remiss of him to make an old girlfriend pregnant, leaving us a man short for Christmas Eve dinner really was the act of a complete bounder.

Dinner, however, left in the hostess trolley by Consuela, was delicious. This had a soporific effect on us all, and even Laura exchanged a joke with Sandy before disappearing upstairs early to feed Hero. Laura never usually retired to feed her babies, often exposing a breast like a vast, blue-veined melon at the table, nipple occasionally popping out and dripping copiously with milk. However a coarse, appreciative joke from Sandy about tits after Zack was born had cured her of that while he was around. I was relieved. My own breasts were inclined to start nervously at the sight, prickling painfully and hardening into reminders of what I had lost.

Washing up, by tradition at Christmas, was never done by Mothers, in spite of what Laura had said. Usually Dad, Paul, Will and myself finished off wine as we washed and dried, forming an incongruous but merry group, singing carols drunkenly under our breath and wiping the same surfaces over again by mistake, teasing each other and exchanging gossip. This year, without Will, and with Dad officially labelled 'tired', Paul and I tackled the marathon ourselves. Carols sounded silly with only two reedy voices, and I could see that all Paul wanted was to get to bed before Hero woke for one of her two-hourly feeds. After ten minutes, I sent him off, claiming to find it easier if I did it all on my own.

Lindsey came in. 'You're not doing this alone, are you?' She seized a tea-towel.

'Really. I'm fine. You've done enough.'

But no. Lindsey wanted to talk. 'Sandy thinks Ella should go away to school. He thinks she's being distracted here.'

'What do you think?'

'I don't know,' admitted Lindsey. 'I don't get home till 8 p.m., and it's impossible to get a word out of her.' She dried and re-dried the same plate so often that I felt like taking it out of her hands, and giving her another one, but she was obviously trying to say something. 'The awful thing is,' she said, finally, 'that I think he wants her to go to boarding school so that she stays a virgin. You know, my pure daughter, fit to marry a prince, that sort of thing.'

I was shaken. 'Surely that's outdated now? And isn't she more likely to go off the rails in the end if she's starved of boys from the beginning?' I re-filled the bowl with steaming hot water. 'She's not at it already, is she?'

'I haven't the faintest idea.' Lindsey sounded exhausted. 'Perhaps you could talk to her. She's always been so fond of you.'

Considering that asking Ella about school was like pulling teeth, the thought of asking anything more intimate filled me with alarm. I shook my head. 'She hardly says anything to me at all these days. Except that she's going to Fiona's party on New Year's Eve.'

'Fiona?' Lindsey squawked. 'Who the heck is

Fiona? I knew she'd tell you things she won't tell me. Oh, God, that sounds like Daisy. She can't wait for tomorrow morning, so she's got thoroughly over-tired.' She put down the tea-towel and disappeared, leaving me feeling thoroughly guilty about betraying Ella.

Laura appeared with an enormous amount of equipment to wash up or sterilize. I always thought the point of breast-feeding was that you didn't have to do that sort of thing, but somehow Laura managed to combine the earth-mother role with as much technology as possible. It was something to do with expressing milk so that Paul could give Hero a bottle at four in the morning.

'Isn't anyone helping you?' she demanded, as if it was my fault that I was doing the washing up alone. 'God, I'm tired.' I was so used to Laura's moaning that I almost missed the tears in the corners of her eyes.

My first thought was, uncharitably, that I had no more room for tears, my own or anyone else's. Then I rallied. 'What's up?'

She leant her forehead on the fridge. 'Nothing. You wouldn't understand. But if only Paul would pull his finger out and earn more. I just feel I'll never be able to escape and have a life of my own. It's not about buying things, it's about freedom. I don't have any.'

I touched her lightly on the shoulder. 'Look, I know I'm not one to talk, and I don't know what's really wrong, but it's not fair to expect Paul to put it right. You're the only one who can do that. You didn't marry a knight on a white charger.'

She gave a twisted smile. 'I certainly didn't. Nothing could be further.'

'Neither did I,' I reminded her gently. 'We both married nice men.'

Laura was amazed. 'You call him nice after what he did to you? I don't believe it.'

I shrugged. Quite often I didn't either. 'But Lindsey's the only one of us who married someone who could have been a knight on a white charger, and look how he's turned out.'

Laura thought for a moment. 'Yes, I remember being really envious when he married Lindsey. He seemed like a real princeling. Rich, indulgent . . .'

'Madly in love with her,' I added. 'Even good-looking, then.'

'He wasn't!' Laura was incredulous. 'No, you're right, he was. Do you remember him wearing that kilt for his wedding? Like a cross between a Russian emigré and an English aristo. You could imagine him sweeping across the Highlands raping and pillaging. Terribly tall, with that pale skin and blond hair. I wouldn't have minded being raped and pillaged by him in those days.'

We giggled. 'Well, the hair's gone, anyway,' I muttered. 'And now he has to decide whether to wear his sporran above or below his bulge.'

'Well, even if he is pompous, he's still very rich,'

said Laura resentfully. 'Lindsey doesn't have to keep going like a one-woman powerhouse.'

'I think she's frightened to stop,' I mused. As I said it, I realized I hadn't thought of it like that before.

Laura blew her nose and cheered up. 'I suppose I have to remember things could be worse,' she added. 'After all, I could be you.'

Thanks, Laura, I murmured under my breath after the door had closed. Thanks a bundle.

When I finally got to my sofabed, I discovered that Sandy had turned the radiator off in the study, presumably because he didn't plan to work over Christmas. I peered at it, but turning radiators on was the sort of thing Will had always done, and, although I fiddled with anything that would move, I couldn't work it out. It was the most exposed room in the house, being at the top on the back extension, so it was absolutely freezing. I didn't dare wake anyone to find any more bedding, so I slept in my tights and a jumper, trying not to think about the warm, solid lump of Will's body against Saffron's gently swelling one in Northamptonshire. Jennifer, I suspected, was the sort of person who would remember to give them hot-water bottles or electric blankets, and, besides, they had each other.

The last thing I thought, before dropping into a troubled, restless, thirsty sleep, punctuated by Hero's thin wailing cry and the occasional rumble of children's feet scampering up and down the stairs, was that

Lindsey seemed to be cracking up. First she forgot Hero, and now my bedroom was unheated. And she'd admitted to being bewildered by the situation with Ella. In anyone else I'd scarcely have noticed, but Lindsey didn't earn a six-figure salary by overlooking small details or being bewildered.

The following day, however, I decided that this was unfair. Even Lindsey couldn't be perfect all the time, and she was still running closer to it than anyone else I'd ever met. I staggered down, hair in a mess and mascara clogged on my eyelashes, at what seemed to me the horribly early hour of 9 a.m. because it was impossible to go on ignoring the squeaking, squealing, thumps and occasional wail that had been shaking the house since 5.30 a.m. Lindsey was sitting at the kitchen table (also laid for breakfast by Consuela before she departed) in a floral housecoat, her hair and face already immaculate.

'Ah, Leonie. Happy Christmas.' I goggled at the housecoat. I didn't think they existed any more, except in 1960s sitcoms.

Having disposed of the formalities, she then decided to run through the arrangements with me, and a sulky-looking Ella.

'Because Mum should do as little as possible,' concluded Lindsey, at the end of a formidable list of instructions, 'and Laura's hopeless when she's breast-feeding. Do buck up, Ella, you're old enough now to be a help.'

There were a number of hurdles to the morning, culminating in lunch in the big dining room. Everyone except Sandy was allocated a task, even Zack and Phoebe. 'I believe in giving children a sense of responsibility early on,' Lindsey told Laura, whose mouth twitched up at the corners.

'This should be interesting,' she hissed at me, as the door closed on Lindsey's back. 'Honestly, Lindsey thinks you can bring children up as if they were in the army. She's going to come a cropper when they all rebel.'

Zack, on being told by Lindsey that he had to help, merely threw himself on the ground screaming, drummed his heels on the floor, and had to be carried off by Paul like a rolled-up carpet. Phoebe accepted the job of filling bowls full of peanuts and crisps suspiciously quickly, spent about half an hour stuffing herself instead of the bowls she was supposed to be filling and was sick all over the kitchen floor. Apparently the Parker children had been mainlining chocolate all morning, while the Lucas-Whites had dutifully handed in the contents of their Christmas stockings to the sweetie jar, from which rations would be doled out over the next few months. Daisy, dressed in a smocked floral dress with her hair neatly scraped back in an Alice band, did look rather wistful.

'Really,' murmured Lindsey. 'Those children are completely out of control. Laura ought to be much firmer with them. She's just laying in trouble for later on.'

I didn't see how Phoebe and Zack could possibly be any worse later on than they were now.

The doorbell shrilled, and I opened the door to find the first of the selection of people that Lindsey had decided to reach out to at Christmas. One was an alcoholic and was therefore to be placed next to Laura at lunch.

'Now, Laura, I know you won't be drinking because you're breast-feeding . . .' Lindsey had explained.

Laura had looked rebellious, opening her mouth.

Lindsey had swept on. 'So it's important to make sure that the wine bottle doesn't go down that end of the table.'

'I'm sure that's not quite the way to . . .' I'd murmured, having once written an article on alcoholism, in which various experts had made it clear to me that alcoholics must take responsibility for themselves.

Lindsey had silenced me with a glance.

The other was a neighbour whose wife had died a few weeks earlier.

'Poor man, we can't leave him on his own at Christmas.' She'd looked cunningly at me. 'Perhaps you could look after him, Leonie.'

I did think Lindsey could refrain from match-making at Christmas dinner.

She trilled on. 'Isn't it extraordinary how tragic this time of the year always turns out to be? She died of breast cancer only six weeks ago,' she reflected. 'There are three little girls, who'll be able to play with Phoebe and Daisy.'

I could feel my throat constrict at the thought of three bewildered little girls trying to open their Christmas presents without their mother, and inevitably it tightened further at the thought that I'd never be opening any presents with the little baby I'd lost. I swallowed, and tried to distract myself by calculating how many sprouts everyone might need each, and then multiplying it by seventeen.

'Still, God's will, I suppose,' chirped Lindsey. Then she added in a much more normal voice. 'Now, Ella, do brush your hair before everyone comes. And wear something nice for a change, not that dreary black.'

We had drinks in the drawing room, where the alcoholic, a whiskery spinster in her seventies called Madeleine Smith, managed to slip under Lindsey's guard by getting Sandy to pour her a large gin. The bereaved man, who looked utterly forlorn and slightly unwashed, turned out to be called Dick someone, with three little girls who scampered readily upstairs with Phoebe and Daisy. He sipped a sherry with the shocked, blank look of someone who has recently been buried alive. I wondered why everything seemed so mixed up and muddled. Christmas seemed like one of those pocket puzzles that you shake and rotate to get dozens of tiny balls in the right holes. Only it never works, and everyone is left stranded, an insignificant ball that has accidentally got stuck in the wrong place or with the wrong people.

By the time we all sat down at lunch, even Lindsey,

dressed in a red silk dress with a pussycat bow, was looking frazzled. Serving out seventeen portions of turkey and all the trimmings took ages, by which time Zack was throwing his sprouts across the table ('yucky'), and picking up the turkey in his fingers, announcing loudly that he 'didn't like chicken'. Phoebe simply shovelled food into her mouth from the moment a plate arrived in front of her, and had finished by the time Lindsey rose and said Grace. Madeleine Smith's hand shot out and grabbed the wine bottle, ignoring flinty looks from Lindsey. There was a gurgle as she filled her glass to the top. Laura seized the bottle as soon as Madeleine put it down and filled her own glass. Lindsey got up and edged down the side of the table, purportedly to re-distribute dishes of sprouts and carrots. Just as she was stretching her hand out to retrieve the wine, Madeleine re-filled her glass again, emptying the bottle. Lindsey's hand paused fractionally, then carried on smoothly to remove the empty bottle.

'Sandy,' she spoke in the icy tones that neither Laura nor I had ever dared ignore.

Sandy munched away oblivious, wincing as Zack let out a shrieking burble and waved his spoon violently in the air, knocking Sandy's glasses off. His colour rose as he retrieved them.

'Darling!' The tones were cut-glass by now. 'Perhaps you could look after the wine from now on?' She signalled furiously over Madeleine's head, mouthing 'Don't let her have any more.'

Even Dick had woken up to an atmosphere by now. His head shot up as he looked from Sandy to Lindsey and back again. Lindsey smiled crisply back at him. He sagged over his roast potatoes in defeat.

'I'm so sorry to hear about your wife,' I murmured softly.

He looked up, and, for a brief moment, I saw such terrible emptiness in his eyes that I flinched. 'Thank you,' he said, touching my hand for a moment. I think he wanted to reassure himself that he was still alive by feeling the warmth of my skin. As a gesture, it certainly bore no resemblance to Sandy's investigative groping. Dick gently pushed the roast potato from one side of the plate to another with his knife to imitate eating. 'You're all very kind.'

Perhaps I didn't need to dole out tea to the homeless to realize that other people were worse off than me. Here, in Lindsey's immaculate dining room, eating her perfectly crispy potatoes, succulent turkey and cranberry sauce from a top delicatessen was someone suffering far more deeply than I'd ever imagined possible. I had to admit that I'd rather Will was exchanging meaningful glances with Saffron under paper hats than lying in his grave like Dick's wife. I could see it in my imagination, surrounded by dead flowers with cellophane still on them, the writing fading in the rain as surely as the image of his wife's face was evaporating in Dick's mind. I didn't think I'd ever seen a human being in such pain. It was as if my misery over Will had ripped away a curtain between me and people like

438

Dick. But I told myself that my problems were trivial compared to his, like a headache compared to brain cancer.

However the fact that I would rather know that Will was alive, even if he was with Saffron was an interesting thought and I examined it carefully. Did it mean that I still loved Will? Did it mean I really, really loved him in a sort of selfless way, like the real mother in the biblical tale of Solomon, who would rather lose her baby than have it sliced in half? Or did it mean that I still believed we could get back together?

I shuddered. If I thought we could get back together, I was in worse denial than Madeleine Smith. He was having Christmas with the mother of his child. The woman he had loved before he knew I existed.

The plate of turkey congealed sickeningly in front of me.

Madeleine Smith spoke for the first time. 'Delicious sprouts, Lindsey. Do you mind if I help myself?'

Lindsey was gracious. 'Do, Madeleine. Brassicas are full of anti-oxidants.'

Madeleine ignored the latter remark, and swooped on the sprout bowl, scooping up a bottle of wine at the same time.

Lindsey breathed in deeply as Madeleine poured it out, and added one sprout to her untouched plate.

'Sandy!'

He swivelled his eyes round. 'Dearest?'

'You're not looking after our guests with the wine.' She flared her nostrils meaningfully.

He waved a hand in the air. 'It's Liberty Hall round here, dear.'

Zack shrieked.

Phoebe's hand snaked out and removed a sausage from his plate.

Zack howled.

Lindsey's eyes watered with the effort of making herself heard because she never raised her voice. 'Laura . . .'

Mum quietly steered Zack and Phoebe out the door. 'I think they've had enough to eat, Lindsey, and as they're so very young, perhaps they could play with their toys?'

Daisy looked imploring and Oliver slouched in despair. Dick's girls were just bemused.

Mum ushered them all out too. 'I think Dad would like some peace,' she murmured tactfully to Lindsey, who usually insisted that the children wait politely until everyone had finished. 'He's rather tired.'

At least Lindsey was off Ella's case for five whole minutes. She never let up on her, not for one moment, I'd noticed.

I decided to try to draw her out. 'How's school?' Wasn't there anything else I could think of to ask her?

'It's all right.' Ella sounded neutral. The hubbub around us rose again.

'Your mother said you weren't all that happy.' It wasn't exactly what Lindsey had said, but I wanted to open up a channel of communication between us.

Ella stopped looking at her plate and spoke in an undertone, 'Mum's a control freak.'

I couldn't help smiling. 'I know,' I said with feeling, and was rewarded with the first smile I'd had from her this Christmas. 'Where are the lip rings?' It suddenly occurred to me that her face was completely free of any sign of piercing.

'They're fakes.' There was another fleeting smile. 'Look.' She took a handkerchief out of her pocket and produced what looked like two silver curtain rings, keeping her hand concealed under the table. 'It's all done on springs. They just slot back again when I want them.'

'Ella!' Lindsey might not raise her voice but it certainly carried. 'Who was that on the telephone earlier?' This was cunning of her, as she had answered the phone herself and had asked who it was at the time. Lindsey timed her interrogations with the skill of Military Intelligence.

Ella stuffed the hankie and rings back in her pocket. 'Fiona.'

'Fiona?' Lindsey asked in a silky tone. 'Fiona? I didn't know you knew a Fiona.'

'Vienna's changed her name. To Fiona. It sounds the same, but less embarrassing.' This was quite a long speech from Ella these days.

Lindsey looked as if someone had shoved a carrot up her bottom. Frankly, if Ella was hanging around with people who thought Fiona was a less embarrassing name than Vienna I didn't think there was a lot to worry about.

'I'm sorry, but I think Vienna's a lovely name.' Laura was on Lindsey's side over this one. 'Perhaps . . .'

Paul shot her a warning glance. 'We can't afford any more children, Laura.'

'No,' said Laura bitterly. 'We can't afford anything.'

Dick looked at the Christmas pudding on his plate with increasing despair and then picked up his spoon to plough bravely through it. I could see that it might as well have been Kapok for all the taste it had for him. I wondered if perhaps Lindsey hadn't been rather cruel in forcing him out to face the world.

'How are your children coping?' I asked him quietly.

He shook his head. 'Hopelessly. We just feel lost.'

Lost. That just about summed everything up. Will and the baby were lost. Maybe this Christmas lunch, unlikely as it seemed, was the beginning of acceptance and a willingness to move on. My heart lifted slightly, like a jumbo jet being hauled out of a terminal nose-dive, before spiralling down again as I remembered the baby. It had never even had a name.

'You two are very quiet down that end,' remarked Lindsey brightly. 'Let's all pull our crackers.'

I could feel Dick sigh beside me, and knew he was counting the minutes until he could decently escape. Madeleine caused a flurry, pretending to be confused about which cracker she should pull, and used the confusion to switch her empty wine glass surreptitiously with Dick's untouched one.

Lindsey spotted it, and her eyes glittered.

I was outside in the front garden getting some fresh air when Dick thanked Lindsey formally and started out down the steps. She hastily shut the front door behind him, presumably to give him the opportunity to take my telephone number in private. It was absurd. The man could hardly remember his own number, he was so desolate.

But he stopped and took my hand.

'Thank you.' Once again, I had the sensation of being able to see right down into his soul. It was a bleak and terrible sight.

'What for?' I was genuinely surprised. I had hardly spoken to him.

'For understanding. For not . . .' He spread his hands as if he had run out of words.

I smiled, and squeezed his shoulder. 'Good luck. I'm sorry about your wife. Really sorry.'

He nodded and turned away, taking two of his daughters by the hand. The third trailed behind him, scuffing her shoes on the pavement. They looked as lonely as I felt, walking down the street. At least he had them.

Lindsey and Laura waited expectantly on the other side of the door. 'Well?'

'For God's sake.' I brushed past them. 'He's only just lost his wife. He adored her.'

'Well, I'm sorry but you have to get in quick,' said Laura. 'Snap up a spare man before someone else does.'

'Widowers are in terrific demand,' added Lindsey. 'They haven't had to divide their property in half like divorcees.'

I looked at them both in amazement. 'I think I'll have another drink.'

'Well, if you're asking, I'll share the other half with you,' squeaked Madeleine, showing blackened teeth in a bird-like smile. 'It's been a lovely Christmas.'

This was what it would be like from now on. I wondered if I could ring Will to wish him a Merry Christmas. Better not. I didn't want Saffron – or Jennifer, for that matter – to answer the phone.

31

Christmas, of course, is not supposed to be enjoyed by the single or the childless. So it didn't much matter if people like Dick, Madeleine or me felt a bit lonely during the festive season. It was expected of us.

However New Year's Eve is quite another matter. It's the Saturday night from Hell, the no-holds-barred, all singing, all dancing, super-evening where anyone admitting to staying in on their own and watching the fireworks on the TV risks being labelled a saddo for the rest of their natural lives.

And New Year's Eve – a gapingly empty New Year's Eve – was only three days away when I opened my own front door again. I knew I should have gone for the bank loan and the Caribbean cruise, no matter how difficult it might have been to prise the money out of the bank. The house smelt damp and fusty after nearly four exhausting days at Lindsey's. In retrospect it seemed like one interminable cycle of eating, washing up and separating children from each other.

There weren't any messages on the answering machine. Two or three late Christmas cards, plus a Barclaycard statement, lay on the mat along with a few pizza delivery leaflets. There was nothing from Will.

I told myself that I hadn't expected anything. I hadn't given him anything. What did you give an ex-husband or wife for Christmas?

An old bunch of flowers wilted in stinking water on the mantelpiece, and a fine layer of dust lay untouched over everything. Fortunately I was due back in the office when it opened tomorrow. At least there I had a role, and was needed.

I'd only got about an hour into my bleak, half-hearted unpacking and clearing up when Laura rang. 'I hope you're okay. I was a bit worried about you. You were awfully quiet over Christmas.'

I must have been extremely quiet to penetrate Laura's maternal hormones. I reassured her that I'd just been tired. She invited me to dinner on New Year's Eve – 'just us and the next-door neighbours, and their children, but it's better than being alone'. I wasn't sure about that, because I knew that Laura and the other mum would talk babies, probably rather competitively, that both would be either pregnant or immediately post-natal, and that the children in question would keep interrupting for cuddles, fruit juice, nappy changes and other excuses to come downstairs, so that no one would ever finish a sentence. But it was kind of her.

Lindsey rang up to thank me for my help and offered an open invitation to a restaurant they were all going to on New Year's Eve. It would be bankers and their smart, over-dressed wives, plus a few high-powered women like her with their matching husbands.

Not an evening for those with flagging confidence.

'I wanted to ask your advice,' added Lindsey.

This was most unusual.

'I've found a magazine in Ella's room,' she announced with all the gravitas of someone who has discovered Category A drugs in the house.

Ah. I was being consulted in my magazine capacity. I couldn't imagine why.

'It's called *front*,' said Lindsey grimly. 'It doesn't seem to have a capital letter on the f.' This obviously mattered a lot. 'It's a boys' magazine. It's most unsuitable. It's got articles about sex in it. And bikes. Something quite ghastly about drugs.' She was obviously flicking through it in fascination as we talked.

'Well, perhaps it isn't hers.'

'Of course it isn't Ella's.' Lindsey sounded shocked at the very thought. 'But someone has obviously given it to her. The question is who.'

I agreed, very much against my better instincts, to find out what sort of readers *Front* had (it did have a capital letter, in spite of Lindsey's worst imaginings). 'I hope it isn't bought by married men or perverts,' she added. 'Or white slave traders.'

I refrained from saying that the ABC circulation figures broke readership down into BC12s or AB1s due to income and geographical location, rather than by sexual orientation. I made reassuring sounds about just a stage Ella was going through, and muttered something about *Front* having won awards in case that impressed her.

She snorted in disdain. You'd have thought it was hard-core pornography for all the fuss she was making. I really did think she should calm down and just let Ella grow up. Perhaps I would tell her this at our next lunch.

The third call that morning was from Corinne.

'Corinne!' I could hardly remember who she was. After she had married her Mike, and I'd married Will – she'd enjoyed going round our wedding explaining that she'd introduced us – we'd drifted apart, mainly because they'd gone to live in Somerset. They'd sent us two – or perhaps three – birth announcement cards, with 'do come and see us soon' scrawled on them. Somehow we never had.

I wondered what she was ringing about, out of the blue.

She was one of those people who have a nose for trouble, and always surfaces when something terrible happens. She's a sort of Fifth Horsewoman of the Apocalypse, riding ahead to inform everyone of impending disaster.

'I just thought you'd like to know,' her usually cheery voice dropped a few octaves, 'that Simon Hastings has been killed. In a car crash. It's awful how these things always happen at Christmas, isn't it?'

Simon Hastings had been someone I'd known at parties – mainly Corinne's – while I was single. He'd married about the same time we all had and had disappeared entirely from my orbit. I'd never expected to see him again, and wouldn't have considered myself on any list to hear about his death. But I was sorry. He was a very nice man, self-effacing but intelligent, and surprisingly gentle. I was sorry he'd gone. I pressed my face to the cold window with the walkabout phone still attached to my ear. Outside it was almost dark, although it was only eleven o'clock in the morning. A few London lime trees swayed dangerously leafless in the wind, but I wasn't afraid. You'd need a hurricane to uproot the London lime.

I told Corinne about Will. Perhaps I'm being unfair, but her voice seemed to sharpen at the news of another tragedy.

'Oh Leonie, I'm SO sorry. Are you alone at New Year? Do come to us. We're having a dinner party. And we could use a spare girl. We've got an old friend from Hong Kong staying with us without his wife.' The voice dropped again. 'His mother died. Long expected but still very sad. He had to fly over at the last minute.'

Corinne obviously still swooped down on people with problems and gathered them under her wing. You knew you were in trouble when Corinne reappeared in your life again.

But that wasn't fair. After all, I was now one of the dispossessed, and I ought to be grateful for being included in Lame Duck Shoots. I accepted. After all, I'd had enough of Laura and Lindsey, kind as they were, and the chance of getting a fourth New Year invitation at this late notice seemed remote. It would be good to meet new people. Part of the healing process.

The window began to steam up with my breath, and I wrote my name in the mist. It looked very solitary.

A party in Somerset it would have to be. Once again, I'd be sitting next to someone bereaved – perhaps that was my fate from now onwards – but at least, thank God, he and I wouldn't be required to have a sexual interest in each other. I mentally thanked the wife in Hong Kong, and sent up a prayer for her continued safety. Perhaps she could just stay in one piece until the First of January.

I imagined Corinne putting down the telephone with satisfaction before rifling through her address book for people we used to know, dialling again, and starting with the words 'I thought you ought to be told . . .' Will and Leonie's separation would be tagged after Simon Hastings' death as a lesser tragedy, and everyone would agree that Christmas could be such a sad time of year.

The drive to Somerset was terrifyingly wet and windy, but stopped irritatingly short of AA warnings for people to stay at home unless their journey was absolutely necessary. I tried every traffic news and radio channel in the hope of such a directive, but all I got were injunctions to drive carefully. The car swayed across the motorway every time I had to overtake a large lorry.

I was trembling by the time I drove up to Corinne and Mike's, an imposing Victorian vicarage just slightly set back from an exposed, windy main road. It was at the edge of a dear little village built in pale, local stone, and I could imagine Corinne skittering from one painted wooden door to another, passing on news of impending and doom-laden motorway schemes and road widenings, painful illnesses and, very occasionally, delicious gobbets of sexual scandal. It was the kind of place that Will liked. I tried to imagine us there, middle-aged before our time, focusing our lives around the Gardens Open Scheme or the Am Dram society. Because without children, that's what you're left with. If we had children, kept dogs or rode horses, well, that might be different. If there had been some way I could work . . . well perhaps different again. Otherwise I'd have been like Corinne, looking for a buzz through other people's misfortunes.

I visualized Saffron stepping out of a stone-grey former vicarage for a Sunday afternoon walk. She'd be wearing wellington boots, the red hair streaming in the wind. She and Will would wear waxed jackets, and their toddler would be strung between them, one mittened hand for each. Saffron would play the piano in the village hall for the school concert. It was not the Saffron I knew, but I suspected that she was ready to play a new role. She was a performer, after all. She would have an Aga like Corinne, and talk about having found a life with real meaning. She'd tell people that she'd never regretted the move for one moment. She'd probably even appear in the odd magazine, explaining that she had given up her chance of stardom for the only job really worth doing.

Corinne dragged me back to the present by enfolding me in a particularly warm hug.

'You poor darling. Mike and I have been talking about it all, and we're so, so sorry.'

I disentangled myself. Pity is the worst.

Corinne took a singing kettle off the Aga and poured it into a blue stoneware teapot.

'Now you sit down, and tell me all about it before Nicholas Burns gets back.' She lowered her voice again. 'His mother's funeral's today. A terrible, terrible way to end the year. Dreadfully sad.' So Nicholas Burns was the bereaved Spare Man.

I didn't, in fact, get much of a word in edgeways, although even Corinne was briefly silenced by the announcement of Saffron's pregnancy.

'How simply awful.' She recovered her powers of speech fairly quickly. 'Do you think she did it on purpose?'

I had often asked myself that. But she couldn't have known that I wouldn't be with Will on 27 May. She did know I didn't care for concerts, but it was a big leap for her to connect my dislike of being cooped up in theatres to getting impregnated by my husband.

'Probably not.' I stirred my tea and inspected the swirling brown liquid for clues. There were none.

'I didn't like Saffron, I must say,' declared Corinne, in an unasked-for declaration of loyalty. 'Mike always said that she wouldn't marry Will because he was only a doctor, not someone influential in the music business. She turned him down three times, apparently.' This was an almost exact echo of Jennifer's words, and I felt a searing, physical pain seize me deep down inside.

I sipped my tea, not trusting my voice to answer.

'It was one of those interdependent, self-destructive relationships.' Corinne's voice drilled on and on. 'They'd split up, then they couldn't leave each other alone, and one would call the other, and then before you knew it, they'd be in bed together again.' She sighed. 'But we thought he was through it when you two got together. He told Mike he was ready to settle down and forget her before he even met you. I mean . . .' she folded her arms in consternation, 'only two weeks before that double date we all had when he met you, he went out drinking with Mike and said he was determined to meet someone else and make it work with them. I can't believe it went so wrong.'

The side door of the kitchen opened and a well-dressed man in his forties – Savile Row suit, Burberry mac, athletic body and a streak of grey in his well-cut dark hair – stood outlined in the grey afternoon light.

'Nick!' cried Corinne, rushing towards him and embracing him as if he'd just been rescued from drowning. 'How are you?' She looked meaningfully into his eyes, obviously hoping for signs of great emotion.

He looked blank for a moment, as if he'd been miles away, and our eyes met briefly with a flicker of recognition. Two people in pain. I saw him re-arrange

453

his face quickly into a polite semblance of normality. He detached himself kindly but gently, peeling her off like a layer of clingfilm.

'I'm fine, Corinne, sweetheart,' he said mechanically, obviously abstracted. 'Just fine.' Then he sharpened up, and looked at me again as if he really saw me. 'And who is this?'

'This is Leonie, you know . . .' I suspected she was making signalling faces at him, with inaudible 'you-remember-the-one-whose-husband-ran-off-with-his-ex-girlfriend-terribly-sad' messages being transmitted rather too obviously.

I was horrified to see that my hand, extended towards him, was shaking. And he'd noticed it.

He took my hand in both of his, an almost priestly gesture. 'You're cold. You've obviously had a terrible journey. Corinne, shall I take Leonie's luggage in and give her a chance to catch her breath before dinner?'

And before Corinne could suggest something more sociable and gossipy – I knew she wanted more gruesome details about how Will had betrayed me with Saffron – he'd opened the door politely to usher me out into the hall.

'This your case?' He picked it up briskly. 'I know which room you're in. The ground-floor study. If you don't like sofabeds you can share my double.' A hint of a grin crinkled the corners of his eyes.

As he closed the door, he popped his head back. 'Sorry to be bossy, but I thought you needed rescuing.

454

Corinne can be hell when she's full throttle on sympathy.' And he shut the door with a soft click.

I couldn't help giggling before I started to cry, truly and properly, for the first time since the frantic festivity of Christmas had shut off all my emotions. If you believed Corinne, Will and I had never had a chance. Never had a real marriage at all. I'd just happened to come along conveniently when he'd resolved to forget Saffron.

Dinner was a lot better than I expected, although Corinne was clearly thrilled by my swollen, red eyes. No amount of cold water splashes had had the slightest effect. She fussed around me until Nick took over, and introduced me to a florid, stocky couple. The wife, who looked like a man in drag, was something in computers, and the husband ran a self-publishing company from home.

'I thought people in the country were farmers and market gardeners. All those traditional country pursuits.'

She laughed. 'Self-publishing and computers are very much country pursuits these days.' They seemed delightfully uncluttered by tragedy, and very much at home with themselves. I liked them. If Will and I ever had moved to the country, they'd have been the sort of people we'd have liked as friends. I reminded myself to stop thinking of everything in the context of Will. There was no Will any more. We chatted about business, and another younger couple, tense with babysitting problems, briefly joined us before fluttering off to the phone again.

Eventually the babysitting situation – whatever it was – resolved itself, and we all sat down to endless courses of creamy, rich food, every dish flanked with at least two other side dishes that would have made a meal on their own. Barrels of cream had obviously been lavished on the menu, and gallons of alcohol were poured down our throats.

But as Nick pointed out in an undertone, the one advantage of suffering is that you're allowed to lose your appetite.

'Just push your food around your plate and look tormented,' he advised. 'I shall. Breaking off mid-sentence and staring into space is a good one.'

A large lump of something creamy nearly choked me when he tried this a few minutes later, with such a convincing show of deep, inner sorrow that I rather thought he might have overdone it. The whole table looked stupefied with alarm at the prospect of seeing grief openly displayed.

'You're embarrassing everyone,' I murmured, when the babble started again. 'Leaving your food is about as far as you can really go in public.'

'Do you think so? They're not so much embarrassed as stuffed so full of cream they've lost the will to make facial expressions. I think, with Corinne around, we could go much further. Which of us is actually going to shed a tear?'

By now the others did look as if they'd been to a

taxidermist, who'd preserved them for posterity as 'Dinner-party revellers, New Year'.

Corinne pressed a choice of three puddings on me. I stopped smiling, and gave her a sincere, caring look. 'I find I've . . .'

'Lost your appetite?' She pressed my arm sympathetically. 'Of course. I remember what Marian Grant was like when her husband ran off with the au pair. We had to spoon feed her, really we did.'

'You're so kind.' Thus I weaselled out of having to block my arteries even further.

'See,' said Nick. 'It's easy. You just have to be ruthless enough.'

I was greatly cheered by the thought that Saffron was being compared to an au pair.

We even got to bed reasonably early, without 'Auld Lang Syne', and with a very restrained, civilized amount of kissing at midnight. There was the faintest roughness to Nick's cheek, and the scent of cigars on his breath.

Not too bad at all, I thought, and crashed into a deep, exhausted sleep.

Less than an hour later I lay there with my heart thumping, straining my eyes into the black velvet night. Something had woken me. I sat up and turned on the light, listening to the rustling country darkness outside. There was a howling noise, which could have been the wind, or an owl, or some more sinister animal. Not burglars, I told myself, not in the middle of nowhere on New Year's Day. Stories about country house murders flooded into my mind.

There was a soft tap on the door. That's what the noise had been.

'Hello?' I knew my voice sounded frightened.

The door opened quietly. It was Nick, wearing a dark red dressing gown.

'May I come in?'

I nodded.

He came in and sat on the side of the bed. 'I just wanted to hold you.'

It seemed a perfectly natural request. I moved aside.

He turned out the light and slid in beside me, naked. At first I thought he was laughing, until I felt his wet cheeks.

'She's gone,' he murmured. 'Just not there. I don't believe it. She was always there for me. Even if I didn't see her very often.'

His shoulders shook in my arms, and I kissed the top of his head. Perhaps suffering was a club, like motherhood, and your card was automatically issued through some kind of invisible post. Pain was its own Masonic handshake. Perhaps Corinne perceived this, and wanted to belong. Perhaps she felt left out.

He kissed me back, his mouth seeking mine in the darkness, tasting of cigars, salty tears and good red wine. I could feel the unfamiliar rasp of his face, the dampness of his cheeks slippery in my hands.

We clung together, Nick and I, on the wreckage of the year, hands and lips discovering the parts of each other's bodies that needed to be loved and comforted. I needed his hands on my breasts and his lips on my nipples. He needed softness, to feel welcomed, not judged or pitied. I wondered if this was what Corinne wanted from her lame ducks, a kind of total loving that stands alone in time and place, that can never be repeated and never be betrayed. Perhaps Mike did not love her deeply or often enough.

Nick's hands stroked such thoughts away. I wanted him.

'Wait,' he murmured. 'You're not ready.'

'I am. You don't know me.'

'I do,' he said, tracing my lips with his finger and pressing it gently against them to silence me. 'Wait. I'll know when you're ready. I can feel it. Forget all those busy thoughts, and follow me.'

Perhaps this was what married men always did when they were away from their wives.

I did not care. I trusted him completely, and shuddered with pleasure as he finally moved on top of me and wound his fingers into mine.

We wrapped ourselves in Corinne's spare blankets and smoked tiny, slender cigars sitting up in bed. I hadn't smoked for years, and just took the odd puff because I felt like it. He talked about his mother, how she'd looked when she'd kissed him goodnight in her balldress so long ago, scented, laughing, dazzling the child who'd loved her so much. And how she'd diminished in size, but never in stature, as he grew. The first time he realized she was frail, the last time she saw him through a crisis.

'I can't believe she's gone,' he kept saying, over and over. 'Just gone.'

He asked about Will, and listened. I told him everything, including Corinne's assertion that he'd never been able to forget Saffron and that he'd deliberately met and married me to provide a new start. Her insinuation that true love came once in a lifetime, triumphed over all, and that Will's and Saffron's love had been too strong.

'That bitch, Corinne,' he said, viciously stamping out the cigar end. 'So that's what she was doing when I came in this afternoon. I knew you needed rescuing.'

'I don't think she does it on purpose.'

'No, you're probably right.' He lit another cigar. 'It's just her way of staying on top. I suppose everyone has to have their survival techniques. Frankly, she probably needs a good shag.'

I was startled. 'Funnily enough, that's what I was thinking.'

He looked delighted. 'Really? Did you really? I didn't know women thought like that.' He kissed me thoroughly and said, 'If I wasn't so old, we could start again.'

'I didn't think like that until tonight,' I admitted. 'It's not at all politically correct of me. Anyway, forty-five isn't old.'

'It isn't, is it?' He sounded delighted again. 'So it isn't.'

Later he said, 'You mustn't take Corinne's remarks at face value, you know. I know quite a few men who took a calculated decision to walk away from their usual girl, or their usual kind of girl and find someone who'll really be there for them. I did. It was the best choice I ever made. And I do really love her.'

'But here you are,' I pointed out. 'Having a one-night stand with someone you've only just met.'

'That's different. You're different.'

'And I'm here, and she's there,' I added without rancour. 'The night your mother was buried.'

He looked at me for a moment and then nodded. 'Yes. You're here, and she's there.'

'Will you ever tell her?'

He shook his head. 'No.'

'I won't tell anyone.'

He grinned at me. 'I knew I didn't need to ask. Will you tell your husband?'

'He's not mine any more.'

Nick studied my face. 'I don't think you've really given him a chance yet, have you? Since you split up, I mean?'

'She's pregnant with his child,' I reminded him.

'Yes.' He looked serious. 'I'm afraid that does matter. It makes all the difference in the world.'

We curled up together, with the smell of six or seven cigars in an ashtray beside the bed, and slept until the sun streamed between the slats of the venetian blinds.

'Christ,' he said, waking up to the sound of Corinne's children screaming. 'For God's sake, we'll never have any peace if she finds us.'

Giggling, I was despatched to distract her, while Nick slipped upstairs. Apparently he bumped into Mike, who looked puzzled but made no comment.

We decided that Mike survived by keeping quiet about anything that seemed at all unusual. The last thing he wanted, we suspected, was another thrilling instalment for Corinne's telephone round.

'I hope I don't hear about you through Corinne,' Nick said to me. 'You know what she's like.'

Nick and I would probably never speak to or see each other again, but we both knew that one day, twenty, thirty, or forty years down the line, Corinne would be getting in touch after a long silence to tell one of us that the other had 'passed away'. Not because she knew we mattered to each other, but because we'd met each other.

We had a long, last, lingering hug before he went out to the car, and I walked off down into the village, into the churchyard, to cry beside the gravestones. In a full house, in a crowded world, it's almost the only place left. I just sat on a bench in the rain, under the spreading, graphic elegance of an ancient yew tree and wept.

After half an hour, I made a conscious decision. I had learned from Nick that there is more than one kind of love. I no longer felt that what Will and I had had was a sham, just desperately sad that it was all over. I looked at the gravestones. There was an old stone memorial with a winged eagle on top, commemorating a whole family, their dates spread over a thirty-year period and starting in 1892. Ebenezer, Louisa and Wilfrid aged eighty-two, sixty-seven and forty-eight, and two little children, Henry, aged five and Elizabeth, two months. There isn't much time, murmured the names and the ages. Don't waste it crying and hating.

It was time to get on with my life. There's nothing like a good cliché to keep you going, and for someone from the world of magazines 'New Year New You' – belonging as it does to all those giving up chocolate or taking up exercise resolutions – would do nicely to fire my resolve. I would come back one day, I decided, with some flowers for Ebenezer, Louisa and Wilfrid and the two little children.

32

I escaped from Corinne's New Year's Day brunch as soon as I politely could. Most of Somerset's lame ducks were there, forking kedgeree on to their plates as if they hadn't eaten in weeks, and washing it down with copious quantities of Bucks Fizz. I exchanged information on who I was and where I had come from with two alcoholics, three divorcees, a husband-and-wife couple who had both recently been made redundant, and someone whose only claim to tragedy seemed to be that his barn door had blown off in the recent gales. Corinne glowed with competence and confidence amongst this wild-eyed, odd-socked crew. As I accelerated away, craving the jerky, unsatisfactory traffic and grimy shop windows of London, I reminded myself that I was being unnecessarily cruel about someone who was doing her best to be a warm and wonderful person. It was just that I didn't intend to play the part of victim for any longer than I had to, and I suspected it was the role that Corinne felt most comfortable with.

She reached inside the car to kiss me goodbye. 'Take care of yourself.' She spoke in her 'special' tones, the slightly lowered, intimate nuances reserved for suffering and sympathy.

I assured her that I would, rather cheerfully, and reminded her that there was always a bed for her in south London.

She looked uneasy, and promised to look me up some time.

There was a present for me in the hallway at 37 Branworth Terrace. He must have let himself in, and left it there. It was a long, thin, brown-paper parcel, baggy and insubstantial. He had scrawled over it in pencil: 'Sorry, this is late. It reminded me of you. Happy Christmas. All my love, Will'.

All his love indeed. I tore open the top and drew out what looked like several large, prickly twigs with labels attached, and quite a lot of soil flaking off from the roots. I peered at one. It had a little white label, inscribed in pen and ink in old-fashioned writing, the ends of the letters blurred with damp: 'Paul's Himalayan Musk'.

I looked at the bare, thorny stalk, remembering the magic of Rosse Manor's gardens, and the abundant pink of the roses climbing over the pergola. I wondered what I should do with it. We'd always wanted to grow Paul's Himalayan Musk so that it could cascade through the cherry tree on our tiny patch, but I'd never found one in a garden centre or had time to find a specialist rose grower. But now was the wrong time of the year to plant it, and, anyway, it wasn't something you'd plant in a house you were about to sell. It took several years to grow. I didn't want to read anything into that. Will knew nothing about gardening, and was quite likely to have bought it on the spur of the moment, although exactly how you found a specialist rose on the spur of the moment in the middle of winter, I couldn't imagine. In Northamptonshire, perhaps. I visualized them buying it together.

'Oh God, I ought to buy a present for Leonie,' Will would say, his arm round Saffron's shoulders, as they scrambled through a field after a good lunch, keeping to the grassy edges so that their boots didn't sink into the unploughed mud. They'd be sketching out their future together under a brilliant blue sky, and Jennifer's dogs would be circling them, diving down into rabbit holes and barking furiously when they saw a crow.

'She likes gardens, doesn't she?' Saffron would say. She always ascribed homely qualities to me, ones I didn't particularly associate myself with. 'What about a plant? Wasn't Jennifer telling us about some kind of wonderful rose place near here?'

And later he'd pick out a Paul's Himalayan Musk, remembering the conversations that we'd had about growing it through the tree. 'She's mentioned this one a few times.'

'Buy it then,' Saffron would say carelessly. 'I meant to ask you, darling, shall we have blue in the nursery? Even for a girl, it always looks fresh.'

And neither of them would stop for long enough to think about whether you could plant a bare-rooted rose in January or that I would have to leave it behind when the house was sold.

The picture was so vivid that I jumped when the telephone cut shrilly into the empty hall.

'Yes?' I knew my voice sounded tense.

It was Lindsey, incoherent for the first time in her life. I really couldn't understand what she was saying at first. Eventually, I managed to grasp a few facts. It was Ella. She was in hospital.

'She's unconscious,' said Lindsey, her voice clearing, but trembling with fright. 'She's been unconscious for eight hours.' She gave a frightened sob. 'We don't know what to do. We got a call early this morning. I've been trying to phone you.'

It seemed that Ella had been allowed out to Vienna/ Fiona's house for a New Year sleepover and that the two girls had never actually got to bed. The early part of the evening, apparently, had been a disco party for thirteen- to fifteen-year-olds, supervised by Vienna's parents, but they had turned in at around 2 a.m., instructing the four remaining girls 'to behave'.

'Apparently, they started mixing cocktails, raiding the fridge and the bar,' wailed Lindsey. 'We don't know what they had, because Vienna's parents can't work out what's missing.' Vienna herself had been extremely sick, which was what had got the parents up at 8 a.m., and at first they'd assumed that Ella had simply fallen asleep on the floor.

'When they couldn't wake her, they called an ambulance.' Lindsey blew her nose. 'It's all my fault.'

'Lindsey! For God's sake. It's not your fault.'

Lindsey blew her nose again. 'It is. I haven't been

a good enough mother. Please come. She might wake up when she hears your voice.'

'Of course.' I took down the address of the hospital, dropped the rose plant in the hall and almost ran to the Tube station, trembling with tiredness and shock, knowing that if I took the car I would never find a parking space, that the hospital would be a maze of badly signposted corridors and cranky lifts, and that I, running against time as if I was on a nightmare treadmill, might get there too late. My heart thumped, and my mouth was dry.

Too late! It was ironic. What Ella needed was medical intervention – drips and stomach pumps – rather than the sound of my voice. Voices seemed pathetically inadequate and squeaky against the dark cloud hanging over her. Surely children didn't die from alcohol poisoning? But they did, occasionally, I knew, and eight hours of unconsciousness was a long time.

When I got to the hospital, Sandy was pacing up and down, threatening to sue anybody and everybody, and Lindsey was weeping silently. 'If she lives, I'm going to give up work and be a proper mother,' she sobbed.

'For God's sake, woman,' roared Sandy. 'Have some sense. She'd never have a moment's peace with you organizing her every minute of the day. No wonder she isn't regaining consciousness.' He strode off to berate some poor young junior doctor.

I drew up a plastic-covered seat beside Lindsey and

took her hand. 'No, really,' she took out another lace handkerchief. 'It just shows you that that Elaine woman was right. You have to make choices. And I've made the wrong ones.'

'Listen,' I tried to tell her that Elaine was at worst a hypocrite, and at best someone making the most of something she hadn't sought. That, had the sales figures of *My Life* continued to soar as they had done under her predecessor, she would still be behind her editor's desk, freezing out anyone who dared to mention her children. I thought, too, of my chance to talk to Ella, and how I'd always been too busy, accepting calls in the middle of sentences, always meaning to get down to being with her and never quite doing it. I should have made time. I'd had a whole week to set aside half an hour just for her, and I hadn't managed it.

'Lindsey. Please.' I thought of telling her that we'd all let Ella slip through our fingers, in one way or another, but I didn't see how that would help. 'It isn't your fault.'

Lindsey was beyond listening. Now was hardly the time for rational thought, let alone explanations about sales figures.

There was a flurry at the door and Laura appeared, her dark, unbrushed curls bursting everywhere. 'Lindsey!' She rushed up and hugged her, and Lindsey virtually disappeared into her voluminous bosom. We are not a touchy-feely family, I don't know where Laura gets it from. She's the only one of us who genuinely thought Princess Diana was a saint, rather than an unhappy, unloved woman doing her best to survive. 'This is awful!' Laura exclaimed. 'I couldn't bear it if it was one of my babies! Was it alcopops? Apparently children as young as five are being brought in drunk these days. It's too terrible, too terrible. Someone ought to do something.'

Lindsey rallied at this. 'Now, Laura, don't worry.' She slipped back into her familiar role as the protective older sister again, patting Laura's arm once she'd disentangled herself from the fleshy folds of a capacious cable knit sweater. 'She has a very good chance of recovery.' Her voice faltered at the end of this confident speech, and she looked again at Ella lying there, so terrifyingly still. Even Laura stopped talking and swallowed.

'What do they say?' Laura looked around for someone who might know something, and merely found our frightened faces again.

I thought of Ella, aged three, holding out a grubby sweet she wanted to share with me; aged five, pale and swamped by her first school uniform; aged eight, and insisting on reading *Black Beauty* to me out loud; aged ten, with her serious concerns about the environment and pollution, sensibly and maturely thought out. And now? I didn't know what she cared about now. I remembered the way she used to run into my arms, cover me with kisses and tell me, over and over again, that I was the bestest aunt that ever lived. I hardly deserved that now. Lying in the narrow hospital bed, she looked like a little girl again under the oxygen mask, not a sulky teenager any more.

'I shall sue,' hectored Sandy, who'd come back into the room again. 'I shall sue.' He didn't even pretend to suggest who this suit might be directed against. We all knew that anger was one of the few ways he had of expressing himself. He crouched down beside her bed and stroked her slender soft white arm, just above where it was hooked into the drip. 'My little sugar plum fairy,' he murmured. 'I'll take you to the *Nutcracker* again soon.' I obviously wasn't the only one who was a bit out of date with Ella's interests.

The door opened, and I could see the outline of a tall man against the flat, yellow lighting. Lindsey jumped up and flung herself into his arms. He held her tight, and I caught sight of a fraying cuff as he stroked her hair. 'It'll be all right,' he murmured. 'I promise. She'll be fine.'

Lindsey drew back. 'Sorry to be so silly.' She wiped her eyes. 'I was so frightened. But she will get better, won't she?'

'I'm sure she will.' But I saw his eyes. He looked worried, as he moved over to the bed and took Ella's hand gently.

'Ella? Poppet?'

She opened her eyes. 'Uncle Will?' she whispered.

Laura burst into noisy tears and I led her out to a stairwell, littered with cigarette butts, dust and torn chocolate wrappers. 'It's so awful,' she sobbed. 'If it was Phoebe or Zack lying there . . .' She re-doubled her sobs. 'Or Hero . . .'

I patted her back while she got out a piece of paper she'd cut out of a newspaper. 'Look.' She handed it over to me.

'Wanted,' it said. 'Negotiator for weekends/evenings to work with full-time staff. Basic and commission.' There was the name of a firm of estate agents at the bottom.

'I've been for the interview,' sobbed Laura. 'And they say the job's mine if I want it. But suppose they all start drinking alcopops when Paul isn't looking.'

'For God's sake,' I scrabbled around down my sleeve and found another tissue to hand to her. 'Paul's a wonderful father. He's not going to let anything happen to them.'

'No,' she replied doubtfully. 'He is a good father.' She rolled her eyes, looking much more cheerful. 'And unless I earn something, we won't even be able to afford alcopops.'

'Will you and Paul have enough time together? If you're working at weekends?'

'Less time to argue.' Laura sounded almost brisk. 'Well, I'd better be getting back.'

'But what's Will doing here?' I asked Lindsey later, when Ella was sitting up in bed, sipping water, still white-faced but clearly on the mend. Will had disappeared off to have a doctor-to-doctor chat with someone he knew vaguely.

'He called me. And anyway he is a doctor,' pointed out Lindsey, patiently, as if I was slightly slow.

'There are plenty of doctors in a hospital.'

'He's also a member of the family,' she added. 'And he always will be, even if you divorce. I'm not going to stop seeing him just because he's made his ex-girlfriend pregnant. The children love him, for a start.'

'What was he calling you about?'

She looked evasive. 'Oh, you know. Things.'

'What things?' I did not want to be talked about behind my back.

'Oh, all right.' Lindsey was pushed beyond endurance, or she'd never have given in so easily. 'He wouldn't let me tell you, but he phones me almost every day to find out how you are. He always has, right from the start.' I remembered Lindsey visiting me in her lunch hour, the day after my miscarriage. It had been very out of character, I'd thought at the time. It looked very much as if Will had sent her.

'Well, why doesn't he phone me?'

She rolled her eyes. 'Because,' she spoke extremely slowly, as if talking to someone who didn't understand English, 'you won't let him. You may think he should ignore everything you say about staying away from you, and you may even think he should just come galloping into your office on a white charger to carry you out screaming, but, Leonie, HE IS NOT LIKE THAT. And you wouldn't like it if he was.'

We glared at each other for a few minutes and she added, 'If you want him back, you'll have to talk to him, you know. He's not just going to materialize in your bedroom as if he'd been beamed down from Outer Space.'

'I don't . . .' I spoke just as slowly, 'want . . . him . . . back. And, in case it had escaped your notice, he's with Saffron, and she's having his baby.'

There was a movement from Ella, and Lindsey rushed over. 'Darling?' She bent over her. 'Sweetheart?'

She looked back over her shoulder. 'Anyway,' she concluded defiantly, 'he'll be able to find out if the hospital is keeping anything from us. About long-term recovery, for example. And whether she's getting the best treatment. Or if she should be transferred somewhere better.'

Still shaken by Lindsey's bluntness, it occurred to me that she had more in common with Sandy than I'd thought. They both seemed to think that hospitals were places you had to keep a constant eye on, where professional negligence and collusion might stand in the way of Ella getting the best possible treatment. I didn't agree with them, but at least it was something you could say for their relationship.

Sandy put his head round the door, and summoned me into the corridor, like a prefect ordering a junior to fetch something. 'Leonie, I'm relying on you. You need to get this absurd idea about giving up her job out of Lindsey's head. She was going on about it before you arrived. You know what she's like. It won't do, it just won't do. I know her, she'll go home now

474

and fax her resignation straight to the board. You've got to stop it.'

'But Sandy,' I felt it was important to make a stand for women at home, 'it might be time for her to re-assess her life. She probably needs to think through what she really wants. Achieve a balance.'

'Yes, yes.' He waved away such delicate consider-ations. 'Get her to do all that tree-hugging stuff if you like, career consultants and what have you. Even a therapist, if you must.' His pink eyes accused me of being the sort of person who urges people to visit therapists. 'Just don't let her give up that job.'

I wondered if they suddenly needed the money. Perhaps Sandy had spent his inheritance on claret and was about to be sacked. Anything could have happened.

Sandy glared at me. 'She loves doing it, you see. Just loves it. She'll hate being at home. Not a woman to be left in charge of a house. Some women do it well. Very well indeed. Not her.'

I realized that, in spite of his grumbling, Sandy really did love her.

'There'll be no peace for the wicked,' he added, opening the door. I saw his face soften as he saw Ella. 'Now you're a very silly girl, you know . . .' But he sat down beside her, and drew her to him, patting her back as if she was Hero. 'Don't give us a fright like that again . . .'

I closed the door quietly, and turned around.

'Why have you been avoiding me?' It was Will, looking grim.

I flinched. 'I should have thought that was obvious.'

He took my elbow. 'Come down to the canteen. The food's so disgusting, there's never anyone in there.'

As he frogmarched me downstairs, our feet pattering on the lino, I heard myself twittering on about Lindsey. 'Sandy wants me to make sure she doesn't leave her job, and I don't know how, and anyway, it might be better if she did, she's never there, doesn't have the faintest idea where Ella is all the time . . .'

Will sat me in the chair. 'Stop interfering. She's an intelligent woman. She'll work it out. I'll talk to her again.'

I wondered what he was going to say, as he went off to buy two thick white china mugs of lukewarm tea that tasted of iron filings.

'Or do you think we all ought to just leave it, not try to influence her?'

'Look,' he slammed his mug down. 'The best thing I can do for her is just to listen.'

The way he said it made listening sound quite aggressive. I decided it would be better not to say anything more.

'I'll just listen,' he repeated more quietly. 'I'm not going to lecture her. There are too many of you doing that as it is. She's been heading for collapse for some time now. But you know Lindsey. She needs help, but she'll be back on her feet with a new life-plan before you can say board meeting. I'm just trying to stop her from doing it in such a hurry that she doesn't really change anything except the labels.'

Will could never resist anyone who needed help. Perhaps that's where I'd gone wrong. Not needing enough help. I thought of the time he'd told me about his night with Saffron. 'She needed me,' he'd said. I'd never told him how much I needed him too. Perhaps I'd been too busy to allow myself needs.

'How is Ella?' Anything to avoid having to ask Will how he was. Whether he had had needs too, which I hadn't met.

'She'll be discharged later on today. They'll give her an injection to stop her vomiting, and after a few days she'll have forgotten this ever happened.'

'Thank you for the rose.' I knew I sounded stiff, not thankful at all.

'You can't plant it yet.'

'No,' I agreed. 'I'll have to put it in a pot temporarily to keep it alive.' By then, of course, the house might be sold. I could plant it in my new garden. I didn't think I would, though.

We were silent for a moment.

'Well,' he said finally, 'have you thought about what you want to do? Properly that is, rather than just throwing plates at me?'

'They weren't plates.' I bit my nails, avoiding his eye. 'What do you mean? Whether I'm going to go for a quickie divorce or draw it out? Whether I keep the house? All that sort of thing?'

'That sort of thing,' he agreed. 'And the rest.'

I wasn't sure what he meant. 'When do you want to marry Saffron?'

He sounded exasperated. 'I am not marrying Saffron. If I had wanted to marry Saffron, I would have done so long ago. You're the only woman I've ever wanted to marry.'

'Why not?' I wasn't sure if I believed this. I thought he'd always loved her.

He stirred the murky tea too vigorously and it slopped onto the table. 'Shit!' He took a crispy white paper napkin from the dispenser – you know, the kind of things that always fall apart unless you use about ten of them, and tried to mop it up.

I seized a handful of napkins and finished the job for him, removing the fast-dissolving white lump of paper from his hand and throwing it away. 'Living alone hasn't made you any more practical.'

'I don't care about being practical,' he said, with extreme patience. 'And in case that was a disguised question, yes, I have been living alone. Now could I possibly have your attention for five minutes? Or is that too much to ask?'

Oh dear, he was cross. I sat on my hands, like a good girl.

'Saffron and I go back a long time. We met when I was eighteen and very impressionable, and she was a mixed-up, vulnerable – but extremely glamorous – twenty-four year old. She played at a concert in my first year at college. There was a party afterwards. I never expected her even to notice me.'

I hadn't really realized it had been such a long time. Twenty years. Almost half his life.

'She dazzled me. And I did love her. Or rather, I was in love with her.'

This was an interesting twist on the more common male cry of 'I love you, but I'm not in love with you', a phrase which had driven us all demented in our single days. Many evenings had been spent in wine bars trying to decipher what it really meant, before concluding, sadly, that it meant 'I want out'. Presumably Saffron and her female friends sat in wine bars worrying about men being in love with them, but not loving them. Perhaps we could have swopped notes.

'That may not make much sense to you,' he conceded.

'Not exactly.'

'It was . . .' he sighed, and I realized that it wasn't that he didn't want to talk about Saffron. He just didn't know how to. 'It was a very passionate affair between a younger man and an older woman. At the start.'

I flinched.

'As I grew up, she started to need me, need things I couldn't give her. We started to grow apart. It seemed perfectly natural to me. Even when I'd been unable to think about any other woman, it had never occurred to me that we might spend our lives together. We wanted different things.'

'She wanted composers and conductors.'

His face was thoughtful. He seemed to be looking down the long dark passage of the years for the ghosts at the end of it. 'Yes. Those. Or at the very least, she wanted fame.'

I thought of her claim to be a very private person, and raised my eyebrows.

He read my thoughts. 'That *Harpers & Queen* piece. She thought it would make her fortune. But, you know, there's always another talented, beautiful thirty-something coming along next month. Everyone read it. Everyone feted her. Her potential looked very exciting. But her performance didn't quite match up to the beautiful photograph in the end. Not as a pianist. Then the fuss just died down. I think she felt humiliated by that. That's why she always pretended to despise publicity.'

'And she always came back to you.' I wondered if these shadowy music men, too, had been in love with her without loving her. Will had obviously been her long-stop, the one who could always reassure her that she was irresistible.

He nodded. 'At first, that was fine. I'd never expected anyone like her to settle for someone like me. I was just happy to have her back, but it never seemed real. More like a dream. She didn't hang around with my friends, because she knew they thought she was using me. Perhaps she was. I didn't care. She was different. That was all that mattered then.'

I could see that.

'At one point, she said she'd come back for good. I was so happy. We seemed, at last, to be equals, the same age. For a while, I thought everything was fine, that she'd changed. That I'd grown up. That it would work after all. Then she started to accuse me of not being committed. And she'd walk out again. And I'd discover she was with another tenor, or a record producer. It never lasted. She'd ring up, crying, ask to see me, and we'd be back in bed again.'

I didn't say anything. I knew relationships like that. I could see the years rolling back, with Saffron growing increasingly restless and desperate, hiding her fears behind her cool exterior.

'She had a way of making me believe in her, and, until I met you, the other women I met didn't mean much anyway.'

I accepted the tribute quietly. 'Why did you let it go on?'

'Love. Then habit. Then . . .'

I looked at him steadily.

He took a deep breath. 'Pity. And guilt. I don't know if you know many anorexics or addicts but they can be very manipulative. As a doctor, I should have been wise to it, but . . .' He spread his hands in regret for the time we'd wasted. 'I thought I could help her. I thought I could make a difference. I suppose that was my vanity. I'm sorry.'

Pity. Guilt. Vanity. Very simple, human emotions. I just hadn't thought of them, when I was trying to make sense of the tentacles she'd wound into our lives. I'd visualized something much darker and more complicated than that. I would say more powerful, except that you should never underestimate pity and guilt. If only I'd looked at it that way before. But I hadn't had time. I'd been thinking about other things.

He continued. 'It was fascinating at first, but I grew so very tired of it all. I'd explain to her that the last thing she wanted to be was a country doctor's wife, and she'd ask me to give her a chance to prove that she could be. And I'd say that I wouldn't marry her because it would be trapping her into a life she'd grow to resent. Then she'd walk out again.'

I could see her point. Men do things like that. Say things like 'I love you too much to tie you down'. It's code for goodbye. I felt a brief spasm of sympathy with her.

'You never asked me to be a country doctor's wife.'

'You're different. I thought we could find a way between us somehow.'

'It all got worse when I took the job at *How?* didn't it?'

I hadn't, in fact, meant to speak out loud, but I saw an answering flicker of response in his face. 'You're not to blame.'

Blame? I wasn't talking about blame, but . . . 'There were two of us in that marriage,' I reminded him. Three if you count Saffron, but I didn't add that. 'And I was too busy all the time. And tired.'

'I don't think you had any other option,' he spoke gently, but he didn't deny it. 'It's a tough job.'

So there you have it. Pity and guilt. Tired and busy. Lack of trust and lack of time. Not major crimes any of them. Just sharp little splinters in our lives, working their way deeply under the skin.

'Why didn't you tell me all this years ago?' I tried to prevent the sadness scarring my voice. 'Explain it properly?'

'I tried to,' he said miserably. 'But it always came out wrong, as if I was taking her side. I told you she was damaged. But after she was so awful to you on that villa holiday, you didn't want to know. I could understand that. I thought it was better to leave it.'

I thought about it all for a bit. I'd thought he was defending her, rather than trying to help me. And, on the whole, he'd been right about leaving it. We'd gone through months, even as much as a year sometimes, apparently without either of us thinking about her. If it hadn't been for that one night, if it hadn't been for the way she kept popping up in our lives, she'd probably, eventually, have drifted out of my consciousness.

'I didn't realize you cared so much,' he added. 'You never seemed hurt by her. Just impatient. And I did feel I owed her something. If I'd been tougher, less selfish at the beginning, I'd have broken it off with her earlier than I did, and not kept drifting back with her. By going along with it all, I took up so much of her life. She had nothing left when I married you.'

Hardly, I thought. Hardly. 'She had James.'

'James?' He gave a short laugh. 'Do you know what

James did? He was into S&M.' I raised an eyebrow.

'He likes games.'

'Well, he's always been very sporting . . .'

'Not those sort of games. Sexual ones. He has a toybox.' Seeing my look of puzzlement, he added, 'Sex aids. He liked to tie her up and smack her with a ping-pong bat.'

I thought of mumsy Jennifer and smothered a smile. I thought of the way Saffron had taunted James at the villa in the south of France, and wondered if Will, even now, knew how much Saffron used her fragility to manipulate people.

I tried it out on him as a theory. 'I sometimes think Saffron is a professional victim, you know. Some women get beaten because they're powerless. But, there, in the villa, she had power. She didn't have to be hit.'

He nodded. 'I know that now. In a way, I've always known. But there's something about victims that makes you want to help them. It's difficult to resist.'

So many misunderstandings. So much pride. So little trust. If I'd asked him, back then, to choose, to cut Saffron out of his life entirely, he would have done it, I think. He wouldn't, perhaps, have gone to the concert.

As for their night together – one thing I had realized, since New Year's Eve, was that our sex life had become so regimented and dutiful after six years of trying to have a baby that a night of real passion must have been irresistible, if it had been offered. And

Saffron had made sure that it was offered. Nick had taught me that being there is what counts when the times are bad. And I hadn't been there. I'd been in Paris. I didn't think I was wrong to go, but it's the price you have to pay.

But it was still too late for us. There was the baby. Saffron had won, after all.

'It was very hard to say "no" to her,' he mused. 'Because, in a way, she asked for so little.'

I remembered the call about the stop tap. The return from the round-the-world trip, when she brought us presents. The long discussion about whether she should accept an offer from a new orchestra. I could, in fact, remember every single time she'd contacted him in eight years of marriage. You could count it on the fingers of two hands.

'She's clever,' I told him. 'In that way.'

'She's ruthless,' he said. 'So ruthless. I don't know if she even means it when she says she wants the baby,' he continued, 'or, if it's just another of her games. You do understand, don't you? You are the only one who does, I think.'

I did. 'That's why you've got to stay in touch with her. To protect the baby.'

He nodded.

Ruthless, he'd said. She was a ruthless victim. It was a powerful combination. Explosive, even. I couldn't bear the thought of Will's baby suffering from the fallout. It would be so small and helpless in the face of Saffron's whims. There were enough lost children

485

around without Will's baby being one of them. I knew that Will would never let that happen. She'd bound him to her as irrevocably as if they had married.

I rifled in my handbag and found a crumpled tenner, as I got up to leave. 'My share.' I put it on the table.

He gave it back to me. 'No.'

'I insist.'

He stuffed it back in my bag. 'Don't forget, it's still our money, not yours or mine. We haven't divided it yet. So it doesn't really matter who pays. But you need it for the taxi back.' He smiled. 'You never have more than a tenner on you.'

He knew me so well. I could have used the bus, but the walk back, late at night, with its rustling shadows and distant shouts, frightened me. And he knew that too.

'Don't go.' He took my hand, as I turned away. 'Please don't go.'

I left my hand in his for a moment, then took it away before it started to feel as if it might belong there. I wanted to think. And besides, I couldn't be late. 'I'm flying to Milan at 6.30 tomorrow morning for a presentation.'

'Ah,' he said, releasing the hand and kissing its palm. 'Milan.'

Just as I reached the door, he called out to me. 'Leonie?'

I turned.

'Will you plant the rose?'

'I don't know.'

*

486

I didn't go to Milan. I went to his surgery, and was waiting there when he arrived.

'Leonie!' He looked haggard, as if he hadn't slept.

Sally, the receptionist, bustled nervously about, rustling appointment papers and signalling discreetly over our heads to someone else. The patients, coughing, wiping their children's noses, or sprawled despairingly across several seats, looked up resentfully as I was ushered in ahead of them. An ashen child with twig-like legs stared at me, hollow-eyed, like a scrap from Eastern Europe. This was the sickness and poverty that Will spent his days trying to fight, trying to cure. It must be hard to make any kind of impact. No wonder trying to help one person, Saffron, seemed more achievable.

I sat down in the patient's chair. The rooms had been re-designed according to some psychological grid, to be more people-friendly, and a laminated curving half-desk had been instituted in place of the conventional square barrier desk between doctor and patient. He shifted his chair close to me, so that our knees touched.

'I've got a proposal for you.' I took his hand, just to feel its warmth.

He sat quite still.

'I used to want everything,' I said. 'You, a brilliant career, and a family. But I've thought about it really carefully. About what I really want most of all. I want you, and my work. Two out of three. And the price

I'll pay is that I'll be there for your baby, if that's what you need in return.'

He turned my hand over, as if reading my palm, and stroked it gently, as if trying to find out if I really meant it.

'But,' I added. This bit was my price, the complete and unquestioning acceptance I needed to make it work. 'I can't go through any more fertility treatment. I want to make a decision, then make the most of it. I can't go on hoping any more. And trying to do too much, to do it all, means we're always too tired for each other. All I can offer is to be the best part-time stepmother I can manage. If you want that. If you can settle for that.'

I waited for him to realize what he would be missing. The chance to have his own children, to see their faces every day at breakfast, the right to take them to the park when he wanted to. Even if he didn't make it with Saffron, he could start again. His time hadn't run out. He could have a real family life with children he didn't have to make appointments to see.

I waited for him to say that he loved me but wasn't in love with me. Or that it was too late.

And I waited for him to say that the situation with Saffron was too delicate. I'd learned enough now to realize, finally and far too late, that she had declared war, all those years ago, beside the glittering swimming pool in France. Now she had a hostage.

'I need you,' I added. 'More than anything else in the world.'

He pulled me to him. 'Welcome home.'

'Two out of three,' he said later, picking me up from work to take me out to dinner. 'Do you mind that I've got two-and-a-half out of three? You, my job, and a bit of a family.'

'Two-and-a-half out of three.' I tried to calculate in decimal points and failed. 'You can't have two-and-a-half out of three. Statistics don't work like that.'

'How do they work then?' He squeezed my shoulder, as we walked over Blackfriars Bridge, passing an *Evening Standard* seller. I could see a photograph of Saffron on the front cover. 'Opera house under threat'. It wasn't a big story but Saffron's looks – the photograph from the cover of the Bellingham brochure had been re-used – had ensured that it had been transferred from the centre section of the paper to the front page, where the caption linked her to the story by citing her as one of the pianists who might lose work if the opera did close. It was a very tenuous link – she'd only played there twice – but on a quiet day, beautiful women, rather than indifferent news, sell papers. It looked as if Saffron, too, had had some of her dreams come true. She was being talked about.

'Oh, I don't know how statistics work.' I took some coins out of my pocket and bought the paper, shoving it in my bag to show Will later. He didn't seem to have noticed. I snaked my arm back around his waist and tightened it. 'But definitely in our favour.'

Epilogue

It wasn't, of course, quite that easy. There were so many decisions we hadn't foreseen back there on Blackfriars Bridge, when we'd been so happy that we hadn't even noticed it was raining. We talked and talked to find the best way of making each other happy. Will's job. Mine. Where we would live. How we would live. We wanted to change quite a lot. I needed to go on going up, taking the challenges that were offered, no longer holding back because I might be pregnant one day. He wanted to scale back, live more quietly, do some research and combine it with being a GP. He said that if he went on giving everything to his patients, day after day, he'd have nothing left for me. We worked out the mechanics. They weren't perfect, but then, neither were we. We made ourselves allocate time, precious inviolable time, just for each other. We had to decide whether Will was going to be Saffron's birth partner. Will made sure his name was on George's birth certificate.

It would be heart-warming to say that Saffron changed with motherhood, but she didn't. If it hadn't been for the irresistible offer of free childcare and babysitting, she'd never have cared whether George saw his father or not. Will was no longer her knight in shining armour, or perhaps, with her new-found fame, she no longer needed one. At any rate, the deadly push-me-pull-you between them had ended completely, but there was still little George, deliciously chunky and cuddly, but ultimately so vulnerable. We managed an alternate-weekends deal, which was punctuated by Saffron suddenly dropping him on us without notice because she had to film or tour. Sometimes our work commitments meant we couldn't just take him at the drop of a hat, but I could always ring Lindsey, who, now that she ran three consultancies part-time, considered herself a mother at home, or Laura, who grumbled furiously, but secretly adored being needed. With a frantic series of phone calls and assignations ('I'll meet you halfway,' was the phrase I most often seemed to be saying), George would be parcelled off to one of their houses for the day while Saffron did some filming or appeared on a chat show.

For her career, at last, had taken off for good. Ever since the Bellingham Glass supplements she had been seen everywhere. She'd become an icon for beautiful older women, and famous for being famous. She was on chat shows and at celebrity recitals. She probably earned more money opening supermarkets than playing the piano. The talk of a novel had just been a tease, but she managed a couple of quite successful health and beauty books, plus a short series on daytime television. The older woman's guru. She became the only celebrity I'd ever heard of to add to her age rather than subtract from it, edging straight into the

'Fabulous at Fifty' genre a few years before she had to. She'd leave George with us for days, even weeks, then swoop back, incandescent with charm and gratefulness, to scoop him up for a feature in *OK!* or *Hello!* I'd open a magazine to find her telling the world that since she'd had a child, she'd become a more centred person and it had transformed her career. 'Women say you have to choose between work and motherhood,' she'd say dewily into the camera. 'George and I are proof that you don't. I'm so much more grounded now that I have to put his needs first.' I'd have liked to have torn the features up, but I kept them for George, in case he ever needed written proof that his mother loved him.

Once she phoned from Paris. 'I'm at the airport, darling,' she told Will. 'George is with the manager of the hotel. I said you'd collect him.'

Will, trembling with fear and rage, took four and a half hours to get there, to find a round-headed little boy of three, the tears still drying in streaks on his cheeks, sitting bravely on a pile of suitcases in the porter's room. His small warm hand slipped into Will's. 'Daddy's here,' he told the porter happily.

Several times we wondered whether to sue for custody, but Will had no legal rights, and a battle could only hurt George. We could have lost him altogether. So we muddled on, as parents do, hoping we were doing the best we could. If I have to drop everything at work to go to the Nativity play, or to work at home because Saffron's left him in the lurch again, I do. And

I don't lie about it all any more. *My Life's* sales – I took over from its editor, Belinda Bracken, when she left to join her husband abroad – are at a record high. The way in which I, and the rest of us – mothers or non-mothers, or even, like me, half-mothers – achieve that is our business. If Peter Rennie questions it, I remind him that he doesn't care whether the staff come in at midnight and work standing on their heads if it gets the magazine out. Oddly enough, now that I've stopped agonizing over motherhood, the rest of the office has more or less calmed down too. I simply tell the singles that their time will come, and that even if it doesn't, being a parent needs society's support. I try to sort out when the mothers do need special treatment and when they're just playing motherhood as a card. I see the single girls playing with the babies that come into the office, and exclaiming over the photographs of first birthday parties, and the mothers wistfully admiring the flowers that arrive in reception for the singles. Camilla still gets in late, but she stays late, too. The mothers get in promptly and are out on the dot of five-thirty. We try to understand each other. Most of the time.

Sometimes I see the head of a tiny baby nestling in the crook of a woman's neck, and I catch my breath. It still hurts. Perhaps it always will.

But the best part about it is George, who is a happy, loving, clever little boy. Before I first saw him, I worried that he'd be a permanent reminder of Saffron. But when Will stood at the door, alone, with George as a tiny baby in his arms, I realized that George was completely and only himself, without any kind of past, the way babies are. He needed us, and we needed him, and that was all anybody needed to know.

These days he hurtles in the door, with Will's intense blue eyes and floppy blond hair, and his own permanently filthy knees and huge appetite for life. He emanates energy, a pure burning hunger for action and discovery, and throws himself at me like a solid little fireball, pulling Will behind him. All I can think, as I smell the clean, soapiness of his head next to mine, is that we're so lucky to have him.

One Saturday afternoon, Laura rang me to say that she'd sold an absolutely huge house, jointly, with one of the full-time girls. She calls everyone a 'girl' even if they're a stout matron of forty-five.

'My share of the commission means, well, at least a holiday for us all. And perhaps a new sofa as well.' She was doing rather well at her part-time job. So was Lindsey, whose 'portfolio' career as a consultant had had an uncomfortable six months to begin with ('the worst time of my life,' muttered Ella), but she was now so much in demand that she wasn't at home any more than she had been when she worked for the bank. Not that she seemed to notice, and was often found explaining how much better 'balanced' her life was now to strangers at parties. If it felt balanced to her, that's all that matters, I suppose. It seemed completely manic to me.

'Well done.' I was pleased at Laura's success.

'Mind you, not the kind of lovely holiday you can afford. Not having children.'

I took a deep breath. 'We do have George. Whenever we can.'

'Oh that doesn't count.'

Before I could tell Laura that it did count, to me, anyway – in fact, George counted for an awful lot – she burbled on, 'Still, George is obviously a Very Good Thing.' I could hear the capital letters in her voice. 'Now that you're so much more relaxed about the baby thing, you might even get pregnant. You never know.'

'Laura.' I tried to sound firm, but really, she is impossible. You can't help laughing. 'I will never, ever be that relaxed about not having a baby.'

'Oh.' She sounded crestfallen. 'I'm sorry. I didn't mean to be tactless.'

I teased her for a bit, and placed the phone gently on the receiver.

The next call, of course, was Lindsey. 'Now you're to say if it's too much trouble,' she began in her most commanding tones, making it clear that I had no such option, 'but I've got Ella for you.' Ella, who'd emerged painfully from her chrysalis of self-consciousness, had taken to dropping in to see me from time to time. She'd perch on the edge of my kitchen table, swinging endless slender legs or propping enormous feet on a chair, talking about make-up and a succession of 'cerool' boys. She was constantly interrupted by phone calls from Vienna/Fiona – now renamed Fifi – or one of the suitors, all of whom seemed to know exactly where to reach her all the time. She was back to giving me kisses and hugs, but they were conspicuous media displays of AbFab affection: resounding air kisses on both cheeks accompanied by screeches of how wonderful I was looking, or, occasionally, the sincere shoulder-wrestling hugs of the intellectual sisterhood accompanied by an intense 'How are you, really?' I suspected she was trying different personalities on for size, but it was good to have her back.

'Leonie,' she sounded slightly breathless and childish again, the way she did when she was nervous, 'I've got into art college. Can I come and live with you? It's much nearer, and besides . . .'

I knew what she meant. No Lindsey on her back. My heart warmed. She could have the top floor to herself, like a little flat. She could come and go as she pleased. 'We'd love to have you,' I told her. I knew Will would be delighted, because we'd occasionally talked about it, when Ella and Lindsey had been getting on particularly badly. 'We'll install a separate telephone line.' She and I made excited, delicious, decorating plans, which would probably be funded by Lindsey. I put the phone down. I knew she wouldn't stay long, only a year or two, before getting unsuitably entangled in some love affair, but I knew that from now on, she'd be back, treating my home as hers from time to time throughout her life.

I sighed with pleasure as I looked out the window, spotting a red plastic ball of George's that had got wedged in the cherry tree last weekend. A family was an attitude of mind, perhaps, rather than an exact quantity of people related in a very fixed way.

And then I got the call from Saffron. Even now, I couldn't prevent a tightness in my diaphragm at the sound of the low, caressing voice.

'Yes?' I knew I sounded sharp.

'I've got the most wonderful news,' she breathed. 'Hiram and I are getting married.' I knew she'd been seen around with an immensely rich, short, fat man called Hiram something III, whose power in the media world was immense. My belly clenched into spasm. Hiram, I knew, from the extra weekends we'd had with George recently, did not care for children. I feared, suddenly and passionately, for George's innocent, loving little personality in all of this. He would get left with nannies, sent to boarding school, left alone in big, impersonal houses around the world with women who barely spoke English. And we would gain Ella, but lose George.

'We'll mainly be based in New York and the Bahamas, of course,' she rolled out the names with immense satisfaction, 'but Hiram's going to buy us a little something in London, too.'

Clouds scudded across the sky outside, grey and menacing. It was as if someone had switched off a light.

'The thing is . . .' I could hear a faint wheedling

tone in her voice. 'I can't bear to disrupt poor darling George's education (this was rich, as he was barely four), so we wondered if perhaps you and Will might be able to take him.'

Only Saffron could offload her child permanently on to someone else in the same tone of voice that another mother might use for arranging a convenient weekend sleepover. I was temporarily winded.

But I gathered my thoughts together quickly. I'd learned enough about the way she operated not to give her any clues about how desperately we both loved George. I didn't want him used as a pawn in the negotiations.

'I'll do all the legal stuff, of course,' she added, with an edge of anxiety in her voice, clearly concerned that I was going to refuse. 'So that you can all travel together and make decisions and everything.'

Everything. That sounded perfect. I arranged my voice to sound calm. 'I don't see why not.' I left another judicious gap. 'I'll have to ask Will, of course, but I'm sure he'll be delighted.' I was careful to make 'delighted' sound like a formality, the response to a dinner invitation.

'That's so sweet of you.' She was all honeyed charm again, the famous person granting favours to a fan. 'I'll get my lawyers to contact yours as soon as possible.'

I smiled as I put the phone down. 'My lawyers' indeed. Then I punched the air. It looked very much as if we were going to be allowed to adopt George, or as close as. He would be ours.

I went happily upstairs to his bedroom. I was going to take down the teddy bear wallpaper we'd put up when he was born, and re-paint the room in strong bright colours. He could help choose them, and he had some posters he wanted up, too. On the floor there was a Thomas the Tank Engine jigsaw he'd nearly completed before going out to the park with Will. Children's puzzles are irresistible. I knelt down and began to finish it. Will and I. Ella. And now, George. I fitted the last few pieces into place, and went downstairs to make tea.